KU-071-343

Paradise

LIZ FIELDING
NICOLA MARSH
JOANNA NEIL

First Published in Great Britain 2016
By Mills & Boon, an imprint of HarperCollins*Publishers*
1 London Bridge Street, London, SE1 9GF

IT HAPPENED IN PARADISE © 2016 Harlequin Books S. A.

Wedded In A Whirlwind, *Deserted Island, Dreamy Ex* and *His Bride In Paradise* were first published in Great Britain by Harlequin (UK) Limited.

Wedded In A Whirlwind © 2008 Liz Fielding
Deserted Island, Dreamy Ex © 2010 Nicola Marsh
His Bride In Paradise © 2012 Joanna Neil

ISBN: 978-0-263-92086-4

05-1016

Our policy is to use papers that are natural, renewable and recyclable products and made from wood grown in sustainable forests.The logging and manufacturing processes conform to the legal environmental regulations of the country of origin.

Printed and bound in Spain
by CPI, Barcelona

WEDDED IN A WHIRLWIND

BY
LIZ FIELDING

Liz Fielding was born with itchy feet. She made it to Zambia before her twenty-first birthday and, gathering her own special hero and a couple of children on the way, lived in Botswana, Kenya and Bahrain— with pauses for sightseeing pretty much everywhere in between. She finally came to a full stop in a tiny Welsh village cradled by misty hills, and these days mostly leaves her pen to do the travelling. When she's not sorting out the lives and loves of her characters, she potters in the garden, reads her favourite authors and spends a lot of time wondering 'What if. . .?' For news of upcoming books—and to sign up for her occasional newsletter—visit Liz's website at www.lizfielding.com.

CHAPTER ONE

MIRANDA GRENVILLE stood through the double baptism, holding each baby in turn as she made the promises, heard the vicar name names…

Minette Daisy…

Jude Michael…

Stood with each glowing mother—first her sister-in-law, Belle, and then Belle's sister, Daisy—smiling as everyone took photographs. Even took some herself.

It was, without doubt, the most joyous occasion and her smile never faltered despite the turmoil of feelings that, inside, were tearing her apart.

Keeping her emotions hidden had been a hard-learned lesson, far more difficult than anything that came out of books; books were easy. But when, finally, the pain had become so great that hiding it had become essential for survival she had found the strength from somewhere.

It hadn't always been like that.

There had been a time when she had let everything show, let her emotional need hang out for all the world to see. It had been a slow and painful lesson—one she'd learned from watching Ivo, her brother. She'd thought he was immune, but the power of a love that was beyond her comprehension, the joy of fatherhood, had shattered the ice cage that once held her brother a fellow prisoner in emotional stasis. Now she was isolated, bound and shackled by the one secret she had never shared with a living soul—not even with Ivo.

And so she smiled for him on this joyous day. Not that he was fooled. He knew her too well for that. Recognised her smile for the brittle thing that it was, sensing a fragility beneath the controlled veneer.

To see his puzzled watchfulness, his anxiety for her, clouding his eyes on what should have been the happiest of days made her feel like the spectre at the feast. She had to get away before he sought her out and asked the question she could see in his eyes.

Is there something I can do?

The answer was—had to be—no. He had already done more than enough. He'd been there with the tough as well as the tender love. He had been her lifeline, keeping her afloat, even when she'd come close to dragging him under with her.

He had a new life now and it was time to cut the ties, set him free of all that chained him to a painful past. She had to convince him that she didn't need him any more, so she smiled until her face ached, toasted the babies, snapped pictures on her cellphone, tasted a crumb of each christening cake.

She was on the point of breaking when her sister-in-law announced that Minette needing feeding and she seized her chance.

'Belle, I have to go,' she said, following her into the nursery.

'So soon?' Belle took her hand, not to detain her, but in a

gesture that was utterly natural to her, full of warmth, a kindness she knew she didn't deserve. She had bitterly resented the glamorous Belle Davenport's intrusion into her brother's life. She'd hated her for being the kind of woman who drew people to her, hated her because Ivo couldn't live without her, and she'd gone out of her way to make her feel like an outsider in her own home. Drive her away.

Stupid.

She, of all people, should have known that, once given, Ivo's love was unshakeable.

'I've got a plane to catch,' she said, moving away. She didn't want or need kindness. Didn't deserve it. 'It's been a hectic few months researching the documentary on adoption and I thought I'd take the opportunity to grab some time for myself before we start filming.'

While Belle and Daisy were taking maternity leave from the television production company the three of them ran as a team.

'What bliss,' Belle said. 'Anywhere interesting?'

'Somewhere without a telephone,' she replied. The caustic edge to her voice had become as natural as breathing. Actually it wasn't such a bad idea. Then, as Minette searched hungrily for her mother's breast and began to suckle, the sharp, woman-of-the-world act buckled and she had to look away. 'Tell Ivo for me, will you?' she asked through a throat that was thickening dangerously. 'And Daisy.'

'You're not going to say goodbye?'

'It's better if I just slip away.' She managed a shrug. 'You know what Ivo's like.' He'd see right through her. 'He'll want to know where I'm going. Make me promise to keep in touch.'

A promise she couldn't keep.

She needed to get away completely. Give him space to enjoy his new family. Escape from an excess of consideration, warmth, kindness and go somewhere where no one knew her. Where she could stop smiling, be angry, be herself...

About to say something, her sister-in-law changed her mind, instead squeezing her hand. 'Thank you, Manda.'

'What for? I promise you're going to regret inviting me to be Minette's godmother. I plan to set both my godchildren a thoroughly bad example.'

Belle shook her head, not taking her in the least bit seriously. 'Not just for being Minette's godmother, but for being so brilliant with Daisy, giving her a job, a purpose when she most needed it.'

'I wouldn't have kept her on if she hadn't proved her worth,' she lied.

She'd taken on Belle's damaged little sister for her brother's sake, her attempt to atone a little for the hurt she'd caused him, make amends, but in truth she understood Daisy in ways that Belle never could. She'd been in the same dark places, knew what worked and what didn't, had known how to be tough when Belle had been emotionally racked.

'Just warn Daisy from me that if she has any idea of becoming a stay-at-home mother she'd better think again,' she said, sidestepping the soft-centred mush. 'I've spent too much time training her in my little ways to let her off the hook.'

'And thank you for not making a fuss when Ivo sold the house,' Belle continued, refusing to be distracted from saying exactly what was on her mind. 'I know how hard that must have been for you.'

Hard...

The Belgravia mansion that had been in her family for generations—a backdrop for the financial and political dinners, receptions, she'd arranged for her brother—had been her whole life when she didn't have a life and she'd lavished all she had in the way of love on its care.

Belle, who'd hated the house from the minute she'd stepped over the threshold, hadn't the faintest idea how hard it had been to let it go, but still, with a throat that ached and a heart like lead, Manda held her smile.

'It would be a bit big for one.' Then, 'I've got to go.'

'Manda…'

'Now,' she said, turning away and heading for the door before Belle did something stupid, like hug her. Before the tears stinging her eyelids spilled over and the ice cool image, the touch-me-not façade she'd built so carefully over the last few years cracked and she made a total fool of herself.

Nick Jago slid on to a stool and the barman, a leathery Australian whose yacht had been wrecked off the coast of Cordillera ten years earlier and had never found the energy to move on, poured him a small cup of thick black coffee and pushed it across the counter.

'It's a while since you were in town,' he said.

'I just came in to pick up my mail. There isn't much else to tempt me into what passes for civilisation around here.'

'Maybe not, but stuck out there by yourself you tend to miss the news.' He produced a month-old copy of an English newspaper from beneath the counter. 'I hung on to this for you.'

Jago glanced at the headlines of a tabloid that had the nerve to call itself a newspaper. Another politician caught with his pants down. Another family torn apart.

'No, thanks, Rob,' he said. 'I'm not that desperate for something to read.'

'Not that,' he replied dismissively. 'Inside. There's a picture that I think'll interest you.'

'And you can keep your page three girls. Fliss will be back soon and I'd rather wait for the real thing.'

'You sure about that?'

He shrugged. He was sure of nothing but death, taxes, and that her goodbye had been accompanied by a hot, lingering kiss that had been better than any promise. But Rob clearly knew something he didn't.

'Why do I have the feeling you're about to disillusion me?'

'I hate to be the bearer of bad news, mate,' Rob replied, 'but I have to tell you that your Fliss might have other things on her mind.' He opened the paper at a double page spread. '*"Sex, Slavery and Sacrifice... Exclusive excerpts from the sensational diaries of beautiful archaeologist Fliss Grant..."*', he read out loud.

Jago, his cup halfway to his mouth, slowly returned it to its saucer.

Archaeologist?

She'd been a postgrad student when she'd turned up at his dig. A volunteer, working for food and experience. There were a hundred more like her—well, maybe not exactly like her—but he wouldn't have paid her, no matter how hot her kisses.

Rob, under the mistaken impression that he wanted to hear more, continued.

'*"Discover the secrets of Cordillera's long lost Temple of Fire. Win a holiday on this exotic island paradise and see for yourself the ancient sacrificial stone—"*'

'What?'

Jago grabbed the paper.

One look at the photograph of the sexy blonde, one look at her khaki shirt, held together only by a knot beneath generous breasts and exposing a lot more flesh than the average archaeological assistant would sensibly display on a hard day at a dig, was enough.

Not that Fliss Grant was average in any way.

He hadn't heard from her since she'd left the island at the end of the digging season when the rains had set in, but then he hadn't expected to. There was no mobile phone signal up in the hills.

He hadn't been bothered—honesty compelled him to admit that conversation had never been the attraction—and he'd had plenty of other things to keep him occupied.

As for the Cordilleran postal service—well, even if she had been moved to write, it was something of a hit-or-miss affair. It was why, when she'd offered to deliver copies of disks containing his diaries and photographs to his publisher, he'd handed them over without a second thought.

He stared at the photograph.

The very brief shorts, a slick sheen of sweat, the wet-look lips and provocative pose had been used to set the tone for diaries written '... *by this dauntless female "Indiana Jones" who braved spiders, scorpions and deadly snakes to uncover the secrets of the island's mysterious past...*'

There was a photograph of a large hairy spider to ram the message home.

'*I knew the temples were there...*'—She knew!—'*...and I was determined to prove it. Now you can read for yourself what I had to endure to discover the terrible truth behind the sacrificial stone...*'

'Give me strength,' he muttered as he attempted to get his head around what he was seeing. And then, when he did, something painful squeezed at his chest and his mouth dried. She hadn't simply taken the chance to make a heap of money using his diaries, his work.

He could have understood the temptation and, wrapped in her hot thighs, he might even have forgiven her. But there was another smaller photograph of Fliss and Felipe Dominez, Cordillera's playboy Minister of Tourism, snapped as they'd left one of London's fashionable nightclubs. She was wearing a dress that left little to the imagination and they were exchanging the kind of intimate look shared only by two people who knew one another very well.

So the only question left unanswered was when had Dominez and Fliss met?

Had it been by chance on one of her little excursions into town for supplies? Had Dominez sought her out and made her an offer she couldn't possibly refuse?

Or had he been set up from the very start?

It wasn't that unusual for postgraduate archaeology students to turn up out of the blue, having paid their own way to the site. They needed field experience to boost their CVs and he needed all the help he could get. The fact that Fliss Grant had a mouth, a body, as hot as sin that she'd been willing and eager to share with him had just made having her around that much more pleasurable.

No, he decided. This hadn't been chance. The speed with which she'd achieved publication suggested that it was the culmination of a well thought out and efficiently executed plan.

Fliss Grant, it seemed, had 'endured' and 'endured' in order to get her hands on his diaries, his notes, his photographs and why would he be surprised by that? Women, as he was well aware, would endure anything to get what they wanted.

Not that she'd actually used any direct quotes, but then why would she bother? This publishing venture had nothing to do with dry scholarship.

He had no doubt that some hack, paid by Dominez, had ghosted this fairy tale from the bones of his excavation diaries, just as someone had been paid to make sketches from his photographs, producing an impression of the temple complex peopled with priests and sacrificial figures that had more in common with a fifties Hollywood epic than reality.

Not that he'd been credited in any way.

From this account, anyone would think Fliss had excavated the temple single-handed, enough to warn anyone with an atom of common sense that this was all hokum. But then this was straight out of the 'God was an astronaut' school of archaeology.

As he scanned the prurient accounts of priestly rites, he knew he should be grateful that his name had been omitted from this tabloid version of the temple's history with its sexed-up versions of the images carved into the stone walls. The 'naked virgins', 'bloody sacrifice' scenarios, the sexual innuendo, were not something he'd want his name attached to.

But somehow, at that moment, gratitude of any kind was beyond him. This rubbish would reduce him to a laughing stock within the academic archaeological world and, without a word, he reached for the bottle of local brandy that Rob pushed in his direction.

* * *

It was unbelievably hot. No temple, no matter how ancient, was worth this kind of suffering, Manda decided, wiping the back of her arm across her forehead to mop up the sweat.

'Come along, keep up,' the guide called, with an imperious gesture. 'There's a lot more to see.'

He was evidently new to the job and hadn't quite got the customer service thing nailed.

Since rebellion in the ranks was apparently unthinkable, he didn't wait to ensure that he was obeyed but plunged further along the path in the direction of yet more ruins, his charges meekly trailing after him. Well, most of them.

Manda was not meek. Far from it. And she'd already had enough of this particular ancient civilisation to last her a lifetime.

Refusing to move another yard, she sank on to a huge fallen chunk of dressed stone that someone, long ago, had started to chisel into a representation of some beast. He'd evidently given up halfway through his task and if it had been a day like this, he had her sympathy.

She leaned forward, unfastening another button of a limp linen shirt that had not been designed for this kind of sweaty exertion, flapping the two edges to encourage what air there was to circulate and cool her damp skin.

Next time she grabbed the first flight on offer to the Far East, she'd take more notice of where she was going. Cordillera, she'd been assured when she'd called the booking agency, was going to be the next 'big' destination. She had caught part of a chat show interview with some impossibly glamorous female archaeologist who'd written a book about how she'd personally—and apparently entirely unaided—uncovered some ancient civilisation on the island, so maybe it was true.

Not really her thing; she'd been more interested in promises of unspoiled palm-fringed coves and white sand. Unspoiled was a euphemism for a lack of amenities, she discovered. They were trying, but the 'resort' at which she was staying was, so far, little more than a construction site.

Normally one look would have been enough. She'd have turned right around and caught the next plane out of there, flown on to somewhere where luxury was guaranteed.

But she'd cut and run from feelings she couldn't handle, had told herself she didn't care where she was going and, having stuck the equivalent of a metaphorical pin in the map, fate had brought her here.

Maybe this was fate's idea of a joke but it had fulfilled a major part of her desire to be out of contact and its awfulness had, somehow, seemed exactly right.

But the lack of facilities, and an airport blockbuster that hadn't lived up to its blurb, had left her bored enough to break the habit of a lifetime and allow herself to be persuaded by a representative from the tourist office, eager to promote the island, that it was something of a privilege to be one of the first outsiders to see the ruins. A real adventure. Something she'd tell all her friends about when she got home.

She hadn't been totally convinced but at the time anything had seemed better than sitting alone with nothing but her thoughts for company.

Big mistake, she thought, pushing back damp strands of hair that were sticking to her forehead and pulling a face. Unfortunately, thirty miles inland, halfway up the side of a mountain on a route march around the seemingly endless maze of what they had been assured were the ancient temples and palaces, it was too late to change her mind.

Jago had been sitting on the altar stone for what felt like hours still holding the bottle of local brandy that Rob had slid across the bar, muttering, 'On the house, mate…'

One more season was all he'd needed and then, come the next rains, he'd have returned to London and published his findings in the academic journals. Written a book that would never have made the bestseller list. There was nothing here sensational enough for that. No treasure. No startling revelations.

He wasn't interested in sensationalism, bestseller lists, anything that would expose him to the glare of celebrity. If he'd wanted them, they could have been his for the asking any time in the last fifteen years.

All he'd wanted was to drop out of sight and lose himself in the work he loved.

He looked down at the bottle in his hand and finally broke the seal.

For a while Manda remained where she was, perched on her stone, quite content to wait until the rest of her party returned, idly tracing the outline of the half-finished figure with the tip of her finger. It was the head of a bird, she realised, a hawk of some kind, and she glanced up at a sky almost crowded out by the thick canopy of the forest.

When their pitiful little band of tourists—a couple of dozen people who were staying at the same complex, boosted by a group of captive businessmen whose plane had been delayed—had walked up from a clearing where they'd left the bus, she'd noticed a hawk, its wings outstretched and seemingly motionless as it rode the currents of air, quartering the side of the valley in search of prey.

She searched the small patch of sky that was now streaked with pink, but the bird had gone and the forest was wonderfully peaceful. She could no longer hear the tour guide's singsong voice pointing out the details they were expected to admire enthusiastically when, in truth, all they'd wanted was to be back at the coast with a very cold drink within easy reach.

She sipped at the bottle of water she carried in her shoulder bag before pouring a small amount on to the hem of her shirt to wipe over her face. Then, wondering how much longer she would have to endure this 'privilege', she glanced at her watch.

Three o'clock? Was that all it was?

She frowned. The pink streaks in the sky suggested it was later. She'd reset her watch to local time when she'd landed, but maybe she'd got it wrong; she hadn't actually been paying much attention to the time.

She stared up at the sky for a moment longer, then at the path taken by her companions. Night fell with stunning rapidity in this part of the world and she listened for any sound that might indicate their imminent return.

There was nothing. The birds had fallen silent, the insects had stopped their apparently ceaseless stridulating as if they, too, were listening.

The absolute quiet that a minute or two earlier had seemed so welcome now seemed strangely eerie, prickling her skin with goose-flesh, setting up the small hairs on the back of her neck at some unseen, unknown danger. A feeling that the earth itself was holding its breath.

'Wait!' Her urgent cry seemed pathetically small, smothered by the density of the vegetation and, in a sudden burst of panic at the thought of being left on her own in that ancient, ghost-filled place, she leapt to her feet and, quite oblivious of the heat, began to scramble up the steep path after the others.

'Wait,' she cried out again. 'Wait for me.'

She had covered perhaps twenty yards when she staggered slightly and, stumbling, put her hand to the ground to save herself. She didn't stop to wonder at such unaccustomed clumsiness, she was in too much of a hurry to catch up with the rest of the party. Then, as she took another step, she lost her balance again and grabbed for a tree as she was overcome with dizziness, staring down at the forest floor, which appeared to be rippling beneath her feet. Puzzled, but not yet alarmed.

Leaves, small pieces of twig and bark began to tumble from the dense canopy high above her and she gave a startled little scream as something hit her shoulder and bounced to the ground. It was a large spider and, for a moment, they stared at one another, both of them confused by the earth's uncharacteristic behaviour. Then the tree she was clinging to began to shake and Manda forgot all about the spider.

For a moment she hung on, clinging to the thick trunk regardless of the debris raining down on her head and shoulders, unable to concentrate on anything but the absolute necessity of remaining on her feet as the earth shook.

If she could just hold on, it would stop and then she would walk slowly back down the path to the tour bus and wait for the others to return.

Except that it didn't.

Instead, the shaking grew steadily worse until the ground beneath her felt as if it were surging in great undulating waves and the tree she was clinging on to for dear life lurched sideways as the path split open with a great jagged tear.

For a frozen moment in time Manda hung on, staring down into the thick green forest that carpeted the valley wall rippling beneath her like some storm-tossed sea. Then, as she realised she was about to be tipped into that maelstrom, she let go of the tree and flung herself across the gaping path a split second before the tree, its roots and the ground to which they were attached, fell away like a stone.

She was screaming now. Seriously screaming.

She knew she was screaming because, although she could not hear herself—all she could hear was the crack and roar as the earth split and tore about her—she could feel the harsh vibration in her throat.

Lying where she had thrown herself in her mad leap for safety, her arms wrapped around her head, her eyes tightly closed, she shrieked, 'Enough! No more, God. Stop it! Please!'

Then the ground beneath her gave way and she, too, was sliding into the abyss.

CHAPTER TWO

MANDA had no way of knowing what time it was, or how long she had been lying on cold stone. She was just grateful that the earth had stopped shaking.

After a while, though, she lifted her head, gingerly feeling for damage. Her fingers were stiff, sore as she tried to move them and there was a tender spot at the back of her head. A dull throbbing ache. Nothing that she couldn't, for the moment, live with, she decided. And she seemed lucid enough.

Lucid enough to know that she had lived through an earthquake and be grateful to have survived.

Lucid enough to know that living through the initial catastrophe might not be enough. She had been alone, separated from her party…

She let her head fall back against the stone and lay still for a moment while she gathered her wits, her strength, knowing that she should move, shout, do something to make herself heard, alert searchers to her presence.

In a moment.

She would do all that in a moment.

It was dark. Pitch-dark. There were no stars, no moon,

which suggested dense cloud cover. Was that normal after earthquakes? Tropical rain would be the absolute limit, she thought, as she tried to piece together exactly what had happened.

The earth shaking. The path splitting. Her fingers clawing at the earth as she had begun to fall.

She went cold as she relived that moment of terror as she'd been carried down on a torrent of earth and stones. As she realised just what that meant. Why there was no sky.

It wasn't cloud that was blocking it out. She'd fallen into some cavity. Into one of the temples? Maybe even one that hadn't been excavated. Or even discovered...

She was beneath the ground. Buried. Entombed. Locked in...

Panic sucked the breath from her. Her cry was wordless and, while every instinct was urging her to fling herself at the walls, claw her way out, she was unable to move.

She knew this feeling. The claustrophobia. The desperation to escape. Her body and mind too numb to do anything about it.

She'd been here before.

She swallowed hard, forced herself to concentrate on breathing...

In. One, two, three...

Told herself that it wasn't the same.

Hold. One, two, three...

That had been a mental lockdown. She'd been confined by the darkness in her mind.

Out. One, two, three...

This was physical.

She could do something about this, dig herself out with her

bare hands if need be, she told herself, even as she strained desperately for the comfort of voices, the clink of stones being turned. A promise that there was someone there. A hand in the darkness.

There was nothing. Only a blanketing silence. Only the rapid beating of her pulse in her ears.

For a moment she lost the rhythm of her breathing, gasping for air as fear began to overwhelm her.

She couldn't afford to panic. It would be a waste of energy, a waste of time, and if there was one thing she'd learned, it was how to take control of her body, her emotions.

Breathe in to the count of three…

She had to shut down everything but the core need to concentrate.

Hold to the count of three…

After that she could make a careful assessment of her situation. Decide what action to take. If ever there was a time to use everything she'd learned—to block out emotion by fixing on what had to be done, making a plan and carrying it through, this was it. If she once succumbed to mind-numbing, will-sapping terror…

Easier said than done.

Control was easy when you were calling all the shots, when you were the one directing events. But it was a long time since she'd been thrown entirely on her own resources.

In the metaphorical dark.

At least this dark was physical. Not that it was much comfort. She was miles from anywhere and even if any of her party was capable of making it to the nearest village it would take time for help to arrive.

She blotted that out.

She mustn't think about that.

Breathe, breathe… The air, at least, was fresh. For now.

She tried to swallow but her throat was dry. There was water in her bag. She had to find her bag. Concentrate on what she could do to keep herself alive because it was far too soon for any serious attempt at rescue.

If she was ever going to get out of here, the important thing was to keep calm. Conserve her strength.

She listened for the smallest sound.

The silence was so dense that it was like a suffocating weight against her eardrums, her chest and once again it almost overwhelmed her and she had to force herself to focus on normal, everyday things. Good things.

Ivo and Belle.

Daisy.

The precious new babies…

At least they didn't know where she was. Wouldn't be glued to news reports, worrying themselves sick. Ivo wouldn't be flying here to take charge…

No. On second thoughts that didn't help. She needed someone out there moving heaven and earth to find her. Lots of earth and stone.

But it wasn't going to happen.

She'd cut loose, broken the ties, had wanted to prove that she was capable of standing of her own feet.

Great timing, Manda…

Maybe she should see if she could stand up, try exploring her surroundings. Maybe she could find her own way out.

'See' being the operative word.

Alone in the dark, it was as if she had suddenly been struck blind and deaf. She lifted a hand but couldn't see it until it was right in front of her face and even then she wasn't sure if she could actually see it, or whether her brain was providing a picture of what she knew was there.

She'd never been in such absolute darkness, the kind of darkness that made an overcast night in the depths of Norfolk seem bright as day.

Maybe, she thought, with a rising tide of panic, she really was blind. Or deaf. Or both. Maybe she'd banged her head harder than she'd imagined and lost those precious vital senses. Maybe she'd been unconscious for hours.

In a sudden desperate need to remind herself that this wasn't so, she shouted, 'Help!'

Trapped in the confined space, her voice echoed and reverberated back at her, again and again until she covered her ears.

There was nothing wrong with her hearing.

She was just alone and in the dark. It might be her worst nightmare, but she wasn't about to wake up and find Ivo waiting to pick up the pieces and put her back together again. Not this time.

There would be no Belle to reach wordlessly for her hand.

No Daisy to grin at her, say something utterly outrageous.

A groan escaped her and suddenly her precious lucidity did not seem such a prize.

Muddle-headed, her memory would not be quite so painfully sharp. Confused, she wouldn't be quite so aware of the danger of her position.

Fear, real icy-cold fear, began to seep into every pore as she realised that, separated from her companions, no one would even know where to begin looking for her...

'Shut up, Manda,' she said. Then tried to decide whether talking to herself was a good sign or a bad one.

Rubbing briskly at her arms, she made a determined effort to exclude the building terror by thinking of something else.

Working out exactly where she was.

Okay.

She'd been standing on a forest path, so logic suggested that she should now be buried beneath tons of earth and vegetation. But she wasn't. Which was a good thing.

Instead, she was in a dark, echoing space, which presumably meant she had fallen into one of the temples.

Which was not...

The path had twisted and turned as they had climbed up the side of the hill and she tried to remember the temple they had visited before she had rebelled against so much enforced culture. Tried to remember which way the path had turned, but the darkness was confusing, blocking her thoughts.

If only she could see!

'Stop it, Miranda Grenville,' she told herself sternly. So she couldn't see. Tough. For her it was just a temporary inconvenience. There were millions of people who were forced to live with it every day of their lives. They coped and so would she.

Her eyes would adapt to the darkness in a few minutes.

She'd get herself out of there...

She stopped the thought before it reached the inevitable... *if it was the last thing she did.*

There was no point in tempting fate. Fate, it was clear, was already on her case in a big way. She had to treat this as if it were some organisational problem. The kind she'd handled for Ivo every day of her working life until she'd made the move to set up her own television production company with Belle and Daisy. Proving to herself, to everyone, that she no longer needed her brother as a prop.

Except that so far it had been a one-show wonder and without Belle...

No! Belle was brilliant in front of the camera, but she was the one who'd made it happen. That was what she did. Give her a goal, a project to bring in on time and she'd deliver the goods and she'd get herself out of here, too.

Breathe!

One, two, three...

Get up!

Rubble rattled off her as she finally managed to sit up; small pieces of stone, along with what felt like half a ton of fine cloying dust that rose up to choke her.

Coughing as the dust filled her nose, her throat, filtered down into her sensitive bronchial passages, Manda groped around for her bag. She'd been holding on to it as she'd taken off after the rest of the party and it must have fallen through the gap in the earth with her, although obviously not conveniently at her side.

Her left arm buckled a little as she eased herself forward to spread her arc of search, her elbow giving way when she put weight on it. Prompted by this, all her other joints decided to join in. Her left knee began to throb. Her shoulder. Her fingers were already stinging...

She stopped making a mental inventory when she realised that she hurt pretty much everywhere and instead congratulated herself that nothing seemed to be broken, although she hadn't actually tried to stand up yet. She flexed her toes but nothing too bad happened.

She had, it seemed, been lucky.

The last thing she remembered was the ground heaving upwards, shifting sideways, tipping her through into the earth's basement like so much garbage, but at least she was in one piece and able to move about.

Check out her surroundings...

She spread her hands and began to feel around for her bag. That had to be her first priority. She had water in her bag.

No luck.

She carefully eased herself to her knees, then cautiously to her feet, feeling above her for the roof, blinking rapidly as if that would somehow clear her vision.

Her hands met no resistance, but maybe her eyes had adjusted a little because the darkness didn't seem quite so dense now. Or were those shapes no more than her brain playing tricks?

She swallowed, inched forward, hands outstretched, letting out a tiny shriek as her palms touched something. For a moment her heart went into overdrive, even while her head processed the information.

Cold, flat. It was a wall.

Once she'd regained her breath, she began to edge her way carefully around the boundary of her underground prison.

She was certain now that she was in one of the temples. They had passed a truly impressive entrance that had been more thoroughly cleared than the rest, but the guide had hurried them past, nervously warning that it was 'not safe' when one of the businessmen had stopped, wanting to go inside.

At the time she hadn't questioned it; she'd just been grateful to be spared yet more of the same. But, before they'd been hurried on, she had glimpsed tools of some kind, a work table.

The tools would be very welcome right now. And if someone was working there, presumably there'd be a lamp, water…

She tried not to think about what would happen if she didn't find her bag with her water bottle. She'd find it…

Every now and then her fingers encountered sharply cut images carved into the walls. Protected from the elements within the temple walls, they were as clean-edged as the day they had been chiselled into the stone.

She had seen enough of them before she'd abandoned the tour and her brain, deprived of light, eagerly supplied pictures of those strange stylised creatures to fill the void.

In the powerful beam of the guide's torch they had seemed slightly sinister.

In the blackness her imagination amplified the threat and she began to shiver.

Stupid, stupid…

Concentrate. Breathe…

She counted the steps around the edge of her cell. Two, three, four… Her mind refused to co-operate but took itself off on a diversion to wonder about her companions. Had they survived? Were they, even now, being picked up by some rescue team? Would they realise that she wasn't with them?

One of the businessmen had been eyeing her with a great deal more interest than the ruins. Maybe he would alert the rescuers to her absence. Assuming there were any rescuers.

Assuming any of them had survived.

That thought brought the fear seeping back and for a moment she leaned against the wall as a great shuddering sigh swept through her and she covered her ears as if to block it out.

There was no point in dwelling on such negative thoughts. She had to keep strong, in control, to survive. But, even as she clung to that thought, the wall began to shake.

'No!' She didn't know whether she screamed it out loud or whether the agonised word was a whisper in her mind as an aftershock flung her away from its illusory protection.

She used her hands to protect herself, landing painfully on palms and knees.

Dust showered down on to her, filling her eyes and, as she gasped for air, her mouth. For a moment she was certain she was about to suffocate and in sheer terror she let rip with a scream.

That was when, out of the darkness, fingers clamped tightly about her arm and a gravelly voice said, 'For pity's sake, woman, give it a rest…'

CHAPTER THREE

JAGO appeared to have the hangover from hell, which was odd. Getting drunk would have been an understandable reaction to the discovery that Fliss had been using him and he'd certainly had the means, thanks to Rob. But he was fairly certain that, on reflection, he'd decided he'd taken enough punishment for one day.

Or maybe that was simply wishful thinking because there was no doubt that right now he was lying with his face pressed against the cold stone of the floor. Not a good sign. And he was hurting pretty much everywhere but mostly inside his head, where an incompetent but unbelievably enthusiastic drummer was using his skull for practice.

He would have told him to stop, but it was too much trouble.

That was the problem with drinking to forget. While it might seem like a great idea when you were swallowing the hot local liquor that offered instant oblivion, unfortunately it was a temporary state unless you kept on drinking.

He remembered thinking that as the first mouthful had burned its way down his throat and then…

And then nothing.

Dumber than he'd thought, then, and come morning he'd be sorry he hadn't made the effort to make it as far as the camp-bed, but what was one more regret? He'd scarcely notice it amongst the pile already waiting to be sifted through.

Right now, what he needed was water and he groped around him, hoping to find a bottle within reach. Aspirin would be good too, but that was going to have to wait until he'd recovered a little.

His fingers encountered rubble.

Rubble?

Where on earth was he?

His forehead creased in a frown which he instantly regretted, swearing silently as the pain drilled through his skull. It didn't take a genius to work out that if a simple frown caused that kind of grief, anything louder than a thought would be unwise.

He closed his eyes and, for the moment, the pain in his head receded a little. But only for a moment. The ground, it seemed, had other ideas, refusing to leave him in peace, shaking him like a dog at a bone. And, if that wasn't bad enough, there was some woman having hysterics practically in his ear.

Oblivion was a lot harder to come by than you'd think.

He turned over, reached out and, as his palm connected with smooth, firm flesh he wondered, without too much interest, who she was. Before growling at her to shut up.

There was a startled yelp and then blissful silence. And the earth had finally stopped making a fuss too.

A result.

He let his head fall back against the floor.

It was too good to last.

'Hello?' The woman's voice, now she'd stopped scream-ing, was low, a little bit husky, with the kind of catch in it that would undoubtedly ensnare any poor sap who hadn't already learned the hard way that no woman was ever that vulnerable.

It wasn't that he was immune. Far from it.

He might be feeling awful, but his body still automatically tightened in hopeful response to the enticing warmth of a woman's voice up close in the dark.

It was over-optimistic.

A grunt was, for the moment, the limit of his ambition but he forced open unwilling eyelids and lifted his head an inch or two to take a look.

Opening his eyes didn't make much difference, he discov-ered, but since light would have only added to his pain he decided to be grateful for small mercies. But not that grateful. Women were definitely off the agenda and he said, 'Clear off.'

Having got that off his chest, he closed his eyes and let his head drop back to the floor.

'Wh-who are you?' She might be nervous but she was ir-ritatingly persistent. 'Are you hurt?'

'Terminally,' he assured her. 'Body and soul. Totally beyond saving, so do me a favour. Go away and leave me to die in peace.'

No chance. She was a woman so she did the opposite, moving closer, finding his shoulder, feeling for his neck. She was checking his pulse, he realised. The stupid female had taken him seriously...

Apparently satisfied that he wasn't, despite his protesta-tions, about to expire on her, she slid her hand up to his cheek, laying long cool fingers against it, soothing his pounding head which, if he were honest, he had to admit felt pretty good.

'Who are you?' she persisted, her voice stronger now that she'd satisfied herself that he was in one piece. In fact, she had the crisp enunciation of a woman who expected an answer. Without delay.

Her touch wasn't *that* good.

Delete vulnerable and caring, replace with bossy, interfering, typical of a particular type of organising female with whom he was very familiar. The ones he knew all had moustaches and chaired committees that allocated research funding...

He didn't bother to answer. She didn't give up but leaned over him so that he was assailed by the musky scent of warm skin before, after a pause, she wiped something damp over his face.

'Is that better?' she asked.

He was getting very mixed messages here, but provided she kept the volume down she could carry on with her Florence Nightingale act.

'Were you on the bus?' she asked.

Jago sighed.

That was the trouble with women; they couldn't be content with just doing the ministering angel stuff. They had to talk. Worse, they insisted you answer them.

'Don't you understand simple English?' he growled, swatting away her hand. The price of comfort came too high.

She didn't take the hint, but laid it over his forehead in a way that suggested she thought he might not be entirely right in it. The head, that was. Definitely one of the moustache brigade, he thought, although her hand had the soft, pampered feel of someone who took rather more care of her appearance. Soft and pampered and her long, caressing fingers were giving his body ideas whether his head was coming along for the ride or not.

Definitely not yet another archaeology student looking for postgrad experience, then. At least that was something in her favour. Not even Fliss, who had lavished cream on every part of her body—generously inviting him to lend a hand—had been able to keep her hands entirely callus-free.

But she *was* female, so that cancelled out all the plus points. Including that warm female scent that a man, if he was dumb enough, could very easily lose himself in…

'Read my lips,' he said, snapping back from temptation. 'Go away.'

'I can't see your damn lips,' she replied sharply. The mild expletive sounded unexpectedly shocking when spoken in that expensive finishing school accent.

And she didn't move.

On the contrary, she dropped her head so that her hair brushed against his cheek. He recognised the scent now. Rosemary.

It was rosemary.

His mother had planted a bush by the garden gate. Some superstitious nonsense was involved, he seemed to remember. It had grown over the path so that he'd brushed against it when he wheeled out his bike…

This woman used rosemary-scented shampoo and it took him right back to memories he thought he'd buried too deep to ever be dredged up again and he told her, this time in the most basic of terms, to go away.

'Can you move?' she asked, ignoring him. 'Where does it hurt?'

Woman, thy name is persistence…

'What I've got is a headache,' he said. 'You.' He thought about sitting up but not very seriously. 'I don't suppose you've come across a bottle around here by any chance?'

Since she insisted on staying, she might as well make herself useful.

'Bottle?' She sniffed. Then the soft hand was snatched back from his forehead. 'You're drunk!' she exclaimed.

Unlikely. Headache notwithstanding, he was, unhappily, thinking far too clearly for it to be alcohol-related, but he didn't argue. If Dame Disapproval thought he was a drunk she might leave him alone.

'Not nearly drunk enough,' he replied, casting around him with a broad sweep of his hand until he connected with what he was thinking clearly enough to recognise as a woman's breast. It was on the small side but it was firm, encased in lace and fitted his palm perfectly.

Alone and in the dark, Manda had thought things couldn't get any worse until cold fingers had fastened around her arm. That had been the realisation of every childhood nightmare, every creepy movie she had watched from behind half-closed fingers and for a blind second her bogeyman-in-the-dark terror had gone right off the scale.

Then he'd spoken.

The words, admittedly, had not been encouraging, his voice little more than a growl. But the growl had been in English and the knowledge that by some miracle she was not alone, that there was another person in that awful darkness, someone to share the nightmare, dispel the terrible silence, had been so overwhelming that she had almost blubbed with sheer relief.

Thankfully, she had managed to restrain herself, since the overwhelming relief appeared to have been a touch premature.

It was about par for the day that, instead of being incarcerated with a purposeful and valiant knight errant, she had stumbled on some fool who'd been hell-bent on drinking himself to death when the forces of nature had decided to help him out.

'I think you've had quite enough to drink already,' she said a touch acidly.

'Wrong answer. At a time like this there isn't enough alcohol in the world, lady. Unless, of course, you're prepared to divert me with some more interesting alternative?'

And, in case she hadn't got the point, he rubbed a thumb, with shocking intimacy, over her nipple. And then, presumably because she didn't instantly protest, he did it again.

Her lack of protest was not meant as encouragement but, already prominent from the chill of the underground temple, his touch had reverberated through her body, throwing switches, lighting up dark, long undisturbed places, momentarily robbing her of breath.

By the time she'd gasped in sufficient air to make her feelings felt, they had become confused. In the darkness, the intimacy, heat, beating life force of another body had not felt like an intrusion. Far from it. It had felt like a promise of life.

It was no more than instinct, she told herself; the standard human response in the face of death was to cling to someone, anyone. That thought was enough to bring her back to her senses.

'I don't think so,' she said, belatedly slapping his hand away.

'Please yourself. Let me know if you change your mind.'
He rolled away from her and, despite the fact that it was no
more than a grope from a drunk, she still missed the human
warmth of his touch.

She *wanted* his hand on her breast. Wanted a whole lot
more.

Nothing had changed, it seemed. Beneath the hard protective shell she'd built around her, she was as weak and needy as
ever.

She'd quickly slipped the buttons on her shirt so that she
could lift up the still damp hem to wipe his face. Now she used
it to wipe her own throat. Cool her overheated senses.

'It would please me,' she said, 'if you'd give some thought
to getting us out of here.'

She snapped out the words, but it was herself she was
angry with.

'Why would I do that?' he replied, as she struggled with
sore fingers to refasten the small buttons. 'I *like* it here.' Then,
'But I like it here best when I'm alone.'

'In that case I suggest you stay exactly where you are and
wait for the next shock to bring the rest of the temple down
on top of you. Then you'll be alone until some archaeologist
uncovers your bones in another two or three thousand years.'

Jago laughed at the irony of that. A short harsh sound that,
even to his own ears, sounded distinctly unpleasant. 'That's
an interesting idea, lady, but since I'm not the butler you'll
have to see yourself out.' Then, as an afterthought, 'Although
if you see that bottle it would be an act of charity…'

'Forget the damn bottle,' she retorted angrily. 'It may have
escaped your notice, but you can't see your hand in front of
you in here.'

'It's night,' he muttered, finally making an effort to sit up, ignoring the pains shooting through every cramped joint as he explored the floor about him. 'And now I really do need a drink.'

'Only a drunk needs a drink. Is that what you are?'

'Not yet. That takes practice, but give me time…'

He stopped his fruitless search for a bottle of water and stared in the direction of the voice. She was right; it *was* dark. On moonless nights the stars silvered the temple with a faint light and even here, in the lower level, they shone down the shaft cut through the hillside that was aligned so that the full moon, at its highest arc in the sky, lit up the altar.

He blinked, rapidly. It made no difference. And as his mind cleared, it began to dawn on him that something was seriously wrong. The dust. The rubble…

He put his hand to his head in an attempt to still the drummer. 'What day is this?'

'Monday.'

'It's still Monday?'

'I think so. I don't know how long I was out and it's too dark to see my watch, but I don't think it could have been long.'

He propped himself against the nearest wall and tried to remember.

Something about Rob…

'Out?' he asked, leaving the jumble to sort itself out. Definitely not alcohol in Miss Bossy's case. 'What happened to you?'

'Work it out for yourself,' she snapped.

She was halfway to her feet when his hand, sweeping the air in the direction of her voice, connected with her leg and grabbed it. She let out a shriek of alarm.

'Shut up,' he said tightly. 'I've got a headache and I can't think with all that noise.'

'Poor baby,' she crooned with crushing insincerity. Then lashed out with her free leg, her toe connecting with his thigh.

He jerked her other leg from beneath her, which was a mistake since she landed on top of him.

He said one word, but since she'd knocked the breath out of him, only he knew for certain what it was.

Manda considered kicking him again but thought better of it. They needed to stop bickering and start working together and, whoever he was, he had an impressively broad shoulder. The kind built for leaning on.

His shirt, beneath her cheek, had the soft feel that heavy-duty cotton got when it had been worn and washed times without number and the bare skin of his neck smelled of soap.

Maybe he wasn't going to be such a total loss after all...

'Make yourself at home, why don't you,' he said, taking her by the waist and shifting her a little to the right before settling his hands on her backside, at which point she realised that it wasn't only his shoulders that were impressive and...

And what the heck was she thinking?

She rolled off him, biting back a yelp as she landed on what felt like the Rock of Gibraltar. If he knew, he'd laugh.

'Who the hell are you?' she demanded.

'Who the hell are *you*?' he retaliated, definitely not amused. On the contrary, he sounded decidedly irritable. 'And what are you doing here?'

'I asked first.'

There was an ominous silence and it occurred to Manda that, no matter what the provocation, further aggravating a man already in a seriously bad mood was not a particularly bright idea.

It wasn't that she cared what he thought of her, but those broad shoulders of his were going to be an asset since it was obvious that their chances of survival would double if they worked together.

Tricky enough under the best of circumstances.

Team-building was not one of her more developed skills; she tended to work best as top dog. Issuing orders. It worked well with the TV production team she'd put together. Belle, in front of camera, was undoubtedly the star, but she was a professional, used to taking direction.

Daisy... Well, Daisy was learning.

Sensing that on this occasion she was going to need a different approach, she began again by introducing herself.

'Look, we seem to have got off on the wrong foot. My name is Miranda Grenville,' she said, striving, with difficulty, for politeness. 'I'm here taking a short break...'

'In Cordillera? Are you crazy?'

She gritted her teeth, then said, 'Undoubtedly. It has possibilities as a holiday destination, admittedly, but so far none of them have been successfully exploited.'

'Oh, believe me. They've got the exploitation angle covered.'

He didn't sound happy about that, either.

'Not noticeably,' she replied. 'And tourists tend to have a bit of a phobia about earthquakes.'

'In that case they—you—would be well advised to stick to somewhere safer,' he retaliated. 'Try Bournemouth next time.'

'Thank you for your advice. I'll bear it in mind should there ever be a "next time".'

His bad mood was beginning to seriously annoy her, a fact which, if he'd known her, should worry him. That she suspected it wouldn't bother him in the slightest made him interesting. A pain, but interesting…

'Meanwhile, since I'm here—we're here—in the middle of the earthquake that happened while you were sleeping off…' politeness, Manda, politeness '…whatever you were sleeping off, maybe you'd like to help me figure out how we're going to get out of here?'

She spoke in calm, measured tones. Dealing with an idiot had the advantage of making her forget her own fears, it seemed.

He replied briefly in a manner that was neither calm nor measured. Then, having got that off his chest, he said, 'There's been an earthquake?'

'By George he's got it,' she replied sarcastically.

He repeated his first thought, expressing his feelings with a directness that she'd have found difficulty in bettering if she wasn't making a determined effort to play nice. Clearly, this was not the moment to point out that he hadn't completed their introductions.

Whoever he was, he didn't seem to have much time for the social niceties, but the silence went on for a long time and, after a while, she cleared her throat—just to get rid of the dust.

Manda heard him shift in the darkness, felt rather than saw him turn in her direction. 'Tell me,' he said, after what seemed like an age. 'What, in the name of all that's holy, are you doing in a Cordilleran temple in the middle of an earthquake?'

For a moment she considered telling him that it was none of his damned business. But she needed his help, whoever he was. So she compromised.

'I'll tell you that,' she informed him, 'if you'll tell me what the devil you're doing, drinking yourself to perdition in a Cordilleran temple. At any time.'

Despite the pain in his head, Jago had to admit that this woman had a certain entertainment value and he laughed.

This was not a wise move as his head was swift to remind him. But something about the way she'd come back at him had been so unexpectedly sharp, so refreshingly astringent that he couldn't help himself. And if she was right about the earthquake she got ten out of ten for…something. If only being a pain in the butt.

Admittedly it was a very nicely put together butt…

He began, despite every cell in his body clamouring a warning, to wonder who she was, where she had come from. What she looked like.

Had he, despite his best intentions, started drinking in Rob's bar and been so lost to sense that he'd picked up some lone female tourist looking for a good time and brought her back here with him? If so, he'd signally failed to deliver, he thought, as he searched his memory for a picture to match the voice.

His memory refused to oblige so he was forced to ask, 'Did I pick you up in Rob's bar?'

'Who's Rob?'

'I guess that answers that question…'

'Don't you remember?'

Great butt, smart mouth. Tricky combination. 'If I remembered I wouldn't ask,' he snapped right back, but the scorn in her voice warned him that he was on dangerous ground. And, remembering that kick, it occurred to him that insulting her might not be his best idea.

But where the hell had she come from?

Everything after Rob had thrust that bottle at him was something of a blur, but he hadn't been in the mood to pick up a woman, no matter how warm and willing she was—and actually he was getting very mixed messages about that—but then he'd be the first to admit that he hadn't been thinking too straight.

If only his head didn't hurt so much. He needed to concentrate…

He had a vague memory of driving back up the side of the mountain in a mood as grim as the pagan gods that had guarded the temple and he glared into the darkness as if they had the answer.

It really was dark.

Of his companion he had no more than a vague impression, amplified by that handful of a small, perfectly formed breast. Two handfuls of neat little butt. Tallish, he thought, a bit on the skinny side, but with hair that smelled of childhood innocence…

He stopped the thought right there.

Women were born devious and he was done with the whole treacherous, self-serving sex.

He'd driven back from the coast on his own, he was certain of that, but if he hadn't picked her up, where the devil had she come from?

He scrubbed at his face with his hands in an effort to clear away the confusion. Then, dragging his fingers through his hair, he winced as he encountered a damn great lump and a stickiness that couldn't be anything but blood.

It seemed that the throbbing ache in his head was the result of a collision with something hard rather than the effects of

Cordilleran brandy. Unless he had fallen out of the camp-bed he'd set up down here after the rest of the team had left when the rains set in. Going home to their families.

It was drier than his hut in the village during the rains. Quieter. And, without Fliss to distract him, he'd got a lot of work done.

He blinked. The lack of light was beginning to irritate him. He wanted to be able to see this woman. Was she another student backpacking her way around the globe? If so, she'd chosen the wrong day to drop in looking for work experience…

'Okay, I didn't pick you up in a bar,' he began, then stopped. That was too loud. Much too loud. 'So where—?'

'You didn't pick me up anywhere.' Her disembodied voice enunciated each word slowly and carefully, as if speaking to someone for whom English was a foreign language. 'I'm fussy about who I hang around with.'

'Really? My mistake,' he said, heavy on the irony. 'So how did you get here?'

'By bus.'

Jago laughed again and this time he was genuinely amused at the thought of this hoity-toity madam flagging down one of the island's overcrowded buses and piling in with the goats and chickens.

Apparently she didn't share his sense of humour.

'What's so funny?'

'Not a thing,' he said, meaning it. Then, 'What did you say your name was? Amanda…?' The effort of remembering her surname was too much and he let it go.

'Miranda,' she corrected. 'My friends call me Manda but, since I have no plans for a long acquaintance with you, whoever you are, we might as well keep it formal.'

'Suits me,' he replied with feeling. Then, 'I'm Jago,' he said, begrudgingly giving up his name at the same time as he remembered hers. Grenville. That was what she had said. The name was vaguely familiar, but he didn't recognise her voice. Maybe the face... He could strike a match, he supposed, but really it was too much effort and, despite his desire to see her, he wasn't ready for anything that bright. 'No,' he said. 'Sorry. I give up. I've forgotten where we met.'

'It sounds to me as if you gave up a long time ago but I'll put you out of your misery. We've never met.'

'I may be careless, lady—'

'Will you please stop calling me that,' she interrupted crossly. 'My name is Miranda—'

'I may be careless about some things, *Miranda*,' he said, with heavy emphasis on her name, 'but I've given up on inviting strangers home to tea.'

'Why is that, I wonder? Are you frightened they might steal the silver?'

He wished, but confined his response to, 'Who are you? What are you?'

CHAPTER FOUR

GOOD question, Manda thought. One to which the people she lived and worked with could give any number of answers, most of them wrong.

'Does it matter? I promise I won't run off with the spoons,' she said, pulling a face, confident that he would not see it.

It was a long time since afternoon tea had been part of his social life if she was any judge of the situation. But although a little verbal fencing in the dark with an unknown, unseen man might have been amusing at any other time, she'd had enough. She'd had enough of the dark, enough of being scared, enough of him.

'Oh, forget it. Just point me in the direction of the nearest exit and I'll be only too happy to leave you alone.'

Jago was beyond such politeness. His head was pounding like the percussion section of the London Philharmonic and all he wanted to do was lie down and close his eyes. 'You got yourself in here. Reverse the process,' he advised. 'You'll be home in no time.' Then added, 'Don't forget to shut the door on your way out.'

An explosive little sound echoed around the dark chamber. 'Sober up and look around you, Mr Jago. There aren't any doors.'

He groaned.

Why was it, with the whole world of wonderful things to choose from, God had picked women as the opposite sex?

'Time and white ants have done their worst,' he admitted, 'but I was speaking metaphorically. Entrance. Opening. Ingress. Access. Take your pick.'

'What on earth is the matter with you? Did a lump of stone fall on your head? Or have you drunk yourself quite senseless?'

'That was the plan,' he said, hoping that she might finally take the hint, shut up and leave him in peace. 'It doesn't seem to have worked. How did you get in here, anyway? This area is restricted.'

'To whom?'

To whom? He rubbed his hand over his face again—carefully avoiding the lump on his hairline this time—in an attempt to bring it back to life. Whoever this female was, she couldn't be a student. No student he'd ever met could be bothered to speak English with that precision. He eased himself into a sitting position. 'To me, Miranda Grenville. To me. And you weren't invited.'

'I wouldn't have come if I had been,' she declared. 'This is the last place I want to be, but I'm afraid you'll have to stand in line to send your complaint to a higher authority.'

'Oh? And which higher authority would that be?' he enquired, knowing full well that it was a mistake, that he would regret it, but completely unable to help himself. There was something about this woman that just got under his skin.

'Mother Nature?' she offered. 'I was simply standing on

a footpath, quietly minding my own business, when the ground opened up beneath me and I fell through your roof. As I believe I've already mentioned, while you were busy drowning your sorrows there was an earthquake.'

'An earthquake?' He frowned. Wished he hadn't. 'A genuine, honest-to-God earthquake?'

'It seemed very real to me.'

'Not just a tremor?'

'Not a tremor. I was in Brazil last year when there was a tremor,' she explained. 'I promise you this was the real deal.'

Jago fumbled in his pocket for a box of matches. As he struck one, it flared briefly, for a moment blinding him with the sudden brightness so near to his face, but as his eyes adjusted to the light, he stared around, momentarily speechless at the destruction that surrounded him.

The outside walls of the temple, with their stone carvings, had been pushed inward and the floor that he had spent months digging down through the debris of centuries to clear was now little more than rubble.

The woman was right. It would have taken a serious earthquake to have caused this much damage.

It had, all in all, been one hell of a day.

A small anguished sound caught his attention and he turned to his unwelcome companion, temporarily forgotten as he had surveyed the heartbreaking destruction of the centuries-old temple complex built by a society whose lives he had devoted so much time to understanding. Reconstructing.

He swore and dropped the match as it burned down to his fingers.

The darkness after the brief flare of light seemed, if anything, more intense, thicker, substantial enough to cut into slices and in a moment of panic he groped in the box for another match.

It was empty.

There was a new carton somewhere, but his supplies were stored at the far end of the temple. And the far end of the temple, as he'd just seen, was no more…

'We're trapped, aren't we?'

Her voice had, in that instant of light, lost all that assured bravado.

'Of course we're not trapped,' he snapped back. The last thing he needed was hysterics. 'I just need a minute to figure the best way out.'

'There isn't one. I saw—'

Too late. Her voice was rising in panic and his own clammy moment of fear was still too close to risk her going over the edge and taking him with her.

'Shut up and let me think.'

She gave a juddering little hiccup as she struggled to obey him, to control herself, but he forced himself to ignore the instinct to reach out, hold her, comfort her.

She'd said she'd been standing on the path, presumably the one leading to the acropolis, but she couldn't have been alone.

'How did you get up here?' His voice was sharper this time, demanding an answer.

'I told you,' she said. 'By bus.'

His head still hurt like hell, but the realisation that he was caught up in the aftermath of an earthquake had done much to concentrate his mind. He'd broken the seal on the bottle of brandy, but the minute the liquor had touched his lips he'd set it down, recognising the stupidity of drinking himself into oblivion.

That was what Rob had done when his yacht had gone down in a storm. Was still doing. Washed up on the beach and pretty much a wreck himself…

'What kind of bus?' he demanded. 'Nobody lives up here.' The locals avoided the area, ancient folk memory keeping them well away from the place.

'Not a local bus. I was on a sightseeing trip.'

He grunted.

A sightseeing trip. Of course.

The government was trying attract tourism investment, but Cordillera would be hard pushed to compete with the other established resorts of the Far East unless there was something else, something different to tempt the jaded traveller.

The ruins of a sexed-up ancient civilisation would do as well as anything. And once the finance was fixed, the resorts built, the visitors would flood in.

He hadn't wanted hordes of tourists trampling about the place disturbing his work. As archaeological director of the site he had the authority to keep them out and he'd used it.

He'd seen the damage that could be done, knew that once there was a market for artefacts, it wouldn't be long before the locals would forget their fear and start digging up the forest for stuff, chiselling chunks of their history to sell to tourists.

He'd known that sooner or later he would be overruled, but in the meantime he'd kept everything but the bare bones of his discoveries to himself, delaying publication for as long as possible.

Impatient for results he could exploit to his advantage, it seemed that Felipe Dominez had looked for another way.

'I hadn't realised that we were already on the tourist route,' he said bitterly.

'I don't think you are,' she assured him. 'If a trade delegation whose flight was delayed hadn't been shanghaied into taking the trip, it would have been me, a couple of dozen other unfortunates who believed that Cordillera was going to be the next big thing and the driver-cum-tour-guide. Why the business people bothered I can't imagine.'

'I can,' he said sourly, 'if the alternative was the doubtful comforts of the airport departure lounge.'

'Maybe, but at least there they'd be sure someone was going to try and dig them out of the rubble. Here—'

He didn't think it wise to let her dwell on what was likely to be her fate 'here'.

'What happened to the rest of your party?' he cut in quickly.

'It was hot and sticky and I was suffering from a severe case of ancient culture fatigue so I decided to sit out the second half of the tour. When the ground opened up and swallowed me I was on my own.'

'But you'll be missed?'

'Will I?' Manda asked.

In the panic she knew it was unlikely. Even supposing anyone else had survived. They could easily have suffered the same fate as she had and she was unbelievably lucky not to have been buried beneath tons of debris… Maybe. That would at least have been quick.

Trapped down here, the alternative might prove to be a lot worse, she thought, and dug what was left of her nails into the palms of her hands.

Breathe…

'I suppose that eventually someone will wonder what happened to me,' she admitted. 'Right now, I suspect they'll all be too busy surviving, Mr Jago, so if you could put your mind to the problem of how we're going to get out of here I really would be grateful.' There was a long pause. 'Please.'

That belated 'please' bothered Jago.

His uninvited guest had not, so far, displayed any real inclination to politeness. On the contrary, she'd been full of spit and fire, swiftly recovering from that momentary wobble a few moments ago.

'Miranda?'

'Yes?'

About to suggest that under the circumstances they could probably both do with a drink, he changed his mind. In the unlikely event that he managed to find the bottle of brandy in one piece, it might be wiser to hang on to it. Maybe later she would be grateful for the possibility of at least temporary oblivion. Maybe they both would.

Instead he said, 'Most people just call me Jago.'

There was a small silence. 'And what does everyone else call you?' she asked, still fighting a rearguard action against the fear, keeping the edge going.

Soft, sweet words, he thought. All of them lies. 'Nothing fit for the ears of a lady.' Then, eager to change the subject, 'Were you hurt when you fell?'

'Just a few bruises,' she said, with a carelessness that suggested she was being economical with the truth. 'What about you?'

'Not bad, apart from a pain in my leg where someone kicked me.' Keeping it sharp was good. She was keeping up a great front so far; kindness might just have her in pieces, which was something he could do without. 'And a headache which probably has more to do with the large lump on my forehead and less to do with alcohol than I originally supposed. But I'll probably live.'

'If we get out of here.'

'We'll get out. I just need to get my bearings.'

'Maybe you should light another match.'

'I would,' he replied. Then, since there was no way to save her from reality, 'Unfortunately that was the last one.'

'What?'

It took a moment for the disaster to sink in. Despite the devastation revealed in those few moments as the match flame had burned away the darkness, the very promise of light had driven back a little of Manda's fear. But no more matches meant no more light and all at once the blackness, thick enough to touch, seemed to be pressing against her face, smothering her.

She scrambled to her feet, brushing frantically at her face with her hands as if somehow she could rid herself of it, rid herself of the sense of being suffocated.

'Don't stand up!'

Jago's urgent warning came too late and, stumbling on the uneven, broken floor, she saved herself by grasping a handful of cloth as she fell against him.

He grunted as she went down, collapsing against him, taking him down with her. He flung his arms about her in an attempt to stop her from hurting herself further, but in her panic she began to fight him, threshing about to free herself.

'Steady now,' Jago muttered into her hair as he hung on, recognising the mindless fear that had overtaken her. 'Calm down, for pity's sake. You'll only hurt yourself.'

And him. He didn't bother to mention that just in case it gave her ideas.

It made no difference since she didn't seem to hear him, but continued to struggle fiercely like a trapped animal and he winced and swore as she broke free, her elbow catching him a glancing blow on the jaw.

'We'll be all right,' he said, keeping his voice low, doing his best to reassure her. 'I'll get us out of here.'

She wasn't listening. Beyond simple reason, she was fighting blindly to escape and, swearing as he took another blow, he pressed his face into her breast to protect himself as he struggled to hold her.

'Let me go!' she demanded. 'I don't need you to get me out of here. Stick with your bottle…' And she continued to kick and writhe until she connected solidly with his shin.

It was enough. The girl was slender but she had a kick like a mule and he rolled over, pinning her to the ground.

'Be still,' he warned, abandoning reassurance, making it an order. She continued to heave and buck beneath him, uncaring of the dust rising in choking clouds around them, too lost in her own spiralling hysteria to hear him, or to obey him even if she could.

He'd have to let go to slap her and while the temptation was almost overwhelming—he was still feeling that kick—he chose the only other alternative left open to him and kissed her.

It was brutal but effective, cutting off the stream of invective, cutting off her breath and, taken by surprise, she went rigid beneath him. And then, just as swiftly, she was clinging to him, her mouth hot and eager as she pressed against him, desperate for the warmth of a human body. For comfort in the darkness. A no-holds-barred kiss without a hidden agenda. Pure, honest, raw need that tapped into something deep inside him. And for a seemingly endless moment he answered it without question.

As suddenly as it began it was over. Miranda slumped back against the cracked and—now—sloping floor of the temple. Jago, his body flattening her to the ground, was horribly aware of the huge shuddering sob that swept through her.

'I'm sorry,' she said and for a hideous moment he thought she was apologising for kissing him. 'I thought I had it.' She shivered again. 'I thought I had it under control…'

'Hey, come on. You're doing fine,' he said, lifting his hand to her face in a gesture that was meant to offer comfort, re-assurance but she flinched away from him.

'Don't! Don't ever do that again!'

'I could just as easily have slapped you,' he said.

'I wish you had.'

'Fine. I'll remember you said that the next time you get hysterical.'

'In your dreams, Mr Jago,' she declared fervently.

'In yours, Ms Grenville.'

In truth they were both breathing rather more heavily and her verbal rejection was certainly not being followed up by her body. Or his. Being this close to a stranger, to a woman who was no more than curves that fitted his body like a glove, soft skin, a scent in the darkness, was doing something to his head.

Her hair, a short, sleek bob, was like silk beneath his hand and she smelled so sweet and fresh after the damp, cloying air of the jungle; a primrose after the heavy, drugging scent of the huge trumpet lilies that hung from the trees, drenching the air of the forest.

She was slender but strong, with a firm leggy body that he guessed would be perfectly at home on horseback. He knew the type. Had grown up with girls who sounded—and felt—like this. Haughty girls who knew their worth, girls bred for men who had titles, or with bank balances large enough to cancel out the lack of one. Made for swish hotels and six hundred-thread Egyptian cotton sheets rather than a stone floor and a man who'd walked away from such luxuries, from everything that went with it, a long time ago.

He knew—they both did—that if he kissed her again, it would be slow and hot and she'd be with him every step of the way and the thought of taking a woman like her on the cold stone, amidst the rubble, without any pretence, any of the ritual dance that a man was expected to go through before he could claim such a prize, was a temptation almost beyond measure.

'Jago?' Her voice, soft and low, pulled him away from his dark thoughts and he finally moved, putting an inch between them, knowing that it was his damaged ego, pride rather than passion, that was driving his libido. Demanding satisfaction. 'Who are you?'

He'd asked her the same question. Her reply had been to ask whether it mattered.

Did it?

He'd grown up knowing exactly who he was, what his future held. He'd walked away from all of it, built another life. Now he was just a fool who had allowed a girl with a hot body to take him to the cleaners.

A fool who was about to become a serious embarrassment

to a Cordilleran government minister who he suspected might find it very convenient if he never emerged from the ruins of his own excavations.

'Me?' he said. 'I told you. I'm the man who's going to get us out of here.'

'Right.'

'You don't sound convinced.'

Oh, she was convinced, Manda thought. If it was possible, he would do it.

She'd briefly glimpsed Jago's silhouette in the flare of the match; a dark mop of hair, a strong neck, broad shoulders that, as the light had gone out, had remained a ghostly negative imprint in the darkness.

The impression had been of power: not the weakness of a man who'd surrendered to the easy oblivion of drink. His face had been taut, firm to the touch. Beneath her fingers, his body had the sinewy, muscled strength of a man who knew how to work. And his mouth—she felt the weakness return; his mouth had not tasted of stale alcohol, but had the clean, hard, demanding authority of a man who was confident of his power to overwhelm all and any objections.

But what woman would object?

Despite their bad start, every instinct told her that he was the real deal, a true alpha male, and she'd come within a heartbeat of succumbing to an intimacy that she'd denied herself for so long, aware that, if only for a little while, this man had the ability to wipe out the darkness.

She had resisted the temptation, knowing that when the darkness returned it would be even worse.

Realising that she was still pressing herself against him, clinging close for support, warmth, comfort—something darker and more compelling—she pulled away and he didn't make any move to stop her.

'Convinced?' she said, using the words, a disparaging tone to her voice, to put more distance between them, distract herself from the throbbing of lips that hadn't been kissed that way in a very long time. Actually, had never been kissed that way. No gentleman ever kissed a woman like that. More was the pity... 'Oh, please! I can tell when it's the drink talking.'

'Really?' There was a long pause and in the darkness Manda fancied he was smiling, if a touch grimly, not fooled for a minute. 'Well, maybe you're right, but since I'm the only help you're going to get, you might be wise to brush up your manners, Miranda Grenville.'

'Why?' She just couldn't stop herself... 'Will they help us burrow our way out of here?'

'No. But it might make the time spent doing it a touch less disagreeable.'

Manda cleared her throat of dust. She knew she wasn't behaving at all well, but then behaving badly had been her default mode for a very long time. She really would have to try and do better now that she was a godmother, even one whose avowed aim was to lead her little charges astray.

As if...

Unless spoiling them rotten came under that heading. Not just with toys, sparklies, outings and treats. She was going to *really* spoil them with words, hugs, being there for them when they needed a hand in the dark, by giving herself. She was going to love them, cherish them. And make sure they knew it.

Given a chance.

She sucked in her breath as she faced the very real possibility that she might never see them again. The knowledge that if she didn't she would have no one to blame but herself. She'd been weak, running away, unable to face up to the demons that haunted her.

Who was she to judge a man like Jago?

If she had to spend much time in this ghastly place, she would probably be driven to blur reality by whatever means came to hand. Or leave.

But maybe he couldn't do that.

He was after all working here...

'O-okay,' she managed. 'Pax?' He responded with a grunt. Obviously she was going to have to work harder on her social skills. 'So, macho man, what's the plan?'

'Give me a minute.' Then, 'I don't suppose you have pain-killers about your person by any chance?'

'In my bag,' she said. 'Wherever that is. Until we get some light you'll just have to suffer.'

No. Even *in extremis* she just couldn't bring herself to play nice...

'That's a pity. I don't think too well with a headache.'

'That must be extremely limiting.' Then, as he began to move, 'Where are you going?'

'Not far,' he assured her dryly at the sudden rise in her voice. 'My supplies were stored at the far end of the temple. I want to see if I can find anything useful.'

'Another bottle of cheap brandy?'

'This isn't the Ritz, lady. You'll have to take what you can get.'

'Mine's water, since you're offering.'

The drink thing was getting old, Jago thought. Okay, she was scared—she had every right to be; he wasn't overcome with an urge to burst into song himself—but a woman with a smart mouth wasn't about to provoke much in the way of sympathy. Even if it was a mouth that had promised heaven on earth.

'If I find any, I'll save you a mouthful,' he said, making a move.

'No! Hold on, I'm coming with you,' she said, grabbing a handful of shirt, and the sudden note of desperation in her voice got to him.

'There's no need, really,' he said. Disengaging her hand from his shirt front and putting his mouth to her ear, he whispered, 'I promise if I find some I'll share. Scout's honour.'

Furious, she backed off. 'You've never been a scout. Anyone less "prepared"…'

'Tell me, are you always this disagreeable?' he enquired.

'Only when I've been trapped underground by an earthquake.' He didn't answer. 'Okay. I have a low tolerance of incompetence,' she admitted. 'Not that I'm saying you're incompetent. I'm sure you're very good at…'

'Getting drunk?'

She gave a little shivery sigh. 'N-no. You're no more drunk than I am.'

'No,' he said, 'although I'll admit that I did consider drowning my sorrows if it'll make you happy. Fortunately for both of us, I thought better of it but it's likely the bottle broke when the earthquake hit so be careful where you put your hands and knees. And don't grab at me, okay? I'm not going anywhere without you.'

'No,' she said again. Then, 'I'm…sorry.'

Anything that difficult to say had to be sincere and by way of reply he wrapped his fingers about her wrist.

It was slender and he could feel the delicate bones beneath

her skin, the rapid beat of her pulse. It was a wonder that something so fragile could have survived undamaged as she had fallen through the roof. She had been lucky. So far.

'Yes, well, maybe we could both do better. Now, let's see if we can find a light.' As she made a move to stand up, he held her down. 'On your knees, Miranda. Breaking an ankle down here isn't going to improve matters.'

'Know-all,' she muttered.

'You know, maybe you should try not talking for a while,' he suggested.

'You should be so lucky,' she replied, grinning despite everything. Riling this man might be the last fun she ever had so she might as well enjoy it. 'So, have you any idea where you are?'

'I know where this was yesterday,' he replied, bringing her back to earth with a bump. 'Once we reach one of the walls I'll have a better idea of the situation.'

Keeping his free hand extended in front of him, Jago swept the air at head height; it would be stupid to knock himself out on a block of stone. Easy, but stupid and he'd used up his quota of stupid for this lifetime.

Despite the blackness, he sensed the wall a split second before he came into contact with it and, placing his hand flat against the surface, he began to feel for the carvings that would tell him where he was.

'I'll need both hands for this,' he said, but rather than abandoning her while he searched for something that would tell him where he was, he turned and pressed her fingers against his belt. 'Just hang on to that for a moment.'

Manda didn't argue. His belt was made from soft, well worn leather and she hooked her fingers under it so that her knuckles were tucked up against his waist as he moved slowly forward, her face close enough to his back to feel the warmth emanating from his body.

'Well?' she demanded after what seemed like an endless silence. He didn't answer and that was even more frightening than his silence. 'Jago!'

'I think I've found the eagle,' he said.

'The eagle?' Manda remembered the unfinished carving on the stone beside the path.

'It had a special place in the life of the people who lived here, watching over them.'

'In return for the entrails of young virgins?' she asked, trying to recall the stuff she'd heard in the television interview of the well-endowed archaeologist.

'You read the *Courier*?' He didn't bother to disguise his disgust.

'Not unless I'm desperate. Should I?'

'Someone wrote a book about this place and the *Courier* ran excerpts from it. It was pitched at the sensational end of the market.'

'They wouldn't be interested otherwise. And no, I didn't read it, but I did catch a few minutes of the author when she was doing the rounds of the television chat shows a few weeks back. Very striking. For an archaeologist.'

'Yes.'

'I take it you know her?' Then, when he didn't answer, 'Who is she?'

'No one who need worry about becoming a virgin sacrifice,' he replied and there was no disguising the edge in his voice. He was, it seemed, speaking from experience. Was she the reason he'd been thinking about taking to the bottle? She didn't ask. She didn't want to know and, rapidly changing the subject, she prompted, 'Tell me about the eagle. The one that you've found.'

He turned away from her, looking up. 'It used to be above the altar stone.'

'So?'

'In the ceiling above the altar stone.'

Earlier that day Jago had been certain that life didn't hold much meaning for him. The sudden realisation of how close he had come to losing it put a whole new slant on the situation.

'Okay, let's try this way,' he said, moving to the left too quickly, catching Miranda off balance and she let out a yelp of pain.

'What is it?' Jago demanded impatiently.

'Nothing. I jabbed my hand on something, that's all—'

'Glass?' Jago reached back, took the hand she was cradling to her breast and ran his thumb over her palm and fingers to check for blood. If the bottle had broken, if she'd cut herself... But her hand was dry. 'It must have been a piece of stone. Be careful, okay?'

She just laughed, deriding him for a fool and who could blame her?

'I mean it!' he said angrily, knowing full well that what had happened had been his fault. 'I'm sorry.'

'It's okay. I understand. It's worse than you thought, isn't it?'

'It's not great,' he admitted.

'So? Are we going to get out?'

She spoke directly, her voice demanding an honest answer from him, but Jago had spent a lot of time working alone in the Cordilleran temples and his hearing had grown acute in the silence. He heard the underlying tremor, the fear she was taking such pains to hide.

CHAPTER FIVE

'We'll get out. I'm not promising you that it will be quick, or easy.' Jago knew there was little point in putting an optimistic gloss on it. She had seen the devastation for herself in the flare of the match. 'Even if, in the confusion, your tour party don't immediately miss you, I have no doubt that your family are already making things hot for officials at the Foreign Office.'

Her response was a tiny shivering sigh. 'I'm afraid if you're relying on that to get us out of here, we really are in trouble. I...I'm sort of taking time out from my family. They have no idea where I am.'

'Are you telling me that you didn't even send your mother a postcard?' he asked, tutting.

'I don't have a mother, but even if I had...' She broke off. 'I mean— Wish you were here? Would you?'

'Point taken,' he said, his pitiful attempt at levity falling flat. He should have known better. He hadn't just taken time out from his family, he'd walked out of their lives fifteen years ago and never looked back. 'Not to worry. If no one misses you, there are plenty of people who know I'm out here.'

He hoped that would hold her for the moment. That she

wouldn't realise that if the whole island had been hit as hard as this there wouldn't be anyone with the time or the energy to care what had happened to him, to any of them. Not until it was too late, anyway.

He continued to hold her hand. Her skin, beneath his own callused palms, was soft. Her fingers long and ringless. Then, as his thumb brushed over the pads of her fingers, he realised that they had taken a pounding. They were rough, the skin torn, her nails broken where she'd clawed at the ground as she'd fallen.

She must have been hurt, he realised, but she wasn't complaining.

'Come on,' he said, with a briskness he was far from feeling. 'This won't buy the baby a new bonnet.'

And this time when she laughed it was with wry amusement. 'When was the last time you bought a baby a bonnet, Jago?'

'Now that, Miss Grenville, would be telling.'

'Manda.'

'Excuse me? You've decided that I'm a friend?'

'I've decided that I don't like being called "lady" or Miss Grenville and I never liked Miranda.'

'Why not?'

'It doesn't matter. Please yourself. Shall we get on?'

There was a long pause, then he released her hand. 'I'm moving to the left.'

She shuffled after him, studiously ignoring a stream of muttered oaths as the floor shook beneath them once more. He turned and caught her before she went down this time, holding her against him, tucking her safe against his shoulder. With her face pressed into his chest, his body protecting her from falling debris, Manda felt ridiculously secure, despite the fact that some vast megalith could at any moment crush the pair of them.

'We really must stop meeting like this,' Jago murmured when everything was quiet, continuing to hold her, her face buried in the hollow of his shoulder, her cheek tight against the heavy cotton of his shirt. The beat of his heart a solid base counterpoint to her own rapid pulse rate and in the darkness she clung to him as if to a lover.

She should move but, afraid of more aftershocks, her courage failed her and she couldn't make herself pull away.

It was Jago who moved first. 'Keep your eyes closed,' he said, shaking off the grit and rubble that had fallen on him.

'Okay, now?'

'No. Wait…' He rubbed his hands clean against his shirt then, very gently, laid them over her face, brushing away the dust from her lids and lashes.

'Okay?' he asked.

'Okay,' she said, close to tears as she slid her hands into his hair, a thick mop of unruly curls, using her fingers to comb out the small pieces of stone. Sweeping her fingertips across a wide forehead, pausing at an impressive bump.

It was little wonder he had a headache, she thought, wishing she hadn't been quite so horrible about that, and on an impulse she kneeled up to kiss it better, before sweeping the pads of her fingers over dusty eyelids, bony cheeks, down the length of a firm jaw. Feeling the stubble of a day-old beard. Discovering the landscape of his face, imprinting its contours in her memory.

He grasped her wrist as she rubbed her thumb across his mouth, stopping her, and for a moment they remained locked together, the pad of her thumb against his lower lip. Then, without a word, he dropped her hand, looped his arm about her waist and turned away, moving slowly along the face of the wall, apparently exploring the carvings with the tips of his fingers as he continued to try and make sense of their surroundings.

'My stuff should be along here,' he said after a while.

'Well, let's get to it,' she said, feeling as if she'd been holding her breath since that moment when anything might have happened. She made a move forward but he didn't let go, stopping her. 'What are we waiting for?' she asked scratchily. 'Your pack of matches won't crawl out all by itself and jump into your hand.'

'True, but blundering off into the dark isn't going to help and if we're not careful we could bring the whole lot down on us.'

'True. And if we stay here talking about it long enough another aftershock might just save us the job,' she replied impatiently. His closeness had become too intimate and she tried to tug free. His grip tightened just enough to warn her to keep still.

'Slow down,' he said, his arm around her waist immovable, powerful. Controlling. Their brief moment of rapport now history.

'Why?' she demanded. 'Despite your little pep talk back there, I do realise that no one is likely to be looking for us any time soon.'

'Do you? Really?'

'What's to understand?'

She'd been in the wrong place at the wrong time. Only time would tell whether she had been lucky or unlucky, but one thing was sure, she wasn't going to sit around and wait for someone to come and dig them out.

'I've seen these things on television, Jago. I know that out there it'll be total chaos and, until we get any indication to the contrary, we have to assume we're on our own. The longer we sit around doing nothing, the weaker we'll get.' Then, with a surge of excitement. 'No, wait!'

'What?'

'In my bag! I've got a cellphone…'

'Miranda—'

'If it survived the fall.'

'And if we could get a signal up here,' he replied heavily, brutally crushing the wild surge of hope.

'There's no signal?'

She felt, rather than saw him shake his head, heard the muttered oath as, too late, he recalled the blow he'd sustained.

'Are you okay?' The chances were that he was suffering from concussion at the very least.

'I'll live,' he replied. 'Is there anything else that might be useful in this bag of yours?'

She suspected he'd asked more to keep her from falling apart again than for any other reason. She wasn't fooled into thinking that it was personal, that he'd felt anything beyond lust when he'd kissed her. She mustn't make that mistake ever again.

He'd protected her from falling masonry because, injured, she'd be even more of a liability. Even a speck of dust in her eye could have caused problems and he needed her fit and strong, not a feeble hysteric.

Heaven forbid he should feel obliged to kiss her again.

Heaven help him if he slapped her.

'Water,' she said. 'I've got a bottle of water.' She thought about it. 'Make that half a bottle of water.' Right now she would have given anything to have a mouthful of that. 'Some mints. Pens. Wipes.' She could really use one of those right now, too. What else? Her journal—no, forget that. 'A foot spray—'

'A *foot spray*?'

'To cool your feet. When you've been walking in hot weather.'

'Right. So, apart from the water and mints, that would be a "no" then,' he said, definitely underwhelmed.

Just as well she hadn't mentioned the deodorant and waterless antiseptic hand wash.

'No matches, torch, string?'

'String?' She very nearly laughed out loud. 'We're talking about a designer bag here. An object of desire for which, I'll have you know, there is a year-long waiting list. Not the pocket of some grubby little boy.'

'So you're the kind of woman who spends telephone numbers on a handbag. I hope I'm not meant to be impressed.'

'It's a matter of supreme indifference to me—'

'I'm glad to hear it,' he said, cutting her off. 'I'm far more interested in its contents.'

And he was right, damn him…

'I've got one of those little travel sewing kits,' she offered sarcastically. 'It has some cotton in it, if you're looking for an Ariadne solution to finding your way out of this maze of ruins.' Then, 'Ruined ruins…'

'A pick and shovel would be more useful, but I accept that's too much to expect. I'll bear the offer of needle and thread in mind, though, in case I'm driven to the point where sewing your mouth shut seems like a good idea.'

'There are safety pins in the kit for that, always assuming I don't use them on you first.'

'Well, now we've got all that out of the way, is there anything that might be in the slightest bit of use to us, because I'm not wasting time hunting for it in the unlikely event that my feet get hot.'

'Wait! There's a mini-light on my keyring,' she replied, as she continued to mentally sift through the contents of her bag. 'It came out of a Christmas cracker, but it's better than nothing.'

'A Christmas cracker?'

'You have a problem with Christmas crackers?' she demanded.

Last year had been her first ever proper family Christmas. Tinsel, a tree covered with bright ornaments, silly presents stacked beneath it. It had been Daisy's idea of a good time, but they'd all been seduced by the complete lack of sophistication, the simple joy of a big fat turkey with all the trimmings, the bright red and green crackers for them to pull, the paper hats, silly jokes and plastic gifts.

Her cracker had contained a tiny light for illuminating locks that she'd hung on her silver Tiffany keyring.

'There's an attack alarm, too,' she offered.

'Did that come out of a cracker, too?'

'No. That wouldn't be very festive, would it?' Then, 'What about you? I saw some tools in one of the temples when we passed the entrance earlier. Was that this temple?'

'The upper chamber, yes.'

'Upper?' Then they were underground? She didn't ask. She really didn't want to think about that. 'The guide said it was too dangerous to enter.'

'He was right. I tend to get seriously bad-tempered when heavy-footed tourists tramp all over my work.'

'Oh. I assumed it was something to do with engineering works.'

'Engineering?'

'Making the place safe for people dumb enough to think this was a good way to spend an afternoon?' Then, when he didn't bother to answer, 'Obviously not. So—what? You're an archaeologist?'

'Not *an* archaeologist. *The* archaeologist. The archaeological director of this site, to be precise.'

'Oh…' She frowned. All feminist ideals aside, she had to admit that it sounded rather more likely than that female in the clinging frock raising a sweat wielding a shovel. 'So who was the woman on the television chat show?'

She felt him stiffen. 'An opportunist with an agenda,' he said tightly. Then, 'I'm sorry. An engineer would undoubtedly be a lot more use to you right now.'

'I don't know about that.' Those sinewy arms were clearly used to hard physical work. 'At least you know your way around, although, since I'm a heavy-footed tourist, maybe I'd better go and hunt for my attack alarm.'

'Please yourself, but if you think setting it off will bring someone rushing to your rescue—'

'No.' And, pressed hard up against him, deprived of sight but with all her other senses working overtime, she said, 'I seem to be in rather more trouble than I thought.'

'You have no idea,' he murmured, his mouth so close to her ear that the stubble on his chin grated against her neck and she could feel his breath against her cheek.

She remembered the feel of his lip against her thumb and it was a struggle to keep from swallowing nervously.

Nerves might be a justifiable reaction under the circumstances, but he'd know it was prompted by her nearness to him, rather than the situation they were in, and that would never do.

Instead, she turned her head so that she was face to face with him in the dark, so close that she could feel the heat of his skin and, lowering her voice to little more than a whisper, she said, 'Do we have time for this, Jago?'

In the intensity of the silence, she could have sworn she heard the creak of muscle as his face creased into a grin. A grin that she could hear in his voice as he said, 'Tough little thing, aren't you?'

And, in spite of everything, she was grinning herself as she said, 'You have no idea.'

For a moment they knelt in that close circle with every sense intensified by the darkness, aware of each other in ways that only those deprived of sight could ever be.

The slight rise and fall of Jago's chest, the slow, steady thud of his heartbeat through her palm.

She could almost taste the pulsing heat of his body.

There was an intimacy, an awareness between them that, under different circumstances, would have had them ripping each other's clothes off.

Or maybe these were exactly the circumstances...

'Okay,' Jago said abruptly, leaning back, putting a little distance between them. 'We need your light, no matter how small it is, and the water. I want you to quarter the floor. Keep low, hands flat on the floor to steady you in case there's another shock. Watch out for broken glass.'

'Yes, sir!' If her knees weren't so sore, she'd have snapped them to attention. 'What are you going to be doing in the meantime?'

'Putting my feet up and waiting for you to get on with it?' he offered, since they were back to sarcasm city. No doubt it was a lot safer than the alternative. 'Or maybe I'll be trying to find a way out. There must be an opening somewhere.'

'Wouldn't we be able to see it if there was?' she asked, in no hurry to let go of her only contact with humanity. To be alone in the darkness.

Or was it letting go of Jago that was the problem? Maddening and gentle, dictatorial and tender by turns, she was becoming perilously attached to the man.

'This chamber is at a lower level so it may not be obvious, especially if it's dark outside. The chances are that we're going to be climbing out, so you'd better be wearing sensible shoes.'

'Perish the thought.'

'I hope you're kidding…'

Of course she was kidding! As if anyone with an atom of sense would go walkabout wearing open-toed sandals in a tropical forest that was undoubtedly infested with all manner of creepy-crawlies.

'Leave me to worry about my feet,' she replied. 'Just get us out of here.'

'Trust me.'

'Trust? Trust a man?' And, suddenly aware of the ridiculous way she was clinging to his hand, she let go. She did not cling… 'Now you're really in cloud-cuckoo-land.'

'Believe me, if I was in the mood to laugh, I'd be in hysterics at the irony of being forced to rely on a woman,' he assured her without the slightest trace of humour, 'but in the meantime I suggest we both take a trip with the cuckoos and pool our resources until we get out of here.'

And, as if to make his point, he found her arm, sliding his down it until he reached her own hand, picking it up and wrapping his fingers around it. Reconnecting with her in the darkness.

An unexpected wave of relief swept over her and it was all she could do to stop herself from tightening her grip, holding him close.

'What do you say, Miranda? Shall we suspend hostilities, save the battle of the sexes for the duration?'

She wanted to ask why he insisted on calling her Miranda. A compromise between Ms Grenville and the 'friendly' diminutive, perhaps. Couldn't he bring himself to be that familiar?

Instead, she said, 'Sure. Consider it a date.'

'It's in my diary,' he assured her, 'but right now we need to move.'

'Yes. Move.'

Having let go once, put on the independent act, Manda found it much harder to prise herself free a second time. That was how it had always been. Pretending once was easy...

He made no attempt to rush her or, impatient, pull away as she slowly prised her fingers free, one at a time. Amazingly, he remained rocklike as she forced herself to peel herself away from the warmth of his body. While she fought the desperate need to throw herself at him as a cold space filled the vacuum where, a moment before, there had been warmth.

Fighting a slide back into the dark sink of desperation, the clinging neediness.

She'd been there and knew how far down it could take her, but it was a tough call. The darkness amplified everything. Not just the tiny sounds, the movements of another person, but the emotion. The fear. And, as she finally let go, mentally casting herself adrift, she sat perfectly still for a moment, taking time to gather herself as Jago moved away from her.

Holding in the scream.

She needed no one. No one...

'Any time in the next ten seconds will do.'

Jago's voice came out of the darkness as astringent as the bitter aloes that one especially hated nanny had painted on her fingernails to stop her biting them. She'd chewed them anyway, refusing to submit, suffering the bitterness to spite the woman. Five years old and even then using her body to take control of her world.

The memory was just the wake-up call she needed and, using the wall as her starting point, she began to edge carefully forward on her hands and knees, casting about in wide sweeps, seeking her bag. Distracting herself from the pain in her knees as she shuffled along the broken floor by thinking about Jago.

So he found her response about trusting a man worthy of derision, did he? It had to mean that some woman had done the dirty on him in the past. The sexy creature selling her dumbed-down book on the ancient Cordilleran civilisation? He'd sounded bitter enough when she'd raised the subject.

She stopped herself from leaping to such obvious conclusions.

To the outside world she had no doubt that her trust problems would have looked that simple, too. Dismissed as the result of a couple of disastrous relationships with men who had commitment problems. She'd seen the grow-up-and-get-over-it looks from people who hadn't a clue.

Nothing was ever that simple.

It wasn't the men. They were no more than a symptom...

She jumped as loose stones fell in a clatter.

'Are you okay?' she asked nervously. What would she do if he wasn't?

'Just peachy,' he replied sarcastically.

Cute. 'You don't actually live down here, do you?' she asked in an effort to keep him talking.

'No. I've got a house down in the village,' he admitted, 'but I keep a camp-bed here. I can get a lot more writing done without the constant interruptions.' His voice seemed to come from miles away. And above her. 'It's about fifteen miles back.'

'Yes, we drove through it.'

She hadn't given a thought to the villagers. She'd seen them working in their tiny fields as they'd driven by. Small children, staring at the bus. Skinny dogs, chickens, goats...

'I hope they're okay down there,' she said.

'Me too, even though they're probably blaming all this on me. Stirring up the old gods. Making them angry.'

'Is that what you've been doing?'

'Not intentionally. They'll have to look further afield for those who've been taking their name in vain.'

Definitely the blonde, then...

'They're not getting excited about the possibility of getting rich off tourism?' she asked.

'The younger ones, maybe. The older people don't want to know.'

'Oh.'

Manda's fingers brushed against something on the floor. A bottle. Glass and, amazingly, intact. She opened it, hoping it was water. She sniffed, blinked. 'I've found your hooch,' she said. 'The bottle wasn't broken.'

'Good. Take care of it.' His voice came from above her. 'We're going to need it.'

She didn't ask why, afraid that she already knew the answer.

CHAPTER SIX

JAGO'S foot slipped, dislodging more loose rubble that rattled down to the temple floor, eliciting a small, if quickly contained, cry of alarm from his companion.

'Are you okay?' he asked. The pause was a fraction too long. 'Miranda!'

'Y-yes… Sorry. I thought it was another aftershock.' Then, 'Can you see anything?'

By 'anything' she undoubtedly meant a way out.

'Not a lot,' he replied, relief driving his sarcasm.

He was prodding gently, hoping to find a way through, but having to be careful that he didn't bring the rock ceiling down on top of them. As far as he could tell, however, the far end of the temple where his working supplies were stored was completely blocked off.

Their only escape route appeared to be up through the shaft, always assuming that it hadn't collapsed. He couldn't see the sky. And just for a moment he considered what it would have been like to come round, alone in the darkness, not knowing what had happened.

'I could really do with that light,' he said. Then, 'Any chance in the near future, do you think?' No reply. 'Miranda?'

'I've found my bag.'

She didn't sound happy.

'What's up?'

'Everything is soaking.'

'You can't expect me to get excited about a ruined bag, no matter how expensive.'

'No. It's just… The water bottle split when it fell.'

He just about managed to bite back the expletive that sprang to his lips. It was not good news. 'If there's anything left, drink it now,' he instructed.

'What about you?'

'I'll manage. Just tell me you've found the light.'

In the silence that followed, his mind filled in the blanks; a picture of her tilting her head back as she swallowed, the cool, clean water taking the dust from her mouth.

'What about the damn light, Miranda?' he demanded in an effort to take his mind off it.

In answer, a tiny glow appeared in the darkness.

A really *tiny* glow that did no more than light up the tips of ghostly pink fingers, shimmer off the pale curve of her cheek.

She'd said it was small, but he'd been hoping for one of those small but powerful mini-torches. The kind of sterling silver gizmo that came in expensive Christmas crackers. Women who carried designer bags that had a year-long waiting list didn't buy cheap crackers for their Christmas parties. They bought the kind that contained expensive trinkets for people who had everything. At least they did back in the days when he had been on the guest list.

Maybe she'd gone for some kind of kitsch irony last Christmas because this light must have come out of the budget variety sold in supermarkets, just about powerful enough to illuminate a lock in the dark.

He fought down his disappointment and frustration. This was not her fault. Miranda Grenville had come out on a sight-seeing trip, not equipped for a survival weekend.

'Well, that's great,' he said, and hoped he sounded as if he meant it. 'I thought it might have been ruined.'

He eased himself back down to the temple floor and carefully made his way across to her with the light as his guide.

'Here,' she said, handing it to him. It went out. 'You have to squeeze the sides to make it work.'

'Very high-tech,' he observed, then wished he'd kept his mouth shut as she found his wrist, slid her fingers down to his hand and guided it to the bottle she was holding.

'Here. I saved you some water. Careful, it's on its side.' Then, before he could take the drink that he was, admittedly, desperate for, she said, 'Wait. I've got some painkillers in here somewhere. For the bump on your head.'

'You don't have faith in the kissing-it-better school of medicine?' he asked, while she fumbled about in the dark for a pack of aspirin, popped a couple of pills from the plastic casing. It was extraordinary how, deprived of sight, the other senses became amplified. How, just by listening, he could tell exactly what she was doing.

'Yes. No...' Then, 'No one ever kissed me better...' she placed the pills into his hand, taking back the light so that he had both hands free to swallow them '...so I couldn't say how effective it is. It's probably wiser to be on the safe side and use the pill popping approach, wouldn't you think?'

He tossed back the pills, swallowed a mouthful of water. 'Never?'

'My family didn't go in for that kind of kissing.'

'No?' His were good at all that stuff. As far as the outside world was concerned, they had been the perfect happy family. 'It's all in the mind,' he said. 'An illusion. If you believe in it, it works.'

'And do you?' she asked. 'Believe?'

'If I say yes, will you kiss me again?'

'I'll take that as a "no".'

Jago wished he'd just said yes, but it was too late for that. 'It got an eight out of ten on the feel-good factor.'

'Only eight?' she demanded.

'You expected a straight ten?' he asked, clearly amused.

In the darkness Manda blushed crimson. Whatever had she been thinking to get into this conversation? Attempting to recover a little self-respect, she said, 'Hardly ten. But taking into account the guesswork involved, the dust, maybe eight point…'

But he didn't wait for her to finish, instead laying his hand against her cheek, brushing his thumb against the edge of her mouth before leaning forward and kissing her back.

Jago's lips were barely more than a breath against her own—a feather-light touch that breathed life, his own warmth into her. Nine point nine recurring…

While she was still trying to gather herself to say something, anything, he saved her from making a total fool of herself and saying that out loud.

'You said you had a phone,' he prompted casually. As if nothing had happened. 'I don't suppose, by any chance, it's the kind that takes photographs?'

Nothing had happened, she reminded herself. He was just trying to keep her from thinking about the situation they were in and she responded with a positively flippant, 'Don't they all?' Then, 'Why? Do you want a souvenir? Pictures to sell to the tabloids.'

'Would the tabloids be that interested?'

Pictures of Miranda Grenville, one-time society hostess, adviser to the Prime Minister, now businesswomen in her own right, filthy and dishevelled in an underground hell? Oh, yes, they'd love those. But clearly he hadn't a clue who she was and she was happy to leave it that way.

'There's always a market for human interest stories,' she told him as she dug the phone out of her bag, wiped it dry on the sleeve of her shirt and turned it on for the first time since she'd arrived in Cordillera. It lit up, then beeped. 'I've got messages,' she said.

'They'll keep,' Jago replied, taking it from her. 'This is more important. Shut your eyes.'

'Why? What are you—' A bright flash wiped out all the night sight she'd slowly built up. 'Idiot!'

'I told you to shut your eyes,' he said, looking at the image on the screen for a moment before turning slightly. 'And again,' he said.

This time she didn't hesitate as she caught on to what he was doing. With the camera in her cellphone he could take pictures, use them to 'see' exactly what the situation was, maybe find a way out. Or at least locate anything that might be of use to them.

He stared at the third image for so long that she leaned forward to see what held his attention.

'What's that?' she asked, after a moment staring at the picture and trying to make sense of the vast piece of stone that was lying at a broken angle from the floor to the roof.

'The eagle.'

'The one that was part of the ceiling?' she asked, shocked. To see something that huge just tossed aside was chilling.

'I climbed up part of the way just now,' Jago said. The screen lit up the tip of his finger, a short clean nail, as he pointed at the photograph. 'There's a shaft that leads directly out to the forest, but I couldn't find a way through. It may be blocked with debris. Or the eagle might have fallen across it.'

'Oh.'

He took another photograph, and then another. It seemed forever before he grunted with something like satisfaction. 'Keep it pointed that way so that I know how far I've got,' he said, carefully handing her the phone. 'I'll be right back.'

She looked at the photograph, trying to work out what had got him so excited. Had he seen some prospect of escape? No matter how hard she stared, all she could see was a jumble of stone piled almost to the roof.

She heard him pulling at it, the rattle as smaller stones moved. 'Be careful!' Then, letting out a breath of relief as he made his way back to her, 'What was it? What did you see?'

'The handle of a trowel,' he said, passing it to her. It was one of those fine trowels that archaeologists used to scrape away the layers of soil. Pitifully small, but better than nothing. 'Put it in your bag. Did you put the brandy in there?'

'Yes.'

'Good. Put the strap over your head so you don't get parted from it again. There are bound to be more aftershocks.'

He used the same take it or leave it tone with which he'd told her to close her eyes and her first reaction to any kind of order had always been to ignore it. This time, however, she didn't hesitate, putting the trowel in her bag, placing the strap over her head.

And she didn't speak again until he'd painstakingly photographed all three hundred and sixty degrees of what remained of the temple. Kept her bottom lip firmly clamped between her teeth, containing her impatience as he carefully examined each image, instead fixing her gaze on the dark angles and planes of his face in the shadowy light from the small screen. Watching for the slightest sign that he'd found some way out.

Without a word he stopped looking, then turned his attention to the roof and carried on taking photographs.

She did her best to smother a pathetic whimper but he must have heard her because, without pausing in what he was doing, he reached out, found her hand in the faint light from the screen.

He didn't say anything. He didn't have to.

'Well?' she asked, unable to contain herself when, finally, he stopped, looked through all the images and still said nothing.

'Is this you?' he asked.

'What?'

She leaned forward and realised that he'd found the pictures taken at the christening. She'd taken a picture of Belle holding Minette.

'No. That's my sister-in-law. I was godmother to her baby last week.'

'Why do I think I know her?'

'I couldn't say,' she replied, unwilling to add glamour to her sister-in-law by telling him that, until recently, she had been the nation's breakfast television sweetheart. 'Maybe you've a thing for voluptuous women?'

'If I have, believe me I'm over it. What about this?' he asked, flipping on to the next picture.

'That's Daisy. She's my assistant. My sister-in-law's sister. It was a joint christening and I was godmother to her little boy too.'

'So where's number three?'

'Three?'

'Doesn't everything come in threes? Wishes? Disasters? Babies…'

'Not in this family,' she said sharply.

'That would be the family you're taking a break from?'

Had she really said that? To this total stranger. Except that when a man had kissed you—twice—he could hardly be described as a stranger. Even when you didn't know what he looked like. Anything about him. Except that he knew when to be tough and when to be gentle. And when a girl needed a hand to hold in the dark.

Maybe that was enough.

'The same family whose photographs you carry about with you?'

'It's…complicated.'

'Families usually are,' he said with feeling.

'What about you? Will your family be glued to the twenty-four hour news channels? Or flying out to help in the search?'

'It's unlikely. They have no idea I'm in Cordillera.'

'Really? I assumed you'd been here for quite a while.'

'Nearly five years.'

'Oh.'

'We're not what you could call close.'

'I'm sorry.'

'It's my choice.'

'Right.' Then, 'Mine don't know, either. Where I am.'

'You said.'

She had said rather a lot for such a short acquaintance, but then the circumstances had an intensity that speeded up the normal course of social intercourse.

'Of course I've only been gone a few days,' she added, feeling guilty.

'I'm sure you'd have got around to sending a postcard eventually.'

'I don't send postcards.'

'Or call? They seem to have been calling you.'

'Those messages? Probably business,' she said dismissively. 'Belle and Daisy and I have a television production company. We're due to start work on a new documentary soon.'

'Oh, well, the good news is that we needn't worry about them worrying about us.'

That was the *good* news?

'Okay, Miranda Grenville. We seem to have just two options. I may have found a way through the roof. The first part of the climb would be fairly easy. Up the back of the eagle where it's sloping to the ground. But after that it's going to be a tough climb, finding footholds in the dark. See?'

He showed her the picture of a dark gash in the roof where the light hadn't reflected back, suggesting space.

'Unfortunately I can't say what we'll find when we get there. We might still be—'

'What's the alternative?' she asked.

'We could try and clear this corner.' He flipped forward to a photograph that showed a corner where the wall had subsided. 'The ground falls away there, so it's unlikely to be blocked with debris once we're through.'

'If we can get through,' she said.

'If we can get through,' he confirmed. 'The third option is to stay put and hope that the sniffer dogs are on their way.'

'I don't think I'll hold my breath on that one.' Manda did her best to swallow down the fear. 'I imagine they already have their paws full.' She tried not to think about what was going on outside. The suffering… 'Which would you choose? If you didn't have to think about me?'

There was a telling pause before he said, 'I think clearing the corner might be the most sensible option.'

He was lying.

'If you were on your own you'd go for the climb. Admit it.'

He hesitated a fraction too long before saying, 'In the dark it could be suicide.'

'You think I'm not up to it, is that it?'

'I've no idea what you're up to, but it's not that. If there's a shock while we're up there—'

'Shut up, Jago.'

'Miranda…'

'If there's a shock it could all come down on top of us.' He didn't say anything. 'And climbing would be quicker.'

'True,' he admitted. 'Did you say something about a packet of mints? Or did they dissolve when the water leaked?'

'You're in luck, they're the chewy kind.' She felt around in her bag until she found them, unwrapped two mints and handed him one. Then she snapped the rest of the pack in two and gave half to him. 'Here. Don't eat them all at once.'

'No, ma'am,' he replied and her eyes were now so accustomed to the low light levels emitting from the phone that she clearly saw him tuck the sweets into his shirt pocket. 'Okay, here's the plan. I'll go up and take a look to see if it's possible, then I'll come back for you.'

'Leaving me down here? No way!'

'You want your mints back?' he asked.

'Stuff the mints…' She didn't care a fig about them. 'Stuff you.' He wasn't going to abandon her. 'Give me my phone back and I'll find my own way.'

As she made a grab for it, he moved it out of reach. 'You think I'd abandon you?'

'Not intentionally. But once you're up there…' He'd be exhausted. It would take a superhero to climb back down into the dark. Not that it mattered. It wasn't going to happen. 'Let's just say that experience has led me to have very low expectations of the average male.'

'Then it's your lucky day. The one thing I'm not is average.'

'No?' Actually, she probably thought he was right, but she wasn't about to pander to his ego. 'So where do you fit? Above or below the median?'

'You'd better hope that it's above.'

'I'll let you know.'

'Cat,' he replied, but softly so that she was sure he was smiling. Then, leaning into her so that she could see the screen, 'Okay. This is the way we go,' he said, pointing out the route he'd chosen.

'What about this way?' she suggested, pointing to what looked like a fissure. 'It looks easier.'

'Did I ask your opinion?'

'But—'

'This isn't a committee, lady.' She hadn't realised the voice could reflect the expression so clearly, but it was obvious that he wasn't smiling now. 'Pay close attention because I'm going to say this just once, then I'm going, with you or without you.'

Damn...

She hadn't meant to do that. It wasn't that she doubted him or his good intentions but she was so used to people listening to her opinions. Being in control...

Whatever he thought, he didn't wait for her to answer one way or the other but, having made his point, he looped his arm over her and pulled her closer. Then, with her chin pressed against his shoulder—she hadn't imagined the strength—he laid out the route they'd take, pointing out crevices for hands and feet that she'd never have seen. Finally, when he was done, he took her hand and placed the phone into her palm, pressing her fingers around it.

'You should keep it,' she said. Doing her best to make up for... Well, just about everything.

'Probably,' he admitted, wrapping her fingers around it. 'Keep it safe.'

His way of proving that she could trust him not to abandon her? Or, having picked out his escape route was he simply freeing up his hands for the climb?

It didn't matter, she decided, as she slipped it into the large breast pocket of her shirt where it would be easily accessible. Then she looked up into the dark void and knew exactly what he'd done.

He'd given her the best light source in case she needed it to find her way and, feeling really bad for doubting him, she said, 'Here, take the mini-light.'

'Sure?'

She didn't answer, but pressed it into his palm. Then, as he turned it on to light his way, she looked up. 'How high is it?'

'Just be grateful these people didn't build on the scale of the Egyptians,' he replied, evading the question.

'How high?' she insisted.

'About ten metres,' he replied, far too glibly, not looking back.

'Don't patronise me, Jago.'

He was close enough for her to feel him shrug, then he turned slightly so that she could see his spare, finely chiselled profile. 'Does it matter?' he asked.

'I like to be in possession of all the facts.'

'A bit of a control freak, are you?'

'Not at all. You can ask anyone. I'm a *total* control freak.'

'Then here are the facts for you. We start at the bottom and we keep going until we reach the top. Simple.' Then, 'What did you do with that bottle of brandy?'

'Need a stiffener before you face it?' she asked, passing it to him.

The light went out and she heard him unscrew the cap. 'Give me your hands.'

About to ask why, she thought better of it and held them out without a word as he placed one of his own beneath them. Then he poured the spirit over both of their hands and she let slip something brief and scatological as the spirit found its way into the scrapes and grazes, bringing tears to her eyes.

'Antiseptic,' he said. 'And it'll dry out your skin. Help with grip.'

'Thanks,' she said cryptically.

'Don't mention it.' He tucked the bottle back into the bag hanging from her back, then said, 'You'd better give me that.'

'Are you sure about that? It'll be a bad look,' she warned

as she lifted the strap over her head and surrendered it to him. 'It definitely won't match your shoes.'

'You know that for a fact, do you?'

'I can't believe you're wearing silver sandals.'

'Please tell me you're kidding.' Then, 'No. Don't say another word. I'd rather not know.'

He didn't wait but, using the small light, he began to move away from her. Having mentally slapped herself on the wrist for being a bad girl—but honestly, any man who seriously believed any girl with a grain of sense would wear silver sandals in the rainforest deserved to be teased—she began to follow him, further scuffing the toes of her expensive loafers as she crawled after him on her hands and knees.

Sensible, after all, did not have to be cheap. Or lack style.

Ahead of her, Jago stood up, turning back to take her arm and help her to her feet. About to remind him that she could manage, she felt her knee buckle slightly. Muffled by all the other aches and pains she was suffering, she'd forgotten about her knee.

'Okay?'

'Fine.' There was a long moment of silence and she knew he was looking at her, trying to gauge just how fine she really was. 'Absolutely dandy,' she assured him. 'No problem. How's your head?'

'I'll live.' Then, 'Let's get on with it.'

In the darkness she found her ears filling in the pictures; the sound of cloth brushing against skin as he moved, of muscles stretching as he reached up, using the tiny light to illuminate the first of the hand-holds that he'd pinpointed on the photograph. Then everything went dark again.

He didn't begin to climb away from her, however, but

reached back and found her hand, lifting it to a narrow crack so that she could feel it for herself, would know how far to stretch, what she was looking for. Have a starting point.

'Got that?' he asked.

'Got it,' she assured him.

'Okay. We'll take it one move at a time. I'll give you a running commentary of my moves so that you can follow them.' Then, 'We're climbing blind and it's not going to be easy and it's not going to be quick. Stop for rests whenever you need to. Don't try to rush it.'

'Yes, sir.'

She didn't actually leap to attention and salute, but the voice implied it and he didn't actually sigh. His momentary pause was enough.

'I hear you, Jago,' she added quickly, wanting him to know that she was with him every step of the way.

'Right.' Then, 'Whatever you do, don't panic. If you're in trouble, tell me. I'd rather come back a few feet to give you a hand than climb back down to the bottom after listening to you scream all the way down.'

She swallowed, lifted her chin.

'If it helps,' she replied, 'you have my promise that I'll do my best not to scream.'

CHAPTER SEVEN

MANDA bit back a yelp as her hand slipped, scraping her knuckles against sharp stone.

It had seemed easy enough at first. The back of the eagle had formed a slope, a fairly steep one, and there were plenty of hand-holds—fissures, small ledges just big enough for her feet, where it had cracked as it had fallen.

But then they reached the wall itself and the climb became harder. Her muscles began to burn with the effort of pulling herself up, her arms to shake and it soon became obvious that all the hand-holds in the world wouldn't get her to the top if she didn't have the strength to hold on.

Breathing was becoming a problem too, her chest aching with the strain. Only by concentrating on the calm, steady voice of Jago, guiding her onwards and upwards, was she able to block out the worst of it. Keep moving.

She didn't manage to completely stifle her difficulty in breathing, however, and finally he paused above her and said, 'Are you okay?'

'Peachy,' she managed, going for sarcasm in an attempt to disguise her pain.

'There's a good ledge here. We'll take a rest…'

'Right.' Excellent. Except that her fingers were numb and she didn't have the strength to move. Instead, she leaned her face against the cold, damp rock wall.

'A couple of feet,' he prompted.

Forget the comfort of the ancient leather sofa in the Belgravia mansion that she had, until recently, called home, his rock ledge sounded like heaven right now.

And about as close…

Above her, small stones were dislodged from the wall and for a moment she thought that he was moving on without her.

'Jago…'

Even as the word was involuntarily torn from her he was at her side, his arm, then his body at her back, holding her tight against the wall. Taking the strain.

'Let go,' he said, his mouth so close to her ear that his neck was tight against her head, his breath, no more than a gasp, warm against her cheek. 'I've got you.'

'I can't…'

'Trust me.'

How many times had she heard those words? How many times had they been hollow lies?

'I'm okay,' she told him, hating this. 'Just catching my breath.' She hated being weak, hated needing a prop. Just once she yearned to be the strong one, but she did as she was told, flexing her fingers, so that the blood flowed, painfully, back into them.

'Where did you put your mints?'

'What's the matter? Have you eaten all yours?'

Jago shifted, crushing her against the temple wall as he struggled to reach his own, slipping the wrapper with his thumb, praying that they weren't sugar free—how likely was that?—as he found her lips.

'Take it!' he said, but instead of just doing as she was told, she bit it in two, leaving half behind for him. Always having to have the last word... 'Miranda!'

'Shares...' she gasped, and Jago didn't have the breath to argue, but palmed it into his mouth before grabbing for a small crevice in the wall, his muscles screaming as he bore her weight as well as his own for what seemed like hours.

In reality it was only seconds before she said, 'Okay. I've got it now.'

'Sure? If you can just make the next move...'

'Go!'

Tough. Foolhardy. Determined not to slow him down. Miranda Grenville might be the most irritating woman he'd ever met, but she still earned his grudging respect as he edged carefully back to his original position on the ledge.

He reached out instinctively to grab her as he heard her foot slip, her grunt as some part of her anatomy collided painfully with stone, afraid that her mouth had finally out-reached her strength.

All he got was a handful of air and then, somehow, she was there, alongside him.

'Shall we go mad and have another mint?' he asked.

'My treat,' she managed, biting one of her own in half and sharing it with him.

They both sat there for a while, side by side, their backs against the temple wall, chewing slowly while their breathing recovered and the feeling began to flow back into tortured limbs.

From above them a few small stones rattled down the face

and Manda stopped breathing as Jago threw his arm across her, pinning her back against the wall, waiting for another aftershock.

Waited. And waited.

Finally she shuddered as she let out the breath she was holding and Jago slumped against her. 'A bird,' he said. 'It must have been a bird. Good news. If a bird can get in, we can get out.'

'Sure,' Manda agreed.

She wasn't entirely convinced. The bird could have been trapped like them. Or it could be a bat. One of those big, hairy, fruit-eating bats...

'Why don't you talk to your family?' she asked, into his neck, not wanting to think about bats, or what else might be tucked up with them. Lurking in the crevices into which she was blindly poking her fingers. Not wanting him to move. Wanting to stay exactly where they were.

His only response was to remove the arm he'd thrown protectively across her and say, 'We'd better get on.' But even as he made a move she caught at his sleeve.

'Tell me!' Then, shocked at herself, knowing that she could never talk about her own miserable childhood, she apologised. 'I'm sorry.'

'It's okay. I'll tell you when we get out of here. Over a cold beer.'

'Another date?'

'It sounds like it.'

The climb was both mentally and physically exhausting. Feeling in the dark for each hold, convinced that every dislodged stone was a new tremor, Jago's worst fear was that he'd reach up in the darkness and find only chiselled-smooth rock.

He'd done some rock climbing as a young man and field archaeology was for the fit, but he understood why Miranda wouldn't wait for him to make the climb, find help and come back for her.

He didn't think he could have remained at the bottom in the darkness either, but with every move he was waiting for the slip behind him, tensed for her cry. He was unable to do anything but keep going and guide her to his own footholds. Praying that he wasn't just leading her into a dead end.

At least she was listening, didn't panic when she couldn't immediately locate the next hand- or foot-hold.

'How're you doing?' he asked.

If it had been physically possible, Manda would have laughed.

Doing? *Doing?* Was he kidding?

A muttered, 'Fine…' stretched her ability to speak to the limit.

It was a lie. She wasn't 'fine'. Not by any definition of the word.

The muscles in her shoulders, arms, back were quivering with exhaustion. Forget the 'burn'. Her calves and thighs were on fire and she couldn't feel her feet. She was just moving on automatic.

Then, as her fingers, wet with sweat—or blood—slipped, her forehead came into sharp contact with smooth stone and for a moment everything spun in the dark. As she sucked air into her lungs, hanging on with what felt like the ends of her finger-nails, she managed to gasp, 'If I fall you're not to climb down.'

He'd stopped moving. 'You're not going to fall.'

'Promise me,' she demanded. 'You have to get out. I want my family to know what happened to me.'

'Like I could look them in the eye and tell them I'd left you lying on the floor of the temple, not knowing if you were dead or alive.' His breath was coming hard too. 'Stop gassing and move. You're nearly there.'

'Of course I am,' she muttered. Did he think she was totally stupid?

'Reach out with your left foot and you'll find a good ledge. Carefully!' he warned, as she felt for the ledge, thought she had it, only for it to crumble away, leaving her scrabbling for purchase. What was left of her nails scraped across chis- elled-smooth stone as she fought to hang on, suspended by one toe and raw fingertips over a blackness that seemed to be sucking her down.

She'd been there so many times in her head but this was real. This time she really was going down and never coming up again. All she had to do was let go…

'Stop pussy-footing about and move, woman!' Jago's harsh voice echoed around the ruined temple, jerking her back. How dared he?

Ivo had never shouted at her. He'd been gentle. Coaxing her back from the brink…

'Any time in the next ten seconds will do!'

But anger was good, too…

'You pig!' she cried, as her toe finally connected with something solid, but her leg was trembling so much that she couldn't make the move.

'Come up here and tell me that!'

'What's the matter, Jago? Are you in a hurry for another kick?'

'Looking forward to it, sweetheart!'

'I'm on my way!'

'Promises, promises. Are you ready for another kiss?'

The adrenalin rush got her across and she didn't wait for him to guide her, but reached up, seeking the next move without waiting for guidance. She'd survived her moment of panic. The black moment when falling would have been a relief.

She'd come through…

He'd brought her through.

Jago.

'The next bit is a bit of a stretch,' he said as she groped in the darkness for a hold in the darkness. 'Reach up and I'll pull you over the edge.'

Edge? She'd been that close?

And now she was out here alone?

Without warning, the blackness sucked at her and she made a desperate lunge upwards, seeking his hand. For a moment his fingers brushed tantalisingly against hers.

She was alone. Out of reach…

'It's too far…'

'Hold on.' She was showered with a fine film of dust as he moved closer to the edge above her. 'Okay. Try again.'

His palm touched hers. Slipped.

He grunted as he grabbed for her wrist, his fingers biting hard as he held her.

'Give me your other hand,' he gasped.

Let go?

Put her life entirely in his hands?

In the millisecond she hesitated, another aftershock ripped through the wall and the ledge on which she was standing gave way beneath her, tearing her hand away from the wall so that she was left hanging over the empty temple.

Somehow, Jago managed to hang on, his arm practically torn from its socket as he stretched out over the chasm, taking her full weight with one hand as Miranda struggled to find some kind of footing. Slipping closer and closer towards the tipping point when they'd both fall.

Stone was crashing around them, filling the air with dust. Something—someone—was screaming. Then, mercifully, the shaking stopped, Miranda's feet connected with something solid and, bracing her feet against the wall, between them they managed to get her over the edge.

He caught her, rolling away with her from the precipice, holding her, even as the pain exploded in his shoulder, his head. As her voice exploded in his ear.

'Idiot!'

'Without a doubt,' he managed as she sucked in a breath, presumably to continue berating him. The dust caught in her throat and she began to cough. Not that she let a little thing like that stop her.

'Don't you ever do that again!'

'I promise.' He might have laughed if it didn't hurt so much. Maybe it was hurting so much because he was laughing, he couldn't tell.

'I mean it! I'm not worth dying for, do you hear me?'

He heard her, heard a raw pain as the words were wrenched from her. It wasn't just reaction, he realised. Or shock.

She truly meant what she'd said and, despite his own physical pain, he wrapped his arms around her and held her close even though she fought him like a tiger. Held her safe until she stopped telling him over and over, 'I'm not worth it…'

Until she let go, subsided against his chest and only the

slightest movement of her shoulders betrayed that she was weeping.

It was her struggle to conceal the hot tears soaking into his shirt as they lay huddled together on the earth that finally got to him.

She had every right to howl, stamp, scream her head off after what she'd been through. She certainly hadn't shown any reticence when it came to expressing her feelings until now. In truth, he would have welcomed the promised kick, or at least a mouthful of abuse. Anything that would stop him from asking her why she wasn't worth dying for.

He didn't want to know. Didn't want to get that involved.

But, even as he fought it, he recognised, somewhere, deep down, that it was a forlorn hope. Her life belonged to him, as his belonged to her.

From the moment he'd reached out in the dark and his hand had connected with this woman, their survival had been inextricably linked. Whatever happened in the future, this day, these few hours would, forever, bind them together.

And they were not home free yet. Not by a long way.

'Hey, come on. No need for that,' he said, tugging out the tail of his shirt and using it to wipe her face, as she'd used hers to wipe the dust from his in what now seemed like a lifetime ago.

Kissing her cheek. Kissing her better.

'Don't!'

His kiss was almost more than she could bear. The gentle innocence of it. Almost as if she were a child. It nearly undid all his good work in putting her back together. It took what little remained of Manda's self-control to stop herself from grasping handfuls of Jago's shirt, holding on to the solid human warmth of his body. Clinging to the safety net that he seemed to offer.

'Enough,' she said, scrubbing at her face with her sleeve to eradicate the softness of his shirt against her skin. The softness of his lips.

Wiping out all evidence of her own pitiful weakness.

She hadn't cried in years. She'd been so sure there were no more tears left in her. But this stranger had risked his own life to save her...

'You should have let me fall,' she said. 'I told you to let—'

'Next time,' he cut in, stopping the words.

Damn him, she meant it!

She closed her eyes in an attempt to stop more tears from spilling down her cheeks, took a breath, then, when she could trust herself to speak, said, 'Is that a promise?'

'It's a promise.'

'Right. Well, okay... Good.'

'You have my word that the very next time you're climbing the wall of the inner sanctum of the Temple of Fire you're on your own.'

'What? No!'

'Isn't that what you meant?'

'You know it isn't. We're not out of here yet and what's the point of us both dying?'

'No one is going to die,' he replied with a sudden fierceness. 'Not today. Not here. Not in my temple.'

'I wish I had your confidence.'

'You've got something better, much better than that, Miranda Grenville. You've got me.'

It was a totally outrageous thing to say, Jago knew. His shoulder was practically useless and the headache that had never entirely eased was now back with a vengeance. But a spluttering laugh that she couldn't quite hold in reassured him.

'So I have. While you, poor sap, are stuck with me. Useless at taking orders and with a trust threshold hovering on zero.' With that she stilled. 'I could have got us both killed back there.'

'Don't beat yourself up about it. We react in the way we're programmed to.'

'And you're programmed to be the hero.' She laid her hand against his chest. 'Thank you for holding on.' Then, as if embarrassed by her own gratitude, she said, 'So? What next, fearless leader? We're not out of the woods yet.'

He caught her hand before she could move and lay back, taking her with him. Closing his eyes. 'We rest. Try and get some sleep.'

'Sleep?'

'What's up, princess? Missing your silk sheets and goose down pillows?'

'Silk sheets? Please…' But she shivered.

'You're cold?'

'Not cold, although it is colder up here. There's more air, too. Do you think there's a way out?'

'Part of the roof has gone. Look, you can see a few stars.'

'Oh…' Then, eagerly, 'Can't we press on?'

'We need to recover a little before we attempt another climb,' he said. He needed to recover. 'And when the eagle collapsed it took part of the floor at this level with it. It seems solid enough here, but…'

'We could take more pictures.'

'If we wait, we'll have daylight,' he said. 'There's no point in taking any risks.'

'I'm not sure about that. It's easier to be brave when you can't see the danger.'

'Trust me.'

'You keep saying that.' She shrugged. 'I guess it makes sense,' she said, but not with any real enthusiasm and who could blame her? 'It's just this place. It gives me the creeps.'

'Afraid of the dark?' He released her hand. 'Come on, cooch up,' he said, holding out his arm so that she could curl up against him, 'and I'll tell you a bedtime story.' She ignored the offered comfort, keeping her distance. He went ahead with the story, anyway. Telling her about the people who'd built the temple. The way they'd lived. What they had worshipped.

He thought she'd be happier if she knew that they didn't go into for bloody sacrifice. That their 'fire' was not a thing to fear. How, when the moon was full, they'd built a fire on the altar at the heart of their temple, then heaped the huge night-scented lilies that bloomed in the forest on to the embers so that the eagle could catch the sweet smoke that was carried up the shaft and fly with it in his wings as a gift to the moon.

'How can you know all that?' she asked in wonder.

'They carved pictures into the walls, drew their ceremonies in pictograms. And laboratories have analysed the ashes we found under centuries of compacted leaf litter.'

'But that's really beautiful, Jago. Why didn't the guide tell us all this?'

'Because the guide doesn't know. I haven't published any of my findings.'

'But what about—'

'Enough.' He didn't want to think about Fliss. He was angry with her, angry with Felipe, but most of all he was angry with himself. This was his fault. If he hadn't been so stubborn, so intent to keeping the world he'd uncovered for himself…

'It's your turn,' he said. 'Tell me what you're running away from.'

CHAPTER EIGHT

'WHO said I was running away?' she demanded.

'"Time out"?' Jago offered, quoting her own words back at her. 'That's a euphemism if ever I heard one. Not checking your messages? Not sending postcards home?'

She drew in a long slow breath and for a moment he thought she was going to tell him to get lost. That it was none of his business. But she didn't. She didn't say anything at all for a long time and when, finally, she did break the silence, it was with just one word.

'Myself.'

'What?'

He'd been imagining a job fiasco, a family row, a messy love affair. Maybe all three.

'All my life I've been running away from this horrible creature that no one could love.'

It was, Jago thought, one of those 'sod it' moments.

Like that time when he was a kid and had poked a stick into a hollow tree and disturbed a wasps' nest. It was something you really, really wished you hadn't done, but there was no escaping the consequences.

'No one?' he asked.

Her shoulders shifted imperceptibly. Except that everything was magnified by the darkness.

'Ivo, my brother, did his best to take care of me. In return I came close to dragging him to the brink with me. Something I seem to be making a habit of.' There was a pause, this time no more than a heartbeat. 'Although on that occasion I was in mental, rather than physical, freefall.'

'You had a breakdown?'

'That's what they called it. The doctors persuaded him to section me. Confine me under the Mental Health Act for my own safety.'

And suddenly he wasn't thinking *sod it*. He was only thinking how hard it must be for her to say that to a stranger. Actually, how hard it would be to say that to someone she knew well.

Mental illness was the last taboo.

'You both survived,' he said, mentally freewheeling while he tried to come up with something appropriate. 'At least I assume your brother did, since you've just been godmother to his sprog. And, for that matter, so did you.'

'Yes, he survived—he's incredibly strong—but it hurt him, having to do that.'

And then, as if suddenly aware of what she was doing, how she was exposing herself, she tried to break free, stand up, distance herself from him.

'Don't!' he warned, sitting up too quickly in his attempt to stop her. His head swam. His shoulder protested. 'Don't move! The last thing I need is for you to fall back down into that damn hole.' Then, because he knew it would get her when kindness wouldn't, 'I'd only have to climb all the way back down and pick up the pieces.'

'I told you—'

'I know. You fall, I'm to leave you to rot. Sorry, I couldn't do that any more than your brother could.'

For a moment she remained where she was, halfway between sitting and standing, but they both knew it was just pride keeping her on her feet and, after a moment, she sank back down beside him.

'You remembered,' she said.

'You make one hell of an impression.'

'Do I?' She managed a single snort of amusement. 'Well, I've had years of practice. I started young, honing my skills on nannies. I caused riots at kindergarten—'

'Riots? Dare I ask?'

'I don't know. How do you feel about toads? Spiders? Ants?'

'I can take them or leave them,' he said. 'Ants?'

'Those great big wood ants.'

'What a monster you were.'

'I did my best,' she assured him. 'I actually managed to get expelled from three prep schools before I discovered that was a waste of time since, if your family has enough money, the right contacts, there is always another school. That there's always some secretary to lumber with the task...'

'You didn't like school?'

'I loved it,' she said. 'Getting thrown out is what's known as cutting off your nose to spite your face.'

In other words, he thought, crying out for attention from the people who should have been there for her. And, making the point that whatever happened he would be there for her, he put his arm around her, wincing under cover of darkness as he eased himself back against the wall, pulling her up against his shoulder.

'Are you okay, Jago?'

She might not be able to see him wince, but she must have heard the catch in his breath.

'Fine,' he lied. Then, because he needed a distraction, 'Ivo?' It wasn't exactly a common name. 'Your brother's name is Ivo Grenville?'

'Ivan George Grenville, to be precise.' She sighed. 'Financial genius. Philanthropist. Adviser to world statesmen. No doubt you've heard of him. Most people have.'

'Actually I was thinking about a boy with the same name who was a year below me at school. Could he be your brother? His parents never came to take him out. Not even to prize-giving the year he won—'

'Not even the year he won the Headmaster's Prize,' she said. 'Yes. That would be Ivo.'

'Clever bugger. My parents were taking me out somewhere for a decent feed and I felt so sorry for him I was going to ask him if he wanted to come along.'

'But you didn't.'

'How do you know that?'

'I wasn't criticising you, Jago. It's just that I know my brother. He never let anyone get that close. Not even me. Not until he met Belle. He's different now.'

'Well, good. I'm sorry I let him put me off.'

He'd meant to keep an eye out for him, but there had been so many other things to fill the days and even a single year's age gap seemed like a lifetime at that age.

'Don't blame yourself. Ivo's way of dealing with our parents' rejection was to put up a wall of glass. No interaction, no risk of getting hurt. Mine, on the other hand, was to create havoc in an attempt to force them to notice me.'

'That I can believe. What did you do once you'd run out of the livestock option? Kick the headmistress?'

'Are you ever going to let me forget that?'

'Never,' he said, and the idea of teasing her about that for the next fifty years gave him an oddly warm feeling. Stupid. In fifty hours from now they would have gone on their separate ways, never to see one another again. Instead, he concentrated on what really mattered. 'Tell me about your parents. Why did they reject you both?'

'Oh, that's much too strong a word for it. Rejection would have involved serious effort and they saved all their energy for amusing themselves.'

'So why bother—to have children?'

'Producing offspring, an heir and a spare, even if the spare turned out to be annoyingly female, was expected of them. The Grenville name, the future of the estate had to be taken care of.'

'Of course. Stupid of me,' he said sarcastically.

'It's what they had been brought up to, Jago. Generations of them. On one side you have Russian royalty who never accepted that the world had changed. On the other, the kind of people who paid other people to run their houses, take care of their money and, duty done, rear their children. They had more interesting, more important things to do.'

What could ever be more important than kissing your kid better when she grazed a knee? Jago wondered. The memory of his own mother kissing his four-year-old elbow after he'd fallen from his bike sprang, unbidden, to his mind. How she'd smiled as she'd said, 'All better.' Told him how brave he was...

He shut it out.

'Chillingly selfish,' he said, 'but at least it was an honest response. At least they didn't pretend.'

'Pretence would have required an effort.' She lifted her head to look up at him. 'Is that what your parents did, Jago? Pretend?'

Her question caught him on the raw. He didn't talk about his family. He'd walled up that part of his life. Shut it away. Until the scent of rosemary had stirred a memory of a boy and his bicycle…

Lies, lies, lies…

'Jago?'

She said his name so softly, but even that was a lie. Not his real name. They were alone together, locked in a dark and broken world, reliant upon one another for their very survival and she had a right to his name.

'Nick,' he said.

'Nick…'

It was so long since anyone had called him that. The soft sound of her voice saying his name ripped at something inside him and he heard himself say, 'I was in my final year at uni when I was door-stepped by a journalist.'

She took the hand that he'd hooked around her waist to keep her close and the words, coiled up inside him, began to unravel…

He could see the man now. The first to reach his door. He hadn't introduced himself, not wanting to put him on his guard. He'd just said his name. 'Nick?' And when he'd said, 'Yes…' he'd just pitched in with, 'What's your reaction to the rumour…'

'My father was a politician,' he said. 'A member of the Government. A journalist knocked on my door one day and asked me if I knew my father had been having a long-term affair with a woman in his London office. One of his researchers. That I had a fourteen-year-old half-sister…'

He caught himself. He didn't talk about them, ever.

'Oh, Nick…' She said his name again, softly, echoing his pain. He shouldn't have told her. No one else had used it in fifteen years and to hear it spoken that way caught at feelings he'd buried so deep that he'd forgotten how much they hurt. How betrayed he'd felt. How lost.

'That was when I discovered that all that "happy families" stuff was no more than window-dressing.'

She didn't say she was sorry, just moved a little closer in the dark. It was enough.

'It must have been a big story at the time,' she said after a while, 'but I don't recall the name.'

'It was fifteen years ago. No doubt you were still at school.'

'I suppose, even so—'

'A juicy political scandal is hard to miss.'

It hadn't just been the papers. His father had been the poster boy for the perfect marriage, a solid family life. It had brought out the whole media wolf pack and the television satirists had had a field day.

'You're right, of course. The fact is that I don't use his name any more. Neither of us do. My father was dignified, my mother stood by him and, in the fullness of time, he was rewarded for a lifetime of commitment to his country, his party, with a life peerage. Or maybe the title was my mother's reward for all those years of keeping up appearances, playing the perfect constituency wife. Not making a fuss. But then why would she?'

It was obvious that she'd always known about the affair,

the child, but she had enjoyed her life too much to give it up. Had chosen to look the other way and live with it.

'She was the one who spent weekends at the Prime Minister's home in the country,' he said. 'Went on the foreign tours. Enjoyed all the perks of his position. Got the title.'

'What did they say to you?'

He shook his head. 'I went home, expecting to find my mother in bits, my father ashamed, packing.' It had taken the police presence to get him through the television crews and the press pack blocking the lane, but inside the house it was as if nothing had changed. 'It was just another day in politics and they assumed I'd come down to put on a united family front. Go out with them for the photo call. My mother was furious with me for refusing to play the game. She said I owed my father total loyalty. That the country needed him.'

He could still see the two of them going out to face the cameras together, the smiling arm-in-arm pose by the garden gate with the dogs that had made the front page of all the newspapers the next day. Could still smell the rosemary as the photographers had jostled for close-ups, hoping to catch the pain and embarrassment behind the composed smiles. As if…

'What I hated most, couldn't forgive,' he said, 'was the way the other woman was treated like a pariah. Frozen out. She had to give up her job, go into hiding, take out an injunction against the press to protect her daughter. Start over somewhere new.'

'You don't blame her at all? She wasn't exactly innocent, Nick, and someone must have leaked the information to the press. Maybe she hoped to force your father's hand.'

'If she did she was a fool,' he said dismissively.

'She didn't go for the kiss-and-tell? Even then?'

'No. Everyone behaved impeccably. Kept their mouths shut and my father was back in government before the year was over.'

'She loved him, then.'

'I imagine so. She was a fool twice over.'

'I suppose.' Miranda's shivering little sigh betrayed her. Was that how she saw herself? A fool?

'If it wasn't for herself, maybe it was for her daughter.'

She swallowed nervously, as if aware of treading on dangerous ground.

'Perhaps she wanted some of what you had,' she said when he didn't respond. 'To be publicly acknowledged by her father. In her place...'

'In her place, what?' he demanded when she faltered.

'It's what I would have done,' she admitted.

'Poking a stick into a wasps' nest,' he said, realising that she was probably right. 'Poor kid.'

'She's a woman, Jago. About my age. Your sister. And you're wrong about your parents losing nothing,' she said before he could tell her that he didn't have a sister. That she was nothing to him. 'They lost you.'

'The people I thought were my parents didn't exist. Their entire life was a charade.'

'Truly? All of it? Even when they came to your school open day?'

'They did what was expected of them, Miranda,' he said, refusing to give them credit for anything. 'It was just another photo op. Like going to church when they were in the constituency. Pure hypocrisy. It didn't mean anything.'

She sucked in her breath as if about to say something, then thought better of it. 'You changed your name? Afterwards?'

'I use my grandfather's name. Part of it, anyway. He emigrated from eastern Europe. Nothing as grand as Russian royalty, you understand, just a young man trying to escape poverty. They put him off the boat at the first port they came to and told him he was in America. We have a lot in common.'

'Don't you think—'

'No,' he said abruptly. 'I don't.' It was the last thing he wanted to think about. 'What about you? Do you see your parents these days? Did they manage to find time for their granddaughter's christening?'

She shook her head, then, realising that he couldn't see, said, 'They died in an accident years ago. When Ivo was just out of university and I was in sixth form taking my A levels.'

Jago found himself in the unusual situation of not having a clue what to say.

To offer sympathy for the loss of parents who had never been there for her would have been as hypocritical as anything his parents had ever done. Saying what was expected. Hollow words. Yet he knew there would still be an emptiness. A space that nothing could ever fill...

'How did you cope?' he asked finally.

Manda caught a yawn. She ached everywhere, her hands were sore, her mouth gluey. The only comfort was the heat of Jago's shoulder beneath her head. His arm keeping her close. His low husky voice drowning out the small noises, the scuffling, that she didn't want to think about.

'Everything suddenly landed on Ivo's shoulders. He'd been about to take a year off to travel. Instead, he found himself having to deal with all the consequences of unexpected death. Step up and take over. He was incredible.'

'I don't doubt it, but I was asking about you. Singular.'

'Oh.' How rare was that...? 'I suppose the hardest thing was having to accept that, no matter what I did, how good I was, or how bad, my mother and father were never going to turn up, hold me, tell me that it was going to be all right because they loved me.'

It was all she'd ever wanted.

'And?' he said, dragging her back from the moment she'd stood at their graveside, loving them and hating them in the same breath.

She wished she could see him. See his eyes, read him... Cut off from all those visual signals that she could read like a book, she was lost. And in the dark she couldn't use that cool, dismissive smile she'd perfected for when people got too close. The one that Ivo said was like running into a brick wall.

She had no mask to hide behind.

'There must have been an "and",' he persisted. 'You're not the kind of woman who just sits back and takes it.'

'Not only a hero but smart with it,' she said, letting her head fall back against this unexpected warmth that had nothing to do with temperature.

No visual clues, but his voice was as rich and comforting as a mouthful of her sister-in-law's chocolate cake. And, like that sinful confection, to be taken only in very small quantities because the comfort glow was an illusion.

She wasn't fooling herself. The magic would fade with the dawn as such things always did in fairy stories, but for now, in the dark, with his shoulder to lean on, his arm about her, she felt safe.

'And...' he insisted, refusing to let her off the hook.

He really wanted to know what she'd done next, did he?

Well, that would speed reality along very nicely and maybe that was a good thing. Illusions were made to be shattered, so it was best to get it over with. The sooner the better.

'You're absolutely right,' she said. 'There's always an "and".'

'You're stalling.'

'Am I?'

Who wouldn't?

'And so I went looking for someone who would,' she said. 'Just one more poor little rich girl looking for someone who'd hold her and tell her that he loved her. Totally pathetic.'

Just how dumb could a girl get?

'You were what? Eighteen?' he guessed. 'I don't suppose you found it difficult.'

'No. It wasn't finding someone that was difficult. There were someones positively lining up to help me out. Finding them wasn't the problem. Keeping them was something else.' Looking back with the crystal clear vision of hindsight, it was easy to see why. 'Needy, clinging women desperate for love frighten men to death.'

'We're a pitiful bunch.'

She shook her head. 'It wasn't their fault. They were young, looking for some light-hearted fun. Sex without strings.'

Something she hadn't understood at the time. And when, finally, it had been made clear to her, it had broken her.

'I think you're being a little harsh on yourself.'

'Am I?' She heard the longing in her voice and dismissed it. 'I don't think so.'

'There's no such thing as sex without strings, especially for women.'

'You're referring to that old thing about men giving love for sex, women giving sex for love, no doubt.'

'I'm not sure anything as complex as the relationship between a man and woman can ever be reduced to a sound bite,' he said.

'It can when you've just taken your finals and the world beckons. No young man with the world at his feet wants to be saddled with a baby.'

'You were pregnant?' That stopped him. She'd known it would.

'My last throw of the dice. I thought if I had his baby a man wouldn't ever be able to leave me. Stupid. Unfair. Irresponsible beyond belief.'

'People do crazy things when they're unhappy,' he said.

'No excuses, Nick. Using a child...' She shrugged. 'Of course he insisted I terminate the pregnancy and, well, I've already told you that I'd have done anything...'

'Where is this child now?'

'You're assuming I didn't go ahead with it.' How generous of him. How undeserved...

'Are you saying you did?'

They were lying quite still but when, beside her, Nick Jago stopped breathing, it felt as if the world had stopped.

'My punishment,' Manda said, at last, 'is not knowing. I was standing at the kerb, looking across the road to the clinic, when I collapsed in agony in front of a car and matters were taken out of my hands.'

And with that everything started again. His breathing, her heart...

'You lost the baby?'

'Not because of the accident. The driver saved my life

twice over that day. First stopping his car. Then realising that there was something seriously wrong and calling an ambulance.'

'You were in that much pain? Was it an ectopic pregnancy?'

She nodded. 'By the time Ivo made it back from wherever he was, I was home and it was over. A minor traffic accident. Nothing to make a fuss over.'

'You never told him? You lost your baby and you never told him?'

'He already had the world on his shoulders. He didn't need me as well. And I was so ashamed…'

'You didn't do anything.'

'I thought about it, Jago. I was so desperate…'

He muttered something beneath his breath, then said, 'And this man who could demand such a thing? Where was he when all this was happening?'

'Keeping his fingers crossed that I'd go through with it?' she offered. Then, with a shrug, 'No, that's unfair. He came rushing to the hospital to make sure I was okay, but I couldn't bear to look at him any more. Couldn't bear to see his relief. Face what I'd done.'

'You hadn't done anything,' Jago said, reaching for her, taking her into his arms in that eternal gesture of comfort.

Did he think she would cry again? Before, her tears had been of relief. A normal, human reaction. But this was different. She had no more tears to cry for herself…

'You would never have gone through with it,' he said, holding her close. And he kept on saying it. Telling her that it was not her fault, that she shouldn't blame herself. Saying over and over, that she would not have rejected her own baby.

This was the absolution she'd dreamed of. And why she'd never told anyone.

She didn't deserve such comfort. It had been no one's fault but her own that she'd been pregnant. It was her burden. Her loss. And she pulled away.

'How did you guess it was ectopic?' she asked. How many men knew what an ectopic pregnancy was, without it being explained in words of one syllable?

'My grandfather was a doctor, wanted me to follow in his footsteps and maybe I would have, if I hadn't been taken to Egypt at an early age...' For a moment he drifted off somewhere else, to a memory of his own. Happier times with his family, no doubt. Then, shaking it off, he said, 'I remember him talking about a patient of his who'd nearly died. Describing the symptoms. He said the pain was indescribable.'

It wasn't the pain that she remembered. It was the emptiness afterwards, the lack of feeling that never ceased...

'What happened to you, Miranda? Afterwards.'

'The next logical step, I suppose. My parents, my boyfriend, even my baby had rejected me. All that was left was to reject myself so I stopped eating.' Then, because she didn't want to think about that, because she wanted to hear about Egypt and Jago as an impressionable boy, however unlikely that seemed, she said, 'What about you?'

'Manda...'

'No. Enough about me. I want to hear about you,' she insisted, telling herself that his use of the diminutive had been nothing more than a slip. It meant nothing...

'In Egypt?' he asked.

Yes... No... Egypt was a distraction and she refused to be distracted.

'When you walked away from your family,' she said.

She felt the movement of muscle, more jerk than shrug, as if she'd taken him unawares. The slight catch in his breathing as if he'd jolted some pain into life. Physical? Or deeper?

Then, realising that she was transferring her own mental pain on to him, that it had to be physical, she sat up. 'You *are* hurt!'

'It's nothing. Lie back.' And, when she hesitated, 'Honestly. Just a pulled muscle. It needs warmth and you make a most acceptable hot-water bottle.'

'Would that be "Dr" Jago talking?'

'I don't think you need to be a doctor to know that.'

'I guess not.' And, since warmth was all she had to offer, she eased gently back against him, taking care not to jar his shoulder.

'Is that okay?'

'Fine,' he said, tightening his arm around her waist so that she felt as if she was a perfect fit against him.

Too perfect.

'So?' she said, returning to her question, determined not to get caught, dragged down by the sexual undertow of their closeness, a totally unexpected—totally unwanted—off limits desire that was nothing more than a response to fear.

She didn't want to like Nick Jago, let alone care about him. Not easy when a man had saved your life. When his kiss had first warmed her, then heated her to the bone.

And the last thing she wanted was his pity.

CHAPTER NINE

'TELL me about your life,' she pressed. 'Away from here. Are you, or have you ever been, married?' she asked, using the interrogatory technique of the immigration form. Turning the question into something of a joke. 'How about children?'

Jago didn't make the mistake of shrugging a second time, just said, 'No, no and none.'

'None that you know of,' she quipped.

'None, full stop. I'm not that careless.'

'I'm sorry…'

'It's okay. It's one of those hideous things that men say, isn't it? As if it makes them look big.'

'Some men,' she agreed. Then, before she could stop herself, 'What about long-term relationships?'

She was making too much of it, she knew. It didn't matter. Tomorrow, please God, they'd be out of here and would have no reason to ever see one another again.

They'd step back into their own lives and be desperate to forget that, locked in the darkness, they'd shared the darkest secrets of their souls with a stranger.

'What about the woman who's been telling the world that

this…' she made a small gesture that took in their unseen surroundings '…was all her own work?'

'Fliss? I was under the apparently mistaken impression that she came under the sex-without-strings heading. She was, allegedly, a postgraduate archaeology student and when she turned up on site looking for work experience I was glad to have another pair of hands. My mistake. I should have made an effort to check her credentials.'

'As opposed to her "credentials",' Manda said, unable to help herself from teasing him a little. 'Which, let's face it, no one could fail to miss.'

'You've got me.' He laughed, taking no offence. 'Shallow as a puddle and clearly getting no more than I deserve.'

'Which is?'

'Being made to look a fool? Although maybe the gods have had the last laugh after all,' he said, no longer amused. 'The temples, as a tourist attraction, which was the entire point of that scurrilous piece of garbage she and the Tourism Minister concocted between them, would seem to be dead in the water. And what does my reputation matter? The suffering caused by this earthquake is far more important.'

He took the bottle of brandy from her bag and offered it to her.

'No. Thanks.'

'Just take a mouthful to wash the dust out of your mouth,' he suggested, 'then maybe it really would be a good idea to try and get some sleep.'

She eased forward, took the bottle, gasping as a little of the hot liquor slid down her throat, for a moment totally unable to speak.

'Good grief,' she managed finally. 'Do people actually drink this stuff?'

'Only the desperate,' he admitted.

'It would be quicker—and kinder—to shoot yourself. Here,' she said, passing it back to him. 'Can you pass me my bag?'

He handed it to her, then eased himself carefully into a sitting position.

He *was* in pain.

Had he just pulled a muscle? Or had he torn something in that long, desperate moment when he'd hung on to her? When he'd helped her over the top to safety.

She didn't ask, knew he'd deny it anyway. Instead, she dug out the nearly empty pack of wipes from the soggy interior of her bag. Then, having used one to wipe the worst of the dust from her face and hands, she took another and, lifting the big capable hand that had held her, had hung on as the earth shook beneath them, she began, very gently, to wipe it clean.

Jago stiffened at the first touch of the cool, damp cloth on his thumb.

'Manda…'

Not a slip, then…

'Shh…' she said. 'Let me do this.'

Even through the cloth, she could feel a callus along the inner edge of his thumb that she knew would be a fit for the small trowel he'd found. The result of years of carefully sifting through the layers of the past.

Pieces of bone, pottery, the occasional button or scrap of leather that had been preserved by some freak chance of nature.

Objects without emotional context. Small pieces of distant lives that wouldn't break your heart.

'Don't worry, I've learned my lesson. I won't throw myself

on you,' she said as she concentrated on each of his fingers in turn. 'I haven't done that in years.'

'No? Just my bad luck.' Then, as if realising that he'd said something crass, 'So what do you do with yourself? Now you've given up on men?'

'I work. Very hard. I used to work for Ivo, but these days I'm a partner in the television production company that I set up with my sister-in-law,' she said, smoothing the cloth over his broad palm. 'I'm the organiser. I co-ordinate the research, find the people, the places. Keep things running smoothly behind the scenes while Belle does the touchy-feely stuff in front of the camera.'

'Maybe you should change places,' he said as, having finished one hand, she began on the other.

She looked up.

'You're doing just fine with the touchy-feely stuff,' he assured her.

'Oh. No. This is…' Then, pulling herself together, 'Actually, since we recently won an award for our first documentary, I think I'll leave things just the way they are.'

'What was it about?'

'Not handbags,' she said. 'Or shoes.'

'I didn't imagine for a minute it was.'

'I'm sorry.'

'No. It's my fault for making uncalled-for comments on your handbag choices. Tell me about it.'

'It was all tied up with one of Belle's pet causes.' He waited. 'Street kids…'

'The unwanted. You're sure this was your sister-in-law's pet cause?'

He was too damn quick…

'She and her sister spent some time on the streets when they were children. Their stories put my pathetic whining in its place, I can tell you,' she said quickly. 'How's your head, Jago?'

'Still there last time I looked, Miranda.'

'Your sense of humour is still intact, at least. Let me see,' she said, cupping his face in her hands so that she could check it out for herself.

It had been so long since she'd touched a man's hand, his face in this way. His lean jaw was long past the five o'clock stubble phase and she had to restrain herself from the sensuous pleasure of rubbing her palms against it. Instead, she pushed back his hair, searching out the injury on his forehead.

He'd really taken quite a crack, she discovered, remembering uncomfortably how she'd taunted him about that.

'I'd better clean that up,' she said, taking the last wipe from the pack.

'I can—'

'Tut…' she said, slapping away his hand as he tried to take it from her.

'I can do it myself,' he persisted. 'But why would I when I have a beautiful woman to tend me?'

She stopped what she was doing.

The crack on his head must have jarred his brains loose, he decided. Despite all evidence to the contrary, he wasn't given to living dangerously, at least not where women were concerned.

Keeping it light, keeping his distance just about summed up his attitude to the entire sex, but ever since he'd woken to the sound of Miranda Grenville screaming in the dark it was as if he'd been walking on a high wire. Carelessly.

Maybe cheating death gave you the kind of reckless edge that had you saying the most outrageous things to a woman who was quite capable of responding with painful precision. A woman who, like a well-known brand of chocolate, kept her soft and vulnerable centre hidden beneath a hard, protective sugar shell.

'You have no idea what I look like,' she said crisply as she leaned into him, continued her careful cleaning of the abrasion. Enveloping him in her warm female scent.

Would her shell melt against the tongue, too? Dissolve into silky sweetness...

'I know enough,' he said, taking advantage of the fact that she had her own hands full to run the pad of his thumb across her forehead, down the length of her nose, across a well defined cheekbone. Definitely his brains had been shaken loose. 'I know that you've got good bones. A strong face.'

'A big nose, you mean,' she said as, job done, she leaned back. 'How does that feel now?'

That she was too far away.

'You missed a bit just here,' he said, taking her hand and guiding it an inch or two to the right. Then to his temple. 'And there.'

'Really?' She slid her fingers across his skin. 'I can't feel anything. Maybe I should have the light.'

'We should save the battery,' he said. 'You're doing just fine. So, where was I? Oh, yes, your nose. Is it big? I'd have said interesting...'

'You are full of it, Nick Jago.'

'Brimful,' he admitted, beginning to enjoy himself. 'Your hair is straight. It's very dark and cut at chin-length.'

'How do you know my hair is dark?' She stopped dabbing

at his imaginary injuries... 'Did you take a sneaky photograph of me?'

'As a souvenir of a special day, you mean?' It hadn't occurred to him down in the blackness of the temple when his entire focus had been on getting them out of there. Almost his entire focus. Miranda Grenville had a way of making you take notice of her. 'Maybe I should do it now,' he suggested.

'I don't think so.' She moved instinctively to protect the phone tucked away in her breast pocket. 'Who'd want a reminder of this to stick on the mantelpiece?' She shivered. 'Who would need one? Besides, as you said, we need to conserve what's left of the battery.'

His mistake.

'I was talking about the light, not the cellphone but I take your point. But, to get back to your question, I know your hair is dark because if it had been fair then the light, feeble though it was, would have reflected off it.'

'Mmm... Well, Mr Smarty Pants, you've got dark hair, too. It's definitely not straight and it needs cutting. I saw that much when you struck your one and only match.' Then, 'Oh, and you're left-handed.'

'How on earth do you know that?' he demanded.

'There's a callus on your thumb. Here.' She rubbed the tender tip of her own thumb against the ridge of hard skin. 'This is the hand you use first. The one you reached out to me when I couldn't make it across that last gap.' She lifted it in both of hers and said, 'This is the hand with which you held me safe.'

It was the hand with which he'd held her when she'd cried out to him to let her fall because she was not worth dying for. Because once, young, alone, in despair and on the point of a breakdown, she'd considered terminating a pregnancy?

Had she been punishing herself for that ever since?

'You are worth it, Manda,' he said, his voice catching in his throat. Then, 'No, I hate that. You deserve better than some childish pet name. You are an amazing woman, Miranda. A survivor. And, whatever it is you want, you are worth it.'

'Thank you…' Her words were little more than a whisper and, in the darkness, he felt the brush of silky hair against his wrist, then soft lips, the touch of warm breath against his knuckles. A kiss. No, more than a kiss, a salute, and something that had lain undisturbed inside him for aeons contracted, or expanded, he couldn't have said which. Only that her touch had moved him beyond words.

It was Miranda who shattered the moment, removing her hands from his, putting clear air between them. Shattered the silence, rescuing them both from a moment in which he might have said, done, anything.

'Actually, I'm not the only one around here with an interesting nose,' she said. Her voice was too bright, her attempt at a laugh forced. 'Yours has been broken at some time. How did that happen?' Then, archly, deliberately breaking the spell of that brief intimacy, 'Or, more interestingly, who did it to you?'

'You saw all that in the flare of a match?' he asked.

'You were looking at your temple. I was looking at the bad-tempered drunk I was unfortunate to have been trapped with.'

'I was not drunk,' he protested, belatedly grabbing for the lifeline she'd flung him. Stepping back from a brink far more dangerous than the dark opening that yawned a few feet away from them.

She shook her head, then, perhaps thinking that because

he couldn't see, he didn't know what she'd done—and how had he known?—she said, 'I know that now, but for a while back there you didn't seem too sure.'

'A crack on the head will do that to you.'

'Concussion?'

'I hope not. The treatment is rest and plenty of fluids.'

'Thus speaks the voice of experience?'

'Well, you know how it is.'

'Er, no, actually, I don't. I suspect it's a boy thing.' Then, presumably because there really wasn't anything else to say about that, 'And, actually, no, I didn't see your nose. I felt it.'

'Yes...'

That was it. How he'd known she'd shaken her head. He could *feel* the smallest movement that she made. Without sight, every little sound, every disturbance in the air was heightened beyond imagining and his brain was somehow able to translate them into a picture. Just as every tiny nuance in her voice was amplified so that he could not only hear what she was saying, he could also hear what she was not.

The air moved and he saw the quick shake of her head, the slide of glossy, sharply cut hair. He touched her face and saw a peaches and cream complexion. Kissed her and—

'I felt it when I cleaned the dust from your face,' she said, her rising inflexion replying to some uncertainty that she'd picked up in his voice. It was a two-way thing then, and he wondered what image came into her mind when he moved, spoke. When she touched him...

'As noses go,' he said, 'I have to admit that it's hard to miss.'

'Oh, it's not that bad. Just a little battered. How did it happen?'

She was back in control now, her voice level, with no little emotional yips to betray her. She'd clearly trained herself to disguise her feelings. How long had it taken, he wondered.

How long before it had become part of her?

How long had it taken him?

'At school,' he said. 'It was at a rugby match. I charged down a ball that was on the point of leaving another boy's boot.'

'Ouch.'

'I was feeling no pain, believe me,' he said, remembering the moment, even so many years later, with complete satisfaction. 'I'd stopped an almost certain last-minute drop goal that would have stolen the match. I don't think I'd have noticed a broken leg, let alone a flattened nose. I was just mad that I had to go to A and E instead of going out with...'

He stopped, his pleasure at the memory tripping him over another, spilling his own emotional baggage.

'Out with?' she prompted, then, when he didn't respond, 'It was your father, wasn't it? He'd come to see you play.'

'Yes...'

How could that one small word have so many shades? he wondered. In the last few moments it had been a revelation, a question, reassurance and now an acknowledgement of a truth that he could barely admit. Because she was right. His father had been there. Even with an election looming, he'd taken time out of a packed schedule to be with him that day.

'Yes,' he repeated. 'My father had come to see the match.'

'Good photo op, was it?' she asked dismissively. 'Senior politician with his son, the blood-spattered hero of the sports field. I bet it looked terrific in the papers the next day.'

'No!' he responded angrily. That touch of derision in her

voice had him leaping to his father's defence. How dared she…?

'No?' she repeated, but this time the ironic inflection didn't fool him.

'There was no photograph,' he said, his voice flat, giving her nothing.

'No photograph? But surely you said that was all it ever was?'

She was pure butter-wouldn't-melt-in-her-mouth innocence, but he knew that it had been a deliberate trip-up. That she'd heard something in his voice—his own emotional yip— and had set out to prove something.

'So—what?' she persisted, refusing to let him off her clever little hook. 'He turned up just to see his son play for his school like any other proud father? No agenda? No photo opportunity?'

She did that thing with her fingers—making quotation marks—and he grabbed at her hands to make her stop.

'You are a witch, Miranda Grenville.'

'I've been called worse,' she replied, so softly that her voice wrapped itself around him.

'I can believe it.' Then, her hands still in his, he said, 'It was my birthday that week. My eighteenth. Dad came down from London to watch the match before taking me out to dinner.'

'You missed your birthday dinner?'

'Actually, it was okay,' he said. 'We sat in A and E, eating sandwiches out of a machine, surrounded by the walking wounded, a couple of drunks, while we waited for someone to fix me up. Give me a shot.'

'Waited? Are you telling me that as the son of a Government

minister you didn't get instant attention?' she said, still mocking him, but gently now.

'The doctors were busy with more serious stuff. It didn't matter. We talked about what I was going to do on my gap year. About the election. It wasn't often I got him to myself like that.'

'So the evening wasn't a total wash-out.'

'Not a wash-out on any level,' he admitted. It had been the last time they'd been together like that. His father had been given a high-powered cabinet job after the election. He'd gone to university.

Manda knelt back on her heels, her hands gripped with painful tightness as Nick, seemingly unaware of her, relived a precious evening spent with his father. Did he, she wondered, realise how lucky he was?

She yearned for just one memory like that.

One day when her mother or father had taken time out of their busy lives to come and see her at school, take her out for tea. For her birthday to have been more than a date in a secretary's diary.

'I suppose now you're going to tell me that I should remember all the good bits, forget the rest,' he said, breaking into her own dark thoughts.

'I wouldn't dream of suggesting any such thing,' she said.

'Don't be so modest, Miranda. We both know that you would.'

'Then we'd both be wrong,' she said vehemently. 'I'd tell you to remember all of it. Every little thing. The good, the bad, the totally average and be grateful for every single moment.' She caught herself. Shrugged awkwardly. 'Sorry. It's none of my business.'

The stone was hurting her knees and she shifted to a sitting position.

'Here. Lean back against me, you'll be more comfortable.' Then, his arm around her, he said, 'Tell me one of your memories, Miranda. Your first day at school. Was that good? Bad? Totally average?'

'Not great. All the other new girls had been brought along by their mothers. Mine was away somewhere.' She had always been away. 'Let's see… September? Shooting in Scotland, probably. Anyway, I told whichever unhappy creature was my nanny at the time to take me home since obviously it had to be a mother who delivered me to school.'

'Did she?'

'What do you think? The poor woman couldn't wait to be shot of me and I was handed over kicking and screaming. No reprieve. A first impression that I strived to live down to. Can you remember your first day?'

'I wish I couldn't. My mother cried. I was so embarrassed that I wouldn't let her take me nearer than the end of the road after that.'

'Oh, poor woman!'

'What about me? I had to live with the shame.'

'What horrible little brats we both were.'

'We were five years old. We were supposed to be horrible little brats.'

'I suppose.'

'Tell me about your first kiss,' he said.

She sighed. 'We're doing all the horrible stuff first, are we?'

'Was it horrible?'

'I was fourteen. That dreadful age when you're pretending to be grown up but you're not. When kissing is a competitive sport, something to be dissected in detail with your friends afterwards and points awarded for technical merit, artistic style and endurance. Mine was with a boy called Jonathan Powell, all clashing teeth and acne. Of course, when we compared notes afterwards I lied through my back teeth. You?'

'Thirteen. Her name was Lucy… Something. I think she must have been practising because I had a really good time.'

'Not just a brat, but a precocious brat and, before you even think of taking this to the next logical step,' she warned, 'forget it.'

'Okay. You choose. Tell me something that happened to you. Something that's stayed with you.'

'My very own heart-warming moment?' she replied, mocking herself.

'I don't know. Have you got a heart to be warmed?'

'Bastard,' she said, but laughing now.

She'd never talked like this to a man. It was as if, sheared of all expectations, freed by the darkness, they could be totally honest with one another. Could say anything.

'And now you've got that off your chest?' he prompted.

'Okay. A memory. Let's see.'

She dredged her mind for something that would satisfy him—something big—and, without warning, she was back on the streets, scouting locations for the documentary. 'At the beginning of the year I took my colleague Daisy on a worldwide recce to find locations where we could film our documentary.'

'The one about street kids.'

'Right. We'd been all over. It was all done and dusted and

we were on our way home from the airport when Daisy told the taxi driver to stop—wait for us—and dragged me down a side alley.'

She could still see it. Smell it.

'We were in one of the richest countries in the world, metres from the kind of stores where women like me buy handbags that cost four figures, restaurants where we toy with expensive food that we're afraid to eat in case we put on a pound or two. And there was this kid, a little girl, Rosie, digging around in a dumpster for food that had been thrown away.'

He let slip the same word that had dropped from her lips. Shock, horror…

'I'd known such things happened,' she said. She shook her head, for a moment unable to say another word. 'I'd known, but blocked it out. To see it with my own eyes…'

'It isn't your fault.'

'Isn't it? Isn't it the fault of everyone who looks the other way? Blocks it out?' Even now, her throat tightened as she remembered the shock of it. The horror. 'I felt so helpless. It was freezing cold and I wanted to pick her up, carry her away, wash her, feed her, make her safe, but Daisy…' she swallowed as she remembered '…Daisy just walked over and joined in, helping her look for the best stuff. It was the most horrible thing I'd ever seen in my life but she'd been there, lived it. Knew how to connect with her. And it was that child's story that touched people, had the country in an uproar, demanding that something be done. Her thin, grubby, defiant little face on the cover of magazines, looking out of the screen, that won us our award.'

'And you feel guilty about that?'

'Wouldn't you? Where was she when I was picking it up at a ritzy awards ceremony decked out in a designer dress?'

'What were you going to do, Miranda? Take in every kid that you saw on the street? Your job was to focus on what was out there, raise public awareness. You helped all those kids, not just one.' Then, when she didn't say anything, 'What did happen to her? Do you know?'

She shook her head. 'As you can imagine, thousands of couples wanted to give her a home. Adopt her.'

'But not you?'

'No,' she said, trying to keep her voice steady. 'Not me.' Then, 'Have you any idea how tough it is to take in a feral child? To make her believe that you'll never let her down, no matter what she does. Because she'll test you...'

She faltered and Jago let go of one of her hands and wiped a thumb over her cheek. It came away wet, just as he'd known it would.

'Something that you'd know all about, right?' He didn't need or wait for an answer, but pulled her into his arms and held her. 'Tough as marshmallow.'

She dug an elbow in his ribs.

'Ouch!'

'Well, what do you expect?' she demanded through a sniffle. 'Marshmallow! I don't think so!'

'No? Maybe not,' he said, remembering his earlier thought that she was like those sugar-coated, melt in your mouth chocolates. All hard shell on the outside... 'Turkish Delight?' he offered, tormenting her to block out the image.

'How about seaside rock?'

'No way.' His head and shoulder hurt when he laughed, but the very idea of her as a stick of bright pink mint-flavoured candy with her name printed all the way through was so out-rageous that he couldn't help himself. 'I'll bet the majority of your wardrobe is black.'

She didn't deny it, but countered with, 'Liquorice. I'll settle for liquorice. That's black. But it has to have been in the fridge.'

'Now you're talking,' he said and his stomach approved noisily too. 'Maybe we should stop talking about food.'

'I've still got three mints left.' She turned her head to look up at him. 'They're yours if you want them.'

'With my three that makes a feast, but let's save them for breakfast.' Then, because he hadn't eaten since early the previous morning and needed a distraction, 'When we get out of here, you should go and find her. That little girl.'

'It wouldn't be fair, Nick.'

'You've thought about it, then?'

She didn't deny it, but shook her head anyway. 'It'll be tough enough for her to move on, for her new parents, without me turning up and bringing it all back.'

'Maybe you could keep an eye on her from a distance. It would put your mind at rest. And you'll be there in case she ever needs a fairy godmother.'

'Kids don't need fairy godmothers, Nick. They need real mothers who are there for them every day, rain or shine, doing the boring stuff. Parents who earn love the hard way every day of their lives.'

He knew she was right. Knew she was talking about more than a little girl whose life she'd changed.

'You think I was hard on my parents, don't you?'

'Yes. No… I don't know.' She drew in a deep breath. 'I don't know anything, Nick. I'm just imagining what would happen if one of them was sick. If your mother needed you. Your father wanted to make some kind of peace...' He thought she'd finished, but then, very quietly, she said, 'Suppose you'd died here without ever having told them how much you love them—'

'I don't!'

'Of course you do, Nick. It only hurts if you love someone.'

Her words seemed to echo around the chamber, filling the space, filling his head, until, almost in desperation he said, 'We're not going to die. Not today.'

CHAPTER TEN

Miranda drew a breath and for a moment he thought she wasn't going to let it drop. Instead, with a little shake of her head, she said, 'Is it still today? It seems a lifetime since I walked up that path, wishing I was somewhere else.'

'You should be careful what you wish for.'

'Thanks,' she said, fishing the phone from her pocket and turning it on to check the time. 'I'll remember that for next time.' Then, with a sigh of relief, 'No, it's tomorrow. Just. How long before it's going to be light?'

He glanced at the screen. 'A few hours yet.' He felt her shiver but not with cold. Shock, hunger and thirst were doubtless taking their toll on her reserves. 'Why don't you check your messages?' he suggested in an attempt to reconnect her to reality, the outside world.

'The battery...'

'We're not going anywhere until daylight,' he assured her, overriding any protest. 'Read them. Text back. Tell them what you're feeling.'

'I don't think so! Besides, what's the point if there's no signal?' Then, catching his meaning, 'Oh. I see. You're suggesting I send them a last message. Something for them to find if we don't make it?'

Did he mean that? Maybe…

At least she had someone to leave a message for.

'We're going to make it,' he said with more conviction than he actually felt. Who knew what daylight would reveal? They might still have to climb their way out and they were weaker now and he'd be operating pretty much one-handed. He wouldn't be able to catch her a second time. 'You'll be seeing them all before you know it, but sending a message will make you feel better.'

'You think? And what about you, Nick?'

'What about me?'

'Is there anyone you want to leave a last message for? What will make you feel better?'

He knew what she was asking him. Telling him. To leave a message for his parents. He could see how she must find it difficult to understand how he could have walked away, how destroyed he'd felt. But they had been his world. They'd brought him up to believe in the cardinal virtues. Integrity, truth. He'd believed in *them*. He'd believed in a lie…

'I'll take another of those kisses, if you've got one to spare,' he said in an attempt to stop her from pursuing that thought.

Manda heard what she was supposed to hear—a careless, throwaway remark, pitched perfectly to provoke her into giving him another poke in the ribs, to distract her.

But she heard more.

Somewhere, hidden beneath the banter, she caught an edge of something she recognised.

Nick Jago, with no other way to push back the darkness, to distract her from her fear, her hunger, had shared his story.

To help her feel a little less alone, he'd exposed a hurt that went so deep he'd cut himself off from his world, even to the point of changing his name.

She understood that kind of pain. How it was tied up with everything you were. Knew how, in order to keep it hidden, you had to wear a mask every day of your life until it became so much a part of you that even those closest to you believed that was who you were.

Until, eventually, you believed it yourself and, unless someone took a risk to save you, took a step into their own darkest place to release a lifetime of unwanted, unused love and give all they had, you would shrivel up until something vital inside you died.

Nick Jago had saved her from certain death. What would it take to save him from the living death to which he'd condemned himself?

He'd answered her question, but could it really be that simple?

'A kiss?' she repeated.

The air was still and, above them, in the small patch of sky that was visible, Venus shone like a beacon of hope.

'Would that be a kissing-it-better kiss?' she asked, softly, lightly, matching his careless tone. 'Or are we talking about a make-the-world-go-away kiss?'

Jago had been deliberately provoking. He'd counted on that to divert her, keep her from the saying the words he did not want to hear, to force him to face a situation that he had blanked from his mind.

He'd anticipated a swift response too. The seemingly endless pause between presumption and response was unexpected, a touch unnerving.

But then her teasing tone as, finally, she'd repeated, 'A kiss?' had reassured him and, braced for whatever she chose to visit upon him, the butterfly touch of her fingers on his cheek, the caress of her thumb over his lips as she took him at his word, asked him what he truly wanted, warned him that this was anything but a reprieve.

He'd barely drawn breath, determined to apologise, reassure her that he'd been joking—put a stop to something that had, in the time it had taken to say it, spun out of control—before her lips touched his with a pressure so soft that he could almost have imagined it.

And then breathing seemed an irrelevance as the slow, penetrating warmth of it heated his lips, seeped into his veins, spread through his body like liquid silk until he was feeling no pain.

It was a kiss of almost unbearable sweetness that gave and gave, growing in intensity while the tips of her fingers slid down his neck, seeking out the pulse point beneath his jaw. And her touch, when she found it, sent a current of pure energy through him, as if she was somehow concentrating her entire being into that one spot.

It was as if, for years, his entire body had been somehow lying dormant, barely ticking over, waiting for this. Waiting for Miranda Grenville to come down into the dark to kiss him into life. Wake him with a touch.

Only her feather-light fingertips, her breath, her lips, touched him, seeking out the hollows, the·sensitive places beneath his chin, his throat, stirring not just his body, but something deeper.

She took endless time, her lips, her tongue, lingering as she made her way down the hard line of his breastbone, slipping shirt buttons as she moved lower, her silky hair brushing against his chest as she laid it bare to the chill night air.

For a moment she lay her hand over his heart and it, too, leapt to her touch. Then it was not her hand, but her mouth against his breast, breathing her warmth, her life into the cold, angry core that had for so long masqueraded as his heart. It was an almost unbearably sweet agony, like that of a numb limb coming painfully to life.

'Miranda...'

He gasped her name out but whether he wanted her to revive him or leave him in the safety of the cold and dark place where there was no feeling he could not have said.

'Nick?' Jago was aware that Manda was speaking to him, that there was an edge of concern to her voice. 'Are you okay?'

Was he? He was feeling a touch light-headed. Not particularly surprising under the circumstances. That hadn't been a mere kissing-it-better kiss...

'Nick!' she repeated more urgently.

'Fine,' he murmured. 'More than fine.' He hooked his arm around her. 'Lie down,' he said, pulling her up to lie against him, her hair against his cheek. 'Try and get some sleep.'

Manda lay with her cheek against Nick Jago's chest, his arm pinning her down so that she couldn't move without disturbing him. And he seemed to have drifted off almost as soon as he'd said the word.

If it was sleep.

For a minute back there she'd thought he'd drifted out of consciousness. But his heartbeat was steady beneath her ear and his breathing seemed okay...

She closed her eyes. Tried not to think of the aches and pains that she'd temporarily managed to block out, but now she'd stopped concentrating on Nick had returned with a vengeance.

The fact that she was hungry. Thirsty. She hadn't had anything to drink other than a few sips of water since lunch. A lunch she'd done little more than toy with. Sleep, if she could manage it, would be a great idea.

She closed her eyes, concentrating on the slow, steady beat of Nick's heartbeat until, gradually, it began to lull her.

It was the light that woke her. Searingly bright against her lids, she moved instinctively to escape it, for a moment completely disorientated. Hurting everywhere. Her neck stiff.

She lifted her head to ease the ache and realised that she was lying against the supine figure of a man.

Nick Jago…

She sat up with a gasp as it all came back with a rush. Tried to speak, but her mouth was dry, her lips cracked and it took a couple of goes before she could manage his name.

'Nick? Wake up! It's morning!'

Manda disentangled herself, scrambling quickly to her feet, forgetting all aches and pains in her eagerness to explore this promise of a way out.

Then, when he didn't respond, she looked back.

'Jago?' He was drowsy, slow to stir. Slow to stifle a groan. 'Are you okay?' she asked, remembering his hurt shoulder. That he'd had a bang on the head.

'Barely,' he muttered. 'There are alarm clocks that use fewer decibels than you. Your wake-up technique could do with a little polishing, Miranda.'

'I just haven't been putting in the practise,' she said, glancing back.

The sun, barely over the horizon, had found a chink in the shattered walls and for a moment it was concentrated on their corner of the dark interior and she caught her first real glimpse of the man with whom she'd spent the long night. Whose hand had brought her from the depths. Whose arm had held her safe.

His face was craggy rather than handsome, not helped by the fact that he needed a shave. His nose was, as they'd already discussed, interesting. His chin, stubborn. His eyes, she saw, in the moment before he blinked and lifted a hand to shade them from the light, were a fine grey. As for his mouth…

His mouth, she thought, looked exactly the way it had felt as she'd traced it with her thumb. The way it had felt when he'd kissed her. Tender, determined, sensuous. As if it had been a long time since he'd smiled.

He leaned his head back against the wall and, suddenly concerned, she said, 'Are you really okay?'

'I'd be better if you sat down instead of flirting with that big empty space out there in the dark.'

She glanced at the wall, with its tantalising promise of light, then dropped to her knees and pushed his hair back from his forehead to check his injury. There was a brutal graze, bruising, a slight swelling. Then, as the rising sun moved, the light suddenly disappeared, plunging them back into deep shadow.

'I think you'll live,' she said, dropping her hand.

'I know I will,' he replied softly. 'You gave me the kiss of life.'

'Did I? When we get out of here…'

'When we get out of here you'll find the child you filmed

on the streets. And I'll get in touch with my parents. Is that a deal?'

'It's a deal,' she said.

And, as if to seal their pact, he reached out and touched her lips with the edge of his thumb. 'Hello, Miranda Grenville.'

'Hello, Nick Jago.'

'No!'

'What? I'm sorry…'

'When someone has saved your life they have the right to know who you really are.' There was a pause, during which she swallowed desperately. 'I was born Nicholas Alexander Jackson—the good, solid English name that my grandfather chose for himself within weeks of arriving in England.'

Jackson… 'But…' She'd actually met his father at some reception or other. Ivo had introduced him, told her afterwards that he and his wife worked quietly these days, without any public fanfare, to raise funds for a charity that helped runaways. Used their own wealth, inherited from the same grandfather who'd gone on to found a giant food conglomerate…

'What?'

She shook her head. Telling him that his father had changed would be pointless. He had to be open to the possibility before he could hear it. See for himself. And he'd made that commitment. It was enough.

'Nothing. Just, thank you for telling me. Nick,' she added.

He drew in a deep breath and it was her turn to say, 'What?'

'It's just been a very long time since anyone's called me that.' Then, briskly, 'Right. So, what do you say? Shall we get out of here?'

'Yes. Please.'

Jago made it to his feet. Last night he'd thought he'd never make it out of here, but now, with even the small amount of light filtering through the broken walls, seeping down the shaft, anything seemed possible.

He looked around. He'd hoped for a way out through the original entrance but, even if it hadn't been completely blocked by falling masonry, it was on the far side of the gaping chasm where the great eagle below had broken away. But above them was the promise of a small patch of sky and he stood up to take a better look.

'Careful,' he said, reaching back to offer a steadying hand as Miranda rose beside him. 'I don't want to lose you now.' And then, as she took it, he turned back.

With the narrow beam of sunlight behind her, her face in shadow, all he'd seen of her had been the halo effect as it had lit up hair that was no longer sleek but suffering from the effects of twenty-four hours without the benefit of a comb.

Thick, dark, tousled.

He'd guessed that she was tall, but not quite how tall. No more than half a head shorter than himself. Tall, slender but with a steel core of strength about her. Well, he knew that. He'd experienced that. As a girl she might have broken down under the twin assaults of rejection and guilt, but this woman had come through a living nightmare with courage, humour, compassion.

Now, the light from above shimmered through the haze of dust motes and he could see that her black halo of hair was veiled with stone dust. There were streaks of dirt, like warpaint, decorating her cheek, her neck.

She did not have the instant, softer sensual attraction of a woman like Fliss. She had a different kind of beauty—taut, tempered in the fire—and she'd still be beautiful even when she was ninety.

She was beautiful now.

'What?' she asked, catching him staring, lifting her hand to her cheek, suddenly self-conscious of how she must look and that was when he saw her hands.

They were small, the fingers long, slender, elegant, well cared for—the remains of polish still clung to what was left of her nails—were a mess. The skin torn, knuckles bruised and broken.

She saw where he was looking and, mistaking his reaction, she spread her hand, regarding it with distaste. 'My manicurist is going to have a fit when she sees this,' she said, taking a step back to that woman who'd roused him with her scream, God alone knew how many hours ago.

Putting the mask back in place before she returned to the outside world.

'Don't!' he said. He was not a man given to fanciful gestures, but he would not let her slide back into that dark place any more than he would have left her to fall and he reached for her hand, holding it across his palm. 'Don't do that, Miranda. You don't have to pretend. Not with me. We have no secrets. We know one another.' And then he bent and kissed her fingers, saluting her wounds as a badge of the courage she'd shown last night. 'We will always know one another.'

'I…'

He saw her throat move as she swallowed, for once lost for words.

He waited.

'I… Yes.' And it was not the sophisticated woman of the world but an echo of the shy young woman she must have been. 'Thank you.'

In danger of saying—doing—something that was totally out of place, he turned and looked up the shaft to the outside world. It seemed a very long way and, having seen the state of her hands, he wondered if she was up to this second climb.

If he was.

But he knew there was no point in suggesting she wait while he went for help.

'Are you ready?'

She nodded. Then said, 'No! Wait!'

And she took her tiny cellphone from her pocket, opened it and quickly entered a brief message. Then, when she saw him watching her, she started to shrug, stopped and said, 'It's not that I doubt we'll do this, Nick. But I could get knocked down crossing the road. Or the plane could—'

'Optimistic soul, aren't you?' he said.

'My parents were killed when the yacht they were on sank. They were just gone. Nothing.' She paused, looking up at him as if asking him to understand. 'Suddenly life seems very precious, Nick. I want the people I love to know how I'm feeling now. That I'm…happy.' And then she reached up, pressed her cheek to his. 'Thank you for last night. For listening. For knowing me…'

For a moment she was in his arms and they clung to one another. Any two people would do the same, he told himself. Except he knew it was more than that. They had connected in the darkness. Bonded. Exposed themselves in ways neither of them had ever done before.

What had happened had forced them to look at their lives, confront the dark spaces, consider a different future.

'Okay. I'm ready now,' she said, taking a step back.

He grabbed her wrist as she disturbed loose stones that, endless seconds later, clattered to the floor below, then, without a word, he took the phone from her and keyed in a message of his own before handing it back.

'I don't have a cell number for my father, so I've sent it via your brother…'

She smiled. 'You won't be sorry.'

He didn't answer, just said, 'I'll go first. Stick close. Whatever happens behind you, just keep going.'

Manda knew how to concentrate.

She concentrated her world into Nick's voice, giving her a running commentary of his moves. She concentrated on his feet, his boots, one step ahead of her. And, one move at a time, she finally found herself not so much climbing out of the shaft as falling, tumbling, rolling sideways down a steep slope until his body brought her to a halt.

He said nothing, just took her hand, and she lay still while she regained her breath. Only then did a giggle explode from her. They'd survived, overcome all the odds, made it back from the dead.

Somewhere above them in the canopy a bird, or maybe it was some small mammal, joined in, setting up a cacophony of raucous laughter that echoed around the forest.

It just made her laugh all the more.

'What?' Nick said, turning to look at her.

She just shook her head, unable to answer him, unable to do or say anything. Laughing so much that tears were pouring down her cheeks.

And after a moment his beautiful, strong, sensuous mouth—the one that looked as if it hadn't smiled in centuries—twitched in sympathetic response. Then widened into a smile and then he too was laughing.

Jago wasn't sure when Miranda's laughter tipped over into tears. It didn't surprise him. There were always two sides of any emotional roller-coaster and hers had been a dark ride. He just held her hand so that she knew he was there and, after a while, hiccuping, sniffling a little, she rubbed a sleeve over her cheek. Then looked at the once white linen, the smears where sweat and tears had mingled with dust, a little blood where a loose stone had caught her cheek.

'I'm filthy,' she said.

'You're gorgeous.'

She turned to look at him. 'So are you.'

'Filthy?'

'Filthy. Gorgeous. Gorgeously filthy. What we could both do with is a shower. You run a very slack establishment if you don't mind my saying so. I was lured to Cordillera with the promise of beautiful beaches, thrilling scenery and every comfort known to man.'

'Put your complaint in writing. I'll give you the name of the Minister of Tourism.' Then, because he didn't want to think about that, because he was alive and he didn't want to feel bad about anyone—not Fliss, not even Felipe Dominez— he said, 'In the meantime, if you can stagger a hundred yards or so, I can offer you the basic facilities, always assuming that nature hasn't messed with the plumbing.'

'Plumbing?'

'There's a stream at the bottom of this hill. Cold and cold running water.'

'Water! What on earth are we waiting for?' She didn't exactly leap up, but made a very good stab at it. She barely winced as her knee buckled. 'Which way?'

He forced himself to his feet. 'This way,' he said, leading her down through the mess of dead leaves and shattered branches that littered the forest floor, towards the sound of running water.

She was limping, he noticed and taking her hand to give her support, he asked, 'How's your knee?'

'Thirsty.'

The walk down the steep path to the bottom of a small side valley nearly finished them both, but the sight of water pouring over a small waterfall and into a pool brought him to a halt.

'What is it?'

He shook his head. 'Nothing.' He'd expected change, devastation. 'Apart from a few leaves floating on the water, it seems untouched…'

'Well, that's great,' she said, urging him on and as one, they flung themselves down beside the pool, scooping up water in their hands to slake their thirst.

Manda drank, splashed water over her face, then lay still, her sore fingers trailing in the cool water.

'Better?' Nick asked.

'I didn't believe water could taste that good. Is it safe?' she asked.

'I've been drinking it for five years without any ill effects. It comes from a spring just below the main building of the temple and I ran a standpipe to the site.'

'Maybe someone should bottle it.'

'Maybe they should.' He rolled on to his back. 'It was

considered sacred by the people who lived here and the original temple building was built over it to protect it. Then, as the power of the tribe grew, new buildings were added and the water was channelled through them for cleansing rituals.'

'So why wasn't there any down in the basement, where we needed it?'

'Over centuries of neglect, the original spring gradually silted up. But water, being water, it found another way.' Then, 'Maybe we should make a move. There will be people looking for us.'

'We'll hear them,' she stalled, not wanting to move.

The pool was unbelievably beautiful. There were ferns growing where the water splashed on to the rocks. Tiny blue flowers, epiphytes growing in the misted air and huge ivory lilies that filled the air with their scent. Trees bearing berries that looked good enough to eat…

It felt untouched, new.

'You know those people, centuries ago, wasting all that time and energy building huge stone temples had it quite wrong.'

'They did?'

'You don't need stone to make a temple. This is the real deal. The sky, the earth. Fruit and flowers…' She stopped, her eye caught by a flash of shimmering colour as a dragonfly skimmed the pool. 'Water.'

She scooped up another mouthful and then, realising that it wasn't enough, she sat up and reached for her shirt buttons.

'Miranda? What are you doing?'

'I'm going to immerse myself. Soak in the water through my skin. And then I'm going to indulge in a little cleansing ritual of my own.'

Her fingers were stiff and awkward and she doubted they'd be up to the task of refastening them, but she'd worry about that later. For now, her only goal was to totally rehydrate herself. Be clean.

Her bra proved more difficult and she turned her back to Jago.

'Are you going to just lie there and watch a woman struggle?' she demanded. Before he could make any kind of move, the hook gave way and she peeled it off, tossed it aside. She'd revealed the darkest secrets of her soul to this man, her body was nothing…

Jago could not take his eyes off her as she stripped off her clothes, transforming herself without a hint of self-conscious-ness into Eve, before she stepped carefully down into the clear water of the pool. Standing for a moment, as if soaking it up, before kicking off to swim across to the waterfall.

The water streamed from her shoulders as she stood up, turning her pale skin to ivory satin against the jet of her hair. And then she turned and looked over her shoulder at him and said, 'This is an equal opportunities cleansing ritual, Nick. There's plenty of room for two.'

CHAPTER ELEVEN

'COLD?'

Manda turned as Jago's broad shoulders emerged from the water to stand beside her beneath the waterfall.

He was lean, sinewy. There was nothing pampered or soft about him. No spare flesh. Lean, hard, with something gaunt, hollow-cheeked about the face that reminded her of an El Greco saint.

'Not now,' she said, and it was true. He did not have to smile to warm her, but when he did it was as if he'd switched on some internal central heating.

'Liar,' he said, ducking his head beneath the shower, dragging his fingers through his hair to shift the dust. And as he bent she saw the mass of purple bruising darkening his left shoulder, his shoulder blade, under his arm.

Without thinking, she reached out and touched him.

'Miranda,' he warned, straightening.

She took no notice but flattened her palms against the bruises as if trying to possess them, take them back. 'I'm sorry,' she said. 'I'm so sorry—'

'No!' He turned to face her, grabbing her, shaking her a little. 'You didn't do this, do you hear me? It just happened.

If I had dislocated it, broken it, if I had died attempting to save
you it would not be your fault.'

'I know,' she said. And she did. 'I just wish I had something to make to better.'

They were close.

The water was cold, but Jago was not. 'There is something,' he said, lifting her from her feet and moving her closer
so that there was nothing between them but a film of water
that was rapidly heating up. 'Your warmth, Miranda
Grenville. And, now that I can see it, your smile.'

She was smiling?

Actually, washed clean, with his body this close to hers,
why wouldn't she be smiling?

'You want another kiss-it-better kiss, Nick Alexander Jago
Jackson? Is that it?' She didn't wait for his answer. Her mouth
was level with his shoulder, inches from his poor bruised
skin, but, as she leaned into it, he backed off.

Startled, she looked up. 'Not this time,' he said. 'This is
an equal opportunity healing ritual. I've been keeping count
and it's my turn.' And, with his gaze fixed firmly on her
mouth, he lowered his lips to hers.

She watched it happen in slow motion. Seeing everything.
The sunlight filtering through the canopy sparkling on the
drops of water clinging to his hair. A petal drifting from somewhere above them as the air stirred. Heard the beat of wings.
And then she slammed her eyes shut. Saw nothing. Heard
nothing. All her senses channelled into one.

Feeling.

His lips barely touched hers—no more than a promise—
before moving on to the delicate skin behind her ears, her
neck. His tongue traced the hollows of her collar-bone while

his fingers eased across her shoulders, the nape of her neck and she discovered an unexpected erogenous zone. That bones truly could melt.

This was not a kissing-it-better kiss. Manda might not know much, but she knew that. This was a make-the-world-go-away kiss that drew from her soft purring sighs that didn't sound like any sound she'd ever made in her entire life.

He kissed every part of her, bringing life flooding to her breasts, blowing softly into her navel as he laid her back in the water to expose more of her body to his lips. Keeping her safe with one powerful arm as he took the concept of kissing-it-better and lifted it to an entirely different plane.

Then, with her shoulders nestled into the soft moss of the bank, she drew him to her, telling him with every touch, every murmur that she wanted more and he gave her himself so completely, so selflessly, waiting and waiting for her, that afterwards she lay in his arms, tears of gratitude in her eyes. Reborn. Renewed.

'Are you hungry?' he asked as they lay on the grass, recovering.

'Starving. Shall we be greedy and eat all the mints?'

'I can do better than that.' He got up and swam across the pool to the waterfall and then began to climb up the rocks to pick the berries that grew there.

'Be careful,' she called out, more nervous now than in the bowels of the temple. But she hadn't been able to see the danger there. Hadn't been able to see him. Or that hideous bruise.

He just smiled and turned, but she couldn't bear to watch and she decided to get dressed.

She recoiled from her underwear and instead slipped into her trousers, then pulled her shirt over her naked skin. Unfortunately, her fingers and the buttons didn't want to co-operate and she was still struggling with them when Nick returned.

'Give me your hands.'

'I just need to—'

'I'll see to it when we've eaten. Here, take them.' He tipped a handful of berries into her hands. 'I've no idea what these are, but they're very high in sugar. The locals dry them and use them for long journeys.'

She tried one. He was right, they were sweet. 'They're very good,' she said, holding them for him to help himself. 'But then I'm so hungry that deadly nightshade would probably taste good right now.'

'Try a little brandy with them.'

'This is a picnic? We can finish it off with the last of the mints.'

After they'd eaten and washed their hands in the pool, they lay side by side, just letting the sun warm them, saying nothing. What was there left to say? They both knew that what had happened had been the final act in a drama that had overtaken them.

Except, of course, for the elephant in the room.

It was Nick who finally broke the silence.

'Miranda—'

She rolled over, putting her fingers on his mouth before he could say the words. 'You're safe, Nick. That's the first time for me in ten years.'

'Ten years? A life sentence,' he said, holding her, kissing her damp hair, her forehead, her cheek, until she had no choice but to look up at him. 'I can't match that kind of celibacy, but I've always used protection. Until today.'

'Today was different. This is the Garden of Eden before the Fall.'

'Maybe, but even the most basic biology lesson would confirm that unprotected sex, wherever it happens, can lead to pregnancy.'

'No.' It was her last secret. Telling him would be like removing the final veil. Leaving her stripped bare, exposed in a way that simple nakedness had not. 'Not for me. The ectopic pregnancy made a bit of a mess when it ruptured, Nick. I will never have a child of my own.'

'I'm sorry.'

That was the thing about learning to control your own feelings—you recognised the real thing when you saw it. When Jago said those two little words, he meant it. Not in a pitying way. But because he understood how much she had lost. Understood everything.

He'd saved her life, brought her from the darkness, given her back the simple joy of her body and with those two words she knew that it would be the easiest thing in the world to fall in love with him.

It was time, in other words, to slip the mask back into place. Not to hide hurt. If she never saw him again after today it would be a cause for regret, but not for pain. He had given her more than he could ever know.

He had been compassionate, kind and, in giving her his own very special version of the kiss of life, he had, quite unknowingly, lifted that dark shadow from her life. The fear that her love was not good enough.

She had trusted him and he had not let her down and now she could trust herself. Trust the love she had been yearning to give and, instead of locking it away, scared of rejection, she would use it. First she'd reassure herself that the child they'd found—Rosie—was safe and happy. Do something for the other children out there, the ones whose thin and grubby little faces hadn't made it into print.

She would wear her mask lightly, and only to protect him from any vestige of guilt for not loving her.

She'd been aware for some time of the sound of a helicopter quartering the ground nearby and she said, 'Time to move, I think. If you'd deal with the buttons?'

'We could just stay here,' Jago replied, keeping a firm hold of her hand. 'Live on nuts and wild berries.'

'We could,' she agreed. 'But I have a documentary to produce and you have a book to write. The real story about the people who lived here.'

'It won't be a sex and sandals bestseller.'

'It will be the truth. You owe them that and I promise I'll be at the head of the line when you have your first book signing.'

'That's an incentive,' he said and his smile formed deep lines down his cheeks. 'Although academic authors tend not to make it out of their own university bookshop.'

'Maybe the rubbish book will provoke interest.'

'Maybe it will. I might sell three more copies.'

'Just tell me where and I'll bring everyone I know. We'll have a party.'

'If I do, will you invite me to the first screening of your documentary?'

She hesitated. 'It's about broken families, Nick. Adoption. The search for birth families. Reunion.'

'Stories which don't always have a happy-ever-after ending?' he suggested. 'Is that why you won't follow up the little girl in your last documentary? In case her story doesn't have a happy ending.'

'I…' She swallowed. 'Yes.' Then, meeting grey eyes that refused to accept anything less than total honesty, 'I've let her down, haven't I?'

'You wanted to believe she was happy. When you're afraid that reality might not live up to your dream, it's tempting to stay where it's safe.'

'With the dream.' She looked around at the perfect vision of paradise that surrounded them. It was lovely for a few hours stolen from life, but the scent that had at first seemed so sweet was now making her drowsy. Was that what the scent of the lilies did? Drug the senses… 'Maybe I've always been hung up on the dream, instead of accepting reality. Yearning for the fairy tale and missing what was in front of me.'

She turned to confront this man who'd given her back her life, both literally and emotionally.

'Isn't that what you've been doing too, Nick? Sticking with the dream of your perfect family, perfect parents. Unable to see your mother and father as just two ordinary people with ordinary frailties. Just like everyone else.'

She didn't wait for him to answer. The question was rhetorical, something for him to think about. Instead, she removed her hand from his and, making a move for her shirt buttons, said, 'It's time to leave, Nick.'

As she fumbled awkwardly, he reached out and stopped her. 'I said I'd do that.'

For a moment Jago thought Miranda was going to resist this final intimacy.

But then she smiled and let her hands drop to her lap. It was a simple gesture of trust and he fastened them carefully, without touching her, knowing that this simple act represented closure. An end to what had happened between them. On an impulse he said, 'I've got an idea.'

She glanced up as a shadow passed over them, a blast of noise, a shower of leaves. The helicopter, directly overhead now. Beneath the canopy they were invisible from the air, but even so it would not be long before the world crashed in on them and, as soon as the beating of the rotor faded, he said, 'Let's come back here. A year from today. No matter what. You bring a packet of mints. I'll bring a bottle of local brandy and we can pick berries. Have a feast. Maybe stay all night, gather lilies to put on a bonfire, give thanks for our deliverance.'

She smiled and for a moment he thought she was going to say that they should stay here now, for ever. But then she seemed to gather herself and, staggering to her feet, shook her head and said, 'The lilies… Did you ever consider they might have some kind of narcotic effect?'

In other words, no.

'Look, can we get out of here?'

She didn't wait, but bundled her underwear, the bottle and sweet wrappers into her ruined bag and slung it over her shoulder and walked quickly up the slope to where, even now, he could hear people shouting her name. His name. Maybe he'd been a little hard on Felipe Dominez.

Leaving him and the glade as apparently untouched as before she'd burst into his life.

He dressed and followed her, reassured the searchers that there was no one left in the shattered building in which they'd spent the night. By the time he reached the clearing where he'd left his Land Rover—now lying on its side at the bottom of a gully, along with the remains of the tour bus—she had been swallowed up by her fellow tourists.

They surrounded her, exclaiming over her, hugging her, treasuring her as someone who'd returned from the dead. Then, before he could join her, he heard his own name ring out.

'Jago!'

And then he had his arms full of woman as Fliss flung herself at him.

'You're alive!'

'Apparently,' he said, putting her down, holding her off. 'I didn't expect to see you here again.'

She had the grace to look embarrassed. 'Felipe wanted photographs of me at the temple. And I wanted to explain about the book. You have heard about the book?'

'Yes, I heard. I hope it's listed under fiction.'

'Jago…' She looked at him, all big eyes and hot lips. There was no doubt about it, she was one hell of a female and despite what she'd done, he grinned.

'What are you doing here, Fliss? Really?'

'When the earthquake hit, everyone was running around like headless chickens. If you were outside the capital…' She shrugged. 'I told Felipe that if he didn't do something I'd tell everyone the truth. That the book was cooked up by some ghost-writer—'

'And then he realised that this place was full of tourists who had families and he actually gave a damn.'

'Well, maybe. I'm sorry, Jago. About the book. Truly.'

'Truly, Fliss, you're not cut out to be an archaeologist and you saw an easy way to make some money. Get the celebrity lifestyle. It's okay. I don't care about the book.'

All he cared about was Miranda, already being ushered towards the waiting helicopter with the other women, some of the older men. He needed to get to her, to say something, tell her…

'You forgive me?' Fliss persisted.

'Yes, yes…' he said impatiently as, over her head, he saw Miranda look back and for a moment hold his gaze.

Manda had practically fled from the glade, afraid of what she might say. Knowing that a year from now they would be different people. That to try and recapture this precious, almost perfect moment would be a mistake.

She wasn't running away from her feelings or protecting herself—she would never do that again. Just running towards real life. Hoping, maybe, that in his own good time he'd follow her. Might remember his promise to invite her to his first book signing.

But then, as she'd stumbled into the clearing, she'd been surrounded by the rest of the tour group, who'd apparently been sheltering in one of the buildings, waiting for rescue. Believing that she was dead.

Being bustled towards the waiting helicopter along with her fellow tourists. Knowing that to delay would be to hold them up when they were desperate for food, hot water and sleep.

Except she could step back, let one of the men take her place and, as the rest of the party pushed by her, eager to get aboard, she glanced back, seeking him out.

For a moment she couldn't see Jago and took a step back. But then she caught a glimpse of his tousled black mop of hair as he lifted his head so that he was standing a little taller than everyone else, right on the edge of the group, and she realised that he'd been talking to someone.

The bus driver, perhaps. He probably knew everyone...

'Miss, can you get in, please...'

On the point of surrendering her seat to someone else—there was a general movement as those remaining were ushered clear of the rotor blades—she saw the someone Nick was talking to. Not the driver, not a man, but the curvy blonde who she'd last seen poured into a clinging gown and flirting with a chat show host on the television. As she stood there Nick said something and then, as if feeling her eyes on him, he glanced up and for a moment held her gaze. Still held it as the woman—Fliss, she had a name—flung herself into his arms.

And, for one last time, she dug deep for the smile that had hidden her feelings for so long. Smiled, mouthed, 'thank you' before turning quickly and climbing aboard the helicopter. She was the last one to board and the door was immediately slammed behind her. It took off almost immediately.

Manda kept her eyes closed as it hovered above the clearing, resisting the temptation to look down, look back. Then, as it cleared the trees, banked and headed into the sun, she opened them and made a promise to herself.

This was a new beginning and from now on it was only forwards, only positive. There would still be dark moments, but she would never again wrap them around her like a cape, but work through them to the light, knowing it would, like the dawn, like spring, always return.

Then they neared the coast and her phone beeped to let her know that she had incoming messages. She flipped it open and read the urgent, desperate messages from Ivo, Belle, Daisy who had, no doubt, been contacted by the consul when the hotel had posted her amongst the missing.

And she hit send on the stored messages that she'd written in the dark, when survival had not been certain. Simple messages that told them how much she loved them.

And then, because it was too noisy to talk, she keyed in another to tell her brother that she was safe. That she was on her way home.

Jago disentangled himself from the embrace of Fliss Grant and watched the helicopter turn and head for the coast, taking Miranda away from him.

'How did you get up here?' he asked.

'I drove up in that Jeep.' She pointed out a Jeep with the Government insignia and a driver. 'The road's a bit torn up but it's passable.'

'And the village?'

'Not much damage. A few minor injuries, that's all.'

'Good. I need to pick up my things and get to the coast.'

'You're leaving? You won't get a flight. It's chaos at the airport.'

That meant that Miranda couldn't leave either. 'Just drop me at the new resort.'

'No problem. I'm staying there myself.'

'Fliss, the book I can forgive, but, as for the rest, I'd advise you stick to Felipe. He's your kind of man.' With that, he swung himself into the Jeep and said, 'Let's get out of here.'

Manda showered, changed and, less than an hour after leaving the temple site, she was boarding a helicopter that Ivo had chartered to pick her up from the resort and fly her to a nearby island where he had a private jet waiting.

He might have stepped back a little from the twenty-four/seven world he'd once occupied, but her brother still knew how to make things happen.

The village might not have been badly hit, but the people still needed help. This had been his home for the best part of five years and Jago couldn't just walk away.

It was a week before he finally made it on to a jet that would take him home. And the first person he saw when he walked through to arrivals was his father.

Older, a little thinner, a lot greyer. For a moment they just stood and looked at one another.

Then his father said, 'Ivo Grenville called me. Passed on your message. Your mother...' He stopped, unable to speak.

'Where is she?' he asked. Then, fear seizing him by the throat, 'Is she ill?'

'No, son. She stayed in the car. She knew she'd cry and she remembers how much you hate that.'

If he'd had any doubts about his promise to Miranda, they were shattered in that moment when he thought he might have left it too late.

'My first day at school. I was telling someone about that only the other day. Miranda. Ivo Grenville's sister.'

'You were trapped with her, Ivo said. I met her once. She's was a tremendous help with one of my projects.'

'She didn't say.' He thought he understood why. 'Will you call Ivo, ask him to thank her for me? For sending the message.'

His father regarded him thoughtfully. 'I think maybe you should do that yourself.'

'I will. Soon. But if you call, she'll know I've kept my word.'

He nodded. Then, 'Shall we go and brave the waterworks?'

'I think perhaps I've finally grown up enough to handle a few tears,' he said. And he flung an arm around his father and hugged him.

It had taken the best part of two months to finish the filming of the new documentary and it was finally in the can. Finished.

Manda sat at her desk tapping the phone with her pen. She'd promised to invite Nick to the private screening. Was it a good idea?

What they'd shared had been no more than a moment in time. A life-changing moment, a moment to cherish, but to try and carry it into everyday life…

She knew he'd seen his parents. His father had called Ivo, asked him to pass on his thanks to her, but he hadn't called her himself even though he was back in London, no doubt working on his book. But then she hadn't called him.

Of course she'd been busy. She'd driven all over the country with Belle and Daisy, putting the adoption documentary together.

No doubt Nick was busy, too. And presumably Fliss Grant was keeping him fully occupied out of working hours. She'd certainly dropped out of the celebrity gossip mag circuit.

Actually, despite the enthusiastic welcome Fliss had received from Nick when she'd turned up with the rescue team, Manda was a little surprised by that.

For a man who held truth in such high regard, it seemed out of character for him to forgive that kind of betrayal.

She dragged her mind back from the memory of the magical moments they'd spent at the forest pool. Maybe that was the lesson Nick had learned in those long hours they'd spent together in the dark. That life is too short. That you had to grab it with both hands, take what it offered. Move on. Looking forward, never back.

Something she was doing herself. Mostly. Not forgetting, she would never forget Nick Jago. He had given her back her life, was part of every waking moment. He always would be; it was something that made her smile rather than cry.

'I'm leaving now, Manda,' Daisy said, wheeling in the stroller containing her sleeping baby. 'We'll be at Wardour Street at eight.'

It took her a moment to readjust to the present. 'Eight? Oh, right. What's the final headcount?'

'I think we've just about got a full house.'

'Well, that's great. Thank you. You've done a great job.' And, glad of an excuse to put off making a decision about whether to call Nick, she dropped the pen on her desk and bent to croon over her sleeping godson.

'Hi, Jude. You just get more gorgeous every day.'

'Manda…'

She looked up, saw trouble. 'What's up?'

'This is a bad time to tell you, but there's never going to be a good one.'

'What?' Then, because she knew the answer, 'It's Rosie, isn't it?'

'You asked me to find out what happened to her.'

'And?'

'It's not good, I'm afraid. You know that she was being held in a care home for assessment while they found a family who would be able to cope? Most of the couples who wanted her didn't have the first clue about what they'd be taking on.'

None of that was relevant and she dismissed it with an impatient gesture. 'She's gone, hasn't she? How long?'

'Months.'

'And they didn't bother to tell us?'

'Manda…'

'I know, I know,' she said, waving away the jargon. She'd heard it all since she'd joined up with Belle to help raise the profile of her causes. 'It's none of our business. No doubt there are laws. Privacy. All that stuff…'

'Yes, there are, but I think the real problem was that they were afraid you'd go to the press. Make them look bad. You can be a bit…well…intimidating.'

'Really?' She combed her hair back with her fingers. 'I don't mean to be. I just don't—'

'—suffer fools gladly. I know. If it helps, you never scared me.'

That was a fact. But then Daisy had been little more than a street brat herself. Full of lip. Terrified beneath all that front. They were total opposites and yet there had been a kind of recognition…

'I have to find her, Daisy. I need to find her.'

'I'll put out the word. It'll take time. If she doesn't want to be found…' She left Manda to fill in the rest. 'I'll catch up with you this evening at the screening.'

'Right.' Then, casually as she could, 'Actually, before you go, would you see if you can find a number for Dr Nicholas Jago, at the University of London?'

'The guy you were holed up with in that temple?'

'Yes.' She avoided Daisy's gaze, picking up her pen again, making a pretence of jotting down a note. 'We talked about the documentary and he said he'd like to see it. He was probably just being polite, but it won't hurt to give him a call and invite him along to the screening tonight.'

'Okay.'

'Tell him that he's welcome to bring a guest.'

The screening was for the network chiefs, the press, overseas buyers. After the awards they'd picked up for their first documentary, there had been considerable interest in the new film and Manda had laid on a buffet and a well stocked bar to keep the hacks happy.

She left Belle and Ivo to greet their guests—she was their 'face' after all—and kept herself busy with the money men. She'd positioned herself with her back to the door, determined not to be caught watching for Nick.

According to Daisy, he'd said he'd be delighted to come. But 'delighted' might just be being polite. Or maybe Daisy was being kind.

Neither Belle nor Daisy had said a word about the fact that she'd been trapped in the dark with a good-looking man for fifteen hours. Which suggested they suspected that the two of them had connected in some way.

Fortunately, she was still scary enough that neither of them had dared broach the subject.

Daisy hadn't said whether he was bringing a guest and Manda didn't ask.

'Manda?'

She turned as Daisy touched her arm, excusing herself, gladly, from a monologue on the necessity of tax incentives for film-makers.

'What's up?'

'Nothing. I could see you were glazing over, but I've been

thinking about Rosie. She'd go back to the places she knew. Where she felt safe. I just thought...'

'What?' But Daisy's attention had been caught by something behind her and she turned to see what it was.

A man. Tall, dark, freshly barbered and shaved.

'Nick...' His name caught in her throat.

'Hello, Miranda.'

Daisy waited for an introduction but she couldn't speak and, after a moment, she said, 'I'll...um...go and start shepherding people through, shall I?' Then, to herself, 'Yes, Daisy, you do that...'

'You look... different,' Manda finally managed. 'In a suit.'

'Good different, or bad different?'

'Good.' In a dark bespoke suit, shirt unbuttoned at the neck, the kind of tan that was so deep it would never completely fade, he made everyone else present look stitched up, dull. No wonder Daisy had been staring... 'Not that you looked bad...' Oh, good grief. So much for walking away, not looking back, just being grateful for that one day. Sophisticated, scary Manda Grenville was behaving like a fifteen-year-old who'd just been smiled at by the hottest guy in school. '...before.'

'Without a suit.'

Without any clothes at all.

She peeled her tongue from the roof of her mouth, rounded up a few brain cells and finally managed a slightly hoarse, 'How's your shoulder?' It wasn't sparkling conversation, but it was safer than the pictures in her head of Nick Jago naked beneath a waterfall. Nick Jago with his mouth...

'How are you, Miranda?'

'Fine,' she said. 'Absolutely great. Working hard, but...great.'

'No nightmares?'

'No…' No nightmares. Just hot, hot dreams… 'You?'

'No nightmares,' he confirmed. 'Just dreams. Did you get my message?'

'Ivo told me. Yes. How is it? With your family?'

'They've changed. I've met my half-sister, too. I've you to thank for that.'

'You'd have got there.' Then the hard question. 'Are you on your own? Didn't Daisy tell you that you could bring someone.'

'Why would I bring someone, Miranda,' he said, 'when the only person I'm interested in being with is here already?'

'Really?' Trying to be cool when you needed a cold shower was never easy, but she did her best, looking around the widest shoulders in the room before saying, 'I haven't spotted the slinky blonde.'

And finally he smiled. As if she'd just told him everything he wanted to know. Well, she had…

'Fliss made her bed with Felipe Dominez, Miranda. I advised her to lie on it. I'd have told you that if you'd hung around for another thirty seconds.'

'Oh.'

'And you could have thanked her. It was down to her that the rescue services reached us so quickly.'

So Fliss Grant was in love with him, Manda thought, feeling almost sorry for the woman. If he'd loved her in return she would never have written the book…

'Did she give you back your documents?'

It wouldn't hurt to remind him of what she'd done.

'There was no need. I had backup copies of everything. She knew that.'

'Of course you did.' Then, 'So, here you are. Finally. It took you two months to make up my head start of thirty seconds?'

'I got held up in the village. It was my home for nearly five years…'

'I'm sorry, Nick. Of course you had to stay. Was it terrible?'

'No. Just a bit of a mess. Nothing that hard work and a few dollars couldn't fix.'

'Money that you supplied.'

He shrugged. 'It was nothing. I stayed for a week, made sure everything was back on track for them, that's all.'

Far from all, she suspected…

'And then?'

'And then…' He looked at her for a moment, the smallest smile creasing the corners of his mouth, his eyes. 'And then, my dearest heart, we both had things to do. Everything happened so fast between us.'

'Was it fast? It seemed like a lifetime, everything slowed down…'

'Facing death, everything becomes concentrated, intense. We needed time to catch up. Time with our families. Time for work.' He took her hand, slid his fingers through hers. 'The future was waiting for us. We've finally caught up with it.' Then, 'Are you free after the screening? Can we have dinner? Talk?'

'Talk? What about?'

'Book signings. Your documentary. The fact that you knew my father and never told me. The rest of our lives.'

The rest of their lives?

She opened her mouth, closed it again.

'The rest of our lives?' she repeated. Then shook her head. 'No… You can't…'

'I've spent the last two months thinking about you in every waking hour. Dreaming about you in every sleeping one. And the truth is, Miranda, I can't not. I want to be with you. Always. Marry me.'

'Manda? We're about to begin.'

She looked round, realised that the room was empty apart from Daisy, who was holding the screening room door open.

'Go ahead without me,' she said.

'But…'

'I'll catch the rerun, Daisy. Right now, I've got the rest of my life to plan.'

They found a small Italian bistro nearby. Manda couldn't have said what she ate, or how it tasted, or even what they talked about. Only that they talked and laughed and that suddenly everything was in its place.

When they finally emerged into the chill of the December night, Christmas lights everywhere, Nick said, 'How did you get here?'

'By cab.'

'Me too.' He looked up and down the street. 'We're not likely to pick one up here at this time of night.' He held out his elbow and she tucked her arm around his. 'Which way?'

'It doesn't matter,' she said, in no hurry to find a cab, let go of this moment. End the evening. 'What will you do now?' she asked as they began to walk.

'I've been offered a chair at the university.'

'Here in London?' She thought about Cordillera. The wildness of the rainforest. A magical pool where a man and woman could pretend they were in Eden. 'It would be very different from what you're used to. Won't you miss field-work?'

'The aching back, the lack of basic facilities, the shortage of funding?'

'The magic moment when you find something that's a piece of the jigsaw,' she prompted, not believing him for a moment. 'That helps bring the picture of ancient lives into focus?'

He glanced at her. 'I'd still get my hands dirty once in a while,' he said. 'Not in Cordillera. The structures are not safe. But we're running other sites. And the slightly higher than average profile I've achieved, thanks to the earthquake, will be a big help in raising funds.'

'So? You're going to take it?'

He shrugged. 'I'm waiting for the right incentive package.'

'Oh.' They turned into a major shopping street. A cab stopped outside a restaurant to disgorge its passengers. They ignored it. Walked on. 'What kind of incentive would it take?'

'I'll know when I hear it.' He glanced at her. 'What about you? Where do you go from here?'

She shook her head, coming back to the real world. 'I can't think of anything but Rosie at the moment.'

'The little girl you rescued?'

Manda stopped.

'What's the matter?'

'She ran away, Nick. Months ago. I only found out today.' Her breath condensed in the freezing air. 'She's out here somewhere, in the city.' Then, looking around, realised where she was. 'Oh, God. This is where we found her. Just down here.'

And she pulled away and ran down a side alley, coming to an abrupt halt as she saw the Dumpster. For one crazy moment she'd thought she be there, digging around for food.

She turned and laid her face against Nick's coat as he caught up with her, put his arms around her.

'She'll die, Nick. I've let her down. I should have been there.'

'Shh.' She felt his breath against her hair as he kissed her, but she pulled away.

'Rosie! Do you hear me?' she called. 'I'm not giving up on you. I'll come back tomorrow. Search every alleyway in London if I have to, but you will not die, do you hear me?'

She clapped her hands over her mouth. Shook her head. Tears freezing on her cheeks.

'Manda…'

'What?' she asked crossly, rubbing a glove across her face. Then she realised that he wasn't looking at her but over her head and swung round, caught her breath as she saw the small, defiant figure standing glaring at them.

'Rosie?'

'Is he your boyfriend?' she demanded.

Manda swallowed.

He'd said 'the rest of our lives' but it was too soon for anything except knowing how much she had missed him. How much she wanted him to stay. How much she loved him.

'This is Nick, Rosie,' she said, grabbing all of those things and putting them together. 'He saved my life.'

'What did he do?'

'I was falling, down into a horrible dark place, but he held on to me even when he might have fallen too. And I'm here to hold on to you.' She crossed to the Dumpster, put her hand on the lid. 'Hungry?' she asked, knowing that she was going to have to open it. Knowing that she would do anything. Then, remembering something that Belle had told her about living on the streets as a child—the one thing they'd have given anything for—she said, 'Or maybe you'd like to come to my place and I'll make you a bacon sandwich. With ketchup.'

'Is your boyfriend coming?'

Nick Jago looked at this beautiful woman. He'd loved her before he'd even seen her, he realised, his heart stolen by the mixture of strength, vulnerability—something more that made her everything she was. Then, when he'd seen her, his eyes had confirmed everything his heart had already known. It was as if his entire world had been shaken to bits and then, when it had been put back together, everything had somehow fallen into place. And then she had gone, whirled away from him in a helicopter before he could say the words. Still running?

He didn't know, but he'd given her space, given himself space for the whirlwind of feelings to be blown away.

But it hadn't happened. Sometimes, in the darkest moment, you met your destiny and he knew, without doubt, that she was his.

'I'm not Miranda's boyfriend, Rosie,' he said, moving to join her. 'I'm the man she's going to marry.'

And when Miranda turned to stare at him, he held her gaze, daring her to deny it. She didn't. Her silence was all he needed and, taking off his coat, he said, 'You know that incentive to stay in London that I was talking about?'

She just nodded as he wrapped it around the freezing child.

'I just heard it.'

'Rosie!' Her room was empty. Her bed not slept in. Manda didn't know what had woken her, only that she'd known, instantly, that Rosie had run again. She turned as Nick joined her in the bedroom doorway. 'She's gone, Nick.'

It had been six months. It hadn't been easy, but they'd made it and, now that Social Services were ready to approve their adoption, she'd been certain they were through the worst. And Rosie had been so excited about being their bridesmaid.

Now, with the wedding less than a week away, she'd run again.

She turned to Nick and buried her face in his chest. 'What now?'

'I think she may have started taking food again,' Nick said. 'I thought maybe she was just a little unsettled—about staying with Daisy while we're on our honeymoon.'

It had taken a while before she'd trusted them enough to stop taking stuff from the fridge to keep in her bag.

'But she adores Daisy. Can't wait to stay with her and Jude next week. I thought she was sure of us. Settled.'

There had been problems before, when they'd set the date for the wedding. She'd run away then too, afraid that they'd have babies of their own and wouldn't want her any more.

But when Nick had told her that wasn't going to happen, had explained that Manda couldn't have children of her own, she'd seemed to settle.

'Don't panic, Miranda. She always goes back to the same place. We'll go and pick her up and get to the bottom of this.' Then, frowning, 'Did you hear something?'

'It sounded like the back door. Burglars?'

Rosie's fiercely whispered 'Shh…' answered that question.

'The kitchen?' Nick suggested.

They opened the door. Rosie had her head in the fridge and didn't see them. The small boy, sitting on one of the kitchen stools, almost smothered by one of Rosie's padded jackets, leapt to his feet, knocking over a mug tree, sending crockery flying as he bolted for the door.

Nick cut him off, scooped him up, holding him easily, despite his desperate struggle. He was about five years old, his mop of black hair a matted tangle and skinny as a lath, but he had huge dark eyes and the kind of beauty that would melt hearts at twenty paces.

Nick smiled at him, tucked him up against his chest and said, 'Who's your friend, Rosie?'

She closed the fridge door very slowly, then turned to face them. 'He was eating out of the bins behind the supermarket. I saw him the other day and I took him some stuff. Clothes, food. On my way to school.'

'You should have told us,' Manda said.

'I thought maybe his mum would come back for him. Sometimes they just get out of their heads for a while, but then they come back. Like my mum did.'

Until, eventually, she didn't, Manda thought.

'But she didn't.' Rosie's shrug was a mixture of defiance and pleading. 'I waited a week and then I thought, since you can't have kids of your own, he should come and live with us. I'll need a brother,' she added a little defiantly.

'Does he have a name?' Nick asked.

'He's called Michael.'

'Rosie,' Manda cut in as gently as she could, 'you know it's not that easy. I'll have to call Social Services. He may have a family…'

'The kind that leaves him on the street. I had family like that too.'

'Even so.'

'I know.' She sighed. 'There are rules and stuff. But you can fix it. You and Nick can fix anything and, besides, you said it was a pity Jude wasn't old enough to be a page-boy.'

'So I did,' Manda said, turning helplessly to the gorgeous man who'd swept her up in a whirlwind of love, made her a family of her own. 'Nick? Do you have any thoughts about how we can handle this?'

He grinned and said, 'I always think best with a bacon sandwich in front of me.' He looked at the child in his arms. 'Michael?'

And Manda felt Rosie's hand creep into hers.

Five days later, Miranda Grenville and Nicholas Jago were married in a centuries-old London church that had been designed by Christopher Wren.

It was one of those rare perfect June days when, even in London, the flower-filled parks still wore the freshness of early summer.

As Miranda emerged from a vintage Rolls Royce on her brother's arm, she paused for a moment while Belle and Daisy, her attendants, straightened the train of the simplest, most elegant ivory silk gown, giving the paparazzi time to take their photographs. This was, after all, the society wedding of the year.

Nothing could have been further from the circumstances of their meeting in Cordillera. Everything pristine, perfect.

Rosie, gorgeous in primrose and white organza, was almost beside herself with excitement. Michael, his hand clutched firmly in hers, was bemused in a tiny kilt and ruffles.

The plan had been to go back, visit their pool, light their fire but they'd put their honeymoon on hold until they'd settled Michael's future.

'Ready?' Ivo asked.

She took a deep breath and said, 'Not quite. I just wanted to say…' She had a load of words, but in the end it came down to two. 'Thank you.' She didn't have to say what for. They both knew. 'Now I'm ready.'

Rosie and Michael led the way, scattering rose petals before them as, to the strains of Pachelbel's *Canon*, Manda walked down the flower-decked aisle towards the man she loved.

She saw nothing, was aware of nothing but Nick waiting for her, his smile telling her that he thought he was the most fortunate man in the world.

Him, and the warm, spicy scent of the huge trumpet lilies entwined along the altar rail. Cordilleran lilies.

'You had them flown in especially?' she murmured as he took her hand.

'We couldn't go to Cordillera, so I brought it to us and tonight I'll light a fire that will keep us both warm for as long as we both shall live.'

DESERTED ISLAND, DREAMY EX

BY
NICOLA MARSH

Nicola Marsh has always had a passion for writing and reading. As a youngster she devoured books when she should have been sleeping, and later kept a diary whose content could be an epic in itself! These days, when she's not enjoying life with her husband and son in her home city of Melbourne, she's at her computer, creating the romances she loves in her dream job. Visit Nicola's website at www.nicolamarsh.com for the latest news of her books.

This one's for all my newfound friends on Twitter.
Tweeting with you is a blast!

CHAPTER ONE

Stranded *Survival Tip #1*
Your past is only a line call away.

KRISTI WILDE picked up the single blush-pink rose, twirled it under her nose, closed her eyes and inhaled the subtle fragrance.

She should call Lars and thank him but... Her eyes snapped open, landed on the trite card he'd probably sent to countless other women, and she promptly tossed the store-bought, cellophane-wrapped rose in the bin.

The only reason she'd agreed to a date with Sydney's top male model was to gain a firsthand look at a rival promotions company's much touted coup in landing the Annabel Modelling Agency as a client.

The fact Lars was six four, ripped, tanned and gorgeous had merely been added incentive.

Walking into Guillaume hand in hand with a guy like Lars had been an ego trip. But that was about as exciting as things got for the night.

Lars had the looks but his personality could put a bunch of hyperactive kids to sleep. While she'd scoped out the opposition, feasted on fabulous French food and swilled pricey champagne, Lars had droned on about himself...and on...and on.

She'd faked interest, been the epitome of a dewy-eyed, suitably impressed bimbo hanging on his every word. She'd do anything for a promotion these days. Excluding the horizontal catwalk, which was exactly what Lars had had in mind the moment they'd stepped into the elevator at the end of the night.

The rose might be an apology. Then again, considering his smug assuredness she'd succumb to his charms next time, he was probably hedging his bets.

Wrinkling her nose, she nudged the bin away with her Christian Louboutin fuchsia patent peep-toes and darted a glance at her online calendar.

Great, just enough time to grab a soy chai latte before heading to the Sydney Cricket Ground for a football promotion.

She grabbed her bag, opened the door, in time for her boss to sweep into the room on four-inch Choos, a swathe of crushed ebony velvet bellowing around her like a witch's cloak, a cloud of Chanel No 5 in her wake.

'Hey, Ros, I was just on my way out—'

'You're not going anywhere.'

Rosanna waved a wad of paper under her nose and pointed at her desk.

'Sit. Listen.'

Kristi rolled her eyes. 'The bossy routine doesn't impress me so much any more after watching you dance the tango with that half-naked waiter at the Christmas party last year. And after that romp through the chocolate fountain at the PR awards night. And that incident with the stripper at Shay's hen night—'

'Zip it.'

Despite her being a driven professional businesswoman, Rosanna's pride in her wild side endeared her to co-workers. Kristi couldn't imagine speaking to any other boss the way she did to Ros.

'Take a look at this.'

Rosanna's kohled eyes sparkled with mischief as she handed her the sheaf of documents, clapping her hands once she'd delivered her bundle.

Kristi hadn't seen her boss this excited since Endorse This had snatched a huge client out from under a competitor's nose.

'You're going to thank me.'

Rosanna started pacing, shaking her hands out, muttering under her breath in the exact way she did while brainstorming with her PR team.

Curious as to what had her boss this hyped, Kristi scanned the top document, her confusion increasing rather than diminishing.

'What's this reality show documentary about?'

It sounded interesting, if you were crazy enough to want to be stranded on an island with a stranger for a week. 'We doing the PR for it?'

Rosanna shook her head, magenta-streaked corkscrew curls flying.

'No. One better.'

Flipping pages, Kristi spied an entry form.

'You thinking of entering?'

Rosanna grinned, the evil grin of a lioness about to pounce on a defenceless gazelle.

'Not me.'

'Then what…?'

Realisation dawned as Rosanna's grin widened.

'Oh, no, you haven't?'

Rosanna perched on the edge of her desk, studying her mulberry manicured talons at length.

'I entered your details for the female applicant.' She gestured to the flyer, pointed at the fine print. 'You've been chosen. Just you and some hot stud on a deserted island for seven days and seven long, hot, glorious nights. Cool, huh?'

There were plenty of words to describe what her boss had done.

Cool wasn't one of them.

Kristi dropped the entry form as if it were radioactive waste, tentatively poked it with her toe, before inhaling deep, calming breaths. Rosanna might be tolerant but there was no point getting wound up to the point she could happily strangle her boss.

'I want you to turn Survivor for a week.'

This had to be a joke, one of Rosanna's bizarre tests she spontaneously sprang on employees at random to test their company loyalty.

Clenching her fist so hard the documents crinkled, she placed them on the desk, desperately trying to subdue the buzzing in her head to form a coherent argument to convince her boss there wasn't a chance she'd do this.

Only one way Rosanna would listen to reason: appeal to her business side.

'Sound's interesting, but I'm snowed under with jobs at the moment. I can't just up and leave for a week.'

Rosanna sprang off her desk as if she hadn't spoken, snapped her fingers.

'You know Elliott J. Barnaby, the hottest producer in town?'

Kristi nodded warily as Rosanna picked up a flyer, waved it under her nose. 'He's making a documentary, based on the reality-show phenomenon sweeping the world. Two people, placed on an island, with limited resources, for a week.'

'Sounds like a blast.'

Rosanna ignored her sarcasm. 'Prize money is a hundred grand.'

'What?'

Kristi tried to read over Rosanna's shoulder. 'You never told me that part.'

'Didn't I? Perhaps I didn't get around to mentioning it, what with your overwhelming excitement and all.'

Kristi stuck out her tongue as she speed-read the prize details.

A hundred big ones. A heck of a lot of money. And if she was crazy enough to go along with her boss's ludicrous scheme, she knew exactly what she'd do with it.

For an instant, the memory of dinner with her sister Meg last night flashed into her head.

Meg's shabby, cubbyhole apartment in outer Sydney, the sounds of ear-splitting verbal abuse from the quarrelling couple next door interspersed with the ranting of rival street gangs outside her window. The threadbare furniture, the stack of unpaid bills on the kitchen counter, the lack of groceries in the fridge.

And Prue, her adorable seven-year-old niece, the only person who managed to draw a smile from her weary mum these days.

After what she'd been through, Meg was doing it tough yet wouldn't accept a cent. What if the money wasn't part of her savings that Meg refused to touch? Would that make a difference to her sister's pride?

'Healthy prize, huh?'

Kristi didn't like the maniacal gleam in Rosanna's astute gaze. She'd seen that look before. Ros lived for Endorse This; the company wasn't Sydney's best PR firm for nothing. While a fun and fair boss, she was a corporate dynamo who expected nothing short of brilliance from her employees.

And every time she got that gleam, it meant a new client was up for grabs, someone whose promotion would add another feather to Endorse This's ever-expanding cap.

Deliberately trying to blot out the memory of Meg's apartment and the unnatural hollows in her niece's cheeks, Kristi handed the flyer back.

'Sure, the money's impressive, but not worth shacking up with some stranger for a week, and having the whole disastrous experience filmed.'

Rosanna's injected lips thinned, her determined stare brooking no argument.

'You're doing this.'

Kristi's mouth dropped open and her boss promptly placed a finger under her chin and shut it for her.

'I had a call from Channel Nine last week. They're checking out PR firms for a new island reality show, Survivor with a twist, they said. That's why I entered you. If you do this, we're set!'

Oh, no. No, no, no!

If the gleam in Rosanna's eyes had raised her hackles, it had nothing on the sickly sweet smile reminiscent of a witch offering Hansel and Gretel a huge chunk of gingerbread.

'And, of course, you'll be in charge of that whole account.'

'That's not fair,' she blurted, wishing she'd kept her mouth shut when Rosanna's smile waned.

'Which part? The part where you help Endorse This score the biggest client this year? Or the part where you're virtually assured a promotion because of it? Discounting the chance to win a hundred grand, of course.'

Kristi shot Rosanna a death glare that had little effect, Ros's smugness adding to the churning in the pit of her stomach.

She had no choice.

She had to do this.

If the promotion wasn't incentive enough, the chance to win a hundred grand was. Meg deserved better, much better. Her sweet, naïve, resilient sister deserved to have all her dreams come true after what she'd been through.

Forcing an enthusiastic smile that must've appeared half grimace, she shrugged.

'Fine, I'll do it.'

'Great. You've got a meeting with the producer in a few hours. Fill me in on the details later.'

Rosanna thrust the flyer into her hands, glanced at her watch. 'I'll get back to Channel Nine, let them know the latest.'

As Rosanna strutted towards the door Kristi knew she'd made the right decision, despite being shanghaied into it.

She'd worked her butt off the last six months, desperate for a promotion, and landing Channel Nine as a client would shoot her career to the stars.

As for the prize money, she'd do whatever it took to win it. No way would she accept anything less than Meg using every last brass razoo of it.

The promotion and the prize money; sane, logical reasons to go through with this. But a week on an island with a stranger? Could it be any worse?

As she rifled through the paperwork, Rosanna paused at the door, raised a finger.

'Did I mention you'll be stranded on the island with Jared Malone?'

CHAPTER TWO

Stranded *Survival Tip #2*
Be sure to schedule your mini-meltdown for off-camera.

JARED strode into North Bondi's Icebergs and headed for Elliott's usual table, front and centre to the glass overlooking Sydney's most famous beach.

His mango smoothie was waiting alongside Elliott's double-shot espresso, his mate nothing if not predictable.

When he neared the table, Elliott glanced up from a stack of paperwork, folded his iron-rimmed glasses, placed them next to his coffee and glanced at his watch.

'Glad you could eventually make it.'

Jared shrugged, pointed at his gammy knee. 'Rehab session went longer than anticipated.'

Elliott's eyes narrowed. 'Hot physio?'

'Hot cruciate ligament, more like it.'

The familiar pinch of pain grabbed as he sat. 'The cruciate healed well after the reconstruction but the ongoing inflammation has the medicos baffled.'

Elliott frowned. 'You're seeing the best, right?'

Jared rolled his eyes. 'Yes, Mum.'

'Putz.'

'The putz that's going to win you another of those film gongs you covet so much.'

Jared jerked a thumb at the pile of documents in front of him.

'Let me guess. The usual disclaimers that anything I say or do on TV, you won't be held responsible.'

'Something like that.'

Elliott pulled the top document, slid it across the table towards him.

'Here's the gist of it.'

Jared barely glanced at the fine print, having already heard Elliott extol the virtues of his documentary at length.

Stranded on an island with a stranger for a week was the last thing he felt like doing, but if it convinced Sydney's disadvantaged kids the Activate recreation centre was the place for them, he'd do it.

He'd spent the bulk of his life in the spotlight, his career and private life under scrutiny, providing fodder for the paparazzi. He'd hated it. Time to put all that intrusion to good use, starting with a week's worth of free publicity money couldn't buy.

Elliott's award-winning documentaries were watched by millions, his cutting-edge work discussed by everyone; around water coolers, at the school gates, on the streets, everyone talked about Elliott's topical stuff.

With a prime-time viewing slot, free advertisements would cost mega bucks so when Elliot had proposed his deal, he'd jumped at it. He'd much rather spend a billion on the centre and equipment than publicity.

Millions would see the centre on national TV, hear about what it offered, and hopefully spread the word. That was what he was counting on.

It was a win-win for them both. Elliott scored an ex-tennis pro for his documentary; Jared scored priceless advertising to tout the kids' rec centre he was funding to the entire country.

'So who's the lucky lady?'

Elliott glanced towards the door, his eyebrows shooting skywards.

'Here she comes now. And wow. You always were a lucky dog.'

Jared turned, curious to see who he'd be stuck with on the island. Not that he cared. He'd socialised on the tennis circuit for years, could fake it with the best of them. Easy.

But as his gaze collided with a pair of unusual blue eyes the colour of the cerulean-blue ocean of Bondi on a clear day, their accusatory gaze cutting straight through him, he knew spending a week on a deserted island with Kristi Wilde would be far from easy.

'I'll deal with you later,' Jared muttered at a confused Elliott as Kristi strutted towards the table on impossibly high heels.

She'd always had a thing for shoes, almost as much as he'd had a thing for her.

'Good to see you—'

'Did you know about this?'

Though she'd cut his intro short, she had no hope of avoiding his kiss and as he ducked down to kiss her cheek the familiarity of her sweet, spicy scent slammed into him with the power of a Nadal serve, quickly followed by a host of memories.

The exhilaration of climbing the Harbour Bridge eclipsed by a laughing, exuberant Kristi falling into his arms, and his bed later that night.

Long, sultry summer nights lingering over seafood platters at Doyles on Watson's Bay, snuggling close in a water taxi afterwards, heading back to his place, desperately trying to rein in their limited self-control.

Best of all, the easy-going, laid-back, fun-filled relationship they'd shared.

Until she'd started clinging, demanding, and he'd bolted.

With good reason. His tennis rankings had been shooting for the stars at the time, he'd had no choice but to repay the people who'd invested their time in him. He'd never wanted to be a user, someone who took their birthright for granted; like his parents.

Ironic, that what had started out as a babysitting exercise, a place the snooty Malones could offload their only child for a few hours a day, had turned into a lucrative career filled with fame, fortune and more women than any guy knew what to do with.

Strangely, only one woman had ever got close enough to see the real him, the guy behind the laid-back smile.

And he was looking straight at her.

While his career hadn't been the only reason he'd left, seeing her here, now, just as vibrant, just as beautiful, reinforced exactly how much he'd given up by walking away from her.

His lips wanted to linger, but she didn't give him time, stepping away with a haughty tilt of her head that might've worked if he hadn't seen the softening around her mouth, the flash of recognition in her eyes.

'Well? Did you know about this?'

Placing a hand in the small of her back to guide her to a chair, unsurprised when she stiffened, he shook his head.

'I just learned my partner in crime's identity in this fiasco a second before you walked through the door.'

'Fiasco is right.'

He smiled at her vehement agreement as Elliott held out his hand.

'Pleased to meet you. Elliott J. Barnaby, the producer of *Stranded*. Glad to have you on board.'

'That's what we need to discuss.'

Gesturing to a waiter, she placed an order for sparkling

mineral water with lime, before squaring her shoulders, a fighting stance as familiar as the tilt of her head.

'Before we begin this discussion, let me make a few things clear. One, I'm here under sufferance. Two, I'm doing this for the money.'

She held up a finger, jabbed it in his direction. 'Three, this island better be big enough for the both of us because I'd rather swim back to the mainland than be cooped up with you for a week.'

Elliott's head swivelled between them, curiosity making his eyes gleam.

'You two know each other?'

She jerked her head in his direction. 'Didn't his lordship tell you?'

Elliott grinned. 'Tell me what?'

'We know each other,' Jared interjected calmly, well aware Elliott would want to know exactly how well they knew each other later. 'Old friends.'

Kristi muffled a snort as he shot her a wink. 'Getting re-acquainted is going to be loads of fun.'

'Yeah, like getting a root canal,' she muttered, her glare mutinous.

After another dreary rehab session with Madame Lash, the physio from hell, Jared had trudged in here, ready to talk business with Elliott, not particularly caring who he'd be stuck with for a week.

Now, the thought of battling wits with a sassy, smart-mouthed Kristi for seven days brightened his morning considerably.

Struggling to keep a grin off his face, he folded his arms, faced Elliott.

'Us knowing each other shouldn't be a problem?'

Elliott shook his head. 'On the contrary, should make for some interesting interaction. The documentary is about exposing the reality behind reality TV. How you talk, react, bounce off each other, when confined for a week without other social interactions should make for good viewing.'

Elliott paused, frowned. 'Old friends? That didn't mean you lived together for any time?'

'Hell, no!'

The flicker of hurt in Kristi's memorable blue eyes had him cursing his outburst, but in the next instant she'd tilted her chin, stared him down, making him doubt he'd glimpsed it at all.

'Cohabiting with a child isn't my idea of fun,' she said, her hauteur tempered with the challenging dare in her narrowed eyes.

She wanted him to respond, to fight back, to fire a few taunts. Well, let her wait. They had plenty of time for that. An entire seven days. Alone. With no entertainment other than each other. Interesting.

Oblivious to the tension simmering between them, Elliott rubbed his hands together.

'Good. Because that would've changed the status quo. This way, your reactions will be more genuine.'

He plucked a folder filled with documents from his pile and slid it across the table towards Kristi.

'I'm aware your boss put your name forward for this, so you need to look over all the legalities, sign the forms where asterisked, we'll go from there.'

She nodded, flipped open the folder, took the pen Elliott offered and started reading, the pen idly tapping her bottom lip. A bottom lip Jared remembered well; for its fullness, its softness, its melting heat as it moulded to his...

Having her read gave him time to study her, really study her. She'd been a cute, perky twenty-one-year-old when they'd dated, her blonde hair wild and untamed, her figure fuller, her clothes eclectic. She'd always been inherently beautiful and while her nose might be slightly larger than average, it added character to a face graced by beauty.

Now, with her perfect make-up, perfectly straight blow-dried hair, perfect streamlined body and perfect pink designer suit, she intrigued him more than ever.

He liked her tousled and ruffled and feisty, and, while her new image might be all corporate and controlled, he'd hazard a guess the old Kristi wouldn't be lurking far beneath the surface.

'All looks okay.'

She signed several documents and, with a heavy sigh, handed them to Elliott. 'Everything I need to know in here?'

Elliott nodded. 'Do you know anything about *Stranded*?'

She shook her head. 'My pushy boss didn't go into specifics.'

Jared leaned across, held his hand up to his mouth, his loud conspiratorial whisper exaggerated. 'Now you're in for it. He'll give you the hour-long spiel he gave me.'

Her mouth twitched before she returned her attention to Elliott, who was more than comfortable to elaborate on his favourite topic.

'While it's basically a competition for the prize money, which will go to the participant who nails the challenges and gains the most hits on their Internet networking sites, I want this documentary to make a social statement on our TV viewing and the way we network today.'

While her heart sank at the conditions imposed on winning the prize—she'd always been lousy at sports and no way could she beat Jared in the popularity stakes on the Net— Elliot continued.

'There's a glut of reality TV at the moment. Cooking, dating, singing, dancing, housemates, you name it, there's a reality show filming it. I want *Stranded* to be more than that. I want it to show two people interacting, without social distractions, without direct interference, without the fanfare, without judges, and see how they get along. I want honest feedback.'

She nodded, gestured to her folder. 'That's where the daily blog and Twitter updates come in?'

'Uh-huh. It'll give the public instant access to your imme-diate feelings, build anticipation for when I screen the docu-mentary a week after you return. Building hype and viewer expectation makes for more interesting viewing.'

'So we're filmed all the time?'

She screwed up her nose, as enthralled with the idea as he was.

Elliott steepled his fingers like a puppet master looking forward to yanking their strings.

'No, the cameras are motion-activated, and only situated on certain parts of the island. If you want privacy or time out, there are designated areas.'

Her relief was palpable, as Jared wondered what would make her desperate enough to do this. Sure, she'd said the money, but she'd never been money-driven so there had to be more to it. Then again, it had been eight years. How well did he really know her?

It was different for him. His life had been laid out for public consumption the last seven years, what he ate, where he went, what car he drove, all open to interpretation.

He'd learned to shut off, to ignore the intrusion, was now using it to his advantage for the rec centre.

But what did she get out of this apart from a chance to win the money?

'Good to know.' Jared tapped the side of his nose, leaned towards her. 'Just in case you feel the urge to take advantage of me, you can do it off camera.'

'In your dreams, Malone.'

'There've been plenty of those, Wilde.'

To his delight, she blushed, dropped her gaze to focus on her fiddling fingers before she removed them from the table, hid them in her lap. He gave her five seconds to compose herself and, on cue, her gaze snapped to his, confident, challenging.

'You really want to do this here?' he murmured, grateful when Elliott jerked his head towards the restrooms and made a hasty exit.

'Do what?'

She was good, all faux wide-eyed innocence and smug mouth. Well, she might be good but he was better. He'd always lobbed back every verbal volley levelled his way, had enjoyed their wordplay as much as their foreplay.

She stimulated him like no other woman he'd ever met and the thought of spending a week getting reacquainted had him as jittery as pre-Grand Slam.

'You know what.'

He leaned into her personal space, not surprised when she didn't flinch, didn't give an inch.

'You and me. Like this.' He pointed at her, him. 'The way we were.'

'Careful, you'll break into song any minute now.'

'Feeling sentimental?'

'Hardly. I'd have to care to want to take a stroll down memory lane.'

'And your point is?'

She shrugged, studied her manicured nails at arm's length. 'I don't.'

He laughed, sat back, laid an arm along the back of his chair, his fingers in tantalisingly close proximity to her shoulder.

'You always were a lousy liar.'

'I'm not—'

'There's a little twitch you get right here.' He touched a fingertip just shy of a freckle near her top lip. 'It's a dead giveaway.'

She stilled, the rebellious gleam in her eyes replaced by a flicker of fear before she blinked, erasing any hint of vulnerability with a bat of her long eyelashes. 'Still delusional, I see. Must be all the whacks on the head with tennis balls.'

'I don't miss-hit.'

'Not what I've seen.'

'Ah, nice to know you've been keeping an eye on my career.'

'Hard to miss when your publicity-hungry mug is plastered everywhere I look.'

She paused, her defiance edged with curiosity. 'Is that why you're doing this? Publicity for your comeback?'

'I'm not making a comeback.'

The familiar twist low in his gut made a mockery of his adamant stance that it didn't matter.

He'd fielded countless questions from the media over the last year, had made his decision, had scheduled a press conference. And while he'd reconciled with his decision months ago the thought of leaving his career behind, turning his back on the talent that had saved him, niggled.

Tennis had been his escape, his goal, his saviour, all rolled into one. While he'd originally resented being dumped at the local tennis club by his narcissistic parents, he'd soon found a solitude there he rarely found elsewhere.

He'd been good, damn good, and soon the attention of the coaches, the talent scouts, had made him want to work harder, longer, honing his skill with relentless drive.

He'd had a goal in mind. Get out of Melbourne, away from his parents and their bickering, drinking and unhealthy self-absorption.

It had worked. Tennis had saved him.

And, while resigned to leaving it behind, a small part of him was scared, petrified in fact, of letting go of the only thing that had brought normality to his life.

'You're retiring?'

'That's the plan.'

He glanced at his watch, wishing Elliott would reappear. Trading banter with Kristi was one thing, fielding her curiosity about his retirement another.

'Why?'

Her gaze, pinpoint sharp, bored into him the same way it always did when she knew he was being evasive.

He shrugged, leaned back, shoved his hands in his pockets to stop them from rearranging cutlery and giving away his forced casual posture.

'My knee's blown.'

Her eyes narrowed; she wasn't buying his excuse. 'Reconstructed, I heard. Happens to athletes all the time. So what's the real reason?'

He needed to give her something or she'd never let up. He'd seen her like this before: harassing him to reveal a surprise present, pestering him to divulge the whereabouts of their surprise weekend away. She was relentless when piqued and there was no way he'd sit here and discuss his real reasons with her.

'The hunger's gone. I'm too old to match it with the up-and-coming youngsters.'

'What are you, all of thirty?'

'Thirty-one.'

'But surely some tennis champions played 'til they were—?'

'Leave it!'

He regretted his outburst the instant the words left his mouth, her curiosity now rampant rather than appeased.

Rubbing his chin, he said, 'I'm going to miss it but I've got other things I want to do with my life so don't go feeling sorry for me.'

'Who said anything about feeling sorry for you?'

The relaxing of her thinned lips belied her response. 'You'd be the last guy to pity, what with your jet-set lifestyle, your homes in Florida, Monte Carlo and Sydney. Your luxury car collection. Your—'

'You read too many tabloids,' he muttered, recognising the irony with him ready to capitalise on the paparazzi's annoying scrutiny of his life to boost the rec centre's profile into the stratosphere.

'Part of my job.'

He laughed. 'Bull. You used to love poring over those gossip rags for the hell of it.'

'Research, I tell you.'

She managed a tight smile and it struck him how good this felt: the shared memories, the familiarity. He knew her faults, she knew his and where that closeness had once sent him bolting, he now found it strangely intriguing.

'We need to get together before we leave for Lorikeet Island.'

Her smile faded, replaced by wariness. 'Why?'

'For old times' sake.'

He leaned closer, crooked his finger at her. 'Surely you don't want to rehash our history in front of the cameras?'

With a toss of her hair, she sipped at her mineral water, glancing at him over the rim.

'The only thing happening in front of the cameras is me pretending to like you.'

Laying a hand on her forearm, pleased when she stiffened in awareness, he murmured, 'Sure you need to pretend? Because I remember a time when—'

'Okay, okay, I liked you.'

She snatched her arm away, but not before he'd seen the responsive glimmer darkening her eyes to sapphire. 'It was a phase in my early twenties that passed along with my passion for leg warmers and spiral perms.'

Not backing off an inch, he shifted his chair closer to hers. 'Didn't you hear? Leg warmers are making a comeback.'

'You aren't.'

Her stricken expression showed him exactly how much she still cared despite protestations to the contrary. 'With me, I meant. Not your career. Sorry. Damn…'

'It's okay.'

Her discomfort, while rare, was refreshing. 'So, about our pre-island catch up?'

She sighed. 'I guess it makes sense.'

'Eight, tonight?'

'Fine. Where?'

Not ready to divulge all his secrets just yet, he said, 'You'll find out.'

CHAPTER THREE

Stranded *Survival Tip #3*
*Pack all your troubles in your old kit bag; but don't forget
protection...just in case.*

'YOU owe me an ice cream for making me wait in the car.'

Kristi grabbed Meg's arm and dragged her away from the all-seeing front window of Icebergs. 'You weren't in the car, you were strolling on the beach.'

'How do you know?'

'Because I saw you craning your neck to get a squiz at Jared and me through the window.'

'I wasn't craning. I was trying to stand on tiptoe.' Meg shook her head, disgusted. 'Still couldn't see a darn thing.'

Perking up as they neared the ice-cream stand, Meg grinned. 'So, is he still as gorgeous in real life as all those dishy pictures in the papers?'

'Better,' Kristi admitted reluctantly, her head still reeling with the impact of twenty minutes in Jared's intoxicating company, her body buzzing with recognition.

She hadn't expected such an instantaneous, in-your-face, overwhelming awareness of what they'd once shared, the memories bombarding her as fast as his quips.

Every time he looked at her, she remembered staring into each other's eyes over fish and chips on Manly beach.

Every time he laughed, she remembered their constant teasing and the resultant chuckles.

Every time he'd touched her, she remembered, in slow, exquisite detail, how he'd played her body with skill and expertise, heat flowing strong and swiftly to every inch of her.

'I could strangle Ros for putting me in this position.'

'And which position would that be? Stranded on an island with Jared? Or maybe back in his arms or—'

Kristi gave her sister a narrowed look.

'If Ros hadn't dangled the promotion, I never would've gone through with this.'

'Even for a chance to win a hundred grand?'

'Even for that.'

A lie, but she didn't want to tip Meg off to her plans for the prize money. Her little sister hated pity, hated charity worse.

When her no-good son-of-a-gun fiancé fled upon hearing news of her pregnancy, it wasn't enough he took her self-respect, her trust, her hopes and dreams of an amazing marriage like their parents had shared.

Oh, no, the low-life scumbag had to take every last cent of her money too, leaving Meg living in a one-bedroom hellhole in the middle of gangland Sydney, footing bills for their cancelled wedding and working two jobs to save enough money to take a few months off after the baby was born.

Life sucked for her pragmatic sister and, while Meg pretended to be upbeat for the sake of the adorable little Prue, she couldn't hide the dark rings of fatigue circling her eyes or the wary glances she darted if any guy got too close.

Trusting the wrong guy had shattered Meg's dreams, her vivacity, her hope for a brilliant future, and Kristi would do anything—including being holed up with her ex for a week—to bring the sparkle back to her sister's eyes.

'What are you going to do with the moula if you win?'

'You'll find out.'

Stopping at the ice-cream stand, Kristi placed an order for two whippy cones with the lot, her gaze drifting back to Icebergs.

She'd left Jared sitting there, all tanned, toned, six four of tennis star in his prime. He'd always been sexy in that bronze, outdoorsy, ruffled way many Aussie males were, but the young guy she'd lusted after wasn't a patch on the older, mature Jared.

Years playing in the sun had deepened his skin to mahogany, adding character lines to a handsome face, laugh lines around his eyes. He'd always had those, what with his penchant for laughter.

Nothing had fazed Jared; he was rarely serious. Unfortunately, that had included getting serious about a relationship, resulting in him walking away from her to chase his precious career.

He'd been on the cusp of greatness back then, had vindicated his choice by winning Wimbledon, the French Open and the US Open, twice. The Australian Open had been the only tournament to elude the great Jared Malone for the first few years of his illustrious career and she'd often pondered his apparent distraction in exiting the first or second round of the Melbourne-based tournament.

The ensuing pictures of him with some blonde bombshell or busty brunette on his arm went a long way to explaining his early departures and she gritted her teeth against the fact she'd cared.

Not any more.

She'd seen the evidence firsthand of what choosing the wrong man to spend your life with could do and, considering Jared had run rather than build a future with her, he had proved he wasn't the man for her.

'Your ice cream's melting.'

Blinking, Kristi paid, handed Meg her cone and headed for the sand.

'You're walking down there in those?'

Meg pointed at her favourite Louboutin hot pink patent shoes with the staggering heel.

'Sheesh, hooking up with tennis boy again must really have you rattled.'

'I'm not "hooking up" with anybody, I'm just going to sit on the wall, take a breather before heading back to work.'

Meg licked her ice cream, her suspicious stare not leaving her sister's face.

'You two used to date. Stands to reason there *is* a fair chance of you hooking up again on that deserted island.'

'Shut up and eat your ice cream.'

They sat in companionable silence, Kristi determinedly ignoring Meg's logic. The sharp sun, refreshing ocean breeze, packed beach were reminiscent of countless other days they'd done this together as youngsters and, later, bonded in their grief over their parents' premature death.

While their parents might have left them financially barren, they could thank them for a family closeness that had always been paramount, ahead of everything else.

'What do you really think about all this, Megs?'

Crunching the last of her cone, Meg tilted her face up to the sun.

'Honestly? You've never got over tennis boy.'

'That's bull. I've been engaged twice!'

Meg sat up, tapped her ring finger.

'Yet you're not married. Interesting.'

Indignant, Kristi tossed the rest of her ice cream in the bin, folded her arms.

'So I made wrong decisions? Better I realised before traipsing up the aisle.'

Meg held up her hands. 'Hey, you'll get no arguments from me on that point. Look at the farcical mess my short-lived engagement turned into.'

A shadow passed over her sister's face as Kristi silently cursed her blundering insensitivity.

'Forget I asked—'

Meg made a zipping motion over her lips as she continued. 'But Avery and Barton were both decent guys and you seemed happy. Yet the closer the wedding got both times, the more emotionally remote you were. Why's that?'

Because she'd been chasing a dream each time, a dream she'd had since a little girl, a dream of the perfect wedding.

The dress, the flowers, the reception, she could see it all so clearly, had saved pictures in a scrapbook.

What she couldn't see was the groom—discounting the magazine pic of Jared Meg had pasted there as a joke when they'd been dating—and while Avery and Barton had momentarily superimposed their images in her dream, they ultimately hadn't fit.

Avery had entered her life six months after her parents died, had been supportive and gracious and non-pressuring. She'd been lost, grieving and he'd helped her, providing security at a time she needed it most.

It had taken her less than four months to figure out their engagement was a by-product of her need for stability after her parents' death and she'd ended it.

Not that she'd learned.

Barton had been a friend, supportive of her break up and the loss of her parents, so supportive it had seemed natural to slip into a relationship eight months after Avery had gone.

While their engagement had lasted longer, almost a year,

she'd known it wasn't right deep down, where she craved a unique love-of-her-life romance, not a comfortable relationship that left her warm and fuzzy without a spark in sight.

She'd been guilt-ridden for months after ending both engagements, knowing she shouldn't have let the relationships go so far but needing to hold onto her dream, needing to feel safe and treasured and loved after the world as she knew it had changed.

Her family had made her feel protected and when she'd lost that she'd looked for security elsewhere. She just wished she hadn't hurt Avery and Barton in the process.

'You know why you really didn't go through with those weddings. It could do you good to admit it.'

Meg nudged her and she bumped right back. She knew what Meg was implying; after Jared, no man had lived up to expectations.

While she'd briefly contemplated that reasoning after each break-up, she'd dismissed it. Jared had been so long ago, had never entertained the possibility of a full-blown relationship let alone a lifetime commitment and he'd never fit in her happily ever after scenario.

Liar. Remember the day he walked in on you in your roommate's wedding dress while she was away on her honeymoon? The day you joked about it being their turn soon?

Not only had she envisioned him as her perfect groom, she'd almost believed it for those six months they'd dated.

Until he'd dumped her and bolted without a backward glance.

'I guess the closer the weddings came on both occasions, the more I realised Avery and Barton didn't really know me. Sure, we shared similar interests, moved in similar social circles, had similar goals but it was just too…too…'

'Trite.'

'Perfect…' she shook her head, the familiar confusion

clouding her brain when she tried to fathom her reasons for calling off her much-desired weddings. '…yet it wasn't perfect. It was like I had this vision of what I wanted and I was doing my damnedest to make it fit. Does that make sense?'

'Uh-huh.'

Meg paused, squinted her eyes in the Icebergs' direction. 'So where does tennis boy fit into your idea of perfection?'

'Malone's far from perfect.'

As the words tripped from her tongue an instant image of his sexy smile, the teasing twinkle in his eyes, the hard, ripped body, flashed across her mind, taunting her, mocking her.

Crunching loudly on the tip of her ice-cream cone, Meg sat up, dusted off her hands.

'You need to do this.'

When Kristi opened her mouth to respond, Meg held up a finger. 'Not just for the promotion or the possibility of winning all that cash. But for the chance to confront tennis boy, finally get some closure.'

The instant denial they'd had closure eight years ago died on her lips.

He'd walked in on her in that dress, had reneged on their dinner plans and avoided her calls afterwards. Except to call her from the airport before boarding his plane for Florida; and she preferred to forget what had transpired during that gem of a phone call.

Meg was right. While the promotion and prize money were huge incentives to spend a week with Jared stranded on an island, getting closure was the clincher.

Standing, Kristi shot Meg a rueful smile. 'Remind me never to ask for your advice again.'

'Don't ask if you don't want to hear the truth.'

That was what scared Kristi the most. In confronting Jared, would she finally learn the truth?

About what really went wrong in their relationship all those years ago?

Elliott ordered another double-shot espresso, slid his wire-rimmed glasses back on, peered over them.

'What gives between you and Kristi Wilde? I've never heard you mention her.'

Jared dismissed Elliott's curiosity with a wave of his hand.

'Old history.'

'A history I have a feeling I need to know before we get this project underway.'

Elliott tapped his stack of documents. 'There were enough sparks flying between the two of you to set this lot alight and I don't want anything threatening to scuttle this documentary before it's off the ground. So what's the story?'

'I met her when I first moved to Sydney. Spent a few months hanging out, having fun, before I headed for training camp at Florida. That's it.'

'All sounds very simple and uncomplicated.'

'It is.'

Jared downed a glass of water before he was tempted to tell Elliott the rest.

The way she was totally unlike any of the women in his usual social circle back in Melbourne. Her lack of pretence, lack of artificialities, lack of cunning. The way she used to look at him, with laughter and warmth and genuine admiration in her eyes. The way she made him feel, as if he didn't have a care in the world and didn't have the responsibility of living up to expectation hanging around his neck like a stone.

No, he couldn't tell his mate any of that, for voicing his

trip down memory lane might catapult him right back to a place he'd rather not be: hurting a woman he cared about.

Elliott rested his folded arms on the table, leaned forward with a shake of his head.

'Only problem is, my friend, I know you, and simple and uncomplicated are not words I'd use to describe you or any of your relationships.'

'It wasn't a relationship,' he said, an uneasy stab making a mockery of that.

While they'd never spelled it out as such, they'd spent every spare moment in each other's company, had spent every night together, had painted this city red, blue, white and any other damn colour, and belittling what they had to assuage his friend's curiosity didn't sit well with him.

'Then what was it?'

The best time of his life.

The first woman he'd ever been involved with.

The first person he'd allowed close enough to care.

The first time he'd allowed himself to feel anything other than caution and judgement and bitterness.

He'd been numb after escaping his parents' bizarre turn-around when they suddenly started acknowledging he existed, had been driven to succeed, to utilise the talent he'd uncovered through their neglect.

Melbourne had held nothing but bad memories and newly clinging parents for him and moving to Sydney had been as much about fresh starts as fostering his career.

Though she hadn't known it at the time, Kristi had been a saviour: a friend, a lover, a distraction, all rolled into one.

And when she'd got too close…well, he'd done the only thing he could.

He'd run.

'Kristi and I dated casually. We had fun.'

'And you didn't break her heart?'

He hadn't stuck around long enough for that; had made sure of it.

'Would she be taking part in your little social experiment if I had?'

Apparently satisfied, Elliott nodded, his glasses sliding down his nose as he absent-mindedly pushed them back up.

'Good point. She seemed feisty. I reckon she would've skewered you if you'd done a number on her.'

'Too right.'

Not that he agreed with his friend's assessment. Back then, Kristi had had vulnerability written all over her. She'd acted as if she didn't care but he'd seen the signs, had caught the unguarded longing stares she'd cast him when she thought he wasn't looking.

Then there was that bridal shower she'd been so hyped about, throwing a huge shindig at her apartment for her roommate, her incessant chatter of gowns and registries and invitations sending a shudder through him.

Marriage was never on the cards for him and just being close to all that hearts and flowers crap made his gut roil.

Then he'd walked in on her one day, standing in front of a cheval mirror, wearing a shiny white wedding gown and a beatific smile. If that vision hadn't sent a ripple of horror through him, her words had.

'It'll be our turn next.'

Not a hope in Hades.

So he'd pulled back, brought forward his departure date to a Florida training camp, said goodbye with a phone call. He'd taken the coward's way out but, the way he saw it, he'd made the right decision.

He'd never promised Kristi anything, had made it clear from the start their dating had a time limit. Wasn't his fault she'd interpreted it as anything other than what it was: a casual fling, fun while it lasted.

'If you two parted amicably, does that mean you're going to pick up where you left off on the island?'

'For your nosy viewers to see? Not likely.'

As the words tumbled easily he had to admit he'd wondered the same thing himself, the thought crossing his mind the instant she'd strutted in here with her shoulders squared for battle and her eyes flashing fire.

'Too bad. Would've been nice to add a little romance to the mix.'

With a shake of his head, Jared stood. 'You're a sap.'

'No, I'm a producer after ratings.'

Throwing a few notes on the table, Elliott hoisted his load into his arms and stood too.

'And sex sells, my friend.'

Jared grunted in response, a certain part of him agreeing with Elliott, with the faintest hope Kristi would too.

CHAPTER FOUR

Stranded *Survival Tip #4*
They're playing our song. Pity it's the theme song from
Titanic.

As KRISTI spritzed her custom-made patchouli perfume behind her ears, on her pulse points, her hand shook, the infernal buzz of nerves in her tummy hard to subdue.

No matter how many times she mentally recited tonight was about fine-tuning details for their week on Lorikeet Island, she couldn't ignore the fact catching up with Jared reeked of a date.

She didn't want to think of it as a date. A date implied intimacy and excitement and expectation, feelings she'd given up on a long time ago where he was concerned.

Jared Malone might have once rocked her world, but she'd got over it. He could flash that sexy smile and charm her with witty wordplay all he liked, it wouldn't change a thing.

She'd seen the way he'd looked at her during their brief meeting at Icebergs; as if he remembered everything about her and would love to take a fast sprint down memory lane.

If he tried, she had four words for him.

Not in this lifetime.

Leaning into the mirror, she tilted her head to one side to fasten an earring. The long, straight silver spiral shimmered as she turned, caught the light, reflected, matching her sequinned halter top perfectly.

She loved the top's funkiness, had offset it with low-slung black hipster formal pants. Chic, without trying too hard. Not that she'd dithered too long on her wardrobe choice. She wanted to speed through this evening, speed through the seven interminably long days on the island and regain equilibrium.

For while she might not have feelings for Jared any more, seeing him again had her on edge, a strange combination of anger, fear and reservation. While he could act as if things hadn't ended badly between them, she couldn't, unable to shake the foreboding that the longer she spent in his company, the more chance she had of making a fool of herself again.

For that was exactly what she'd done last time around.

Made an A-grade ass of herself.

She'd known he'd had to leave eventually, yet had started to cling the closer his departure grew, culminating in that silly, angry ultimatum during their last phone call.

She'd made him choose. Her or tennis. How young and stupid had she been?

When he'd walked in on her in that wedding dress the week before he left, she'd been glad. She'd wanted him to see how she looked, wanted him to envisage the dream of happily-ever-after as much as she wanted it.

So she'd made that flyaway comment about it being their turn next, half hoping he'd sweep her into his arms and take her with him.

Instead, he'd withdrawn, closed off, the last week before he departed, leaving her morose, desperate and hurt, incredibly hurt.

Her ridiculous ultimatum had been born of anger and resentment and rejection, something she should never have done.

But she couldn't change the past; the memory of her naivety made her cringe and seeing Jared again only served to resurrect those old feelings of embarrassment and mortification.

He'd appeared unfazed by their past while she'd sat through their meeting mentally kicking herself all over again.

Now she had to spend a week on a deserted island with him.

Her humiliation was complete.

The intercom buzzed and with one, last quick glance in the mirror she trudged across the room, grateful her platform T-bar metallic sandals only allowed her to move at a snail's pace, and hit the button to let him in downstairs.

She'd wondered if he'd call her at work to get the address, surprised when he hadn't. It meant he remembered, leading to the next obvious question: what else did he remember?

Much to her chagrin, she hadn't forgotten a thing about him.

Avery's shoe size? Erased from her memory banks for ever.

Barton's preferred margarine? Gone.

Yet she could recall in startling clarity how Jared liked his eggs—poached; his coffee—white with one; his side of the bed—right.

Maybe that had been half the problem with both engagements? The guys had been fine, upstanding citizens with good jobs, good looks and good credentials, but they weren't Jared.

The thought had crossed her mind both times she'd broken off the engagements but she'd dismissed it as a young girl's whimsical memory of a brief romance that had been too good to be true.

She'd had genuine feelings for both fiancés, had gone through her version of grieving both times: intermittent crying jags, locked away at home for a week, consumed copious tubs of her favourite Turkish delight ice cream.

She'd pondered their relationships at length, had tried to erase the final departure from both engagements each time: the shock, the bewilderment from the guys, the guilt, the sadness from her.

It had taken her a while to recover from Avery, then Barton, and each time she'd started reminiscing about Jared and hated herself for it.

The girls at work discussed their first loves all the time: the thrill, the newness, the heady sensation of being on heightened awareness every second of every day, how it all faded.

That was the problem. The buzz between her and Jared hadn't had a chance to fade. He'd absconded before the gloss had worn off, left her embarrassed she'd read so much into their relationship, furious how he'd ended it yet pathetically pining when he hadn't looked back.

The memory of their parting doused any simmer of sentimentality she might have felt towards this meeting, annoyance replacing her memories as she yanked open the door.

'Good. You're here. Let's go.'

Her brusqueness evaporated when she saw him leaning against the jamb, wearing a wicked grin that made her facial muscles twitch in eagerness to respond.

'Wow.'

She stiffened as his appreciative gaze roved over her freely, the naughty twinkle in his eyes undermining her as much as that damn smile.

Ignoring the responding quiver in her knees, she dropped her gaze, discovering his designer loafers, dark denim, and cotton shirt the colour of her favourite butterscotch didn't help re-establish her immunity.

He'd always been a great dresser, could wear anything and make it look like haute couture. Yet another thing she'd loved about him. A love that meant jack considering how fast he'd run.

'You ready to go?'

Scanning her face for a reason behind her snippiness, he chuckled, held out his hand. 'Shall we?'

Ignoring his hand, she nodded, needing to wipe that twinkle from his eye, to establish she wouldn't engage in whatever game he intended for tonight.

'If you're planning on flirting your way through dinner, forget it. I'm doing this so we get everything straight before we're stuck on the island. Understand?'

His mock salute and wide grin spoke volumes: he'd do as he damned well pleased tonight, regardless.

'Perfectly.'

She shook her head, frowned. 'I mean it. I'm immune so don't waste your breath—'

'Did it ever strike you I'm uncomfortable about all this and flirting is the only way I know how to ease back into how we were before?'

His honesty surprised her, for, while his tone was light-hearted, she saw the flicker of uncertainty in his eyes.

A sliver of guilt penetrated her prickly armour. If she was feeling uncomfortable about this whole scenario, why shouldn't he?

'We can't go back to how it was before.'

His answering smile elicited a twinge of remembrance, a yearning to do just that.

'We laughed a lot back then, were easy in each other's company. Wouldn't it be great to recapture some of that on the island, especially in front of the cameras?'

Of course, that was what this was about: re-establishing some kind of rapport so they didn't embarrass themselves on camera. She should've known, but for a split second she'd almost wished he were flirting with her because he wanted to recreate some of the other magic they'd shared back then.

'I guess you're right.'

'That's my girl.'

She wasn't, had never been really.

Maybe Jared could ignore the past, could don his smooth, funny, adorable persona and hope she'd forget how things had ended between them, but she had as much hope of that as scaling the Opera House in her favourite four-inch Louboutin's.

Hurt faded but it wasn't forgotten.

Not when the man who'd broken her heart would be in her face for the next week.

Grateful he hadn't chosen any of their old haunts, Kristi stepped through the enormous glass door of Sydney's newest East meets West fusion restaurant and nodded her thanks at Jared. Another thing that hadn't changed about him: his impeccable manners.

'Have you been here before?'

She shook her head, tried not to look suitably impressed as she glanced around at the soaring ceilings, steel beams and enough chrome and glass to build an entire suburb.

'Rumour has it you have to be the prime minister or an Oscar winner to get a booking for the next year.'

She paused, quirked an eyebrow. 'Or apparently a star tennis player?'

Chuckling, he tapped the side of his nose. 'It's not what you know, it's who you know.'

'Obviously.'

She swanned through the restaurant, aware of the not too subtle envious glances cast their way. Not that she could blame the women.

Jared Malone, world-renowned playboy, was a serious babe.

Voted number one sexiest sportsman for three years running in all the top women's magazines.

Not that she'd kept count. Flicking through glossies was a fabulous part of her job, keeping abreast of the latest PR strategies, and while she'd quickly flipped over pages wherever Jared appeared she'd still noticed.

Any woman with a pulse would have to be half dead not to notice him.

And she'd be stuck with him, on a deserted island, for a week. Gain a promotion out of it. Possibly win a hundred grand. So why the reservations?

As they reached the table, his hand guiding her in the small of her back, his breath the barest whisper against her heated skin, she knew exactly why she wasn't doing cartwheels over the next week.

It would've been bad enough spending seven days on an island with some stranger, but a week with a guy she'd once loved, who knew her weaknesses, who knew her intimately?

Heck.

'You're nervous.'

She feigned ignorance as he held out her chair and she sat, grateful for the support when his hand grazed the back of her neck, a particularly sensitive spot as well he knew.

'About our little island jaunt.'

She winced. 'It shows?'

Chuckling, he ran a fingertip just above her top lip. 'You get this little wrinkle right about here when you think too much.'

Brushing his hand away, she gulped from the crystal water glass thankfully filled to the brim.

'Aren't you the slightest bit uncomfortable about all this?

He sat back, folded his arms, that familiar cocky grin making her heart jive and jump and jitterbug.

'No.'

'So it doesn't matter we had…'

'A past?'

His grin widened. 'Surely you'd rather be stuck on Lorikeet Island with me than some stranger?'

She'd debated the fact, hadn't reached any conclusions yet. She could've been distantly polite with a stranger, could've faked enthusiasm for the documentary, could've been totally and utterly uninvolved.

Spending a week with Jared, just the two of them, would render it impossible to stay distant.

She knew so much about this man, remembered details she should've forgotten: how he bounced out of bed every morning and stretched five times, how he hated orange but loved mango juice, how he made adorable little snoring/snuffling sounds when asleep after an exhausting game.

How he devoured sushi like a man starved, how he preferred swimming in the ocean to a swimming pool, how he liked sporting magazines over novels.

So many memories, all of them good. Except the one where he walked away from her without a backward glance.

'If you have to think that long, maybe I've lost my charm.'

She rolled her eyes. 'Nothing wrong with your charm and you darn well know it.'

He wiped his brow. 'Phew, for a second there you had me worried.'

When he'd left, she'd missed many things, his sense of humour being one of them. They'd always sparred like this, swapping banter along with huge chunks of their lives. She'd loved it, loved him.

Which brought her full circle back to her original dilemma: how dangerous would it be being stuck on an island with Jared?

Her sorrow at their break-up and any residual humiliation should ensure immunity to him after all this time. She'd moved on since, had two engagements to prove it.

Broken engagements, her insidiously annoying voice of reason whispered.

Guys she'd fallen for enough to think she wanted to marry,

just not enough to take that final step and actually say, 'I do.' She'd loved both Avery and Barton, loved their gentleness and patience and understanding. They'd reminded her of her high-school boyfriends, the nice guys who'd carry her books and write corny love letters and give her a lift on the handlebars of their bikes.

She'd been horrid to those boys, demanding and snooty and condescending, thrilled to have their attention yet secretly craving the Prince Charmings she read about in her mum's romance novels.

Thankfully, she'd grown up enough to treat her men better, but a small part of her wondered if she didn't end up treating her fiancés as badly in the end.

Yes, she'd definitely moved on from Jared, couldn't have loved those men if deep down in her heart she secretly pined for her first love. Besides, he'd shattered her grand illusions of loving him by choosing his career over her, by not being willing to work out a compromise.

She'd worked through the stages of grief after he'd left: anger, denial, reaching acceptance months later.

Simply, he hadn't loved her.

Yet sitting across from him, in all his confident, laid-back, gorgeous glory, she had a hard time shaking the memories of how it had once been.

Ignoring the nervous churning in her gut, she grabbed a menu and stuck it up, using it as a barrier to hide her readable face, not willing to let him know the turmoil within.

'Shall we order? I'm famished.'

'I took the liberty of ordering the eight-course degustation menu.'

He signalled to a waiter, who instantly bore down on them brandishing an expensive bottle of champagne. 'That way we get to sample a bit of everything. Hope you don't mind?'

Normally she wouldn't but seeing him assume the old role of 'man of the world', a guy who'd been around the block a time or two in comparison to her naivety back then, grated. But what was the point of stirring up trouble? Once their week together was over, she'd go her way, he'd go his. He was an expert at that.

'Fine.'

As the waiter poured the champagne she took the opportunity to glance around. Not surprisingly, every woman within a few feet cast surreptitious peeks at Jared when their partners weren't watching, their eyes predatory until they slid to her, when their gleam became curious, envious.

She'd never had to deal with that before, would've hated it. Working in PR, she'd mingled with the rich and famous, had seen high-profile relationships up close and personal, and had never figured out how the women put up with their partners being fawned over by other women; or, worse, blatantly propositioned.

She would never tolerate it. Thankfully, she would never have to.

'What are you looking at?'

She picked up her champagne flute, raised it in a silent toast.

'All the women around us are making goo eyes at you.'

'Where?'

He looked over his shoulder, caught a woman's eye, winked and smiled as she ducked her head and blushed.

'Oh, you mean her.'

'And her.'

She nodded to the left. 'And her.'

She jerked her head to the right. 'And her.'

'That one's behind you. How can you tell?'

With a wry grin, she raised her glass again. 'Because she's human and female and as smitten as the rest of this room with your presence.'

A corner of his mouth kicked up in that quirky smile she loved as he folded his hands on the table, leaned forward.

'Does that include you?'

She made a loud scoffing noise that descended into an embarrassing snort.

'Do I look like I'm smitten?'

Leaning even closer, so close she could smell his clean lime aftershave, see the familiar green flecks in his hazel eyes, he touched her hand.

'You look incredible, more beautiful than you were eight years ago if that's possible.'

'Been working on those lines?'

Unperturbed, he sat back, resumed his casual relaxed pose, one hand slung across the back of his chair.

'According to you, I don't need lines. Apparently women are smitten just sitting here.'

She made a rude noise that had him laughing as he picked up his champagne flute, touched it to hers.

'To us. And making the most of our island jaunt.'

'To us.'

As she echoed his toast her reservations took a serious hit as a sliver of anticipation lodged where she feared it most.

Her heart.

He took a long sip of his champagne, his eyes not leaving hers, the intensity of his stare making her increasingly uncomfortable.

Lowering his glass, he placed it on the table, leaned forward. 'You know, I was once crazy about you.'

'Yeah, so crazy you moved to the other side of the world to get away from me.'

The heat faded, his eyes instantly guarded.

'My career was taking off. You know that.'

The old familiar resentment bubbled to the surface, obliterating the unexpected joy she'd experienced just by being here, sharing a meal with him.

She had known it but had let herself get caught up in their whirlwind romance anyway. Jared had lived in the moment, wanted instant gratification, didn't want to look too far ahead, whereas she'd had enough dreams for the both of them.

Not that it had mattered. Nothing she could've said or done back then would've changed the outcome.

'Yeah, I know.'

When she wouldn't meet his gaze, he captured her hand, reluctantly releasing it when she tugged hard.

'You sound bitter.'

'You don't think I have a right to be?'

'You knew the score. I never made any promises.'

'Beyond a few months of fun?'

She snapped her fingers. 'Silly me for reading more into us spending every spare second together.'

He shook his head. 'You really want to rehash all this now? Right before we spend a week together in front of the cameras?'

What she wanted was an apology.

What she wanted was some small indication she'd meant half as much to him as he'd meant to her.

What she wanted was to annihilate the crazy, excited buzz deep in her belly that made a mockery of her indignation.

Blowing out an exasperated puff of air, she shook her head.

'No point. Let's leave the past in the past.'

His crooked smile, so familiar, so heart-rending, made a serious dent in her residual animosity.

'Look, I know this is awkward. We were great together 'til that last week, when we both acted a little crazy.'

'You think?'

He laughed and she managed a tight smile. She didn't want to discuss her humiliating ultimatum, how she'd shrieked at him, filled with hurt and anger and resentment. Crazy? She'd acted like a certified lunatic so yeah, this was beyond awkward.

'We were both young, we had different agendas. How about we put all that behind us and try to be friends for the next week?'

Friends. Yeah, she could do friends at a pinch.

Think of the money…think of Meg and Prue…

Unfortunately, all she could think about was exactly how friendly Jared wanted to get on the island.

'Friends,' she said, gulping at her champagne, though it did little to quell her nerves as he held out his hand and, this time, she had no option but to place her hand in his and shake on it.

A simple arrangement, friends for a week.

Pity complication was her middle name.

CHAPTER FIVE

Stranded *Survival Tip #5*
When asked, 'Do you like me?' don't answer, 'I'm here, aren't I?'

FOOTFALLS scuffing the corridor outside his door grabbed Jared's attention as he wrapped up final negotiations for a popular rock band to play at Activate's official opening.

A few local kids had been dropping by since he'd opened the doors a month ago, but not enough for his liking. He still saw them loitering in small gangs on the streets, in the parks, bored, on edge, looking for trouble.

While the original idea for the centre had come to him in rehab, surrounded by partially disabled kids who needed a place to hang out, once he'd investigated sites and discovered the startling number of kids loitering on Sydney's streets he'd known his dream needed expanding.

Through months of painful, monotonous rehab, he'd planned Activate from the ground up, investing an exorbitant sum, determined to give something back to those who needed it the most.

While his parents had been AWOL from the time he could walk, he'd never wanted for anything, their wealth a cushion against the harsher side of life.

From what he'd seen these past few months around Kings Cross, a lot of local kids needed that kind of shield.

So the centre had grown, catering for all disadvantaged kids, physically and emotionally. He'd keep the money coming, grab the free publicity from Elliott, then move on to his next venture. Whatever that was.

'Got a minute?'

He raised his head at the sound of a hesitant voice, tried to place the red-haired kid with enough facial piercings to rival his freckles, and remembered his name after a quick mental rummage.

'Sure, come in, Bluey.'

The flash of surprise in the kid's eyes, along with a quick nod of acknowledgment, vindicated the time he'd spent at the centre. He might only be financing the venture, but if his presence encouraged drop-ins for the simple fact they recognised him from tennis it was time well spent.

The kid slouched across the room, flopped into the chair.

'What can I do for you?'

Bluey picked at a hole in his jeans, plucked at the frayed edges, concentrating on his fiddling rather than looking up.

'Word on the street is you're planning on keeping this joint open day and night. That true?'

'Uh-huh.'

'Why?'

Bluey's head snapped up, fear mixed with mistrust in the furtive shadows clouding his eyes.

'What do you get out of it? You're just some hotshot tennis jock. Why do you care?'

'Because I do.'

A lousy response but what could he say?

He had no idea what it was like to semi-doze on a park bench, night after night, so tired you could fall into a coma, too terrified to sleep for fear of any number of horrors nabbing you.

He didn't understand the pinch of hunger, the hollow, scraping feeling in one's gut that made Dumpster leftovers an appealing feast after a while.

But he sure as hell recognised the fear in this kid's eyes, the lonely emptiness inside that no one gave a damn about you.

He might have had everything money could buy and parents only too happy to splash their cash around, but he'd lived with that same emptiness every day growing up, wishing for acknowledgement, willing them to show some semblance of sentiment rather than treating him as if he were a nobody, as if he didn't exist.

So did he care?

Hell, yeah, but how to get that across to a kid who viewed him as just another adult he couldn't trust?

'This place is here if you want it. Tell your mates. No pressure, no expectations. Just a place to hang out, play some sport.'

Bluey shrugged, resumed picking at his frayed edges. 'Chill, man. Just wondering, that's all.'

Jared couldn't tell the kid's age. Twelve? Fourteen? With his slight build, hunched shoulders, grimy face, he could've been any number of kids that frequented the Kings Cross area.

While his slashed cheekbones highlighted a gauntness honed by hunger, there was resilience about the boy, a toughness that defied anyone to pity him.

That was when it hit him.

Bluey reminded him of himself.

Fierce, determined, resentful, he'd been all that and more before he'd discovered tennis, when being the best at a sport had given him an outlet for his bitterness.

Where would Bluey end up with a little help?

It reinforced he was doing the right thing, investing in this place. Now all he had to do was tell the world about it, and that was exactly what he'd do, starting tomorrow, first day on the island.

'Do you network on the web?'

Bluey glanced up again, curious. 'Like Facebook and MySpace and stuff?'

'Yeah.'

Bluey sent him an 'are you for real?' sneer.

''Course. A few dudes have mobile phones. We get to check stuff out.'

'Good. Make sure you spread the word about this place. And keep an eye on Twitter and a blog I've set up.'

At last, a flash of recognition, of interest, reinforcing he was doing the right thing in taking part in *Stranded*. The kids would definitely sit up and take notice now.

'Yeah, whatever.'

Apparently Bluey had said what he'd come to say because he unfolded his lanky limbs from the chair, raised a hand in farewell before heading out of the door, his scuffed Doc Martens leaving a muddy trail behind him.

With a wry grin, Jared refocused on his paperwork. The sooner he dotted every i, crossed every t, the faster this place could really get off the ground.

'Any last-minute questions?'

Kristi tore her gaze from the distant view of Sydney's city skyline and turned to Elliott.

'No, I think you've pretty much covered everything.'

Satisfied, Elliott glanced at Jared, who shrugged, grinned.

'A-okay here.'

'Good.' Elliott snapped his clipboard shut. 'Then you're on your own.'

'Thanks, mate.'

As Jared slapped him on the back she waved, quickly dropped her hand when it shook with trepidation as Elliott stepped onto the powerboat and shot away from Lorikeet Island, leaving her alone with the man who intruded her thoughts constantly these days.

She'd been a mess at work the last week, Ros plying her with questions and suggestions for her seven days on the island, and Meg hadn't been much better.

If she didn't want the money for Meg so badly, and couldn't almost taste the promotion Rosanna had dangled in front of her, she would've quit this whole crazy scheme.

But the fact remained: Meg was living in a hovel, with a gorgeous seven-year-old to raise who grew faster than her mum could outfit her, and working her butt off to survive.

Enough money could change all that and she could give her that gift. As for the promotion, a girl could never have too many Louboutin shoes.

Slinging an arm across her shoulder, Jared hugged her close. 'Looks like it's just you and me, kid.'

She stiffened, darted a quick glance around. 'Are there any cameras here?'

His eyes crinkled at the corners when he laughed. 'Safe zone. You weren't listening.'

She shrugged out of his embrace on the pretext of studying some particularly riveting marine life at the water's edge.

'I tuned out when Elliott repeated his spiel for the fifth time.'

'He just wants this to be perfect. It's what he does.'

Feeling bad, she turned back to him. 'I know. He's a great producer. Guess I'm just angsty now we're actually here.'

Squaring his shoulders, he dusted off his hands. 'Right. Let's get cracking.'

Now that the moment of truth had arrived, she didn't want

to leave this spot, didn't want to step in front of the cameras to have her every move filmed and scrutinised and analysed.

'First things first. Accommodation.' Jared jerked his thumb east. 'Our humble abodes are that way, apparently.'

'Mmm,' she mumbled, scuffing her sandal in the sand, reluctant to move.

Laying a hand on her shoulder, he squeezed, an innocuous comforting touch that shot a spark of awareness straight through her.

'You can do this.'

Think of the money, think of the promotion.

She'd been thinking of nothing less to keep her motivated—discounting the inordinate amount of time she'd spent thinking about this man and how to approach their enforced proximity over the next week.

She'd replayed every moment of their dinner together, had marvelled at how laid-back he'd been, slipping into comfortable conversation, content to ignore or glide over her silences, her monosyllabic responses.

She'd done her best that night to send him a message: that he could smile and flirt all he liked, she was immune. And while she'd like nothing better than to vent her long-suppressed feelings about how things had ended, harbouring ongoing animosity would make the next seven days unbearable.

So she'd made a decision.

She would be polite but distant.

Respond to his questions but not get too friendly.

Play the part of a woman determined to win the cash while trying to ignore the cameras.

And not, repeat *not*, let Jared and his fabled charm creep under her guard again.

She should've been glad she'd established a cool distance the night at dinner. Instead, a tiny part of her had fallen back under his spell that night and that knowledge was what kept her standing here, her feet riveted to the spot, her heart pounding with fear that the moment she truly embarked on this crazy week would signal the beginning of the end. The end of her peace of mind, the beginning of a possibility. That couldn't last.

'Come on, I'll be with you every step of the way.'

He held out his hand and she stared at it, the broad palm, the long, strong fingers, the curve of his thumb pad.

She didn't want to place her hand in his, to trust him, had learned the hard way it was all an illusion.

Lowering his voice, he said, 'We'll have a ball. It'll be just like old times.'

Old times?

She'd adored him, craved him, loved him so fiercely she could scarcely breathe for wanting him.

He wasn't offering her anything, but for an insane moment, staring into his eyes, so frank, so honest, she wanted to recapture some of that old magic, wanted to feel half as good again.

On a drawn-out sigh, she placed her hand in his, her pulse leaping in recognition as he curled his fingers over hers.

'Okay. Let's do it.'

KRISTI'S BLOG, DAY 1
Lorikeet Island: beautiful views of Sydney, surrounded by the bluest ocean on the planet, perfect weather. I've lasted the first hour without making any major gaffes in front of the cameras. Then again, have sat petrified, sipping soda on the postage-stamp veranda of my 'home' for the next week, watching Jared act all he-man by scoping out the lay of the land.

Don't know why he's bothering. Not like we'll get attacked by any wild animals, right?

Yikes! What was that growling sound?

Oh, only my stomach. Woman does not survive on soda and fresh air alone. Time to rustle up lunch. Baked beans on campfire toast?

I miss Sydney already.

JARED'S BLOG, DAY 1
Not a bad spot. Might take up fishing. Kristi brought too many shoes. She's such a girl.

CHAPTER SIX

Stranded *Survival Tip #6*
Blogging is fun but for ever. Choose your words wisely.

'YOU ever use Twitter before?'

Kristi shook her head, trying to sneak a peek over Jared's shoulder as he fiddled with his iPhone.

'No time. Work keeps me pretty busy. I email. Facebook page. That's about it.'

His eyes not leaving the screen, he said, 'You don't know what you're missing.'

Her scoffing snort had him darting an amused glance her way.

'What's so special about informing the world what you're up to in one hundred and forty characters or less?'

'It's the challenge, to make your tweet interesting in so few words.'

Typing quickly, he finally laid his phone down, his stare loaded.

'Surely you know how much guys like a challenge?'

'Guys or just you?'

He chuckled. 'Last time I checked I was a guy. Or would you care to verify—?'

'Stop that!' she hissed, jerking her head towards one of the not-so-hidden cameras. 'We're live.'

Dropping his voice to a conspiratorial whisper, he leaned forward and spoke behind his raised hand.

'Viewers love this sort of thing. A bit of light-hearted banter, flirting. Good for ratings.'

He wiggled his eyebrows until the unimpressed twist to her lips relaxed into a smile. 'Sex sells, baby.'

Okay, so he was hamming it up for the cameras. Not that she could blame him. There was something so weirdly un-natural about all of this. As to why anyone would be remotely interested in watching the two of them have dinner or quibble over the last Tim Tam was beyond her.

But she couldn't deny Elliott Barnaby was a genius; and the one salient fact: she was in this for the money, and the pro-motion.

Faking a huff, she tossed her hair over her shoulder like any screen heroine worth her salt.

'I'm not your baby.'

'You were once.'

He whispered it so softly the cameras wouldn't have a chance of picking it up, her skin prickling with alarm as he scooted closer, his warm breath fanning her neck as he mur-mured in her ear, 'Want to recreate some of the old magic?'

'No!'

Her body made a mockery of her instant refusal, heat flushing her skin rosy as she inadvertently leaned into him, practically inviting him to slip an arm around her and cradle her close as he used to.

'Liar,' he whispered, his fingertips trailing across the back of her neck and sending a quiver of desire through her as he casually draped an arm over her shoulder, appearing to the whole world as if they were best buddies.

An instant, unexpected, fierce need pounded through her body, setting a relentless tempo, willfully ignoring her supposed immunity to him these days and urging her to be totally reckless, fling herself into his arms, cameras be damned.

But there was a difference between making a fool of herself over this man again and doing it with the general public eagerly looking on, so she slid out from under his arm on the pretext of retrieving his phone.

'Here. Tweet something.'

His low, husky laugh rippled over her, his knowing stare leaving her in little doubt he didn't buy her brush-off for a second.

'Okay. Watch this.'

His thumb flew over the phone's keypad, his grin widening before he handed over the phone.

'Go ahead. Take a look.'

With increasing foreboding she glanced at the screen, her heart skipping a beat, several, as she read his brief message to the cyber world.

Twitter.com/Stranded_Jared
Old flames never die. They just burn brighter if you fan the fire.

Ignoring the irrational leap of her pulse, and the distinct urge to skip the fanning part and jump directly into the fire, she handed him back the phone.

'You sure you're not a pyromaniac? All this talk of flames and your incessant need to poke at the campfire?'

'Being obtuse won't help.'

He pressed the phone into her palm. 'Your turn.'

'I don't have an account.'

'Elliott set one up for both of us. Yours is under Stranded_Kristi.'

'Of course it is.'

Mustering a sickly sweet smile, she tapped at the phone, saw her PR picture on her Twitter home page.

'Remember, play nice,' he murmured, his wink urging her to do the exact opposite.

She searched her brain for something suitably witty to say, something other than the mundane. In the end, she settled for the partial truth.

Twitter.com/Stranded_Kristi
Ever wish an ex could see you now? Be careful what you wish for!

Jared clutched his chest. 'Harsh.'

'Honest,' she said, handing him back his phone with a smirk. 'I think I'm getting the hang of this Twitter thing.'

He slipped the phone into his pocket with a rueful grin.

'Yeah, just don't go singing my praises too much.'

'No risk of that.'

She stilled as he reached out and touched her cheek, a brief brush of his fingertips that tingled all the way to her toes.

'What happened to the girl who used to look at me with stars in her eyes?'

Not liking this turn of conversation, she shrugged, aimed for levity.

'Stars fade, lose their lustre.'

She knew she'd said the wrong thing the instant he stood, his eyes shuttered, his expression deliberately blank.

'I didn't mean—'

'I know you didn't.'

He turned his back on her, strolled towards the water's edge, staring across the water to the Harbour Bridge glittering like a sparkly coat hanger in the distance.

'You miss it, don't you?'

His shoulders stiffened imperceptibly before he thrust his hands into his pockets, his casual stance at odds with his tense posture.

'Everyone has to retire some time.'

'But that choice was taken away from you by the injury. It's different.'

'I could've come back if I'd wanted to.'

His voice held a wistful edge, a hint of vulnerability she'd never heard from the invincible charmer, and the part of her that had once loved him urged her to go to him, offer what comfort she could.

'Why didn't you? Really?'

She laid a hand on his shoulder, willing him to turn around, to let her comfort him. But he didn't move, continued staring out over the water as if she hadn't spoken.

She wanted to push him for answers, wanted to use the old philosophy 'a problem shared is a problem halved', but she had no right.

They'd been apart for eight years and she knew little about him beyond what she'd read in the tabloids, knew little beyond what he'd told her when they'd been dating; and that hadn't been much.

No, she had no right to push him for answers, none at all. For answers would give her a glimpse into the guy behind the confident façade, would make it harder for her to pretend they were nothing more than friends.

Despite the bitterness following their break-up, despite the anger that infused every part of her trusting soul until she wanted to wring his neck, after spending a day with him, she was forced to acknowledge the truth.

A small part of her still cared.

Always had, and spending time with him reinforced Meg's theory: maybe she hadn't gone through with her two marriages because of this man and the mark he'd left on her all those years ago.

Call her crazy, call her corny, but she suddenly understood the quaint term 'being spoiled for any other man'. Jared had branded her heart as surely as if he'd taken a heated iron bar and pressed it there, leaving her burned, marked as his.

Her hand fell from his shoulder and she stepped away, surprised when he turned to face her, his expression inscrutable in the shadows.

'Ever had someone have a profound effect on your life?'

Whatever she'd been expecting, it wasn't that and she cautiously nodded, not wanting to turn this into a conversation about her.

'My folks, I guess. They were amazing.'

'You would've done anything for them, right?'

'Uh-huh.'

She had no idea where he was going with this, assuming he was indebted to a mentor, maybe a coach, which had influenced his decision to retire.

Dragging a hand through his hair, he shook his head. 'Getting injured, going through rehab, seeing all those injured and partially disabled kids gave me time to think about where my life was heading. Through all those boring hydrotherapy sessions I figured it was time to do something else than hit a ball around a court.'

'Something you were darn good at, mind you.'

'I was, wasn't I?'

His proud grin warmed her heart. 'Now that's the modest Jared Malone I know and love.'

Yikes! She'd spoken too quickly, made a gaffe of monumental proportions.

To his credit, his smile didn't slip but she saw caution creep into his eyes.

'Glad to hear I haven't lost any of my multitudes of adoring fans.'

She could've left it there, should've left it there, but she'd never taken the safe option when it came to this man.

'Is that all I ever was to you?'

'You know better than that.'

Did she?

They'd had a whirlwind romance that lasted six months. He'd moved to Sydney, they'd met at a PR event; she'd been smitten the first time he'd smiled at her. And while he'd lavished her with compliments, spent every spare moment off the courts with her, she knew she'd fallen harder.

He'd never said he'd loved her, never made any promises, and watching him walk away had broken her heart. Her gullible, impressionable heart that used to leap into the palm of his hand every time he was near.

Thank goodness she'd grown up, wised up, toughened up.

'It's late. Think I'll turn in.'

She hadn't taken two steps before his hand slid around her waist and she stopped, held her breath, aware of the inky darkness, the soft lapping of waves on the shore and the heat, so much heat, from his simple touch.

'We were good together.'

What the heck did that mean? They could be again? Not bloody likely!

She spun around, expecting to brush off his hand. It didn't move and she found herself tantalisingly close to a body she'd once known intimately, a body giving off signals she didn't have a hope of ignoring.

'What do you want from me, Jared?'

She watched a million responses flicker across his face, before his mouth quirked into that familiar, sexy, heart-rending smile.

Tugging her close, he gazed into her eyes and she knew right that very second, she was in trouble. Big Trouble.

'What do I want?'

His gaze dropped to her lips as anticipation fizzed through her like expensive champagne.

'This.'

His kiss catapulted her back to a time filled with special memories and the sweetness of first love, a time where a charming, gregarious and utterly devastating man had swept her off her feet. A time she'd lost all sense of reason until it was too late.

Which begged the question: what on earth was she doing letting him kiss her now?

CHAPTER SEVEN

Stranded *Survival Tip #7*
Avoid board games to pass time. Arguments assured.

KRISTI'S BLOG, DAY 2
One down, six to go. Honestly, how long can one week drag?

As fellow 'strandees' can't read each other's blogs I'm going to be blunt.

Being stuck on this island is KILLING me!

No Italian milk hot chocolates from Max Brenner, no Caesar salads from my favourite café in Bondi, no lunchtime retail therapy dashes to check out shoes.

Worst of all? No peace of mind.

Word of advice to anyone contemplating a similar madness? Don't do it.

Being cooped up with an ex is similar to getting a bikini wax: pure torture.

Wouldn't be so bad if I didn't like him but we're talking about THE Jared Malone. Ladies, you know what I mean. You've seen him with his shirt off courtside a thousand times, you've seen him interviewed and heard his snappy one liners, and you've seen that killer smile.

Say no more.

I'm a wreck.

Pretending like everything is just oh-so-casual is tough. Staying immune to the damn charmer tougher.

See, this is the problem with no TV. You're forced to read or talk and there are only so many back issues of Vogue I can skim. Which leaves me back at square one: talking to the guy, laughing at his jokes, acting all matey when...when...heck, I'm not supposed to like him any more!

Repeat after me: six days to go...

JARED'S BLOG, DAY 2
Hanging out with Kristi is cool. Like being with an old buddy and not having to make an effort. Next six days going to be a blast.

SHE was killing him.

With every squirt of the suntan lotion tube, every slow, deliberate rub down her arm, down her long legs, with every wriggle of her cute butt as she got comfortable on her beach towel, she was killing him.

So much for a week of banter, flirtation, nothing too heavy.

As Kristi rolled from her back to her front, inadvertently squeezing her breasts together, spilling over the top of the tiniest green bikini he'd ever seen, Jared bit back a groan and resumed the mundane task of gathering kindle.

This was all his fault.

He'd never meant to kiss her, had intended on having a little fun while on the island, had wanted to keep things light-hearted.

Then she'd gone all serious on him, probing into his reasons behind quitting the tennis world, had opened a chasm in his heart he ignored every day, and he'd lost it.

Kissing her had been the lesser of two evils, for he had no intention of delving into his psyche and the constant reminder he would never play tennis again.

His manager and coach had pushed him to see a psychologist after the injury, mandatory for any pro cut down in his prime.

He'd faced the usual questions: how do you feel about your injury? Are you resentful? Angry? Liable to go off the deep end?

Okay, so that last one hadn't been phrased quite like that, but the uptight geek in his fancy glass-enclosed office that hadn't spent a day on a court in his life had prodded and probed his mind until he would've said anything to get out of there.

The thing was no amount of therapy sessions with an elite sports psychologist would ease the ache of losing a part of himself, the only part of him linking him to his flaky parents.

And that was what peed him off the most.

The fact he cared.

After living through the nightmare of their dysfunctional relationship, after surviving their total oblivion to having a son, the second he'd been discovered and won Junior Wimbledon his parents had done an about-face.

He'd initially hated their sudden fawning, had doubted every overture they'd made, until the locked away part of him that had always craved their approval cracked and let them in.

The smart, cynical side of him knew why they'd done it. To bask in the reflected glory of his triumphs, to share in his fame.

Yet the vulnerable little boy desperate for a smidgeon of affection from his parents thrived under their long-overdue attention, enjoyed having them courtside, applauding him, fist-pumping along every hard-fought victory, sharing in his Grand Slam titles.

So what would happen to their tentative relationship now he'd quit? Considering the sparse visits during his rehab, the lack of phone calls recently, he knew. Whoever had coined the phrase *the truth hurt* had a courtside seat to his life.

Now this.

Kristi made an impolite slurping as she guzzled her favourite soda and he raised his head, watching her.

He didn't give a damn what the cameras picked up, didn't care if they captured an image of a schmuck blinded by the only woman to ever get remotely close to him.

He'd flirted with the world's most beautiful women, from film stars to royalty, and contrary to paparazzi reports hadn't slept with them all. He hadn't had the time, focused solely on being the best and obtaining the number-one ranking.

Tennis had consumed his life for so long. Now it was gone. And while his priorities had shifted into the business arena, a small part of him was terrified he'd revert back to that lost kid who wasn't good enough unless he held a racket.

Kristi knew nothing of his past and he'd like to keep it that way. She might be the closest thing he'd ever had to a relationship but that didn't mean he'd lose his head again.

As for his heart, he'd locked that away a long time ago, safe from trust and inevitable pain when people you loved didn't give a toss either way.

'Done with the caveman routine?'

The organ he refused to acknowledge lurched as he glanced up, saw Kristi on her side, propped on an elbow, wearing that sinful green bikini and a reluctant smile.

She'd been frosty towards him over dinner, with more of the same since they'd arrived on the island, but under his constant barrage of teasing she was finally starting to thaw.

Not that he blamed her. From her angry outburst when he'd picked her up the other night, she hadn't forgiven him for choosing his tennis career over her all those years ago.

But he'd had no choice.

Not that he'd go delving into his reasons why now.

For their time on the island he wanted to recapture some of their old magic, wanted to make her laugh and fire back those scathing one-liners as she used to, wanted to see her eyes sparkle just for him, for old times' sake.

Hands on hips, he wrenched his straying gaze away from the tempting expanses of flesh on display. 'Weren't you the one who wanted to toast marshmallows tonight?'

'Did *I* say that?'

She pressed a hand to her chest and his gaze followed, shooting down his intentions to keep his distance.

'Do you even have any?'

She chuckled, lowered her sunglasses to stare at him over the top. 'Maybe you should've asked that before planning to build a bonfire that can be seen in New Zealand.'

Adding another branch onto the growing pile, he feigned indifference.

'I'm surprised you could fit any marshmallows in your case, what with that mobile shoe shop you carry around.'

Her eyes narrowed, the corners of her mouth twitching. 'Are you dissing my shoes?'

'Merely making an observation.'

With a little huff that was so adorable he wanted to kiss her senseless, she pouted.

'I'll have you know it takes effort to look this good.'

His gaze raked her from top to toe, lingering on her curves, the hollow of her hip, the dip of her collarbone, remembering how he'd traced every inch of her once, how he hadn't been able to get enough.

Logically, he knew it would be foolish to resurrect the past, when nothing fundamental had changed. Kristi was a relationship type of girl. He was a guy who had no intention of getting emotionally involved with anyone.

Physically, his body was on memory overload, sifting through every incredible, erotic encounter the two of them had ever had.

'You're not looking at my shoes.'

Dragging his gaze to meet hers, he raised an eyebrow. 'You're not wearing any.'

She scooped up a spangly flip-flop, dangling it from a finger. 'What's this?'

'Suitcase filler?'

'Heathen,' she muttered, sliding her sunglasses back into place and rolling onto her back. 'Get back to your wood gathering. It's what you Neanderthals are good at.'

'Sticks and stones,' he said, much more at ease with this banter than last night's emotion-charged discussion.

Pointing at the diminutive wood pile, she smirked. 'More sticks. Less stones.'

Dusting off his hands, he planted them squarely on his hips, glared her down.

'If someone spent less time criticising and more time helping, we might actually get this fire built before dusk.'

'And ruin your he-man reputation? Not likely.'

With a shooing wiggle of her fingers in a dismissive wave, she rolled over onto her tummy and turned her head the other way, leaving him with an ideal view of her great butt.

He'd like nothing better than to march over there, grab her and pick up where they left off last night. Instead, he clenched his hands several times, shook them out before turning on his heel and heading off in search for more wood.

His sole intention for being stuck on this island for a week might revolve around priceless free publicity for the rec centre, but the more time he spent sparring with Kristi, the further his intentions would evolve.

Into something he couldn't contemplate.

Grateful he'd dropped out of a camera's vision, he roundly cursed as he picked up a piece of wood and hurled it as far as he could.

Twitter.com/Stranded_Jared
Playing best buddies with an ex sucks.

Twitter.com/Stranded_Kristi
Cosy campfire, toasted marshmallows, hot guy. What?
A girl can look, right?

'Don't go getting any ideas.'

'Huh?' Kristi stretched, rubbed her tummy and moaned as Jared popped a marshmallow off the end of the stick, juggling it between hands and blowing on it.

'We are *not* doing this every night.'

'Considering I've just consumed half a bag of marshmallows and can barely move, you won't get any complaints from me.'

Throwing the marshmallow in the air, he tilted his head back, caught it in his open mouth first try.

'That's what you say now but I bet you'll be back to your bossy best tomorrow, making me gather firewood while you loll around.'

Shaking her head as he offered her the last marshmallow, she said, 'Think of the ratings. All those women viewers out there will be glued to their screens, starry-eyed over your flexing muscles as you gather wood.'

Flicking his glance over her denim cargo shorts and white ribbed singlet top, he raised an eyebrow.

'I think you're doing more than your fair share for ratings, what with that scrap of material passing as a bikini you wore today.'

He'd noticed! She'd been furious after that kiss, angrier

with herself than him. She'd expect something like that from him considering his blasé attitude, as if they could pick up their relationship and run with it.

But her responding to the kiss…now that was another matter. Oh, she'd been resistant at first. But the longer his lips had coaxed her, plied her with a skill that still left her breathless after all this time, she'd lost her mind, forgetting every sane reason why she shouldn't respond.

She didn't know what was worse: her mortification that she'd kissed him back or the discovery her resilience against this man was under serious threat now she'd let him in a fraction.

Like any woman scorned, she'd mulled over payback. And deliberately worn the most provocative bikini she owned today. Foolish, maybe, but she wanted to rattle him as much as he'd rattled her last night with that unexpected kiss. What she hadn't banked on was the heat of awareness prickling her body every time he glanced her way.

She'd moved on eight years ago, had two diamond solitaires to prove it, but when Jared looked at her in that special way he catapulted her right back to a time when she'd once been crazy for him.

'It's supposed to be realistic. What else is a girl supposed to wear on an island?'

She only just caught his muttered 'a neck-to-knee bathing suit'.

Oh, yeah, she was getting to him.

She should feel vindicated. Instead, a strange sense of deflation crept over her. What was she doing? Playing some silly tit-for-tat game when she'd vowed to keep her distance.

Her response to his kiss had been an aberration, a reaction of a woman who hadn't had a date let alone a peck of a kiss in ages. Best she ignored it, reverted to her original plan: ignore, ignore, ignore.

Hugging her knees to her chest, she folded her arms, rested her chin on them, watching the shadows from the fire play across his face, highlighting a cheekbone here, a jaw line there.

He'd always been handsome but there was something about him now…an assuredness he'd never had when they'd first met.

Winning a few Grand Slams did that for a guy, but there was more to it. From all reports, and if she believed everything she read, he'd had a cushy life, the Aussie darling of the tennis circuit, the golden boy who couldn't put a volley wrong.

Yet there was a new hardened edge to him, as if life had smashed more than a few aces his way.

'You're staring.'

'At the fire.'

He prodded the fire with a long stick. 'Nope, at me.'

She should leave things alone but the atmosphere, the silence, was conducive to chatting. It was okay to freeze him out emotionally but surely she could make small talk?

Curiosity egged her on; she was dying to ask if all the rumours were true, if he'd done half the things the magazines said he had.

'Can't get enough of me, huh?'

He leaned back on outstretched elbows, the sky-blue cotton T-shirt pulled taut across his muscular chest. For someone who'd been out of the game a year, he hadn't lost his physique. Then again, twelve months of intensive rehab would've kept him fit.

'Your ego hasn't changed a bit.'

She rolled her eyes, bit back the urge to laugh along with him.

'You've changed.'

Despite his light tone, she could sense a serious undercurrent and, while she didn't want to get into a deep and meaningful rehashing their past, he'd piqued her curiosity. How did he see her now?

Playing it cool, she wound a strand of hair around her finger, checked for split ends.

"Course I've changed. New hairstyle, new wardrobe—'

'New attitude.'

'What did you expect? For me to be the same naïve, starry-eyed girl you…hung out with?'

She'd almost said loved but that wasn't true. Jared had never loved her. Despite all the attention, all the good times, all the intimate moments they'd shared, he hadn't loved her. Not enough to stick around.

His eyes narrowed, as if he could see right through her.

'You've got a streetwise edge these days.'

'You don't like it?'

He glanced away, his answer right there before he spoke.

'I liked my old Krissie.'

She bit her tongue to stop blurting she was never *his* to begin with.

Uneasy with this turn of conversation, she needed a diversion.

'Tell me about Florida.'

His shoulders tensed, an instant giveaway he didn't want to talk about it.

'How was it when you first left Sydney and settled there?'

He sat up, dusted his hands off, resumed poking at the fire, staring into the flames.

'Not much to tell. I trained like the devil, hung out with other up-and-comers, did everything my coach and manager told me to, that's it.'

He'd told her virtually nothing. She could leave it at that but, knowing Jared, he'd swing the interrogation right back on her and there was no way she'd dwell on a time they'd been crazy for each other.

'You rocketed into the top one hundred in your first year. Must've been some ride.'

'Pretty boring, actually. Early mornings, rigorous training schedule, strict diet, limited down time.'

He continued to stare into the fire, his face devoid of emotion, which only fuelled her curiosity.

'So all those blondes came later?'

He finally glanced her way, a flicker of a smile tugging his lips.

'Don't forget the brunettes and the redheads.'

'And the princesses, the movie starlets, the supermodels.'

She ticked them off on her fingers, could've easily covered both hands and feet with the reports of playboy Jared and his conquests.

'Yeah, those too.'

He smiled, instantly alleviating the reservations of moments ago.

'Anyone serious among your harem?'

'Hell, no!'

His vehement response startled her but before she could respond, he rushed on. 'Not the relationship type. You know that.'

As if she needed reminding. The day he'd walked in on her in her room-mate's wedding dress was embedded in her memory, an annoying spur that niggled despite the years gone by. His shocked expression, horrified and shuttered when she'd made that half-serious comment about it being their turn soon.

When he'd initially left for Florida she'd spent many wasted hours replaying that moment, wondering if things would've been different if she hadn't said it, if she'd passed it off as a flyaway comment.

Instead, her highly strung emotions had snowballed from that moment. He'd pulled away, she'd pushed for answers he didn't want to give. So, yeah, she knew he wasn't the relationship type, yet hearing him articulate it now after so much time had elapsed still had the power to hurt.

'Hey, if anyone knows what you're like, it's me.'

She inwardly cringed as the words left her mouth, her proclamation sounding too personal, too close for comfort.

He stood, threw his stick on the fire, took a few steps towards the wood pile before turning back to face her.

'Don't go getting any ideas.'

'Like?'

'Like taking our time here as meaning anything more than what it is.'

'And what's that?'

'Two old friends getting reacquainted.'

'Bull.'

She leaped to her feet, marched towards him until she stood two feet away, in his face.

'I bought that trite old line eight years ago but not any more.'

'What line—?'

'The one about you not being the settling type. About not wanting to get involved.'

She gestured towards Sydney's skyline glittering in the distance.

'You wouldn't be back here if you didn't want to settle. You wouldn't be stuck on this island with me if you weren't already involved.'

He swiped a hand over his clenched jaw. 'You don't know what you're talking about—'

'Elliott told me you're doing this because you're backing some youth centre in Kings Cross? If that isn't involvement, I don't know what is! You could've just thrown a zillion dollars their way but, uh-uh, you're here, being filmed for some crazy documentary, to gain some high-priced advertising slots.'

She jabbed him in the chest, twice, for good measure. 'That's involvement! And it's great. So don't spin me some bull about you not getting involved because you do.'

Just not with me.

A realisation she'd come to terms with eight years earlier, yet reinforcing the knowledge didn't make it any easier.

He held up his hands, backed away. 'Look, after what happened last night, I just don't want any confusion.'

Clenching her hands, she deliberately released them before she slugged him.

'I'm not confused. *You* kissed *me*; it's what guys like you do.'

A frown settled between those startling hazel eyes. 'Guys like me?'

'You need me to spell it out?'

'Please do.'

'You're a player. A little charm here, a little flirting there, the odd heated glance, throw in a kiss or two, you like to have women adore you.'

His frown deepened, the groove slashing between his brows not detracting from his good looks one iota.

'Harsh.'

'But true.'

Shaking his head, he said, 'You don't know me at all.'

The realisation slammed into her and she staggered a few steps back, stopping short of slapping her head.

She'd never known him.

Not the real Jared Malone; behind the driven ambition, behind the sexy smiles and laid-back attitude, behind the charming exterior.

He'd only ever let her see what he wanted her to see, holding her at bay emotionally during the time they dated. She'd been so busy nursing a broken heart back then, she hadn't seen the truth.

That she'd never really known this man at all.

Quelling the urge to rub at the ache nestling in her chest, she shrugged.

'You're right, I guess I don't.'

The prickle of tears took her completely by surprise and she blinked, damned if she'd let him see her cry over him. Spinning around, she dashed towards her hut.

'Kristi, wait.'

She didn't.

She was through waiting for anything associated with Jared Malone.

CHAPTER EIGHT

Stranded *Survival Tip #8*
Real men erect tents.

KRISTI'S BLOG, DAY 3
Been the epitome of a polite island companion all day.

*Haven't talked much beyond, 'How are you?' and,
'Nice cup of billy tea.'*

*Safer this way. Last night's chat? Not good. All the
signs of an irrational woman cooped up on an island
with a sexy ex too long.*

*Kinda like that syndrome victims acquire with their
kidnappers, when the proximity gives them the delusion
of falling in love?*

*Yeah, that's exactly it! I'm a woman, he's the only
other guy on the island, stands to reason I want to get
up close and personal, right? Want to delve into his
psyche? Get to know him better?*

*Problem is, have tried this before, eight years ago
to be precise. Didn't work then, what makes me think
it'll work now?*

He's closed up tight. Even got all snotty when I men-

tioned his backing the youth centre. Touchy, touchy, touchy.

With only four days to survive, must stick with plan. Avoid at all costs.

JARED'S BLOG, DAY 3
Have never built a campfire before. Not a bad job. Kept the bugs away.

What is it with women and fires? They want to get all cosy and chatty? Annoying.

Have disassembled wood pile today.

'STUPID challenge, stupid island, stupid man,' Kristi muttered, fiddling with a tent peg for the tenth time and watching the front collapse again.

'Need some help?'

She glared at Jared's perfectly erected two-man tent, pegs spaced equally, ropes taut, royal-blue tarpaulin gaily silhouetting the sun, and bit back her first retort of where he could stick his help.

While concentrating on keeping her distance from him was now a full-time job, she hadn't lost sight of the prize. She needed to win that prize money so proving herself at these challenges was essential. Either that or make such a huge fool of herself people would take pity on her and vote for her anyway.

'No, thanks.'

She ducked her head, concentrated on driving the peg into the ground, only to have the darn thing slip from her fingers and the entire side wall collapse.

She let fly a string of pithy curses under her breath and blinked back the sudden sting of tears, which had little to do with the tent and everything to do with the man offering his assistance.

Yeah, as if he cared. He'd been distantly polite all day, responding to her remoteness with much the same and she'd been glad. If they stayed aloof she could pretend their little heart-to-heart last night had never happened.

After his revelation, should be easy.

'Don't go getting any ideas. Like taking our time here as meaning anything more than what it is.'

Foolishly, that was exactly what she'd done, despite her determination to keep her distance. All the logic in the world hadn't stopped her from reading more into his charm, his flirting, his kiss.

Damn it! The guy had *kissed* her and he expected her not to go getting any ideas?

She was glad she'd blurted the truth about why he was here, despite Elliott mentioning it was a touchy subject and to not let on she knew. What he was doing was admirable, so why the secrecy?

She knew. Just another way for him to maintain his distance, to keep her out of his life. Fine with her.

She stood, gave the peg a childish kick and marched towards the water's edge, grateful the cameras had whirred off a few minutes ago.

If footage of the camping challenge Elliott had set them was interesting, it would've won an Emmy with her petulant outburst. Viewers lapped up all that reality-throw-a-barney rubbish.

'Let me help.'

He laid a hand on her arm and she stiffened, hating how his touch could make her crave him, hating how much she wanted to give in to him more.

Where was her pride? Where was her plan to stay aloof? A bit hard when all she wanted to do was turn around, fling herself into his arms and sob her little bruised heart out.

'Better not.'

She shrugged off his hand, not daring to look at him. 'I might go getting *ideas*.'

'I knew you were still peed off about that.'

'Kudos to you!'

Blowing out an exasperated breath, she folded her arms, little protection against a guy of his calibre.

'I'm just being honest with you.'

'Bull!'

She swung to face him, her plan to stay cool blowing sky-high in the face of his nonchalant self-denial.

Jabbing a finger in his direction, she said, 'You're not being honest with yourself so how the heck can you be honest with me?'

He didn't say a word, merely looked at her with a patient expression, patronising beyond belief.

'Tell me this. What did you think happened between us eight years ago?'

Wariness crept into his eyes, turning them intriguing caramel.

'We had fun.'

'Fun. That's it? Nothing more?'

He shifted slightly, his feet shuffling in the sand. 'I was only ever going to be in Sydney for a short time. You knew the score.'

She thought she had. But in her romantic dreams their score had been love-all instead of deuce, a tie of crazy emotions and cool aloofness when he left.

'So you're telling me there were no emotions involved?'

Another direct hit when his gaze slid away and focused on the shrubbery fringing the beach.

'We had a great six months, Krissie. It had to end eventually. Why dredge up the past now?'

Her eyes narrowed as she took a step towards him, enjoying the flicker of alarm as his gaze refocused on her.

'Because you're a fool if you think for one second that what happened between us in the past isn't affecting us right now.'

His jaw clenched, clamping down on a host of truths she needed to hear; or was that just wishful thinking on her part?

'Aren't you the least bit curious why I'm so peed off at you? The real reason?'

His lips compressed in an unimpressed line, guilt shifting like furtive shadows darting across his face.

'I know you blame me for how things ended—'

'You think?'

She calmed her loud voice with effort, rolled her shoulders to work out some of the tension, all too aware that once she started down this track she'd have to finish it.

In a way, venting might alleviate some of her residual anger, a bitterness that ran so deep she hadn't known it existed until he'd strutted back into her life pretending he'd never been away.

'You knew our dating had a time limit.'

Defensive to the end. Well, she had a few truths for him.

'Yeah, but what I didn't know was that once you reached that time limit you'd cut and run without even seeing me for a proper goodbye.'

'I don't like farewells.'

Unclenching her fist long enough to jab him in the chest, she stepped closer, invaded his personal space, righteous indignation spurring her to make her point, to make the most of this opportunity after all these years.

'That's lame, even by your standards.'

When he didn't venture any further denials, she exhaled on a long, low whistle and pivoted away, taking several steps before swinging to face him again.

'You took one look at me in that wedding dress and had a coronary. You didn't give me a chance to tell you I was joking about us doing it for real, you didn't give me a chance to do much of anything after that.'

Swallowing an unexpected sob bubbling in the back of her throat, she pinned him with an accusatory stare.

'Throwing that ultimatum at you was stupid. But I was hurting. I hadn't seen you. Then you just hopped on that plane and left, just like that, and I'll never forgive you for robbing me of a real chance at closure.'

He opened his mouth, closed it again, shook his head.

What could he say? She'd said enough for both of them, encapsulating their break-up in a few harsh sentences.

Strangely, she felt better, the offloading of her latent resentment cathartic. But she hadn't finished. She'd had her say about their past; time to get the present sorted.

'And you're wrong. Dead wrong. There were emotions involved before so tell me, what's zapping between us now?'

'Sexual attraction.'

It was her turn to flinch as he leaned forward, so close she could smell his crisp, clean cologne, could feel the heat radiating off him.

'As *I* recall, we had that in spades. Good to see some things never change.'

Back on safe turf for him, flirting, using his sexuality as a weapon to avoid anything remotely deep and meaningful. While she might have responded in like eight years ago, what he'd said last night had snatched the sarong from over her eyes.

She'd loved him eight years ago, really loved him in the way a woman pictured herself walking up the aisle in a stunning white dress, having kids with him, growing old with him.

She'd lied to him. That flyaway comment about them getting married in the future? She'd meant every word of it. But what was the point of telling him now? It would undermine her whole argument that he'd robbed her of closure by leaving without giving her a chance.

He'd been her first love, the kind of love a girl never forgot and, while she might have kidded herself into believing those feelings were long dead, it had taken a mere three days in his company to peel away the layers and reveal the truth.

He still had the power to shake her to her very foundations.

Him, a guy who couldn't commit, who didn't do emotions, who had the audacity to tell her, *'Don't go getting any ideas.'*

The bloody cheek of the man!

Stifling the urge to bop him on the nose, she lowered her tone to silky smooth.

'So what you're saying is you want me for my body?'

His intense gaze slid down her body, bold, provocative, setting her alight and almost ruining her determination to take a stance.

But this was too important and no way in hell would she let him get away with it again. Eight years was a long time to wise up and now she'd finally had her say she had no intention of succumbing to his fall-back, fail-safe charm.

When he met her eyes again, his wicked grin sent a shot of pure lust licking along her pebbled skin, leaving her resolve shaky.

'Yeah, I want you.'

Hoping he couldn't see her shift slightly thanks to the sudden wobble in her knees, she took hold of his hand.

'Here's a tip.'

She placed his hand on her hip. 'If you want this.'

She raised his hand and placed it directly over her heart, desperately trying to ignore how it pounded at the touch of his hand near her breast. 'You first have to go through this.'

Surprise parted his lips before he clamped them shut and

snatched his hand. With a shake of his head, eyes wild, he took a step back, drew in a breath, several.

She'd never seen him so rattled and the fact he'd reacted like this confirmed what she already knew.

No matter how aloof or cool he liked to pretend to be, something more than attraction simmered beneath his cool exterior.

When she'd given up hope he'd answer, he finally said, 'I don't want to hurt you. Don't you get that?'

Squaring her shoulders, she went for broke.

'A little late for that, don't you think?'

The horror crinkling his face almost made her laugh.

'Are you saying you're in love with me again?'

'Hell, no!'

Her vehement refusal had his mouth twitching.

'I meant you've already done that. I think I can survive anything you throw my way these days.'

'Even if all I want is a fling?'

She'd never settle for anything remotely like a fling but for a tiny, infinitesimal second, she almost wished she would.

'You're a smart guy, you figure it out.'

She touched his chest directly over his heart, lightly, a brush of her fingertips that jump-started her own and had him leaping back as if she'd electrocuted him.

He turned on his heel and strode away as fast as his long, athletic legs could carry him.

She should've been sad, hurt. Instead, a satisfying vindication had her smiling as she noted every rigid, resistant line of his body.

Jared could verbally deny any hint of emotion between them but he couldn't hide his body language.

She'd seen the same tension in his shoulders, his hands, his face, every time he walked out on the court. He'd given his all to tennis, had played like a man possessed, as if he had something to prove each and every game.

It was what had made him the best, had propelled him to the number-one world ranking and kept him there for years.

He reserved that tension for what he cared about, what he was passionate about and, right now, despite all his protestations, he still cared about her.

The scary thing was, did she really want him to do anything about it?

Jared stomped back to his hut, his bung knee getting a thorough workout while he all but ran across the sand. Away from Kristi and her damn home truths.

It wasn't enough she'd kept him up most of last night, her accusation that he was emotionally invested in Activate resonating for hours.

Uh-uh, now she had to go and rehash the past with her own scathing brand of honesty.

It stung. All of it.

Until now, he'd explained away his actions during their break-up—if only to himself—as justified.

She'd taken a light-hearted fling and read more into it. She'd started to cling and make demands he'd had no hopes or intentions of fulfilling. She'd made that outlandish ultimatum, asking him to choose between her and his career. All her fault.

Or so he'd told himself all this time.

When the reality was something entirely different.

Maybe he'd been young and stupid and driven to succeed at the only thing he was truly good at, the only thing that had ever garnered attention from his folks, but he could've handled their break-up differently.

All the self-justification, all the excuses in the world,

couldn't change the fact he'd been scared, terrified in fact, of how she'd made him feel in such a short space of time.

Being with Kristi had been easy, comfortable, yet filled with a constant buzz that he'd only ever emulated by winning his first Grand Slam title.

She'd made him feel good about himself, as if he could achieve anything. And how had he repaid her? By walking out on her without a backward glance.

When she'd made that demand on the phone during their last phone call he'd given her a quick brush-off, mumbling his obligations to his fledgling career, bade her a trite 'all the best' and hung up.

She'd deserved better.

And now, discovering how much she'd invested in them back then opened up an old wound thought healed. At best, he owed her an apology.

Swiping a weary hand across his face, he turned back, hoping she'd hear him out.

When he reached the beach, she'd vanished. Following her footprints in the sand, he picked up the pace, finally catching her near a rocky outcrop overlooking Sydney city in the distance.

'Krissie?'

She turned, her mutinous expression at odds with the tracks of dried tears running in parallel lines down her cheeks, and something inside him broke.

Even when he'd dumped her on the phone, she hadn't cried. Called him a few choice names, but not a hint of a sob in sight. She'd let him off the hook easily, too easily. Time to make amends.

Wrapping her arms around her middle—to ward off the cold or him, he wasn't sure—she thrust her chin up in defiance.

'Figured it out already, huh?'

'You said I was a smart guy. Why do I feel so dumb?'

She didn't budge an inch, remote, unobtainable, as he silently called himself every kind of fool for hurting this special woman.

'You tell me.'

He took a step forward, held out a hand, which she ignored.

'I owe you an apology.'

'For?'

Damn, she was magnificent. From the top of her wind-tousled wild hair to the bottom of her inappropriately designer-clad feet, every inch of her screamed pride.

She wouldn't let him off easy this time. Uh-uh, this time she'd make him grovel.

'For being a coward. For being dense. For treating you appallingly when we broke up.'

Her mouth softened a fraction and he pushed the advantage.

'I could use the excuse I was young and stupid but the truth is, no matter how brilliant we were together back then, I would've run from commitment. It just wasn't the right time.'

Understanding shone from her eyes, blazing with a jumble of emotions he had no hope of deciphering.

'You weren't the only one who was young and stupid.'

Her arms fell to her sides, her shoulders relaxed and loose. 'That horribly cringe-worthy ultimatum I gave you was just plain wrong. I put you in an impossible position.'

'Yeah, you did.'

He tempered his comment with a soft smile, buoyed when she smiled right back.

'I'm sorry, Krissie. Forgive me?'

This time, he wouldn't offer her his hand in the hope she'd take it. Instead, he snagged her hand, held on tight despite her slight tug of resistance.

'I'll think about it.'

His smile widened. 'Good. While you're thinking about it, want to take a walk?'

Kristi fell into step beside Jared, little rockets of sensation shooting up her arm and into orbit the harder he squeezed her hand.

They shouldn't be doing this, strolling along a moonlit beach, hand in hand. It reeked of romance and she'd given up on that with this man a long time ago.

His apology had softened her, had gone some way to assuaging the resentment lodged in her heart, but she couldn't throw away all her reservations at once.

Jared wanted a fling.

He'd virtually said as much with all that talk of sexual attraction and possible flings. All very cut and dried and easy for him; flirt a little, get physical, walk away at the end. As if she'd ever agree to that! Once was enough.

'I've been thinking about what you said.'

His low tone shattered the companionable silence, shattered the illusion that for a moment they were two people in perfect sync taking a lovely stroll along a deserted stretch of sand.

'Yeah?'

He stopped, leaving her no option but to do the same, giving her opportunity to slide her hand out from his, and she took it.

'About me being invested in the rec centre.'

'And?'

'You're right.'

He shook his head, his tortured expression revealing he was none too pleased with the admission. 'It was about the money at first, giving something back. But seeing all those partially disabled kids in rehab, then the street kids around the Cross when I was scoping sites, really got to me.'

'That's nothing to be ashamed of.'

She touched his arm, trying to convey her admiration, her respect. Many sporting stars financially supported kids' foundations but not many took the time to attend personally, let alone spend a week on a deserted island for publicity.

Pain contorted his features before he carefully blanked them, forced a smile.

'We're just full of confessions tonight.'

It was her turn to feel uncomfortable. He might have unburdened himself, but she still had a few secrets up her sleeve, secrets she had no intention of confessing.

'I'm glad you can talk to me.'

She held her breath as he reached out, his fingertips grazing her cheek in the softest caress. 'I always could.'

But you still left anyway.

It would always come back to that. No matter what he said now, or how far she was willing to forgive him, she could never forget the fact he'd left her.

Battling a surge of heat to her cheeks, she shrugged and turned away on the pretext of staring at the view of Sydney in the distance.

'I guess some things don't change.'

He touched her shoulder and she clamped down on the urge to lean into him. 'We've both changed. Maybe the real question is have we changed enough to move on from the past?'

He used the royal 'we' when he meant her. Had she changed enough to move on from the past, from what they'd shared, from what they'd lost?

Taking a deep breath, she met his curious gaze head-on. 'Honestly? I don't know.'

'Okay, then.'

She had no idea if he'd agreed with what she said, if he was okaying her right to be honest or her right to indecision.

What she did know was the longer they stood here, almost toe to toe, tension crackling between them, the harder it was for her to not say 'screw the past' and jump feet first into the present.

His gaze slid to her lips, lingered, and she inhaled sharply, her lips tingling with expectation.

'Have you figured out what you want?' she blurted, her insides trembling along with her resolve as he leaned towards her, inch by exquisitely torturous inch, lowering his head, the heat radiating off him scorching.

Her eyelids fluttered shut, her head tilting ever so slightly to receive his kiss.

When he rested his forehead against hers and murmured, 'Damned if I know,' she couldn't agree more.

Twitter.com/Stranded_Jared
Get me out of here.

Twitter.com/Stranded_Kristi
Have really started to dig this place. Purely for the scenery, of course.

CHAPTER NINE

Stranded *Survival Tip #9*
Want to humiliate him on camera? Ask him to hold your purse.

KRISTI'S BLOG, DAYS 4–5
Elliott will be lapping this up. Jared has ensured we spend every waking hour in front of the cameras the last two days. An avoidance technique, obviously. Doesn't want a repeat of our little confrontational conversation during the camping challenge. Might start calling him Ostrich Boy...burying his head in the sand and all that.

What he doesn't understand is that he can't avoid me for ever. And the cameras are on timers so if I plan my ambush just right...he doesn't stand a chance.

That, or hog-tie him and drag him to the camera-safe locations on the island.

Of course, I'd get the whole tying-up thing on camera first. Wouldn't that make for interesting TV? Would definitely score points in the prize-winning stakes.

He may have the muscles to erect a tent better than me

but I definitely nailed the swimming challenge. And I caught five fish to his measly two in the fishing challenge.

I rock!

Show me the money!

JARED'S BLOG, DAYS 4-5

Only two days to go.

I've made it through Wimbledon semi-finals with back spasms.

I survived a five-set marathon to win the US Open, twice.

I can do this!

(By the way, aren't girls supposed to be squeamish about baiting hooks with live bait? Can't believe she out-fished me! I'd rather lose the hundred grand than let the boys discover I got whipped with a rod by a girl!)

IT WASN'T in Jared's nature to sulk. But that was exactly what he'd been doing since that little revealing chat with Kristi two days ago.

She'd loved him.

And he'd broken her heart.

He'd seen it in her wounded expression, the vulnerable glimmer in her eyes, and the more she'd pushed him for answers he couldn't give, the more he'd rebelled, desperate to push her away.

Hell, if he'd known how cut up she was about their break-up he never would've agreed to have her here on the island. He would've made Elliott choose an unknown, someone he had no hope of sharing a spark with.

And that was what annoyed him the most; the fact that all the denials in the world didn't change the fact that he was still attracted to her.

Just attracted?

Therein lay the kicker.

As long as he convinced himself it was a purely physical thing, an attraction for a beautiful woman, he could handle this, though deep down he knew better.

He might have grown up avoiding reality, doing his best to lose himself in tennis, but the longer he spent with Kristi, the longer he got to hear her sweet laugh and spar with her and try to elicit those amazing, uplifting smiles she did so well, the harder it was to deny the truth.

That she was right.

He was invested.

And not just in the rec centre.

'You ready to go down in another challenge?'

He stopped, wiggled his backpack higher, hands on hips. 'You just got lucky.'

She held up her hand, counted off her triumphs. 'In the water. While fishing. About to add reaching the top of this mountain first.'

'You think?'

'I know.'

Her self-righteous smirk had him wanting to cross the short distance between them and kiss that smug smile right off her gorgeous face.

'Pride before a fall and all that.'

She waved away his corny cliché. 'Let's just get this show on the road so I can cement my place as the virtual winner.'

He laughed at her audacity, a small part of him hoping she'd win. If he won he'd planned on donating the money to the centre anyway and in the grand scheme of things it wouldn't make much difference considering how much he'd already invested.

But for her to be here, putting up with everything he threw at her, she must really want the money, bad.

He shifted, winced at a slight stab in his reconstructed knee, unprepared for her quick shift from cocky to concerned, the flare of pity in her eyes obvious as her gaze zeroed in on his leg.

'You sure your knee can hold up to this?'

'I'm fine.'

His annoyed grunt could've been misconstrued for pain, but the only ache giving him any grief was the one in the vicinity of his heart.

He'd tried to stay away from her the last few days, tried to ease back into polite small talk and away from anything too personal, but, damn, he missed their closeness, missed seeing her tentative smiles as she slowly opened up to him again.

She narrowed her eyes, dropped her gaze to his knee before pinning him with an accusatory glare.

'Make sure you tell me if you need to rest.'

Hitching his backpack higher on his shoulders, he said, 'You'll be the one begging for a rest.'

Her mouth twitched at his quip as he silently pleaded for one of her brilliant smiles.

'You sportsmen are all the same.'

She fell into step beside him, trudging up the gentle incline, the twang in his chest having little to do with the increasing gradient and more to do with her being involved with other sportsmen.

'Speaking from personal experience?'

'Uh-huh.'

She didn't elaborate, tugging her ghastly floppy flamingo-pink hat lower so he couldn't see her face bar a few shadows.

'Pros?'

His fingers dug into the straps anchoring his backpack, the

thought of Kristi anywhere near some of the sleazebags he'd toured with making him want to punch the nearest tree.

He only just caught her mumbled, 'More like amateurs.'

He should leave well enough alone, had no right to delve into her past. But some curious demon egged him on, demanding answers he knew he wouldn't like.

'Old boyfriends?'

'Old fiancés.'

Her feet picked up speed while he stood rooted to the spot, shock ricocheting through him.

'Whoa!'

She stopped, turned, her face in shadow. 'What? You need a rest already?'

Broaching the short distance between them, he whipped off her hat.

'What I need is to hear more about these fiancés, *plural*?'

She shrugged, her expression carefully blank. 'I was engaged. Twice.'

She said it as if she'd been to the grocery store, twice, as if it was of little importance, a mundane occurrence, as boring as picking up a loaf of bread.

While he still reeled from the shock she snatched her hat out of his hand, rammed it back on her head.

'Any other questions?'

'Why didn't you go through with it, both times?'

He held his breath. What was wrong with him? Did he expect her to say because of him? Did he want her to?

That would be a bloody nightmare, something he couldn't bear to have on his conscience: that she'd once cared so much for him she couldn't go through with a marriage to another guy.

'You really want to know why?'

She flipped the brim back on her hat, raised an eyebrow in challenge, as if taunting him to admit the truth.

That while he wanted to hear her answer, it also terrified him.

Squaring his shoulders, he nodded. 'Wouldn't have asked if I didn't.'

Staring directly into his eyes, she said, 'With Avery and Barton, I mistook caring for love. And I'd never settle for anything but love. An all-consuming, blinding, passionate, no-holds-barred love.'

The scoffing sound he made had her smiling, a smug, patronising smile, as if she pitied him.

'Let me guess. You don't believe in it.'

'Damn straight. No such thing.'

Shaking her head, she said, 'I've seen it firsthand. Believe me, it exists.'

And he'd seen the exact opposite firsthand: a bitter, twisted version of the embroidered emotion love, the likes of which still left him reeling and avoiding it at all costs.

He waved away her explanation. 'Where? With your friends? People think they're in love, go all soft and soppy, spouting it to anyone who'll listen, but behind closed doors they probably hate each other's guts and take it out on those around them.'

Something in his voice must've alerted her he spoke from experience as he silently cursed his wayward tongue.

This was about her, damn it, not him.

'You never talk about your past.'

Yep, she'd honed in on the one area that was off limits, to everyone.

'There's a reason why it's called the past. It needs to stay there.'

This time he kept walking, leaving her standing in the dust, but not for long. He should've known she wouldn't give up so easily.

'My parents had the perfect marriage.'

'No such thing as perfect.'

He didn't break stride, ignoring the twinge of guilt as she all but ran to keep up with him.

'Their love was amazing. Eyes only for each other. Totally besotted. It's the type of love I want.'

'Good luck with that,' he said, all this talk of love and marriage almost as unpalatable as the thought of her loving two jerks called Avery and Barton enough to want to marry them.

'What about you?'

'What about me?'

'Any special someones over the last eight years?'

'Nope.'

'Too bad.'

He heard the underlying hint of glee in her tone, stopped and faced her.

'You sound happy about that.'

'None of my business.'

She waved a hand in front of her face, as if shooing a fly.

'Bet you would've been jealous if I had been.'

The amusement in her eyes faded, her mouth drooped. 'We've already established I cared back then. What do you want to do, ram the point home?'

'Hey, I was joking.'

He laid a hand on her arm and she shrugged it off, stepped away.

'Yeah, that's you, a regular joker.'

She stormed ahead, leaving him more bewildered than ever. *Women.*

If they didn't have to reach the top of this hill to complete the hiking challenge and do a bit of preening in front of the cameras, he would've headed back to camp.

As he contemplated doing just that a scream pierced the air and his heart stopped as he saw the most infuriating woman on the planet go down in a heap ten metres ahead.

'Krissie!'

His knee gave a protesting twinge as he dumped his back-pack and sprinted to where she'd gone down in an ungracious crumple. 'You okay?'

Sending him a withering glare, she winced as she moved her leg.

'Do I look okay?'

'Here, let me help.'

'Don't touch it!' She screamed as he reached out to assist her up.

'Your knee?'

'Ankle,' she snapped through gritted teeth, pain twisting her mouth, her face pale.

'I need to check it out.'

'Let me guess. You can add medico to your many talents.'

'That's Dr Malone to you,' he said, relieved when his lame humour elicited a wan smile. 'Where does it hurt?'

'Here.'

She pointed to the outside of her ankle, sporting a sizeable swelling already.

'Can you point your foot?'

She managed some degree of movement, cringing. 'Hurts like the devil.'

'Side to side?'

She cried out as she inverted her foot, made a grab for it and he stilled her arm with a touch.

'You've strained your lateral ligaments.'

His fingertips traced the swelling, gently probing, as he watched her face for reaction. 'Not broken, thank goodness.'

'Bet that would've sent Elliott's ratings skyrocketing.'

'Stuff the ratings. I'm more concerned about you.'

'Careful. Concern could be confused with caring. And we both know you don't do that.'

'You'll live.'

He released her ankle, ready to spring up and flee as he usually did when emotions entered the conversation.

But something in her expression, an underlying vulnerability, a valiant bravado as she struggled to hide her pain, had him sinking back down to sit beside her, his heart sinking along with his body.

He'd known it would come to this.

All his denials, to her and himself, stood for jack in the face of this woman and what she brought to his life and what she made him feel.

'What do you want me to say? That you're right?'

He threw his hands up in the air in surrender. 'Fine. I care, damn it, I care. Happy now?'

'Getting there.'

Her radiant smile reached out to him, touched him in a way he'd never thought possible.

'Admitting that doesn't mean—'

'Shut up, Malone.'

She placed a hand over his mouth, her palm begging to be kissed. 'Quit while you're ahead.'

What was it about this woman that made him forget everything, made him forget why he couldn't feel, made him forget the pledge he'd made all those years ago?

As her hand slid from his mouth, along his jaw, and came to rest on the back of his neck before she tugged him forward and placed a soft, tender kiss on his lips, he knew.

She made him feel like a better man.

When he was with her, everything seemed brighter and shinier and lighter. It had been like that between them eight years ago and not much had changed.

The connection they shared was way beyond physical attraction; exactly why he'd done his best to deny it.

What if he didn't fight so hard?

Would that be so terrible?

'Stop thinking so much.'

He smiled against her mouth, eased away to stare into her sparkling blue eyes. 'Shouldn't that be my line?'

'No, your line is "where do we go from here?"'

'Right.'

Despite the banter between them, she'd honed in on what he was thinking.

Where *did* they go from here?

They had one night and one day to survive on the island, before back to reality. Was he prepared to start a relationship when he knew it couldn't go any further than casual dating? Would Kristi be up for that?

Her admittance of feelings for him first time around and her recent revelation of waiting for the perfect love should be enough to make him swim back to the mainland.

It didn't need to be so complicated. He'd be upfront from the start so she'd be under no false illusions. They'd date, have fun, nothing too heavy.

But what if she didn't go for it?

'First up, we go straight back down this mountain so I can tend to that ankle.'

Her eyes narrowed, not buying his brush-off for a second. 'How exactly do you propose to get me down there? Piggyback?'

'One better.'

Before she could argue he swept her into his arms, hoisting her in the air as he stood.

'Put me down, you great macho idiot. You'll ruin your knee!'

'I've been lifting weights ten times heavier than you,' he said, tightening his grip behind her knees as she started wriggling. 'And quit that, otherwise I'll drop you, you'll bruise your butt, and I'll have to tend to that too.'

Her mouth opened, closed, her lips compressed while her eyes sparked rebellious fire.

'You're enjoying this.'

'Damn straight.'

He couldn't look her in the eye, what with her face—and lips—within kissing distance, so he tightened his grip under her knees and concentrated on making it down the hill with his precious cargo.

To give her credit, she stopped wriggling and tightened her hold around his neck and for a crazy second he wanted to hold her like this, protect her, cherish her, for ever.

See, he knew admitting he cared was a dumb idea. Now he'd acknowledged the chink in his emotional armour, who knew what else he'd be forced to admit?

Such as how dating would be fun but being truly involved, emotionally invested, could change his life.

'You can put me down now.'

Distracted by his worrying thoughts, he'd made it down the last of the incline and reached their huts.

'Not 'til I get you in bed.'

Her choked sound had him chuckling. 'So I can tend to that ankle properly.'

'No need to clarify. I knew what you meant.'

Bumping the door to her hut open with his butt, he backed into the one-room abode, careful not to hit her head on the way through.

He paused on the threshold, his chest giving a painful twinge at the irony of holding this woman in his arms as he crossed into a room with the intention of getting her to bed.

'Don't worry, there were no vows involved.'

Another thing that scared him. She could read his mind, always could, seemed to know him better than he knew himself.

'And there never will be, not in this lifetime,' he said, crossing the sparse room to gently deposit her on the bed. 'Now sit tight while I grab some ice.'

'Yes, sir.'

She saluted, her eyes twinkling, her mouth curved into a tempting smile and, suddenly, that ice wasn't a bad idea. Not for her ankle though. There were parts of him in desperate need of cooling.

'Lucky there are no cameras in here,' he said, rummaging through the mini freezer for ice, wrapping cubes in a tea towel and heading back to the bed.

'Nothing to do with luck.'

She winced as he elevated her foot with a rolled towel and settled the ice pack over the swelling. 'Having cameras out there for a few hours a day is bad enough. No way would I have done this if they were in my face twenty-four-seven.'

She shuffled forwards, rearranged the pillows behind her back, before sagging against the headboard. 'I'm not some media hound who loves the attention.'

'And I am?'

Shrugging, she plucked at the horrible brown chenille bedspread. 'There must be other ways to get publicity for the centre. Maybe you miss being in the spotlight?'

Silently cursing, he stood, started pacing the room, belatedly realising she was studying his every move.

Dropping into a chair nearby, he crossed his ankles, leaned back, hands clasped behind his head, his posture deliberately relaxed when nothing about this situation was remotely relaxing.

He didn't want to discuss how much he missed the spotlight or why. Kristi was too perceptive, too good at seeing right through him, and if he gave her a glimpse into his insight who knew what she'd uncover?

'You're in PR, you know what grabs kids' attention these days. Media. Social networking.'

'Hence our blogs and Twitter. Yeah, I get that. But why this? Why you? There must be directors and counsellors and any number of staff who could raise the profile. What do you get out of it? And don't tell me it's the prize money, because a hundred grand would be pocket change to you.'

The truth hovered on the tip of his tongue before he swallowed it, the lingering urge to unburden a sign of how close he'd come to blowing it.

She couldn't learn the truth, not all of it.

'Nothing too complicated. I just wanted to squeeze as much free publicity for the centre as possible. You know how much prime-time TV ads cost. Worth every second I'm here.'

'Very noble of you.'

Her eyes narrowed, assessing, and, while she didn't probe further, he knew by the astute gleam she hadn't entirely bought his story.

'Speaking of the cameras, we need to do a Twitter update. I'll grab my phone.'

Eager to escape, he strode to the door.

'Jared?'

'Yeah?'

With his hand on the doorknob, he paused, glanced over his shoulder, surprised by the vulnerable edge to her voice.

'Thanks for taking care of me.'

Thanks for caring about me, was what she really meant and, with a terse nod, he bolted.

Twitter.com/Stranded_Jared
Admitting the truth can't be good.

CHAPTER TEN

Stranded *Survival Tip #10*
Don't hang a 'Sex instructor: First lesson free' sign on your hut.

KRISTI'S BLOG, DAY 6
Hiking challenge didn't happen. Made it a quarter of the way up a very slight slope before my klutz gene kicked in and I fell. Didn't help my pride it happened while storming away from Jared in a huff. Though wasn't all bad. Got him to admit he cared. Shock, horror!

On the downside, that's another challenge I've fluffed so I'm two from four. For my newfound fans reading this, please don't bail now. I need your continued hits! Keep the faith. I'm going to win this comp if I have to swim back to the mainland to do it. Maybe could feed my opponent to the sharks while I'm at it?

JARED'S BLOG, DAY 6
So much for plan to keep distance from Kristi. While her sprain better, she's still hobbling around and I can't abandon her. Cooking her dinner at her 'place'. Will make sure she's comfortable then leave.

*Must repeat that last word several times for good
measure, for I'm having decidedly 'un-leave-worthy'
thoughts...*

'YOU make a mean grilled cheese sandwich.'

Kristi patted her stomach and Jared's gaze followed the
movement, lingered, before he leapt from the table on the
pretext of clearing dishes.

'I'm a man of many talents. Didn't you know?'

She grunted a response and he wondered what it would
take to get her to lighten up.

He'd been cheerful over dinner, flippant, had aimed for
casual, fun, wanting to give her a glimpse of how good they'd
once been together without all the heavy stuff they'd discussed the last few days.

For he'd come to a decision while he'd carried her down
that mountain.

He'd already admitted he cared.

He enjoyed being with her.

He wanted to get to know her again, to date when they got
back to Sydney.

But how to convince her when he'd done everything in his
power while on the island to hide the real him, to evade her
questions, to keep up the pretence that he hadn't changed
from that young, fun-loving guy?

He had one night left. He'd make it count if it killed him.

While he rinsed the dishes, she wriggled around on the
hard wooden dining chair, tentatively moving her ankle
propped on another. Thanks to regularly changing ice packs
and elevating it, the swelling had decreased significantly.

She could probably hobble on it, but with him attending to
her every whim, where was the fun in that?

Sneaky? Too right. He liked having her dependent on him,

having her ask him for help. It soothed his macho soul and went a small way to making up for the last few days.

Another reason he wanted tonight to be special. He had no idea where things stood between them once they returned to Sydney and if the next twenty-four hours were all he had with her, if she didn't go for his dating plan, he'd make every second count.

Stacking the dishes on the side sink, he dried his hands, bending over to grab a tea towel to do so, and heard a muffled groan.

Maybe she was in more pain than she'd let on. Yet when he straightened, turned, her gaze hastily shifting from his butt, he knew her sound had more to do with the tension buzzing between them than any sprain.

Good, time to liven things up a little. Grinning, he thrust his hands into his pockets and leaned against the sink.

'Fancy dessert?'

'What's on offer?'

He watched her eyes widen as she focused on his naughty smile as he pushed off the sink, crossed the small room to squat beside her chair.

'What do you want?'

Her fingers clung to the edge of her chair as he willed her to release them and reach out to his forearm resting near her bare thigh.

Static electricity crackled between them as he shifted a fraction, brushed her thigh, her slight jump nothing on the kick-start to his libido.

He held his breath, wishing she'd take a chance, wanting her to make the first move. After all he'd done in the past, all they'd been through, he couldn't push her; it wouldn't be fair.

'Got any more of that Swiss chocolate?'

'Sure.'

He stood and turned away, disappointed. Then again, what did he expect? For her to forget how he'd treated her and come back for seconds?

'Back in a sec.'

'Okay.'

There was something in her voice…a hint of mischief…and as he paused at the door, shot a quick glance over his shoulder and caught her perving on his butt again, he knew it was time to re-evaluate the situation.

Maybe Kristi wasn't so indifferent to the idea of making this night special?

If that was the case, he had high plans for Miss Wilde and the fine chocolate when he returned. High plans indeed.

Jared thumped around his hut, grabbed his backpack and dumped the contents on the table. He'd clean up the mess later. Something he'd have to do with his life if he continued down this suicidal path.

Spying the chocolate, he left it sitting amidst the mess, jammed his hand through his hair and started pacing.

What the hell was he doing?

He'd played this game with Kristi before, pretending their relationship was oh-so-casual, deliberately ignoring the signs she cared too much.

That twinkle in her eye as he'd left her cabin proved how much she cared, for he knew she'd never consider getting physical unless she was emotionally invested.

She'd told him that first time around and he'd gone ahead and taken advantage of the situation, a young guy crazy for a beautiful woman. He'd kidded himself back then, ignored the signs she cared more than he did, content to coast along, have fun.

But he wasn't that young guy any more. He was wiser,

more mature, knew how much it must've cost her to finally let down her guard and give him that monkey-business look.

So where did that leave his plan to make their last night together on the island special?

Basically, he couldn't keep his hands off her.

She was injured, for goodness' sake! Yet he'd taken every opportunity to touch her, on the pretext of helping her.

Probing her ankle? Yep.

Scooping her into his arms to move her from the bed to the chair? Yep.

Skimming her shapely calf while settling her ankle on a cushion? Done that too.

Sick.

Now he had to march back over there and do it all again, helping her from the chair to the bed, tucking her in, making sure she was comfortable...

Two words stuck in his head, on repeat.

The bed...the bed...the bed...

He wanted to be in that bed with her so badly he ached.

But they hadn't talked yet, hadn't established boundaries about their new relationship and maybe now wasn't the time despite the urge to march back there and lay everything out. He wanted her fighting fit, in full possession of her faculties, painkiller free, so that she couldn't blame any misconceptions on a fogged head.

Listen to yourself. Making excuses for the relationship before it's even begun.

'It's what I do.'

Admit it. Kristi's different. You care. And that scares the hell out of you.

'Damn straight. I don't want to hurt her.'

Is she the only one you're scared of hurting? You're really screwed up since the injury and the fiasco with your parents.

'Shut up.'

Tired of arguing with himself, he snatched several Swiss chocolate bars and headed back to Kristi's hut.

He had no idea what to do about their situation but he'd been under pressure before, had always come out on top.

He'd figure it out. If not, he'd fall back on the old fail-safe that had got him through every convoluted part of his life.

Wing it.

'What do you think you're doing?'

Kristi, propped on her good leg, sent Jared a sheepish smile as he burst through the door. 'Testing out my ankle.'

'Testing my patience, more like it.'

He dumped the chocolate on the table and scooped her into his arms before she could utter a word of protest.

Not that she would have. She was enjoying this whole invalid thing far too much for comfort.

'You really don't have to carry me.'

As he smiled down at her, his face mere inches from hers, she tried to think of every sane reason why he shouldn't, for right this very moment she could think of nowhere else she'd rather be than in his arms.

'Would you rather I slung you over my shoulder like a sack of spuds?'

'Brute.'

'Hey, would a brute do this?'

He lowered her gently to the bed, placed a cushion under her ankle, arranged the pillows behind her, her heart careening out of control and slamming against her chest wall with him in such close proximity.

She knew what he'd do next.

Hand her the chocolate. Pass her the latest romantic suspense novel she'd brought. And leave.

Not while she still had a breath in her body. Staying aloof, maintaining a cool front, keeping her distance, had slowly but surely driven her insane.

She'd wanted closure when she first arrived here? She'd partially got her wish, with him apologising and acknowledging he cared. But as long as her body craved him, confusing her mind with mixed messages, she'd never have full closure, not the way she wanted.

So while he'd gone in search of chocolate, she'd searched her heart, her mind, and come to a decision. Only one way to get the closure she needed to move on with her life since he'd re-entered it.

Get him out of her system once and for all.

As he straightened she captured his hand. 'You're not a brute, far from it.'

His gaze clashed with hers, searching, wary, and she tugged so hard he had no option but to sit on the bed beside her.

'Krissie, don't go building me up into someone I'm not.'

'I'm not a naïve young woman any more. I know what I'm doing.'

His reserved expression softened. 'Do you? Really?'

This was it.

The point of no return.

Every tension-filled minute over the last week, every loaded smile, every flirtatious quip, had been leading to this and her body tingled in anticipation.

Releasing his hand, her fingertips trailed up his arm, across his shoulder, dipping between his collarbones, before resting on his lips, tracing the contours while she moistened her own with her tongue.

Sliding her hand around the back of his neck, she pulled him slowly towards her.

'I know exactly what I'm doing,' she murmured, a second before she kissed him.

His resistance was fleeting, the merest rigidity in his shoulders before his arms wrapped around her and he kissed her with as much passion, as much desperation as she reciprocated, a frantic, explosive kiss filled with hunger and longing and soul-deep need.

His lips left hers all too soon, trailing across to her ear, where he whispered, 'What about your ankle?'

'I won't need my ankle, unless you've turned kinky over the last eight years.'

His joyous laughter burst over her like a warm spring shower and she laughed along with him, their intimacy having more to do with the past they'd shared than shedding their clothes, a long, leisurely, exploratory process that left her trembling by the time they were naked.

'You're so beautiful.'

His hand hovered over her hip as he stared at her, his eyes gleaming with desire before he splayed his hand flat against her belly and she gasped at the heat from his palm branding her his.

'And you still have the power to drive me wild.'

As his hand skated across her skin, exploring, teasing, tantalising, she lost herself in the exquisite rapture, in the pleasure, in the absolute certainty that despite wanting closure, she'd just opened her heart to Jared Malone again.

Twitter.com/Stranded_Jared
What have I done?

Twitter.com/Stranded_Kristi
So much for closure. Start of a beautiful new…day.

CHAPTER ELEVEN

Stranded *Survival Tip #11*
Sharing the last piece of beef jerky is only polite.

> KRISTI'S BLOG, DAY 7
> *The last day on the island passed in a blur of interviews,
> cameras and fake smiles, when all I wanted to do was
> smile for real. In fact, from the moment I woke to find
> Jared's note, I couldn't keep the grin off my face. Then
> Elliott and the media descended and I didn't have a
> minute to myself. Worse, I didn't have a chance to talk
> to Jared in private. That's where the fake smiles came
> in. We acted very chummy, sparring with each other on
> camera, smiles firmly fixed in place. But what was he
> thinking? Really thinking behind that smile? I intend to
> find out. Today.*
>
> *Oh, and hoping my soldiering-on-under-duress rou-
> tine was enough to win the hundred grand!*

> JARED'S BLOG, DAY 7
> *Up and at 'em early this morning, in time for the media
> circus. Did the usual meet-and-greet stuff. Great pub-
> licity for 'Activate'. Looking forward to seeing what's
> been happening at the centre in my absence.*

* * *

'YOUR blog entries were short and sweet.'

Jared drummed his fingers against the table, reached for his latte, pushed it away again, his eyes firmly fixed on the door.

'I'm a bloke. What did you expect?'

Elliott's sly grin alerted him to a veer in topic he wouldn't like.

'Kristi's were interesting.'

'Yeah?'

He grabbed at the latte this time, gulped the lot, scorching his tongue in the process. Good, as he had no intention of discussing Kristi or what happened on Lorikeet Island with his mate.

'Now that you're back, maybe you should read them.'

'Too busy.'

He slammed the glass on the table, glanced at his watch, wishing he could beg off this post-island-wrap-up. He didn't want the first time he saw Kristi to be here, like this.

She deserved more. She deserved an explanation.

Or maybe that should be a clarification. For while they'd done the deed last night they hadn't had a chance to talk, really talk, about where things stood.

And that worried him. He didn't want her getting any crazy ideas.

He wasn't a complete fool. He'd seen the starry-eyed look in her eyes when they'd faced the media, had felt her subtle adoration like a hit over the back of the head with a tennis racket.

While his pulse pounded at the memory of their hot encounter, and the driving need to do it all again, he needed to set boundaries.

'Relax, she'll be here.'

His gaze snapped from the door to Elliot as he deliberately sat back.

'Of course she will. She's a professional.'

'Is that all she is?'

Sending Elliott a glare he'd used to intimidate opponents—considering his record it had worked most of the time—he folded his arms.

'Kristi's a trouper. She handled all those bogus challenges you set up for us, she acted accordingly in front of the cameras to boost *your* ratings—'

'What about when the cameras were off?'

Off camera had been the time he'd enjoyed the most, when she'd slipped off her bubbly PR face and relaxed into the lively, carefree girl he'd known.

He'd dated extensively over the years, had squired movie stars and supermodels and sporting legends to glittering affairs from Monte Carlo to New York, but none of those women could capture his imagination as much as Kristi Wilde in all her natural, vivacious glory.

Elliott held up his hand. 'On second thoughts, don't answer that. I can see your response written all over your face.'

Hoping like crazy his mate couldn't see half of what he was thinking, he deliberately relaxed his shoulders, uncrossed his arms.

'And what's that?'

'Tennis's notorious bachelor boy has fallen.'

'Bull.'

Shoving his glasses up his nose, Elliott leaned across the table, peered into Jared's face as if scrutinising a particularly challenging Sudoku puzzle.

'Nope. No bull. You get this funny look in your eyes whenever I mention her, then there's that goofy grin you had on the island this morning, and you're never tight-lipped about any of your other conquests—'

'She's not a conquest!'

He slammed his palms on the table, rattling the cutlery,

sloshing water from glasses, annoyed as hell at Elliott's knowing smirk.

'Well, well, well, I think your reaction settles that particular question.'

'Smart ass.'

Chuckling, Elliott flipped open his laptop. 'Smart? Yeah. An ass? Not so much.'

Elliott was right. He was the ass. And far from smart if he overreacted at the mere thought of Kristi being anything more to him than a casual girlfriend.

It had all sounded so simple when he'd mentally rehearsed how to handle this relationship. So why was he getting so hot and bothered now?

He'd survived being raised by two narcissists who made boxing championships look like toddlers sparring.

He'd survived being dumped at the tennis club from an early age.

He'd survived his career falling apart when he'd gone down in that twisted, tangled heap on Centre Court at Flushing Meadow.

Surely he could handle one fiery, opinionated woman, no matter how tempting?

'Don't look now but your *friend* has arrived.'

Elliott's not so subtle emphasis on friend earned him another death glare as Jared snuck a quick peek at the door.

So much for quick. The instant Kristi strutted into Icebergs, all legs in a tight black mini dress and killer shoes, a coy smile playing about the mouth he remembered in minute, erotic detail, he couldn't tear his gaze away.

She zeroed in on him, her smile widening as she raised a hand in greeting and something deep down, in a place he didn't acknowledge these days let alone indulge, twanged. Hard.

'She's great.'

'Yeah.'

He couldn't look away, mesmerised by the sway of her hips as she wound her way between the tables, hypnotised by the mischievous shimmer in her blue eyes, as if she had a secret and he was in on it.

Clenching his hands under the table, he inhaled, trying to stay cool when all he wanted to do was leap from his chair, vault the tables and sweep her into his arms.

'You should see the footage. Priceless.'

'Yeah?'

Jared couldn't care less about the documentary footage. All he cared about this very minute was having Kristi sit next to him, her seductive spicy scent enveloping him, reminding him of how close they'd got last night, how her scent had clung to him all morning despite an early shower to clear his head.

'Hey, boys. Haven't we done this before?'

She slid into a chair, dumped her monstrous handbag and signalled a waiter, ordering a soy chai latte while beaming at them.

He loved that about her. Her energy, her pizzazz, her zest for life.

His use of the L word pinged in his brain a second too late and before he could process it she clapped her hands together.

'So, Mr Producer, how did we do? And more importantly, who won?'

Elliott tapped his laptop screen. 'Pure gold. I'm almost done editing and splicing the footage, should have it ready for you to view tomorrow.'

She batted her eyelashes and something twisted inside as he registered Elliott's goofy expression. Not that he could blame the guy. He was only human and what red-blooded male wouldn't be affected by Kristi Wilde at her flirtatious best?

'As for the winner, I've tallied your individual site hits.'

Elliott paused for drama and Jared rolled his eyes.

Taking hold of Kristi's hand, Elliott bowed over it while Jared clubbed the green-eyed monster making him want to box his friend's ears.

'I'm pleased to announce that you, my dear, are the winner.'

Kristi's loud whoop had several nearby patrons craning their heads, frowns easing into patient smiles as they registered her infectious excitement.

'Bloody brilliant!' She pumped her fist in the air, the action drawing his attention to the black dress pulling deliciously across her breasts. 'Thanks so much.'

Elliott grinned like a proud benefactor. 'My pleasure.'

'Congratulations.'

She turned her triumphant smile on him and the impact slugged him all the way to his toes.

With a toss of her hair, she licked the tip of her finger and chalked one up in the air. 'Never in doubt.'

He chuckled, leaned towards her and whispered loudly behind his hand, 'I could've whipped your butt if I'd wanted.'

Holding her hand in his face, she said, 'Talk to this.'

Elliott joined in their laughter at the antics while Jared desperately tried to subdue the wave of longing swamping him.

Last night had achieved what he'd feared most. Opened his heart to Kristi all over again. Left him wanting more. Much more than what they'd shared last time.

'So where to from here? Are you doing a special preview screening just for us?'

Elliott blushed as she added a beguiling smile to the mix.

'And any family and close friends you'd like to bring along.'

Her smile slipped a fraction, but enough for him to recognise the loss of her parents must've hit her hard. Divulging their idyllic marriage to him on the island explained a lot. Her quest for love, for the perfect man, for marriage, all centred on what she'd grown up with.

Which went a long way to explaining his own aversion to the institution.

The marriage he'd been privy to was filled with screaming matches and vitriol and abuse; emotional, psychological, worse than physical.

His parents had been ratbags, certainly not cut out for parenthood and, while he acknowledged not every marriage was a trial, he'd seen enough to know the whole ''til death us do part' thing was not for him.

'I'll bring my sister, Meg, and my boss, Ros. They'll get a laugh out of it.'

Pathetically eager to bustle in on the conversation between the two, Jared leaned his forearms on the table. 'Surely my acting wasn't that bad?'

Her eyes twinkled as she turned towards him, the impact of her dazzling smile hitting him in the chest as only a smile from her could.

'Acting? You mean you were acting all those times you preened and ponced around in front of the cameras?'

She crooked her finger at Elliott, who practically fell over himself trying to lean across the table.

'Have you seen the part where he erected the tents? And gathered wood? And built a bonfire? True he-man stuff. All that posing and muscle flexing had to be staged.'

Elliott grinned, rubbed his hands together. 'You should see the footage now. I've added sound effects and music and—'

'Can you two quit it? You're giving me a complex.'

'That'll be the day.'

Her cute scoff formed her lips into a delicious pout, instantly transporting him back to last night and exactly what she'd done with those talented lips.

The thought had him reaching for his water and draining the entire glass in four gulps.

Elliott closed his laptop. 'Seriously, you two did a great job. Your blogs and Twitter updates have generated loads of talk and interest, so the public are hankering for our official screening next week.'

Elliott reached into his top pocket, pulled out an envelope, handed it to Kristi.

'Here's your cheque. Money well spent if I get another gong for the documentary and guaranteed funding for my next project.'

'Thanks.'

Kristi quickly slipped her cheque into the bag at her feet, but not before Jared had seen the sheen of tears.

Though she hadn't told him what she'd do with the money if she won, he'd bet she'd share some of it. She was that type of person, had a generous heart, a heart he had no intention of breaking this time around, clear warning they had to have a 'talk' before this thing between them went any further.

Sculling the soy chai latte that had been placed in front of her while they'd been chatting, Kristi leaped from her chair, hooked her bag over her shoulder and darted a quick glance at the door.

'It's been a blast, guys, but I have to get back to work.'

Not wanting to let her go so soon, not before they'd had a chance to talk privately, Jared stood.

'It's your first day back and almost four. Surely you can skive off the rest of the day?'

Annoyance contorted her mouth before she slipped a smile back in place. 'No, sorry, gotta go.'

Grabbing her arm before she bolted, he leaned down to murmur in her ear.

'We haven't had a chance to talk after last night.'

'Call me later.'

She tried to twist out of his grasp but he held firm. 'Are you okay? You seemed fine with Elliott but now—'

'I have to get back to work.'

He couldn't hang onto her without causing a scene and he reluctantly released her. Before she could take a step he swooped down for a snatched kiss, his lips meeting hers all too briefly before she stepped away, staring at him with bemusement, shock and just a little fear.

'I'll call you,' he said, holding her answering tremulous smile close to his heart.

When she'd gone, he finally registered he was still standing, while Elliot lounged back in his chair with an aggravatingly patronising smile on his smug face.

'Well, I guess that answers my question.'

Reluctantly taking a seat, he said, 'What question's that?'

Elliott's grin broadened. 'The one about what happened off camera.' He snapped his fingers. 'And the one about bachelor boy falling.'

'Shut up.'

Elliott toasted him with water. 'I won't say another word. Besides, you'll see for yourself once you take a look at the footage.'

Ignoring the niggle of foreboding he'd let on more than he'd wanted to on the island, Jared suddenly couldn't wait for the pre-screening of Elliott's masterpiece.

CHAPTER TWELVE

Stranded *Survival Tip #12*
The camera never lies.

> *Twitter.com/Stranded_Jared*
> *Good to be back to civilisation.*

> *Twitter.com/Stranded_Kristi*
> *Christian Louboutin, oh, how I love thee. Can you tell*
> *I missed my shoes?*

'SINCE when did you become addicted to Twitter?'

'Since the island.'

Kristi barely glanced at Meg as she slipped her mobile into her handbag, wishing Jared's last tweet had been more informative.

'So I have tennis boy to thank for moving you into the twenty-first century?'

'He may have had something to do with it.'

Along with fast-tracking her heart forward eight years and landing her right back where she'd been when they'd first met.

Star-struck. Mooning. Just a tad in love.

She'd had it confirmed the second she'd entered Icebergs

two hours ago, locked gazes with him and lost her breath. They'd only been apart a few hours and the heavy weight of missing him pressing on her chest had lifted the moment she'd seen him sitting oh-so-casually at the table.

It had little to do with a white polo shirt hugging a broad chest, muscular arm draped across the back of his chair or the model-handsome face that had broken hearts of sports fans across the globe, and everything to do with his sense of humour, his sense of honour, his sense of decency.

He made her laugh, he made her cry; with the yearning to get to really know him and, hopefully, keep him in her life this time. For ever.

'Did you two get it on?'

Used to Meg's bluntness, she picked up her sangria, raised the glass in her sister's direction. 'Oops. Did I fail to mention private details of my sex life on Twitter? Silly me.'

Meg chuckled, clinked glasses. 'Ah-ha! So there was sex involved?'

Kristi made a zipping motion across her lips.

Meg sculled half her glass, blinked her eyes at the sting of alcohol, before jabbing a finger at her.

'You better hope there weren't any hidden cameras in your room, that's all I can say.'

Dismissing her spurt of panic as irrational—Elliott would never do that to them—she sipped at her drink.

'Why not? After my documentary experience, I quite fancy a stint on YouTube.'

'You're insane.'

'Right back at you, sis.'

They grinned at each other, their closeness the one thing that had got her through their parents' death all those years ago.

The Bobbsey Twins, everyone had called them, and despite

their age difference they'd been best friends and confidantes from a young age.

It irked what her sister went through every day, all because she'd been foolish enough to chase the same dream Kristi had: craving the perfect marriage, the perfect man, the perfect life. Sadly, in Meg's case, the dream became twisted, leaving her abandoned and pregnant without a wedding ring in sight.

While Jared had broken her heart eight years ago, at least she hadn't been left to raise a baby. Prue was adorable but raising a child didn't fit into her career plans right now.

Thanks to her stint on Lorikeet Island she could now give Meg and her adorable niece some much-needed help.

Reaching into her handbag, her fingers clasped the crisp envelope, pulled it out and handed it over.

'Here. This is for you.'

'What is it? A summons?'

'Better. Go on, open it.'

Meg ripped open the seal, withdrew the cheque, confusion creasing her brow as she scanned it, her eyes widening as she held it up to the light, reread it.

'It has my name on it.'

'That's because it's yours, silly.'

Meg's mouth opened and closed several times, before she dropped the cheque on the table as if burned.

'Don't be ridiculous.'

Picking up the cheque, she unfurled Meg's rigid fingers and pressed it back into her hand. 'It's yours. For you and Prue.'

Giving her sister a hug, and swallowing back tears, she said, 'Take it, Megs. Give that gorgeous girl everything her heart desires.'

'B-but it's a hundred grand!'

'I had to go without Christian Louboutin's latest black ostrich sandal and pitch a tent and suffer a sprained ankle for that money so you sure as hell better use it. I don't want my short-lived television debut to be in vain.'

Meg clutched at the cheque, stared at it for an eternity, before flinging her arms around Kristi's neck.

'You're the best! How can I ever thank you?'

Squeezing Meg tight, she said, 'By being happy and continuing to do a fabulous job raising the cutest niece in the world.'

'I'll do my best.'

Meg hiccuped, sniffled, enough to set off her own crying jag.

'Hey, you're supposed to be doing cartwheels, not bawling.'

'Your fault.'

Meg pulled away, swiped at her nose, her eyes red and puffy. 'You sure about this? You can't use the money?'

'Apart from the promotion, the only reason I agreed to do *Stranded* was for a chance to win the money. I intended to give it to you all along.'

Kristi picked up their glasses, handed one to Meg. 'So drink up. And start planning. Maybe consider changing apartments? Invest some of it? An education fund? How about—?'

'Thanks, sis, I've got it covered.'

Kristi clamped her lips shut. 'I'll drink to that.'

As they sipped at their sangria and Meg's eyes took on a starry gleam, a tiny sliver of apprehension intruded on her magnanimous good feeling.

What if Meg chose to move interstate, where the rentals were much cheaper? Rosanna was a good buddy but she was also her boss and Kristi had held back on loads of personal stuff in the past, not wanting to blur the lines and appear unprofessional.

She'd handled both break-ups with Avery and Barton in the same way: thrown herself into work, attended as many PR parties as humanly possible, filled her wardrobe with new shoes and hung out with Meg and Prue on the weekends.

What would she do this time?

That was her real worry, the expectation she'd break up with Jared and would have to deal with the devastation alone.

The thought had her sculling her drink, her hand shaky as she replaced the glass on the table.

'What's wrong?'

'Nothing,' she lied, not wanting anything to mar Meg's happiness.

'It's tennis boy, isn't it? You never did get around to telling me what happened on the island, what with waving six figures around and distracting me from the goss. How did the closure thing go?'

'Jury's still out on that.'

She could tell Meg nothing, or she could give her the abbreviated version. 'He hasn't changed a bit. Still charming. Still gorgeous.'

'Still has the power to reduce you to mush.'

Kristi nodded ruefully. 'That too.'

Peering over the rim of her glass, Meg mumbled, 'You know he's the love of your life, right? And the reason you didn't hook up with banker boy and number cruncher?'

Kristi laughed. 'Wish you'd called Avery and Barton those nicknames to their faces.'

'I did. Didn't help them get the message though.'

'What message?'

'The one where they didn't have a hope of getting you up the aisle because neither of them could hold a tennis racket.'

'You're harping.'

'I'm also dead right.'

That was the problem. Meg was one hundred per cent right and now she'd finally admitted—if only to herself—that she loved Jared, she could see it so clearly.

She'd given her all to both engagements, had been emotionally invested, had wanted to love Avery and Barton with all her heart. They'd been great guys, cute and reliable and steady.

And not a patch on a charming, confident playboy tennis pro with a hint of something dark and dangerous beneath his smooth veneer.

Had she tried hard enough with Avery and Barton? She'd thought so at the time but something they'd both said niggled… 'Can any guy live up to your expectations?'

Maybe they'd got it right? Maybe she'd been subconsciously comparing them to Jared? Then again, Jared hadn't lived up to expectations either, dumping her in favour of his career.

She'd worked through her guilt at ending both engagements, had analysed them to death. Maybe this time round with Jared, she could put some of what she'd learned to good use?

'You need to talk to him, sis. Make it clear what you want from the start.' Meg patted her cheek. 'You don't get many second chances in a lifetime. Better make the most of this one.'

Kristi had every intention to.

When she plucked up the courage to tell him she'd been foolish enough to fall for him, again.

'You've been avoiding me.'

Kristi jumped as Jared whispered in her ear, taking advantage of their proximity, inhaling her sweet, spicy scent that evoked so many visceral reactions his gut clenched.

'Shh. The documentary's about to start.'

'That's not an answer.'

He vaulted the sofa and plopped into the empty space beside her, desperate to talk after reading her blog and Twitter entries from Lorikeet Island.

They revealed so much and after what had happened their last night on the island…yep, they definitely needed to talk.

'Should you be doing that with your knee?'

Flexing it to prove a point, he said, 'As I recall, my bung knee held up just fine on the island. It was your dodgy ankle that made you wimp out of the hiking challenge.'

'I didn't wimp out! I was injured, you unfeeling—'

He kissed her before she could say another word, a quick, brief kiss that barely lasted a second but enough contact to sizzle his synapses.

'That always was the best way to shut you up,' he murmured as Elliott strode into the room, closely followed by two women.

'You'll keep.'

She bumped him with her shoulder, shared an intimate smile that reminded him so much of the past his chest ached. They'd been in sync back then and he fervently wished they could slip back into an easy-going relationship.

After reading her blog entries, he didn't know what to think. One particular entry stuck in his head.

Problem is, have tried this before, eight years ago to be precise. Didn't work then, what makes me think it'll work now? He's closed up tight.

He cared about Kristi, wanted to give them a shot but if he didn't open up, tell her all of it, would she have a bar of him?

He'd spent a lifetime suppressing his childhood memories, channelling all his energy and frustrations into whacking a ball around a court.

He didn't know what he feared most. Feeling too much for her or opening up an old wound to find he hadn't healed at all. Or, worse, what she might think of him because of it.

They had to talk. When he'd called last night, she'd let it go through to her message bank, probably too physically and emotionally drained to face him yet. Not that he could blame her.

Spending the week with her had seriously disturbed his

equilibrium and he'd needed space to think, time to figure out what he wanted to say before blurting the truth and ruining any chance they had before they really got started.

Nudging her right back, he jerked a thumb at the two women standing in front of them, knowing grins making them look like twin cats that'd swallowed an aviary of canaries.

'Introductions?'

'Jared. Meet Meg, my sister.'

'Nice to meet you.'

He stood, shook Meg's hand and bent to kiss her on the cheek, a gesture that registered approval if Kristi's wide grin was any indication.

'Krissie's told me a lot about you.' Meg smirked, and Kristi shook her head in warning, only serving to stir Meg up. 'Your past together and—'

'And this is Ros, my boss.'

He laughed at her diversion, sending her a wink for good measure.

Pumping his hand, Rosanna pursed her Botoxed lips. 'If you're ever in need of a new PR firm, you know who to call.'

By the predatory sparkle in Rosanna's greedy gaze, PR wasn't the only reason she hoped he'd call. While he hated the term 'cougar' for older women dating younger men, there was something about Rosanna and the way she eyeballed him as prime devouring material that made the analogy apt.

'Thanks, I'll keep that in mind.'

He pulled out nearby chairs for Meg and Rosanna before resetting beside Kristi, his thigh brushing hers, the heat radiating from it sending an answering spark through his body.

Leaning across to whisper in her ear so the others couldn't hear, he said, 'What did you think of my blogs?'

'Typical.'

'Of what?'

She turned her head slightly, caution deepening her eyes to sapphire. 'Of you bolting from anything resembling emotion.'

'Ouch.'

He clutched his heart, faked a smile when in fact her comment hit too close to home.

'But, hey, nothing I didn't know already, right?'

Her light tone hadn't changed but there was something in her eyes, a hint of vulnerability bordering on hurt that made him want to snatch her into his arms and never let go.

'Yours were rather revealing.'

She quickly averted her gaze as a blush stained her cheeks. 'Really? I didn't think they said much.'

'Oh, they said plenty.'

'Maybe you read too much into them?'

Unable to resist teasing her, he ran a fingertip across her collarbone, delighting in the instant pebbling of her skin beneath his touch.

'That's something I'd like to find out,' he murmured, brushing a soft kiss against her cheek.

'Ready?' Elliott rubbed his hands together, glanced at his captive audience, while Jared straightened, then sneaked a hand across and squeezed Kristi's knee in reassurance.

'Later,' he mouthed, relieved when she nodded and placed her hand on top of his.

Rosanna called out, 'Roll the tape, maestro,' as Jared slung an arm over the back of the sofa, his fingertips brushing Kristi's left shoulder, the soft smooth skin beckoning him to continue his exploration, sending blinding need pounding through him.

She leaned into him, snuggling, and as he tightened his grip he wondered what took him so long to figure out this felt right.

As their faces filled the projector screen Elliott had set up for the preview his contentment received a serious jolt.

There she was, on the first day, staring up at him as the boat pulled away, stranding them on Lorikeet Island.

And there he was, looking down on her, his adoring expression so open, so revealing, it snagged his breath in his lungs and held it there until he exhaled in a panicked whoosh.

Heck, if his feelings were that obvious—on the first day!—what would the rest of the documentary reveal?

Over the next hour he sat there, mortified with every passing minute, wondering if the public would see past her initial prickliness, her reticence, the arguments, his jokes, his deliberate flirting, and see what he saw.

A guy in love.

A guy so obviously in love he'd let the whole world know before telling the woman in question.

As the final credits rolled, and Meg and Rosanna hooted, whistled and broke into spontaneous applause, Jared removed his arm, sat up and stared straight ahead, his back ramrod straight, his face deliberately expressionless.

Hell.

Elliott switched on the lights, worry lines creasing his brow. 'Well, what do you think?'

'It's fantastic!'

Meg gave a thumbs-up of approval while Rosanna's eyes glittered with triumph.

'Pure gold,' Rosanna said, leaping up from her chair to grab Elliott's arm. 'Would you like me to put a PR package together for you? Because we're doing one for Channel Nine's new show shortly and…'

He tuned off, his senses on high alert, his attention focused on the woman beside him who hadn't said a word.

Picking up on the tension, Meg cast a worried glance their way before heading for the kitchen. 'I'll grab the pitcher of margaritas. Back in a minute.'

Jared didn't move, bracing his elbows on his knees, leaning forward, his gaze riveted to the screen, shell shocked.

After what seemed like an eternity, Kristi spoke. 'What did you think?'

He blew out a long, low breath, before finally turning to face her.

'I think we need to talk.'

'You're giving me the 'we need to talk' line?'

Her anger spiked in a second, her lips compressed, her eyes flashing fire, as he silently cursed his inability to comprehend what he was feeling let alone communicate it to the woman he loved.

The woman he loved.

Hell.

'I wanted to talk yesterday but you gave me the brush-off. Then last night you didn't answer your phone.'

Straightening as Meg re-entered the room and cast a curious glance their way, he lowered his tone. 'So, yeah, we need to talk. Whether you want to or not.'

Her shoulders slumped as she nodded. 'How soon can we beg off?'

Jerking his head towards Elliott, in his element surrounded by two beautiful women downing margaritas at a rate of knots, he said, 'Fifteen minutes should about do it for politeness. Then we're out of here.'

'You're on.'

Standing, Kristi headed towards the jolly threesome, while he sat there, stunned at what that tell-all documentary had revealed, trying to make sense of it all.

And wondering what the hell he was going to do about it.

CHAPTER THIRTEEN

Stranded *Survival Tip #13*
Falling coconuts not as dangerous as ones thrown at you in exasperation by fellow island inhabitants.

> *Twitter.com/Stranded_Jared*
> *Been kidding myself. About everything.*

> *Twitter.com/Stranded_Kristi*
> *If the camera never lies, maybe it should tell a few fibs.*

JARED knew this spot.

They used to come here all the time. Picnics by the harbour, wine at dusk, strolling along the water's edge hand in hand.

A good spot for what he had to say. If he could get the words straight in his head.

What he'd seen on that film hadn't just confused him; it had detonated every preconceived notion he'd ever had about love clear out of this world.

'I'm not interested in taking a stroll down memory lane.'

Jared stared out over Sydney Harbour, his gaze fixed on the lit bridge, his knee giving a twinge as he rocked on the balls of his feet.

'Neither am I.'

He turned to face her, hoping he didn't make a mess of this. 'I want to discuss our future.'

'Wow, that's a surprise.'

Kristi's voice held a dubious edge and he couldn't blame her. Last night, he'd been ready to lay it all out: them dating, having fun, nothing too heavy.

All that had changed since he'd seen Elliott's documentary. He could spout all he wanted about keeping their relationship casual, dating, hanging out, whatever he wanted to call it, but he knew without a doubt that however he dressed it up, Kristi would see right through him.

He loved her yet he didn't want to marry, ever.

Where did that leave him? Them?

What could he say without coming across as a selfish jerk who wanted her, just not enough?

If he hadn't seen the evidence with his own eyes, seen how much he loved her, sat through the excruciating hour of watching them interact on the island, his feelings etched on his face for the world to see, he wouldn't have believed it.

Though that was a crock and he knew it. There'd been signs on the island: the emotions she dredged up from deep within him, his admission he cared, the certainty that when she was with him, he was a better man.

All fine and good but if they reunited for real this time, she'd want more. She'd want it all, just as she'd hinted at when he'd walked in on her in that damn wedding dress.

He couldn't give her what she wanted and he shrivelled inside at the thought of breaking her heart all over again.

'Jared? About the documentary—'

'I know.'

A wary frown eased across her brow. 'You know what?'

'What it looked like.'

Even saying the words out loud squeezed his chest in a vice, tight, uncomfortable, strangling the very air from his lungs.

'Like…?'

'Don't.'

He held up a hand, jammed the other through his hair. 'We know each other too well to play these games.'

'I'm not—'

'I looked like an idiot.'

He pronounced it like a terminal condition. Exactly how he viewed the ludicrous emotion and all it stood for: control, competition, callousness.

He couldn't love.

It wasn't in his genetic make-up.

His father didn't have it: he'd spent his life at his precious men's club, only deeming to acknowledge his wife and child to hurl put-downs or abuse their way.

His mother didn't have it: she'd slept her way through the bridge club, the country club and the polo club before he'd won his first junior comp.

And neither of them had had the remotest love for him. Until he'd hit the big time, though their fawning couldn't be labelled as anything other than what it was: two people trying to cash in on his fame, playing the role of proud parents when in reality they didn't give a stuff.

The closest he'd come to feeling anything remotely resembling the ill-fated emotion was with Kristi eight years ago.

But even she'd disillusioned him at the end, putting her wishes ahead of his, placing him in that ludicrous position by making him choose between her or his career.

'I think you looked fine.'

She sat on the concrete wall edging the path leading down to the harbour, her legs swinging, her face turned slightly to the right so he couldn't read her expression.

Reluctantly perching a foot away from her, he braced his hands on the wall.

'What do you want me to say?'

'Say what you think.'

He couldn't, not without telling her the truth about his past, not without revealing too much of himself and exposing a vulnerability he barely acknowledged existed.

'For goodness' sake, it shouldn't be this hard.'

She slid off the wall, dusted her butt off and swivelled to face him, her cheeks flushed, her mouth twisted in anger.

'What's going on with you?' She jabbed in his direction. 'We reconnected on the island.'

When he opened his mouth to respond, she jumped in. 'And I'm not just talking about the sex! You admitted you cared. It was plain to see on that documentary. So why are you freaking out? Don't you want to give us a go?'

'I did.'

Her face fell as his past tense registered.

'What changed?'

'Damn, this is difficult.'

He slid off the wall too, jammed his hands in his pockets to stop reaching for her.

'Just tell me the truth.'

Her soft sigh tugged at him, hard. She was right about one thing. He cared about her, more than she'd ever know, and he owed her some small snippet of the truth.

'When I said I wanted to talk last night, I wanted to see if you were interested in dating.'

The glimmer of hope in her eyes had him eager to finish the rest of what he had to say. 'Dating, Krissie, that's it. Nothing too heavy, too involved, just the two of us seeing each other casually.'

'Which means what?'

'Exactly that. Hanging out together, going places, having fun.'

Her eyes narrowed. 'Sleeping together.'

He nodded, hating how her less than impressed tone made it all sound so empty, so sordid.

'Just like old times.'

He knew he'd said the wrong thing the instant the words left his mouth, her chin tilting up as she glared daggers.

'Old times?'

Her voice ended on a shriek and she twirled around, stalked a few steps before turning around and marching straight back up to him, her palm slapping against his chest and shoving.

'You expect me to slip back into our old pattern, waiting for when you have a free moment to call, waiting for you to drop around any time of the night just so I can see you, waiting for whatever ounce of affection you throw my way?'

She laughed, a hollow, humourless sound that chilled him. 'I can't believe I've been so stupid. Again!'

'Krissie, it's just—'

'Save it!'

She shoved him again, dropped her hand, her head. 'Go.'

He couldn't leave like this.

'Let me take you home. We can—'

Her head snapped up, the sheen of tears slugging him. 'There is no we! Not any more.'

That was when it hit him.

After tonight, if he walked away from her, he'd never see her again.

Ironic, in putting her needs first—her need for a full commitment, her need for the perfect marriage she craved—he'd lose the only woman he'd ever loved, leaving a giant, gaping hole in his life, his heart.

Grabbing her hands, he tightened his grip when she tried to pull away.

'I don't know how to give you what you want.'

Something in his tone must've alerted her to the seriousness of his declaration for she stilled, her wary gaze scanning his face.

What seemed like an eternity later, apparently satisfied by his sincerity, she said, 'What do you think I want?'

His attention, his love, his ring on her finger. He could give her the first two; the last was non-negotiable.

'All of me.'

'Maybe I'd be happy with some?'

He shook his head. 'You shouldn't have to settle. You deserve more.'

'Spoken like every other guy trying to give a girl the old "it's not you, it's me" claptrap.'

Needing to convince her, needing her to hear him, really hear him, he said, 'Whatever happens between us, I can't promise I'll ever marry you.'

When her mouth drooped he released her hands, stepped away, hating the fact he'd made her look so sad.

'You want the perfect love. You said so. While I'd give anything to explore what we've restarted between us, I can't be that perfect guy for you.'

He rubbed the back of his neck. It didn't help, tension tightening his muscles to the point of migraine onset. 'There's no such thing as perfect.'

She didn't speak, her lips compressed, her eyes downcast, and when she finally raised them her wounded expression had him curling and uncurling his fingers to stop grabbing hold of her hands again and never letting go.

'Krissie, I'm sorry.'

'Not half as sorry as I am.'

He watched her walk away, clamping down on the desperate urge to run after her and take it all back.

CHAPTER FOURTEEN

Stranded Survival Tip #14
Find humour in watching your last bar of soap float away.

> *Twitter.com/Stranded_Jared*
> *Watch* Stranded. *Interesting doco. Gong-worthy. The producer rocks.*

> *Twitter.com/Stranded_Kristi*
> *Private screening party for* Stranded *debut cancelled.*

KRISTI stared blankly at the stack of glossy brochures for the latest mobile-phone technology on her desk. At the start of a PR campaign she'd usually scour whatever promo material she could lay her hands on, get a feel for what the client wanted then brainstorm, allowing her imagination free rein to create a whizz-bang public-relations pitch she could deliver with pizzazz.

Her job was to make the client look good. Pity she couldn't do the same for herself.

Glancing down at her drab navy shift dress and sedate pumps, she grimaced. She hated navy, hated shapeless shift dresses more. But this was her 'I'm having a bad day' dress and people knew it. They steered clear, exactly as she intended.

Being here was hard enough without having to field count-less inane questions about her time on Lorikeet Island; or, worse, her time spent with tennis pro Jared Malone.

She'd faced them all her first hour back: *what was it like being stuck on an island with a hottie? What did you do? How did you pass the time? Did anything happen off camera?*

Rubbing the bridge of her nose, she swung away from her desk, ignoring the stack of brochures in favour of the stunning Bondi view out of her window.

What was wrong with these people? Did she go around asking everyone how they passed the time with their other half or if anything *happened*?

Besides, they'd be able to see for themselves soon enough, considering her star-struck expression would be prime-time viewing for all and sundry this time next week.

Just one look and people would know exactly how she'd spent her time on the island: swinging between moody and resentful to mooning around after a guy who didn't want her for anything beyond *casual*.

'Good to see you hard at it.'

At the sound of Rosanna's gravely voice, she swung her chair around, hoping her smile appeared genuine.

While her boss hadn't said anything after the preview screening, she knew curiosity must be eating away. Rosanna was never backward in coming forward and would have a host of probing questions waiting.

Kristi tapped the mobile-phone brochures. 'Just thinking about a new angle for these.'

'Don't bother.'

Rosanna swept into the room, balancing a thick Manila folder in one arm and a soy chai latte in the other.

'These are for you.'

Kristi's eyes narrowed as she eyed off the latte. Rosanna

never brought her coffee, let alone her favourite; it was always the other way around.

As for the folder, more work. Goody. Might take her mind off the monstrous mistake she'd made in assuming Jared might actually feel something for her, that they might have a future.

Picking up the coffee, she sipped, sighed, savouring the delicious creaminess sliding over her tastebuds.

'Are you buttering me up for something?'

Rosanna perched on the edge of her desk, looking decidedly smug. 'Nope. It's a thank you.'

'For?'

'This.'

Ros tapped the Manila folder, her cat-got-the-cream smile widening.

'Remember that promotion I mentioned? All yours.'

'Really?'

In all the draining tension of the last twenty-four hours, she'd forgotten about the promotion. Once she'd handed the prize cheque to Meg, she'd been happy, her job done.

At any other time, she would've cartwheeled over her desk and high-fived Ros, but now, while she wanted to keep busy, the thought of extra workload merely added to the thick, leaden woolliness in her head.

'I mentioned Channel Nine's upcoming reality show, *Survivor* with a twist? Well, there's another twist. They're syndicating around the world.'

'Great.'

This would be a job opportunity of a lifetime, doing the PR for a project this huge. If only she could summon up suitable excitement.

'It is for you. You're heading to LA.'

'What?'

'You heard me.'

Rosanna slid off the desk, rubbed her hands together. 'A show over there went gangbusters courtesy of some top-notch PR. Channel Nine want you to check it out, do something similar here.'

Rosanna snapped her fingers. 'Did I mention all expenses paid?'

'Wow…'

She wanted to step up the career ladder, take her job to the next level, now she could. So why the fizzle of disappointment that gaining this promotion wasn't all she'd built it up to be?

'Tell me that glum expression isn't because you'll miss lover boy? You don't leave for a few weeks, plenty of time for a long, meaningful goodbye.'

That was when it hit her.

Role reversal. Last time, Jared left because of his career. This time, it was her turn.

She should be glad. She'd wanted closure, now she'd have it, once and for all. So why the uncertainty twisting her insides into a painful knot?

Rosanna snorted, held up a hand. 'Don't tell me. By that faraway look on your face, you're imagining all the ways to say goodbye.'

Wiggling her fingers, she twirled and marched to the door. 'I'm out of here. I'll email you all the details.'

'Thanks for the promotion.'

'You earned it, sweetie. Later!'

She had earned it.

Spending a week stranded on an island with Jared Malone, being filmed, allowing the world to see what a fool she'd made of herself…yeah, she'd definitely earned it.

Time to say goodbye to her past. Permanently, this time.

When she'd walked away from Jared last night, something inside her had broken.

He cared about her, was willing to have a relationship with her, but didn't want to marry her. Which ultimately meant he didn't love her enough, couldn't love her enough.

She should be grateful he was putting her needs first, had listened to her dreams for the perfect love. Instead, all she could think was, *What a damn waste.*

Now she was leaving and, while she'd had no intention of seeing him again after their D&M last night, this time she wanted complete closure.

On her terms.

She didn't want to spend the next six months in LA rehashing every word, every expression, of their last heartbreaking confrontation.

Uh-uh, this time, she wanted to go out knowing she'd slammed the door on any potential relationship between them once and for all.

Jared picked up the phone for the hundredth time that morning before slamming it back down.

He wanted to call Kristi.

He should call her.

Just to make sure she was okay.

Yet every time his finger had hovered over the numbers, he'd hung up, angry with his deliberating, furious with the constant twinge in his breastbone, compelling him to go to see her and apologise.

For what?

Not being able to love her enough?

Not being able to give her what she wanted, what she deserved?

Or for not being the type of man to take a risk on something—*someone*—with the potential to change his life?

He couldn't stop thinking about her.

He'd bounced into Activate at the crack of dawn, eager to bury his nose in work: ordering new equipment, ensuring the financial records were ready for a meeting with the bank, checking over the digital media package.

All perfectly legitimate stuff that could've been handled by the manager but, the more time he spent here, the more he realised the rec centre was more to him than a funding opportunity.

He wanted to be a part of it.

He understood these kids: where they were coming from, what they faced, what they were running from. He could make a difference, and not just with his money.

He had investments all over the world, had used his prize money wisely, but now he was here he had no intention of spending his retirement playing the occasional celebrity tournament or driving fast cars in Monte Carlo.

Sydney was his new home, was a good fit and he'd make sure every disadvantaged kid in the city knew they would always be welcomed at Activate.

Thinking of his involvement here brought him full circle back to Kristi. She'd been the one to open his eyes to his commitment to the place. She'd been the one to open his eyes to a lot of things.

Namely that he could love, despite long-term beliefs to the contrary.

So what was he going to do about it?

He'd rehashed their parting last night a hundred times in his head. Was he being noble in putting her needs first or was he running scared?

Scared of commitment, scared of the future, scared of loving someone so much you had to spend the rest of your life with them or shrivel up emotionally and die.

'Yo.'

Glad for the distraction from his circuitous thoughts, he glanced towards the door where Bluey slouched, his red hair bristling as much as his attitude.

'Hey, Bluey. Come on in.'

The sulky teenager didn't say a word, shuffled into his office and slumped into a chair.

Jared took a seat on the sofa opposite, glad he'd overseen his office personally. Kids wouldn't feel comfortable on the other side of a commanding desk and he hoped the modular lounge suite with comfy cushions might encourage them to heed his open-door policy.

He wanted to be available to anyone and everyone whenever he was in the centre, yet more proof of his commitment.

'Been reading your blog.'

'Yeah? What do you think?'

'Lame.'

Jared stifled a smile as he registered the first sign of anything but indifference in the boy's expression.

'Maybe you should watch the show next week. Might be better.'

'Whatever.'

Bluey focused on the rip in his dirty jeans, picking at the fray.

'Me and some of the guys want to shoot hoops. You have anything like that here?'

Wanting to punch the air in victory, Jared deliberately played it cool.

'Sure, any sport you're into, the rec centre can get equipment, set up courts, whatever you need.'

Keen not to lose the kid now he'd made his first overture, he stood.

'Want to check out the basketball court?'

Bluey glanced nervously around, as if expecting someone to appear out of nowhere and give him a clip across the ear. Poor kid. He'd probably had that happen a time or two.

'We can grab a soda on the way, and a ball, maybe get in a few practice shots?'

Bluey's eyes lit up and Jared drew in a sharp breath at the unexpected surge of emotion making him want to hug the boy tight.

'Okay.'

As he fell into step with Bluey Jared knew sticking around Sydney was the smartest decision he'd made in ages.

Now if he could only solve the dilemma regarding Kristi as easily.

The hairs on the back of Kristi's neck stood to attention as she walked quickly down Darlinghurst Road, staring straight ahead and blocking out the shouts from touts outside strip joints, the abuse hurtling between two homeless guys fighting over a half-empty beer bottle and a road-rage incident between rival bikie gangs.

She'd lived in Sydney her entire life but rarely ventured down to Kings Cross after heeding her parents' warnings of assaults, robberies and drugs.

The occasional visit had been in a big group of friends, usually to the bar with the best bands at the end of the road, and while she shouldn't feel this uncomfortable in broad daylight, she did.

All the hollow eyes peering at her from between buildings, bodies wedged into the darkness, as if waiting for nightfall to come out.

A loud cackle from a nearby doorway made her jump and, feeling decidedly foolish—and more than a tad nervous—she picked up the pace, rounded a corner and breathed a sigh of relief as she spied Activate, a nondescript building with a new whitewash.

Sitting on several blocks, the centre must've been an old

warehouse at one stage: high ceilings, sprawling buildings interconnected, large yard at the front.

Her first impression was welcoming as she hurried through the wide front gate, along a newly paved Bessemer path and up the steps to the double doors, which slid open soundlessly as she approached.

Jared must've spent a fortune on this place, she thought as she stepped inside, breathed in the pungent odour of fresh paint, polished wood and new leather.

The reception area, if one could call the informal entrance area that, consisted of several black and red leather sofas spaced around the walls facing each other, an antique trunk stacked with sporting magazines and a self-serve vending machine that looked as if it operated on a trust system, with a basket in front of it for donations.

While the place was empty, she could envisage it filled with kids lounging around, flipping through the magazines, mouthing off about who could do the biggest motor-cross jumps or do the biggest bombs into Watson's Bay.

The place beckoned, had a warmth missing in most kids' hang-outs, and if it could tempt a quarter of the teens off the streets of Kings Cross into here for even a short time Jared would be doing the area a great service.

Before she could head off in search of Jared, a small plaque tucked behind the front door caught her eye.

DEDICATION TAUGHT ME TO BELIEVE MIR-
ACLES CAN HAPPEN…IF YOU WANT THEM BAD
ENOUGH.

Kristi suspected Jared was referring to his dedication to tennis and, while that dedication had once ripped them apart, she agreed with the sentiment.

Miracles could happen if you wanted them badly enough: just not to her.

With Jared's recalcitrance and her promotion on another continent, it would take more than a miracle to get them back together. Like hell being covered in a layer of thick, solid ice.

Heading down a long corridor, she followed the sound of distant voices and a consistent thumping that could only be a basketball.

The corridor ended, opened out onto a huge indoor basketball court, the squeak of sneakers on floorboards drawing her attention to the far end where two figures shot hoops.

Her heart leapt at the sight of Jared, her predictable reaction having more to do with his patience in showing a young kid how to shoot hoops than his impressive physique.

Even from a distance, she could see the muscle definition in his legs, the tone in his torso, the strength in his arms as he lifted the ball overhead and lobbed a perfect three-point shot.

The kid applauded before snatching the ball out of Jared's hands, dribbling towards the hoop and executing an impressive slam dunk.

They high-fived, resumed positions and Kristi leant against the door jamb, content to watch the man she loved yet couldn't have exhibit yet another wonderful side to him.

Shame about that miracle because, right at that very moment, she wanted it so badly she ached.

CHAPTER FIFTEEN

Stranded Survival Tip #15
Scrapbooking may be fun, but choose the memories you
save with care. Glue lasts longer than first love.

> *Twitter.com/Stranded_Jared*
> *Check out Activate. Shoot hoops, cricket in the nets,*
> *hang out, whatever, it's cool.*

> *Twitter.com/Stranded_Kristi*
> *I'm leaving on a jet plane. Over and out. Definitely*
> *over, worse luck.*

'YOU were great with that kid.'

A genuine smile lit Jared's face as he grabbed a soda, handed Kristi one. Her favourite lemon flavour. Was there nothing he didn't remember about her?

'That's what this place is here for, somewhere kids like Bluey can hang out.'

'I'm not talking about the place.'

She slugged back her soda, locking gazes with him over the can, wondering why he could stand in front of the world and accept a Grand Slam trophy but was reticent to accept praise over a good deed.

Shrugging, he lobbed his empty can into a bin. 'I got to mingle with kids on the circuit. Loads of talented youngsters.'

'A bit different from the street kids around here, I'd say.'

'Kids are kids the world over. Give them a cool place they can blow off some steam, they'll be there.'

'Is that what you did as a kid? Pick up a racket to blow off steam?'

A shadow passed over his face before he ran a hand over it, wiped it clean, his expression frighteningly grim.

'Yeah.'

He didn't want to talk, that much was obvious. She would've ignored his reticence, stepped around it in the past and on the island, but now she had nothing to lose.

She was leaving, and she'd be damned if she went out on a whimper.

'How old were you when you started playing?'

'Nine.'

'Is that late for a champion?'

'Depends. Kids start learning at all ages. Guess I was a fast learner.'

He spun away, his strides long as he headed up the corridor towards what she assumed was his office. She fell into step beside him, her four-inch stilettos not made for power walking as she had to sprint to keep up.

'Hey, slow down a sec.'

He stopped so fast she almost slammed into him. 'Look, I'm really busy so—'

'Too busy to say goodbye?'

'What?'

Frowning, his mouth dropped open before he quickly snapped it shut in a thin, unimpressed line.

'I'm leaving next week. Thanks to our island jaunt I've got a promotion based in LA.'

'Congratulations.'

'Thanks.'

She hated this stilted conversation, wished he would sweep her into his arms and plant a huge celebratory kiss on her lips as he once would've done.

But their time for kissing was long past. They were over, finished, and this time she'd have the full closure she deserved.

'Look, we were friends if nothing else. We shared a past, we shared an interesting week on the island. I just wanted to say goodbye face to face, that's it.'

She didn't have to spell it out for him, a flicker of guilt clouding his eyes.

'You want the goodbye you didn't get last time.'

'Uh-huh. Is that too much to ask?'

'No.'

His gaze locked on hers, the intensity slamming into her.

She opened her mouth to respond, totally losing her train of thought as he stepped closer, her heart jackknifing at the proximity, recognising how much she'd miss him.

He caressed her cheek, the barest brush of fingertips against skin that sent a shudder of longing through her. 'So this is it?'

She managed to draw air into her lungs to form the words 'This is it,' her trembling body making a mockery of her response.

He hesitated a second before crushing his mouth to hers, the impulsive kiss every bit as wonderful, as wild, as unrestrained as she remembered.

She hadn't planned this as part of their goodbye, hadn't thought beyond a civilised parting enabling her to move on with her life, but as he backed her up against the nearest wall, deepened the kiss to the point of no return, she knew her quiet, polite farewell plans had just gone up in smoke.

When they came up for air she took a step back, needing

space to recover, needing air like a diver with an attack of the bends. 'You want the local kids to get some decent sex education too while they drop in?'

He muttered a curse. 'Lost it for a moment.'

'Guess we both did.'

Something she couldn't afford if she was to walk away from him, head held high.

Her first instinct to hold out her hand for a farewell handshake died at the confusion in his eyes, the pain mirroring her own, so she settled for a quick kiss on the cheek.

'Goodbye, Jared. I wish you all the luck in the world.'

While the logical part of her had already mentally rehearsed this goodbye, emotionally, the young woman who'd once loved him with all her heart wished he'd sweep her into his arms and never let go.

When he didn't speak, she turned and walked away, her heels rapping loudly in the silence, echoing the hollowness in her heart.

She'd done it.

Had closure.

So why did it hurt so damn much?

With tears cascading down her cheeks and rigid determination not to look back, she headed for the door, and missed seeing a world champion brought to his knees in defeat.

'I can't believe you're leaving.'

Meg scrubbed the kitchen bench with added vehemence, her pout reminiscent of the many times she'd tried to snaffle one of Kristi's Barbies and failed. 'And for six months! What sort of an aunt leaves Prue for that long?'

'An aunt cementing her career. An aunt hoping to fly her favourite niece over to Disneyland with the hefty raise she's getting.'

Kristi's dry response garnered the slightest smile from her sister.

'We can pay our own way, thanks to your generosity.' Meg's bottom lip wobbled before she clamped down on it with her overbite. 'But honestly, sis, I'm going to miss you.'

'Ditto, kid, but it isn't for ever.'

Unlike her break-up with Jared, the thought, sending a stabbing pain like a stake through her heart.

'Oh-oh.'

Meg ditched her cleaning cloth and flung open the freezer door, passing a tub of Turkish delight ice cream and a spoon.

'Here. Get some of this into you. It'll help whatever just put that look on your face.'

Before she could shovel the first spoonful into her mouth, Meg slapped her head, groaned.

'Tennis boy! How does your leaving affect things between you two?'

'It's over.'

Quickly spooning a mouthful of ice cream into her mouth to prevent talking, she waited for Meg to exhaust her indignation/advice/theories.

'Over? But the guy's in love with you! How could you break his heart like that?'

The spoon clattered to the floor as she gaped in shock.

'*Me* break *his* heart? Are you nuts?'

Shaking her head, Meg grabbed the tub out of her hands, rummaged in the top drawer for her own spoon, before digging it into the soft, creamy ice cream fast melting to goop.

'Tell me what happened.'

'Considering you're on his side, maybe I shouldn't.'

Stuffing a spoonful into her mouth, Meg brandished the spoon like a sword.

'Start at the beginning and don't leave anything out. Otherwise I'll stow away a week's worth of Prue's gym socks in your shoe bag.'

Unable to stifle a grin, Kristi folded her arms and propped against the kitchen bench.

'Fine. You saw how he looked on the doco. He's as smitten as I am. Then later, he gives me some spiel about wanting to date again but not being able to ever promise marriage, about not giving me what I deserve. Lame, huh?'

Meg tapped the spoon against her front teeth, the clatter annoying. 'Hmm…interesting.'

'What?'

Pinning Kristi with a probing stare she had honed to a fine art growing up, when she used to pester her with a thousand and one facts-of-life questions, Meg said, 'What are you afraid of?'

'Nothing.'

'Bull.'

Meg dumped the ice-cream container on the bench top and jabbed a finger her way.

'You must be afraid of something, otherwise why wouldn't you date and see where this leads?'

'Because I want to get married and—'

'Puh-lease! Aren't you a bit old to be hanging onto a pie-in-the-sky dream?'

Shaking her head, Kristi stared at her sister. 'What's gotten into you?'

Holding her hands palm up in surrender, Meg shrugged. 'I just don't want to see you throw something special away on a pipe dream.'

When Kristi opened her mouth to protest, Meg held up a hand. 'Uh-uh, let me finish. Last time you were heartbroken because he didn't love you enough. This time, he loves you yet you still don't want him. What do you want from this guy?'

'I want him to love me enough to give me the world!'

'Get real.'

Meg's cute little scoff would've made her laugh if she'd felt like laughing. As it was, she felt like strangling her relationship-guru-in-the-making sister.

'You're chasing perfect and there's no such thing as perfect.'

Meg gestured around her tiny cubbyhole kitchen, at the pile of homework books strewn across the table, the photos of her daughter in higgledy-piggledy disarray on the fridge, the stack of sporting equipment tumbling over itself near the door.

'This is what chasing perfect got me. You know that. So what are you doing? Giving up on a guy you've loved for ever because of some warped principle?'

Meg shook her head. 'Here's the thing. Not every marriage is as great as Mum and Dad's. They lucked in. Most don't. Surely I'm not telling you anything you don't already know?'

'Of course I know that,' Kristi snapped, hating how Meg sounded older and wiser while she sounded delusional for wanting something most people would class as unobtainable.

'Then what?'

Meg touched her arm, concern etched across her pixie features, features creased beyond their years, and suddenly she knew.

'I *am* afraid…' she murmured, the realisation flooring her.

'Of loving Jared? That's normal—'

'No.'

Kristi grabbed Meg's upper arms, not wanting to put her sister in any pain but needing to voice her fear if only to test it out, to see if it was real.

'Of making the same mistake you did.'

Meg rolled her eyes. 'You're too smart to fall for a dropkick let alone get pregnant by him.'

Kristi gave her a little shake. 'Don't you see? You were doing the same thing I am, chasing the dream, trying to have the type of relationship Mum and Dad had. You weren't to know Duane would be an idiot when you got pregnant and do a runner.'

'Of course I was chasing the dream.'

Meg shrugged out of her grip, dragged a hand through her messy hair. 'That's why I want you to wake up and not let this opportunity slip through your fingers.'

'But he could leave me again…'

'Ah…the real fear.'

Meg snapped her fingers. 'Newsflash. Relationships evolve. Change. Hopefully grow. If not, either of you can leave. Why put all that on him?'

'Because last time—'

'Last time you were both young, immature. He was a superstar with a brilliant career ahead of him. He was *always* going to leave. You knew that.'

Kristi's mouth dropped for the second time in as many minutes as Meg had the grace to look sheepish. 'I didn't say anything at the time because you were heartbroken and later it didn't matter, but now?'

Meg shrugged. 'Now, you need to stop blaming him for walking away and maybe start thinking about why he did.'

'You think *I* pushed him away?'

Stunned by her sister's revelations, she sank onto the nearest chair and rubbed the back of her neck to ease the tension.

'Did you?'

Kristi closed her eyes, transported back to her relationship with Jared, every fabulous, exciting minute.

Sure, she'd always been more touchy-feely than him, but that wasn't a crime. Nor was texting him and ringing him countless times a day; just showed she cared. They'd been besotted, couldn't get enough of each other, yet Meg was right. She'd known he'd leave right from the very beginning, had allowed her sadness and naivety to ruin their last week together.

She jumped and opened her eyes as Meg placed a hand on her shoulder, squeezed.

'How could you have done it differently? To help make it last this time?'

She'd do a thousand things differently: she wouldn't be insecure and immature, she'd be realistic, knowing what she was getting into at the start, accepting him rather than hoping she could change him.

She'd admired her mum and dad's marriage so much, and their relationship had been all about respect, mutual admiration, trust...

'I didn't trust him enough...' she whispered, the knowledge hitting her out of nowhere and making her want to thump her head against the table in frustration.

'I've been an idiot.'

Meg grinned and bent down to give her a hug. 'More like a fool in love. Twice!'

Returning the hug, Kristi pulled back to study her sister's face. 'How did you get so wise?'

Meg wrinkled her nose. 'Try enough self-analysis, after a while you become a know-all on relationships.'

Seeing the shadows shifting in her eyes, Kristi studied Meg's face harder.

'Do you regret your time with Duane?'

'Considering Prue was the result? Not bloody likely.' Meg's heartfelt sigh hid a wealth of emotions Kristi had no hope of tapping into. 'Do I regret being so narrow-sighted in wanting the dream the folks had I was blind to Duane's faults from the start? Hell, yeah.'

Kristi gnawed on her bottom lip, the truth behind Meg's wise words registering.

She'd been blind too, blind to everything but the truth.

She loved Jared.

Whatever he had to offer.

But now she was in a bind. Professionally, she couldn't give up on her dream promotion after she'd worked so long and hard for it.

Emotionally, she wanted to fling herself into Jared's arms and take whatever he could give.

Chuckling, Meg pushed her away. 'What are you going to do?'

'I have no idea.'

Despite everything that had happened, she still wanted that miracle.

Sadly, she'd given up on those a long time ago.

CHAPTER SIXTEEN

Stranded *Survival Tip #16*
When in doubt, run.

> *Twitter.com/Stranded_Jared*
> *Never look back.*

> *Twitter.com/Stranded_Kristi*
> *And they say girls are fickle.*

'ARE you and Kristi watching the premier together?'

Jared shook his head at Elliott, ignoring the jab of disappointment in his gut. 'Nope.'

'Why not? Trouble in paradise?'

Elliott's snigger faded as Jared shot him a death glare.

'She's leaving.'

Elliott's eyebrows inverted in twin comical commas. 'Ironic. Just what you did to her last time.'

His death glare didn't let up as his mate pronounced the fact he'd been pondering himself.

The irony wasn't lost on him either, though he'd been smart enough not to deliver her an ultimatum. Despite his newly awakened feelings for her, despite the urge to beg her not to go and give them a chance, he would never put her in a position to choose.

He knew how important her career was—hell, she'd spent a week on a deserted island with him for it!—and now it was taking off, he'd never hold her back.

Besides, he couldn't give her what she wanted.

She wanted a perfect love, a perfect relationship and, as he'd learned the hard way, there was no such thing.

What he still didn't understand was why she hadn't realised the truth either. She had two failed engagements to prove it, was hell-bent on following some warped idea that only the perfect man would fit her dream of matrimonial happiness, and if he didn't harbour his own doubts from watching his parents' monumental marriage stuff-up, he wouldn't put himself under that kind of pressure anyway.

What happened during their first argument, their first trial? Would she deem the marriage not perfect and bolt anyway?

Uh-uh, no way would he put that kind of pressure on himself. He'd be doomed for failure from the start.

Elliott stirred his double espresso faster. 'You've stuffed up again.'

'What do you mean again?'

Taking an infuriatingly long time to sip his coffee, Elliott finally replaced the cup on the saucer.

'Listen, mate, I didn't buy all that bull about you two just being good friends years ago and I'd be blind not to see what's going on between you now.'

Elliott steepled his fingers, pushed his glasses up with his pointed fingers. 'She's in love with you and you're just as bonkers about her.'

'Your point?'

'Do something about it.'

'She wants to get married, I don't, end of story.'

'Yeah, right, whatever.'

Amusement overrode his anger for a moment. 'You sound like Bluey.'

'The kid from the centre?'

'Yeah.'

Elliott stabbed a finger in his direction. 'See, that's what I don't get. You're prepared to invest in a bunch of kids who, let's be honest, might shove the whole thing back in your face, yet you won't take a chance on an amazing woman like Kristi?'

Elliott shook his head, resumed drinking his espresso with annoying calm. 'Seems pretty dumb to me.'

'Who asked you?' Jared muttered, stirring his latte so fast the froth spilled over the top and splattered on the table.

Wisely, Elliott kept his mouth shut, giving him time to absorb, to mull...

The kids were different. Taking a risk on them was easy because he didn't love them as much as he loved Kristi and the thought of losing her if he went the whole way and gave her what she wanted...

His hand shook so much half the latte joined the froth on the table.

No way.

The M word?

No. Uh-uh. Couldn't contemplate it.

'Why don't you just talk to her? Try to reach a compromise? Perhaps she isn't as hooked on this marriage malarkey as you think?'

His head snapped up to glare at Elliott but he'd resumed drinking his coffee, staring at the next table as if the Parramatta Eels cheer squad were sitting there.

Could he reach a compromise?

Was it possible?

Was he giving up on the best thing to happen to him because of some entrenched fear of an institution that might never eventuate?

She was leaving in a week. Was it long enough to convince her how he really felt, despite doing his best to the contrary all this time?

'I'm off.'

Grabbing his keys and mobile off the table, he saluted Elliot. 'Wish me luck.'

'You're going to need it,' Elliott called out but he'd already gone, eager to tell the woman he loved the truth.

All of it.

Jared sprinted up the last few steps and burst through the snazzy glass door of Endorse This.

His knee had to be at the end of its rehab for the workout he'd just given it; running up three flights of stairs to avoid waiting for the lift had pushed its limits.

He'd been like this as a kid with tennis. Once he'd made up his mind, he threw himself one hundred per cent into a project. His sporting career, the rec centre, Kristi…he just hoped she'd go for his plan.

The outer office was eerily empty, as was Kristi's front and centre glass-enclosed office, so he headed towards the lone voice barking instructions in a nearby room.

Sticking his head around the door, he saw Rosanna on the phone, her hands jabbing the air as she punctuated her points with someone bearing the brunt of her ire.

Cringing at her last particularly nasty outburst, he stepped into the conference room.

'Hope I'm not interrupting.'

Barely glancing his way, she waved him in. 'You've got two minutes before I blast the next slacker.'

'I'll only bug you for a second. Is Kristi around?'

'Nope.'

From meeting her at the preview, Jared thought Rosanna was a garrulous woman who couldn't shut up for more than two seconds, so her brief response puzzled him.

'Any idea when she'll be back?'

A strange smile quirked her red-slicked lips. 'In about six months, give or take.'

His gut twisted as the implication sank in. 'You mean she's left already?'

For a moment, he thought Rosanna wouldn't answer, her lips compressed into a thin, unimpressed line. Then the phone rang and she snapped, 'The LA TV execs wanted her out there ASAP so they moved her departure date up. She's leaving tomorrow but don't you dare do anything to muck that up!'

'Thanks,' he mouthed, as she'd already answered her call, and sprinted back to the stairs.

If his knee had been tested before, it would be pushed beyond limits now as he flew down the stairs, skipping every second one.

Not muck up her departure plans?

He intended to do that and more.

Kristi lovingly wrapped her absolute favourite Christian Louboutin's in a shoe bag and made space for them in her suitcase. Her monstrous suitcase. That only housed shoes.

Luckily she had a matching pair of cases, though she doubted the airline would be terribly impressed with her destined over-the-limit baggage allowance.

C'est la vie—a girl trying to make an impression in LA needed her shoes.

Satisfied she'd packed enough pairs, she flipped the lid, zipped the case shut, wheeled it towards the door and plonked it next to the other.

The two stood guard, like sentinels to her new life; a life that didn't include the only man she'd ever truly loved.

While she'd pondered the revelations gained from her chat with Meg, she'd done nothing about it. She could've confronted Jared but realistically what would be the point?

Could she enter a relationship without marriage being the end game?

She'd contemplated it for an entire night, not sleeping a wink, a million questions and scenarios playing out in her head. Yet when the sun peeped over the horizon, she came to the same conclusion.

She'd be setting herself up for further heartbreak, the ultimate fall, if she opened up to a full-on relationship with Jared knowing it couldn't lead anywhere.

During the long sleepless night, she'd thought about a lot of things. Her two cancelled weddings, the possibility she'd done the same to Barton and Avery as she had to Jared.

The admission didn't sit well with her, the thought she might have inadvertently sabotaged those relationships too.

Avery and Barton had been good guys: safe, steady, with dependable jobs, nice, the least likely to leave her. Exact opposites of Jared in every way. Looking back, she'd probably chosen them for that reason.

When Jared had dumped her and reports of his women started filtering through the magazines, she'd believed herself to be another conquest; he'd made her doubt her own judgement, had driven her to seek out men the opposite.

She'd stipulated long engagements both times, had gone out of her way to be demanding and fussy with the wedding plans. Both guys had been patient, which had only served to rile her further, a thousand and one small things piling up, niggling her, annoying her, until she'd finally called it off.

Yeah, she'd definitely sabotaged those relationships and the truth hurt. A lot.

She'd hurt those decent guys and all because she'd been too immature, too selfish to recognise that Jared hadn't been the only one at fault in their initial relationship; she'd done her fair share.

The thought of weddings drew her gaze to the scrapbook, sitting on the bottom shelf of her bookcase. Sadness filtered through her, wrapped around her heart, settled there like a dead weight as she contemplated what lay between its much-loved pages.

If Avery and Barton had been stand-in grooms after she'd fallen for Jared first time around, what guy had a chance of coming close to that role this time?

She loved him wholeheartedly, unreservedly.

He was The One.

The One her mum had talked about, had demonstrated with her love for her father every day of their lives.

She wanted that. She deserved that. Now, courtesy of one stubborn, commitment-phobe, she'd never have it. For if there was one thing she'd learned out of this fiasco, it was never to settle. Meaning she'd end up a scary spinster living in a tiny apartment with about a hundred cats.

Okay, so that cliché would never come to fruition, as she was allergic to the furry cuties, but she could see it happening: her, old, alone, flipping through the scrapbook and wishing for what might have been.

Turning her back on the scrapbook, she headed for the kitchen before a loud pounding on her door stopped her dead in her tracks.

She'd farewelled Meg, had finished up at the office, so who was trying to break her door down with their incessant pounding?

'Open up, Krissie, I know you're in there.'

Her nerve endings snapped to attention at the familiar voice, her heart clenching in recognition.

She'd said goodbye, didn't want to talk to him, for they had nothing left to say.

As the pounding resumed she knew she had to open the door. If she didn't, and sent him away, she'd for ever wonder why he'd come.

Assuming her best indifferent face, she opened the door.

'You're leaving,' he blurted, his frantic gaze falling on her suitcases, his handsome face haggard.

'Yeah, you already know that.'

'But you brought your departure date forward. I almost missed you!'

She'd never seen him anything other than gorgeous and the fact he looked so awful went a small way to soothing her aching heart.

So he cared about her? Big deal. She wanted beyond caring, would never settle for anything else ever again.

'Can I come in?'

Shrugging, she opened the door wider. He stalked into the room, hands thrust in pockets, shoulders slumped, as if he had the weight of the world on them.

Quashing a surge of pity he didn't deserve, she crossed her arms, propped on the back of the sofa.

'What do you want?'

His gaze met hers, feverish, determined.

'I want you.'

Her heart gave a delighted wiggle before she gave it the proverbial whack. She already knew he wanted her; he'd proved that—and how!—the last night on the island. Problem was he didn't want her enough.

'Doesn't change anything—'

'I'm in love with you!'

Every muscle in her body stilled, along with her heart, as the words she'd been longing to hear filtered over her, processed in her brain, yet came up with a 'this does not compute' message.

How could he love her when he'd spent weeks trying to convince her otherwise?

Curious, she eyeballed him. 'Why now? You've had weeks to tell me how you *really* feel?'

Dragging a hand through his hair, he started pacing. 'I don't blame you for being sarcastic. I've been an idiot.'

'You got that right.'

He didn't halt, his long strides sweeping up and down her apartment.

'Stop that, you're giving me a headache.'

He stopped so suddenly in front of her she didn't have time to react when he swept her into his arms and squeezed the life out of her.

Burying his face in the crook of her shoulder, he murmured, 'I love you. And I'm sorry for putting you through all that crap while I realised it.'

Every cell in her body screamed to give in, to wrap her arms around him and never let go. But words were cheap; and she'd heard them all from this guy and more.

Allowing herself the luxury of momentarily melting into his embrace, she blinked back tears, steadied her resolve, before gently pushing away.

'Apology accepted.'

His eyes lit up, until she added, 'But it doesn't change a thing.'

Slipping out of his personal space, she strode to the door, gave a suitcase a little kick.

'I'm still leaving and your declaration doesn't change that.'

'I see.'

His devastated expression ripped a new hole in her heart, the bleakness in his eyes stabbing another.

'Do you? Really?'

She leaned against the door, mustered every ounce of strength she possessed. She'd need it, to walk away from him once and for all.

'I love you, I've always loved you. And you still walked away from me.'

Taking a deep breath, she deliberately calmed, banishing the hysterical edge to her voice.

'This time, I'm walking away and not looking back.'

Incredulity creased his face. 'So this is payback?'

He would think that. Had nothing she said registered?

'This is me taking control. This is me following my dream, my career. Surely you of all people can understand that?'

She scored a direct hit with her last comment as he nodded, defeated.

He swiftly crossed to the door and, seeing his intent to sweep her into his arms again, she held up both hands to ward him off.

'Goodbye, Jared.'

He hesitated, before swooping in for a blistering kiss that left her tingling all the way down to her toes.

'I'm not going to give up on us,' he murmured, tipping her chin up, maintaining eye contact until she squirmed to escape the burning intensity.

She didn't say, 'You already did.'

Desperate to put some space between them, she headed for the kitchen. 'I need tea.'

Metaphoric speak for 'I need time to think, to assimilate, to process the fact you love me.'

'Want a cuppa?'

'Great.'

By his relieved grin, he expected her to thaw. Not likely. He loved her, she loved him. But she couldn't stop the insidious thought this was his way of issuing an unspoken ultimatum: him or her career.

Maybe it was some warped kind of payback? A thought she discounted in a second. She knew what type of guy he was, and playing games off court wasn't his forte. Whatever his reasoning for blurting his feelings now, she desperately needed time to think, desperately needed a soothing cuppa.

The way she was feeling, hopefully the tea leaves would make more sense of her swirling thoughts than she could.

The moment Jared had stepped into Kristi's immaculate apartment and seen those suitcases, his heart sank.

He'd prepared a speech about long-distance relationships and giving them a try, had wanted to convince her of his feelings, yet when he'd spied those cases all his plans had exploded in a bungled blurted admission he loved her.

He didn't blame her for being cynical. Considering what he'd been saying the last few weeks, he wouldn't believe him either.

Thankfully, she'd needed time out, had fled to the kitchen, giving him valuable space to regroup, marshal his thoughts and hope to God he convinced her to take a chance on them when she returned.

He wandered around her small lounge room, checking out photos, loads and loads of the things depicting a happy family and more recent pics of her and Meg.

In every photo, her parents had their arms wrapped around each other, her dad resting his head on her mum's, their strong bond evident. Kristi and Meg were beaming in every picture. They'd had the perfect upbringing, with parents who loved each other and obviously adored their girls.

Little wonder Kristi had some pie-in-the-sky idea about love and what it entailed.

Turning his back on the photos, he perused her bookshelf, housing everything from thrillers to historical romance.

He loved books, had hid out at the local bookshop as a kid—another escape from his parents—happily spending hours in there, skimming titles, reading blurbs but preferring cartoon magazines, eager to get lost in a world of make believe that was so much better than reality.

Tugging on the latest legal thriller to scan the blurb, he dislodged a stack of books from the top shelf, several tumbling out, knocking more off lower shelves in their journey before landing at his feet.

Squatting, he picked them up, his gaze landing on a giant scrapbook that must've fallen off the bottom shelf.

He wouldn't have noticed it if not for the picture of a young Kristi stuck on the front cover, next to the words 'MY WEDDING'.

Suppressing a shudder, he quickly glanced over his shoulder before flipping it open.

Then wishing he hadn't.

Page after page of white gowns and floral bouquets and towering cakes.

Scraps of lace and satin, old wedding invitations, saved cake bags.

Bad enough in their own right, until he came upon the last few pages…

'My Dream Wedding.'

He shouldn't have looked, should've snapped the scrapbook shut and shoved it back into the bookcase but, drawn by curiosity, he flipped the page.

And his heart stopped.

There, amidst the pictures of a simple white floor-length

gown, a two-carat princess-cut bezel diamond ring and a two-tiered white with black piping cake resembling a fancy hat, was a photo.

Of him.

'You want cookies with your tea?'

He jumped at her voice drifting from the kitchen, bundled the scrapbook and the remainder of the books back into the bookcase and stood quickly.

'No, thanks, I'm good.'

But he wasn't. Seeing him in the role of her groom had shattered every preconceived notion he'd ever had.

She thought he was her perfect groom.

He couldn't be further from it if he tried.

His first instinct was to run. Run as fast and as far as he could.

Then his gaze resettled on the scrapbook and he closed his eyes, seeing every page in crystal-clear clarity as he mentally flipped the pages.

Those pages filled with wedding memorabilia must've taken a long time, must've taken patience and care from a woman who valued an institution as old as time.

As for her chosen dress and cake and ring, someone as special as Kristi deserved those beautiful things, deserved to have the fairy tale come true.

In that second, his eyes snapped open. What the hell was he doing? He'd come here to prove his love, to convince her to try a long-distance relationship, to let her know he'd finally opened his heart enough to consider the possibility of marriage, despite the fact it scared him silly.

So why on earth would he take one look at her wedding scrapbook, a book filled with hopes and dreams and love, and want to turn his back on that?

He was an idiot.

How could he convince her to believe he'd changed his mind when he could hardly compute the change himself?

Unable to tear his eyes from the scrapbook, he stared at it…as if it were trying to send him some kind of obtuse message…and as he heard her footfall it came to him in a flash of pure, inspired brilliance.

He swiped up his keys, glancing at the kitchen in time to see her sashay out with matching teacups on a tray. Her confused gaze landed on his keys before slowly lifting to meet his.

'What's going on?'

'Don't move. I'll be back ASAP.'

'Are you nuts?'

She dumped the tea on a nearby table, disbelief warring with outrage across her expressive face. 'You barge in here, blurt you love me, now you do a runner? What the—?'

'I love you. Trust me.'

He planted a quick peck on her cheek, her spicy fragrance tempting him to linger, to haul her into his arms and never let go. There was time enough for that.

He was a man on a mission.

'Trust you?'

Her raised eyebrow said it all.

'I'll tell you everything as soon as I get back.'

She didn't move, didn't blink, the shimmer of hope in her wide blue eyes enough incentive to send him bolting out of the door.

They'd been through so much, too much. Words weren't enough any more.

She needed proof of his love.

He'd give it to her; show her exactly how much he loved her.

CHAPTER SEVENTEEN

Stranded *Survival Tip #17*
When in need of serious forgiveness, forget the flowers.
Only one thing works. Get down on your knees and start
grovelling.

Twitter.com/Stranded_Jared
Whoever said actions speak louder than words was a
bloody genius.

Twitter.com/Stranded_Kristi
Made a list, checked it twice; typical of a guy to throw
it all into disarray.

KRISTI paced the apartment for hours, wearing tread marks in
her favourite funky rug.

Jared was a certifiable lunatic.

Professing his love one minute, bolting out of here the
next. She should lock the door, refuse to answer it and finish
up her packing.

Instead, his sincerity when he'd asked her to trust him kept
flashing through her mind. And there was that one little salient
point of him saying he loved her...

She pinched herself on the arm, again, just to make sure she hadn't collapsed onto her bed in exhaustion from packing and fallen asleep.

Ouch! Nope, still hurt, which meant she was very much awake and the guy she loved had just told her he loved her right back!

What was he up to?

The selfish part of her—which had botched her previous relationships—wished he could come with her to LA. But she'd never make that demand. She was foolish enough to push him away once, no way would she do it again.

So where did that leave them?

Long-distance relationship? Her losing concentration on the job and getting fired anyway? Exorbitant phone bills? Her life laid out on Twitter again?

None of those options appealed, which brought her back full circle to *what was he up to?*

A loud pounding had her running to the door and flinging it open, totally blowing her intention to play things cool and wait to see what he had in mind.

Before she could speak he picked her up and spun her around, the air whooshing out of her lungs, her whoop of surprise making him laugh.

'Hey! Let go…' she trailed off, her heart ka-thumping at Jared's triumphant grin.

'Sorry for rushing out like that. Important business to attend to.'

'Business? After what you said earlier?'

She shook her head, pushed against his chest until he set her down on her feet. 'You've got five seconds to explain yourself, mister, or I'm—'

'I came to give you these. Some light reading to pass the time on the long-haul flight.'

He ducked down, picked up a pile of magazines hidden behind one of the pot plants framing her doorway, and handed them to her.

Her eyebrows shot heavenward as she flipped through the stack of bridal magazines, all glossy and new and tempting. What she couldn't understand was why.

'And this, to help you hurry back.'

If the magazines confused her it had nothing on the small distinctive blue box from Tiffany resting on the palm of his hand, outstretched towards her.

Taking the magazines and dumping them on top of her cases, he pressed the box into her palm.

'Go ahead. Open it.'

No way.

It couldn't be.

Her fumbling fingers fiddled with the lid and when she finally prised it open she exhaled on a loud woo, not computing what she was seeing.

'It's my ring.'

'I know. Not exactly the same but the closest I could get on short notice.'

He grinned, proud as a kid who'd aced his first test. 'I saw it in your scrapbook.'

If the ring had floored her, the sight of Jared Malone dropping to one knee and taking hold of her hand in her doorway almost made her keel over.

'Because I love you. Because I want to spend the rest of my life with you. Because I want to marry you.'

A faint buzzing filled her head, grew louder, as she blinked away the spots dancing a jig before her eyes.

She'd never fainted in her life but as the world suddenly tilted it looked as if there was a first time for everything.

'Whoa!'

He leaped to his feet, caught her before she slumped to the floor, her head spinning from his proposal more than a lack of oxygen to the brain.

'Not quite the reaction I expected.'

'Not quite the farewell I expected,' she countered, allowing him to lower her onto a nearby sofa where she hung her head between her knees, took great gasps of air, finally feeling strong enough to sit up and face him.

Taking hold of her hand, he sat beside her, his body wedged tight against hers, as if he had no intention of letting her go anywhere.

'I know you think I'm a lunatic, vacillating all over the place, pushing you away one minute, professing my undying love the next. That's where this comes in.'

He toyed with the ring box in his free hand, flipped the lid open and shut, the princess diamond catching the light and sending shards of exquisite brilliance dancing around the room.

'I wanted to show you how I felt. I thought you wouldn't listen to me after the way I've acted. I'm hoping you'll believe me now.'

She didn't know what to believe.

Her dream groom had just proposed, exactly like in her fantasy. Only problem was, it had happened so fast, she doubted any of this was real.

Rubbish! You're doubting yourself as usual, trying to find a reason to sabotage the relationship for fear of making a mistake like Meg, for fear of the relationship not living up to your high expectations, for fear he'll leave you. Again.

Squeezing her hand, he said, 'Say something.'

She blurted the first thing that popped into her head. 'I'm scared.'

He slid his arm around her, hugged her tight. 'Of what? Me walking away again? Because it won't happen. Taking this step has been huge for me, I'm not about to be a runaway groom now.'

She shook her head, desperate to snuggle into him but needing to tell him the truth if they were to have any chance.

'I'm scared of having a real relationship with you.'

He frowned, confusion clouding his eyes. 'I thought that's what you wanted?'

'I do, but…'

The memory of their last phone call eight years earlier echoed through her head, the anguish, the bitterness, the resentment, closely followed by memories of Avery's stunned expression when she'd handed back the ring, Barton's sheer outrage, which had morphed into tears when she'd broken the engagement before he'd had a chance to serve a three-course dinner he'd prepared.

She'd botched those relationships. Her, with her ridiculously high expectations and utter selfishness, not the guys as she would've liked to believe, so what was to stop history repeating?

'But?'

With her mind a whir of confusion, her heart wanted to jump back into the fray. She had to tell him, there was no other way.

Laying her palms against his chest, she pushed lightly, stared up at him with hope.

'I'm terrified of mucking up again, of making you leave.'

His brow creased in confusion. 'I don't get it.'

Inhaling, she let it all out in a rush. 'I blamed you for dumping me last time. Selfish, arrogant, tennis jock choosing his precious bloody career over me when I knew you'd leave, right from the start, I just didn't want to believe it. You never made any promises, you were the dream date for six months, and I became a clinging, pathetic limpet demanding more than you were able to give.'

He opened his mouth to respond and she placed her hand over it, quieting him.

'There's more. I resented you for years, and, whether inadvertently or deliberately, I chose to date guys the exact opposite of you.'

She dropped her hand, winced. 'That didn't help either, because my old attempts to sabotage reared again and I stuffed those relationships too.'

Smart man, he didn't say a word, let her exhaust her cathartic confession.

'So here we are again. I love you, have probably always loved you, you propose and I'm not doing cartwheels. Want to know why?'

He nodded, his tender smile encouraging her to continue.

'Because there's no such thing as perfect. What if I've built up this ridiculous marriage scenario in my head we have no hope of living up to? What if I disappoint you? Or push you away? Or do a million other stupid things that'll give you no option but to leave? What if I—?'

He silenced her with a kiss, a hot, searing kiss that blazed a path directly to her heart, scorching any further protestations along the way.

Capturing her face between his hands, he sat back, stared unflinchingly into her eyes.

'What if we go into this with our eyes wide open? What if we have no expectations other than to love and trust and respect each other? What if we do everything in our power to make each other happy?'

Hope surged through her, making her body tremble.

'I kinda like your what ifs a lot more than mine.'

Rubbing noses with her, he murmured, 'Me too.'

Smiling, she tilted her head slightly, brushed a soft kiss against his lips before pulling away to stare into the handsome face she loved.

'As much as I'd love to get swept away in all this, I'm dying to know. Why the sudden turnaround?'

He grimaced, pinched the bridge of his nose, doing little to ease the sudden frown. 'Thought you might ask that.'

'Well? You going to elaborate any time soon or do I have to torture it out of you?'

He smiled at her levity, but it was a forced smile with a twist of pain.

'Your parents had the perfect marriage. Mine didn't.'

He stood, thrust his hands into his pockets, his pacing a fair imitation of what she'd done earlier. By the time they'd finished, the rug would be for the tip.

'You never mentioned them?'

'Because I preferred to ignore them.'

He stopped, his expression halfway between disgust and embarrassment. 'They were filthy rich. Self-absorbed, bored, hated each other. I was probably a mistake, a mistake that made them pay every day they had to look at me so they chose to ignore me, pretend I never existed.'

Sympathy twisted her belly at his obvious pain.

'When they weren't screaming at each other they were keeping up pretences for their equally narcissistic friends. Empty marriages among the lot of them.'

Which explained his anti-commitment stance. But there was more, she could tell by the rigidity in his shoulders, the clenched fists.

'Best thing they ever did was dump me at their exclusive tennis club. I started taking my frustrations out on a ball, the rest is history…'

'Did your success change their attitude?'

'Oh, yeah, suddenly they couldn't get enough of me. Fawning over me, turning up at all my matches—it made me sick.'

His flat tone chilled her as much as his bleak expression. 'But you know what made me sicker? The fact I cared. Whenever they turned up at a game, I was like a little kid pretending his nightmare childhood never existed, a kid craving his parents' approval.'

'There's nothing wrong with that. They're your parents—'

'Who've barely spoken to me since I blew my knee. Nice, huh?'

He resumed pacing, his expression thunderous. 'They're such screw-ups I didn't trust myself not to be like them. But you know something? I'm nothing like them! I love you and it took the fact of almost losing you to make me realise how damn much. Marriage isn't the problem. It's the people who enter into it.'

He stopped, grabbed her hands, hauled her off the sofa and into his arms.

'We can make this work. Sure, it's not going to be easy, and far from *perfect*, but it's you and me, kid, and that's already advantage Malone.'

His sincerity took her breath away, her heart expanding with so much love she could barely breathe.

'I didn't want to let emotion into my life, didn't want to take a risk on a lifetime commitment.'

He paused, searched her eyes for reassurance.

'Until now.'

Joy clogged her throat and she swallowed, saddened by what he'd been through, when she'd had the fabled perfect life he didn't believe in. For him to tell her this, unburden his soul…she now understood what drove him and all her reservations flew into the sky alongside the latest A380 she'd still have to board tomorrow.

Jared loved her.

She loved him.

What was she waiting for?

'I accept.'

Confusion clouded his eyes for a moment before realisation struck and he let out a wild whoop, kissed her thoroughly, before opening the small blue box and sliding the ring onto the third finger of her left hand.

'There. You can't get away from me now.'

She winced. 'Actually, I can. I need to be on that flight first thing tomorrow morning.'

Crushing her to him, he murmured in her ear, 'Give me a week to get the centre organised and I'll be on the first plane out. Deal?'

'You'd do that for me?'

'You know the centre means a lot to me, but I'm basically the financier. I can do most of the work online, can always fly back when needed.'

Smiling, he cupped her cheek, the love blazing from his hazel eyes toasting her. 'It's you I can't do without.'

'In that case, you've got yourself a deal.'

They sealed it with a kiss. A long, slow, passionate kiss that elicited a long wolf whistle and hoots from her nosy neighbours who were passing by her open door.

Neither cared. They'd already had part of their lives plastered on TV.

What was another public display of affection?

EPILOGUE

Stranded *Survival Tip #18*
An island stay is temporary. A ring is for ever

Twitter.com/Stranded_Jared
Here comes the bride. She's stunning. And she's all mine.

Twitter.com/Stranded_Kristi
*Who needs a scrapbook when you've got the real thing?
Cue the bridal waltz. Lucky me!*

Excerpt from the society pages of the Sydney Morning
Star.

*Fans of sport and television flocked to the harbour-side
wedding of tennis champion Jared Malone and his
stunning bride, PR whiz Kristi Wilde.*

*The couple's relationship blossomed under our very
eyes in the documentary* Stranded, *viewers' interest
enhanced by regular blog and Twitter updates from the
love-struck pair.*

*The entire country waited with bated breath when
our very own golden couple fled to the States for six*

months but in the Aussie tradition they returned for an Australia Day wedding, the hoopla surrounding the private event rivalling the latest A-list celebrity nuptials.

The happy couple released a single photo through their best man and our source, award-winning producer Elliott J. Burnaby. The beautiful bride wore a stunning Vera Wang ivory satin strapless gown with mermaid fishtail while the dashing groom wore an Armani tuxedo.

The bride's sister and sole bridesmaid, devoted single mother Meg Wilde, walked alongside her daughter, Prue, in the bridal procession. Prue, a gorgeous ring bearer, won the crowd over with her impromptu rendition of 'Chapel of Love'.

After the select few guests, including several teens from the Activate recreational centre Mr Malone supports, feasted on roasted half-duckling with seasonal greens, milk-fed veal with Gruyère and a dessert platter featuring warm quince tart, saffron and coconut crème brûlée and dark chocolate semi-freddo, they danced well into the night.

The happy couple are honeymooning at an undisclosed destination.

Stay tuned.

Or better yet, follow the golden couple on Twitter.

Twitter.com/Stranded_Jared
I always thought winning Grand Slams was the pinnacle of success. Marrying the love of my life proved me wrong.

Twitter.com/Stranded_Kristi
Dream wedding, dream man. Perfect love exists. Never give up. Winning is sublime, on and off the court!

* * * * *

HIS BRIDE
IN PARADISE

BY
JOANNA NEIL

When **Joanna Neil** discovered Mills & Boon, her life-long addiction to reading crystallised into an exciting new career writing Medical Romance. Her characters are probably the outcome of her varied lifestyle, which includes working as a clerk, typist, nurse and infant teacher. She enjoys dressmaking and cooking at her Leicestershire home. Her family includes a husband, son and daughter, an exuberant yellow Labrador and two slightly crazed cockatiels. She currently works with a team of tutors at her local education centre to provide creative writing workshops for people interested in exploring their own writing ambitions.

CHAPTER ONE

'I CAN'T believe my luck,' Alyssa said excitedly, cradling the phone close to her ear. 'The house is magnificent, Carys, and it's right next to the ocean.'

'Mmm...that's exactly how I imagined it,' her cousin answered. 'So you managed to find the place all right? How's it all going for you?' On the other end of the line, Carys's voice held a note of eager anticipation.

Alyssa smiled at her enthusiastic tone. Carys lived on the mainland in Florida, some sixty or seventy miles away from here, and she was keen to know everything that was going on.

'Oh, it was easy enough,' Alyssa said. 'The taxi driver dropped me off. Apparently everyone around here knows the Blakeley property.' She adjusted the fluffy bath towel around her damp body. She'd not long come from the shower and had been sitting for a few minutes by the dressing table, blowdrying her long hair so that the mass of chestnut-coloured curls gleamed softly in the lamplight. 'I'm doing just fine,' she added. 'It's lovely here. You wouldn't believe how beautiful it is.'

She left the dresser and went to settle down on the luxurious softness of the large divan bed, stretching out her long, slender limbs. 'I only arrived here a couple of hours ago, so I haven't really had time to look around, but the house is perfect. There are double glass doors everywhere, even in the bedrooms, and when you step out onto the deck you look out over the Atlantic Ocean. It's fantastic, Carys…it's so incredibly blue.'

A faint breeze wafted in through the open veranda doors, and glancing there from across the room Alyssa could see the branches of the palm trees swaying gently against the skyline of the setting sun. Birds called to one another, sleepy in the warm evening air. 'I'm sitting here now, and I can hear the waves breaking on the shore.'

'It sounds heavenly.'

'Mmm, it is.' Alyssa couldn't believe her change in fortune. Within a few weeks she'd gone from enduring a bleak, desperately unhappy situation back in the UK to finding herself in this idyllic haven on a sand-fringed island in the Bahamas. 'I keep thinking that any minute now someone will come along and pinch me and tell me it's all a dream.'

Carys chuckled. 'No, I think it's really happening. Is Ross there with you? I know he was keen to help you get settled in.'

'No. He rang to tell me he'd be along a little later. He had a meeting with the director so that they could iron out a few things before filming starts tomorrow.'

Alyssa stopped to listen for a moment as a faint creaking sound caught her attention, like a footfall on the steps leading to the deck. Was someone walking around outside? Could it be that there was a change of plan and Ross was coming home earlier than expected? Then one of the voile curtains fluttered on a light current of air, distracting her, and she shook her head. Ross had stressed the importance of the meeting. It must have been the door that was creaking, that would be it.

'Well, he'll make sure that everything goes smoothly for you, I'm sure,' Carys murmured. 'You can put all your troubles behind you now, and forget about your awful ex. I've known Ross for ages, and he has a heart of gold. He'll take good care of you. I know he was besotted with you from the moment he set eyes on you.'

Alyssa sat up against the pillows. 'Oh, no...surely that can't be true... At least, I hope it isn't.' Ross knew how she felt. She'd come here to get away from all the mess that relationships involved, clutching at the chance Ross had given her to make her escape. This was her sanctuary.

Her work back in the UK had proved to be a stumbling block, too, and she'd reluctantly decided to put what had once been a promising medical career temporarily on hold. At least, she hoped it was only a relatively short-term move. In the end, things had proved too much for her, and she'd had to accept that she needed to take time out to recover from the burnout that had crept up on her and caught her unawares.

Somehow, she had to try to get herself back together again and she was pinning her hopes on the healing qualities of these next few months. As to the rest...

'I've finished with romance,' she said, her tone quiet and restrained. 'I'm done with all that.'

'So you say.' Carys laughed. 'Anyway, your ex is finally out of the picture, so with a bit of luck you can relax now and look forward to a few months of sheer luxury and self-indulgence.'

'Well, of course,' Alyssa answered, tongue in cheek. 'How could I not enjoy all this? I've got it made, haven't

I? Nothing much to do but enjoy the sunshine and surf and thank my lucky stars. I'll take money and all these rich trappings over love any time. Who wouldn't?'

'Sure you will,' Carys murmured drily. She knew full well that Alyssa was joking. 'Look, I have to go. I'll call you again. You take care. Love you.'

'And you.'

Alyssa cut the call and put down the phone, listening once more as the creaking grew louder. *Was* someone or something out there? It couldn't be Ross, surely? He'd said he would be delayed for at least an hour. Frowning, she went over to the doors and stepped out onto the deck.

A white ibis caught her attention in the distance, wandering along the shoreline, dipping his long red bill into the shallows in search of any tasty morsels that might have been washed up by the sea. She watched him for a moment or two.

'We see those birds quite often around here,' a male voice said, catching her completely unawares. The deep, resonant tones smoothed over her, making her swivel around in startled surprise.

The man moved from the shelter of the open sitting-room door and came to stand just a couple of feet away from her. He leaned negligently against the rail, making himself completely at home.

'Who—who are you…? What are you doing here?' She stared at him, shocked, wide-eyed, a little afraid and uncertain as to what to do. She was completely alone out here. He was at least six feet tall, long limbed, broad shouldered, definitely a force to be reckoned with.

She quickly thought through her options. The neighbours were too distant to hear if she were to shout out, and for an instant she floundered, before self-preservation took hold. Maybe he *was* a neighbour, and she was simply jumping to conclusions. Just because he was standing on Ross's veranda, it didn't have to mean he was some kind of would-be felon...did it?

'I was originally planning on helping myself to a cool drink and something to eat,' he answered with a faint shrug. 'I thought the place was empty, but then I heard a woman's voice and thought maybe I'd better find out who was here.'

His glance travelled over her, gliding along the creamy slope of her bare shoulders, moving down across the brief white towel that clung to her curves and coming to linger for a while on the golden expanse of her shapely legs. His gaze shifted downwards. Her feet were bare, her toenails painted a delicate shade of pink, and there were tiny gemstones embedded in the pearly nail varnish. A faint smile touched his mouth. 'I certainly hadn't expected to find anyone quite so lovely here to greet me.'

Alyssa felt warm colour invade her cheeks and her fingers tightened on the towel, clutching it to her breasts. He seemed to be quite at ease here, yet he still hadn't explained who he was.

'Well, whoever you are, you shouldn't be here,' she said. What kind of person would have the gall to calmly walk in and help himself to a drink? Ross had insisted she would have the place to herself. Her green eyes flashed a warning. 'You'd better go before I call the police.'

Belatedly, she remembered that she'd left her phone on the bedside table. Could she sidle back into the room and dial the number without alerting him to her actions? Hardly. Still, a bit of bravado wouldn't come amiss, would it?

He'd made no attempt to move. 'I can't think why you're still standing there,' she said in a terse voice. 'I meant what I said.'

'Yes, I realise that... I just don't think it's a very good idea.'

'Of course you don't. You wouldn't, would you? Even so...' She took a couple of steps backwards into the bedroom, not taking her eyes off him for a second. The smooth, Italian-tiled floor was cool beneath her feet, soothing to her ragged nerves. Her heart was pounding, her pulse thumping out an erratic beat.

He didn't look the least bit put out. He was dressed in cool, expensive-looking chinos and a loose cotton shirt. His hair was dark, the perfect styling framing an angular face, but it was his eyes that held her most of all... They were narrowed on her now, grey, like the sea on a stormy night, and compelling, a hint of something unknown glimmering in their depths as he studied her.

Slowly, he pushed himself away from the rail and began to move towards her, and her insides lurched in fearful acknowledgement. Instinctively, she recognised that this was a man who knew what he wanted and who was used to getting his own way. He wasn't going anywhere, and it certainly didn't look as though he intended to heed her warning.

She felt behind her for the mobile phone on the bedside table.

'As I said, I really wouldn't advise you do that,' he murmured, his gaze following her actions. 'You might find yourself having to explain to them what exactly you're doing in my house.'

Her jaw dropped a fraction. '*Your* house?' She frowned, then shot him a steely glance. 'No...no, that can't be right. You're the intruder, not me. I'll tell them so.'

There was a glint in his dark eyes. 'Okay, let's get this straight—I'm Connor Blakeley, and this has actually been my home for a number of years. My brother lives here too, from time to time, but it's a fact that it's my name on the deeds of the property.' He studied her. 'So, would you like to tell me who you are and what you're doing here?' His mouth moved in a wry smile. 'Or perhaps I can hazard a guess. This is bound to be something to do with Ross. You must be his latest girlfriend.'

She stiffened. He made it sound as though there had been a stream of them. Deciding to ignore his comment, she shook her head so that her bright curls tumbled about her shoulders. This man had to be an imposter, surely? Doubts were beginning to creep in, but she said cautiously, 'Connor's away for the next six months. Ross told me so. His brother's in Florida, helping to organise a new medical emergency unit over there.'

He nodded briefly. 'That was true. Unfortunately an urgent situation occurred right here in the Bahamas, and I was asked to come back and take over the accident and emergency department at the hospital. So I'll be working here and at the same time I'll be keeping an eye on the Florida unit from a distance.'

Her indrawn breath was sharp and audible. What he said sounded plausible enough. Could it be that she'd made a mistake in doubting him? He did look a bit like Ross, now she came to think of it.

Carefully, she replaced the phone on the table and

straightened up. Now what was she to do? Her cheeks burned with colour. How could she have ended up in such a humiliating situation? Hadn't she put up with cnough of those back in England? This was meant to have been a fresh start, and now it looked as though her expectations of spending a relaxed, trouble-free few months out here were being rapidly consigned to the rubbish bin.

She lifted her chin, determined to pull herself together. It was a setback, that was all. Somehow she would sort this out and find herself another place to stay. She just had to hope that the cost wouldn't be way beyond her means. It had only been Ross's conviction that she could stay in this house rent-free that had persuaded her she could afford to come out here in the first place.

'I'm really sorry,' she said. 'I'd no idea… I wasn't expecting anyone else to be here tonight.' She hesitated, drawing in a calming breath. 'I'm Alyssa Morgan. Your brother invited me to stay here.'

'Was he planning on staying here with you?'

She frowned. 'Not with me, exactly. He said he would take the upper-floor accommodation, and I could have the downstairs apartment.' She looked across the room to where her suitcases stood against the louvred doors of the wardrobe. She hadn't even had time to unpack. 'But, of course, it's all changed now. I'll get my things together and find somewhere else to stay.'

'At this time of the evening?' He raised a dark brow. 'Even supposing you could find anywhere at such short notice, I couldn't let you do that. I've a feeling that an attractive young woman alone in the city would be far too great a temptation for some of our, shall we say, less civilised, male citizens?'

She straightened her shoulders. 'I can take care of myself.'

His glance moved over her. 'Really?'

His obvious disbelief stung. She felt his dark gaze linger on her slender curves, and she hugged the towel to herself in a defensive gesture. With so much pale golden skin on display she felt she was at a distinct disadvantage. 'Anyway, I should get dressed,' she said, with as much dignity as she could muster. 'If you wouldn't mind...?'

He nodded. 'Of course.' He started to walk across the room but stopped by the door to look back and say, 'You seem a bit flushed. Perhaps I could get you an iced drink and maybe something to eat? Or have you already had supper?'

Her eyes widened. She wasn't expecting such generosity, given the circumstances, and it only made her feel worse, after the way she'd spoken to him. 'No...um...I haven't had time... I only arrived here a short time ago, and I was feeling hot and dusty after the flight and so on, so I decided to have a shower before I did anything else. Ross and I were going to have supper when...' She broke off, then added, 'He had to go to a meeting.'

'Hmm.' Connor was frowning as he looked at the suitcases. 'I take it from your accent that you're English. Is that right? Did you and Ross meet over in the UK? I know he was over there scouting for talent for his latest film project.'

'Yes, we did.' Connor was American-English, she knew, as his father had been born in the United States and his mother was from London. 'We...uh...have a mutual friend over in Florida...my cousin, Carys...and she suggested he look me up.'

'Oh, yes. I know Carys.' He made a faint smile as he studied her. 'I expect Ross was glad he took the time to follow up on that.' He started to turn back towards the door. 'Well, maybe I'll make a start on preparing some food and then Ross can join us when he gets here.'

'I... Yes, that would be good. Thank you.' Her head was reeling. How on earth would Ross react on finding that his brother was here? One way or another, he was in for something of a shock.

Connor left the room and Alyssa pulled in a deep breath. It wasn't the best way for her to have met Connor, was it? She'd heard quite a bit about him from Ross, and her overall impression was that Ross was a little in awe of his older brother. Now that she'd met him, she could certainly understand why. There was that quality about him, something that suggested he would always be in complete control of any situation, that nothing would faze him. Everything about him underlined that. He was supple and lithe, his body honed with latent energy, and a calm, inherent sense of authority oozed from every pore.

She dressed quickly, choosing a pale blue cotton dress with narrow straps, cool enough for the warmth of the evening. It wasn't much in the way of a defence, but at least being fully dressed made her feel more in command of herself.

A few minutes later she walked into the kitchen and found Connor busy at the table, adding tomato paste and grated cheese to a large pizza base. He looked up as she entered the room. 'You look fresh and cool,' he murmured. 'That colour suits you.'

'Thank you.'

'Sit down,' he said, waving her to a chair by the pale

oak table. 'Would you like mushrooms with this? And peppers?'

'Yes, please.' She nodded, watching as he deftly cut and sliced mushrooms and then sprinkled them over the cheese.

She glanced around. From here, by the deep, broad window, she could look out over the ocean, and closer to home there was what seemed to be a small kitchen garden just beyond the veranda. The light outside was fading now, but solar lamps sent a golden glow over a variety of vegetables and a small grove of trees laden with plump, ripe oranges.

She turned her attention back to the kitchen. 'You have a beautiful home,' she said. The kitchen was full of state-of-the-art equipment, along with a tiled island bar and glass shelving that housed colourful ceramics and delicately sculpted vases.

'Thanks.' He smiled. 'I must admit I'm pleased with it. When I moved here I wanted a house where I would be able to relax and shrug off the cares of the day, and this seemed to be the perfect place in an idyllic setting...a small piece of paradise, if you like. I sit out on the deck of an evening and watch the waves breaking on the shore. It's very relaxing, especially if you like to watch wildlife, as I do. You sometimes see herons and egrets around here, and there might even be a golden plover that appears from time to time.'

'It sounds idyllic.'

'It is.' He slid the pizza into the hot oven and came over to the table, picking up a jug of iced juice. 'Would you like a drink? I can get you something stronger if you prefer.'

'Thanks...orange juice will be fine.' She made a

face. 'I'm not used to this heat. I seem to have been thirsty ever since I arrived here.'

His mouth curved. 'You get used to it after a while. I have air-conditioning, but sometimes I prefer to throw open all the doors and windows and let the sea air in.'

'Yes, I can understand that. I think I would, too.' She sipped the cold juice, pausing to rest the glass momentarily against her throat to cool her heated skin. His glance followed her movements, but his eyes were dark and unreadable.

'So, you and Ross must be working together on his new film, I suppose?' he commented. He poured himself a glass of juice and took a long swallow, looking at her over the rim. 'He and I haven't talked much about the casting, but I can see why he must have wanted to bring you over here. I imagine you're very photogenic. And I guess you must have auditioned well.'

'Um…that's not exactly what happened,' she murmured. She frowned. He obviously had the wrong idea, if he was assuming she was an actress. 'I'm really not expecting to have anything to do with the filming as such.'

'Ah…that's interesting.' He shot her an assessing glance. 'Still, he must think a lot of you, to have brought you over here and set you up in the family home. After all, you can't have known each other very long.'

Alyssa put down her glass, her mouth firming into a straight line. 'Um…I don't know, but…I think you must have the wrong idea. I get the impression that you've put two and two together and made five.'

'Have I?' His mouth tilted in disbelief. 'I may have some of the facts wrong, but in essence I know my brother pretty well, and this wouldn't be the first time he's fallen for a young woman and gone out of his way to throw the world at her feet.' There was a gleam in his eyes. 'Unfortunately for him, this time he wasn't expecting me to turn up out of the blue. I can see how that might make things a bit difficult.'

She stood up. 'You know, on second thoughts, I don't think this arrangement is going to work out after all. I think I'll go with my original plan and find somewhere else to stay.'

She started to move away from the table, but he caught hold of her, his fingers curving around her bare arm. 'Please don't do that, Alyssa, it's really not a good idea.'

'Maybe so, but that's my worry, not yours.'

She tried to pull away from him, but he simply drew her closer to him, so that her soft curves brushed against his long body. 'I'm afraid it's very much my problem,' he said, 'since my brother has seen fit to install you under my roof.'

'You make me sound as though I'm a package to be parcelled up by your brother and shipped wherever the fancy takes him,' she said in a terse voice. 'That's not only insulting, it's downright chauvinistic. Where have you been living these last thirty or so years? It's obvious to me that your mind-set is stuck somewhere in the last century.'

He laughed. It wasn't what she was expecting, and anger and frustration rose up in her like mercury shooting up a gauge on a blazing hot day. 'You'd better let me go right now,' she said, 'or I swear you won't like the consequences.' When he didn't release her, she started to bring her knee up, ready to deliver a crippling blow, and he swiftly turned her round so that his arms encased her from behind. Frustratingly, she was locked into his embrace, her spine resting against his taut, masculine frame.

'Of course I'll let you go,' he murmured, 'if you promise me that you won't try to leave before morning. I apologise if I've been jumping to conclusions. I've been assuming that Ross is behaving in his usual hedonistic manner, but I have to admit you're very different from what I might have expected. You're not at all like his usual choice of women.'

'Is that so?' She was rigid in his arms, still seething with indignation.

'I didn't mean to offend you,' he said. 'Honestly. I'm trying to explain. Look at it from my point of view. I had no idea that he was bringing anyone home. He usually tells me. So why didn't he do that if everything was open and above board? For all he knew, I might have arranged for a friend to stay here while I was away. That's why we always tell each other about our plans.'

'Perhaps he acted on impulse and meant to tell you later.' Her body relaxed a fraction.

'Yes, I suppose that could be it.' He nodded, and his cheek lightly brushed hers. His hold on her eased a little, and it seemed to Alyssa's heightened senses that it became much more like a caress. She felt his warm breath fall softly on the back of her neck, and his arm brushed the rounded swell of her breast as he held her to him. It was unintentional, she was sure, but the heated contact ricocheted through her body, bringing with it a shocking, bone-melting response. She closed her eyes, breathing deeply. How could she be reacting this way? She didn't even know him. It was unthinkable.

Clearly there was something wrong with her. Jet-

lag, probably. She needed to break free from him, but
the warmth of those encircling arms and the gentleness
of that embrace had taken her completely by surprise.
It seemed like such a long time since anyone had held
her in such an intimate way and, worryingly, she was
discovering that she liked it.

'I'll find somewhere else to stay first thing in the
morning,' she said.

Slowly, almost reluctantly, he released her. 'You
don't need to do that. You're Ross's guest, and there-
fore mine, too. I wouldn't dream of having you go elsewhere. Please stay. I'd like you to stay.'

'I'll think about it.' She dithered for a moment. She
wanted to walk out of the room, but as she stood there,
undecided, she glanced towards the oven, conscious
of the appetising smell of melting cheese and sizzling
herbs and tomato permeating the air. She hadn't realised
until now how hungry she was…her last meal had been
virtually a snack on the plane journey over here.

He looked at her, his head tilted on one side, a faint
smile playing around his mouth. 'You're hungry,' he
said. 'It's no wonder you're feeling a little fractious.
Sit down and we'll eat. Things always seem better on
a full stomach.'

Annoyed by her own weakness, she did as he suggested and went back to the chair. Maybe he was right,
and circumstances had combined to throw her off balance. A long plane journey, a change of surroundings
and the appearance of the proverbial tall, dark stranger
had certainly knocked her for six. Her heart was racing
as though she'd run a marathon, and the world seemed
to be spinning around her ever so slightly. She felt decidedly odd.

There was a noise from across the room and they both turned as the kitchen door opened and Ross came in.

'What on earth…? Connor, what are you doing here? Aren't you supposed to be in Florida?' He was tall, like his brother, with dark hair and the same angular jaw, but Ross had more homely, lived-in features, and generally there was a happy-go-lucky, almost boyish air about him. 'You said you'd be away for several months.'

'I did, but there was a change of plan. It turns out I'm going to be working here, on the island, for the most part.'

'So you'll be staying here.' It was a matter-of-fact statement. Then Ross added, 'I've arranged for Alyssa to have the ground-floor apartment. I'd no idea you would be coming back so soon.'

Connor nodded. 'Yes, she told me. That's okay. That arrangement can still stand. It just means that you'll have to stay at your place near the film studio. That won't be a problem for you, will it?'

Ross's grey-blue eyes narrowed. 'I guess not.' He looked at his brother as though he suspected him of some devious ploy.

'Good. So now that's all sorted, perhaps we can sit down together and enjoy a meal.'

Connor took the pizza from the oven, and Alyssa said quietly, 'Is there anything I can do to help? I could set the table for you, if you like.'

'Thanks. That would be great. There's a bowl of salad in the fridge. You could put that out, too, if you would.'

'Okay.'

They worked together, while Ross went to freshen

up. 'So, if you're not involved with the filming, what will you be doing all day while Ross is at work?' Connor asked. 'Is this meant to be a holiday for you, or a sight-seeing trip, or something like that?'

Alyssa smiled. 'It's nothing like that. I'm going to be working as a medic on the film set. Apparently, the company Ross usually calls on to provide that service is tied up with other projects right now, so when he found out that I was looking for work, he asked me if I'd like to take it on.'

Connor's dark brows lifted. 'You're a nurse?'

She shook her head. 'I'm a doctor. I've worked in the same line as you, accident and emergency, so I should be able to deal with any problems that arise if stunts go wrong, and so on.' She smiled. 'Though, hopefully, that won't happen. Mostly, it'll be a case of handing out headache and sunburn medication, I expect.'

'So now you've managed to surprise me all over again.' Connor stared at her for a moment or two, before starting to slice the pizza into triangular wedges. 'Now I understand what you meant when you told your friend that there would be nothing much to do but enjoy the sunshine and the surf and thank your lucky stars.'

She frowned, sending him a fleeting glance. 'You heard me talking to Carys on the phone?'

He nodded. 'I didn't know it was Carys, but I heard some of the conversation you were having. I came out onto the deck and I couldn't help but hear what you were saying.' He paused as he checked the filter on the coffee pot.

'The only part that bothered me was when you added that you'd take money and all the trappings over love any time.' His gaze meshed with hers. 'I don't know what your plans are, but perhaps I should warn you to tread carefully there. I wouldn't want to see my brother hurt. He has his faults, but he's family and I care about him very much.'

Once again this evening she felt hot colour rise in her cheeks. No wonder he'd been so edgy with her from the beginning. He'd heard what she said and had drawn his own conclusions.

'It was just a joke,' she said. 'The sort of throw-away remark we all make from time to time. It didn't mean anything.'

'Maybe so.' He acknowledged that with a wry smile, but she noticed the warmth didn't reach his dark eyes. 'But the warning stands… I've always looked out for my brother, and I see no reason to stop doing that.'

'Even though he's a grown man who owns a successful film company? Don't you trust him to make his own decisions?'

'Of course I do…to a certain extent. But Ross is a fool where women are concerned. He's made a few mistakes over the years that have cost him dearly. I don't want to see that happen again.'

'And I'm obviously the scarlet woman whose talons cut deep?' She sent him a scornful look.

'You've come all the way from the UK to be with him.' His mouth twisted. 'I don't blame you for that. Who would turn down the chance of living a life of luxury on this beautiful island? But I'm inclined to be cautious all the same.'

Clearly he wasn't going to believe she was on the level. Alyssa opened her mouth to make an answering retort, but Ross came back into the kitchen just then,

and she concentrated instead on carefully laying out
the cutlery on the table.

'I'm starving,' Ross said, eyeing the food with a rav-
enous eye. 'This looks good.'

She smiled at him, handing him a plate, and took her
seat at the table. She didn't need to say anything more
to Connor. They simply looked at one another, and that
glance spoke volumes. They both knew exactly where
they stood. He didn't trust her an inch and for her part
she was ultra-wary of him. The battle lines were drawn.

CHAPTER TWO

'ARE we all clear for this shot?' Ross was talking to the cameraman, making sure that every detail was covered. They were standing just a few yards away from Alyssa, and she could hear every word that was being said. It was fascinating, she'd discovered, to watch a film being put together. In principle, Ross was the producer, but she'd learned that he also had a hand in directing the films.

'Let's start off by letting the audience see the coral reef in the distance,' Ross said quietly, 'and the sheer drop to the sea. Then we can gradually move to the background of the pine forest and sweep down to a view of the lake, so that we see the sun shining on the surface.'

The cameraman nodded, and Ross went on, 'Lastly, I want you to bring in the bridge over the main road and try to give us an impression of the sheer height and majesty of it all. We'll tie all that in with atmospheric music and build up to a crescendo.'

'Okay. And that's where we cut to the car chase?'

'That's right. As soon as that comes to an end, we'll go straight into the stunt scene.'

'You want the lorry to come into the picture from the east? I'll need a clear signal for that.'

'Yes. I'll let you know as soon as the driver starts up the engine.'

'Okay.'

Alyssa watched all the activity around her with interest. The actors who would be needed for the next scene were standing around, chatting to one another, languid in the heat of the sun as they waited to be called. Everyone wanted to see how the stunt would go. The technicians had planned it down to the last detail, and there had been several rehearsals, but now it was time for the real thing, and the stuntman, Alex, was in position on the bridge, a lone, dark figure against the protective rail.

Ross came over to her. He was in prime form, bubbling with energy and totally enthusiastic about the way things were going. 'I'm going to be tied up with this for the next hour or so,' he told her, 'but I thought we might have lunch later at the new restaurant that's opened up in town...Benvenuto. It's down by the marina. They do some great dishes there. I think you'll like it.'

'Sounds great. I'll look forward to it.' Alyssa smiled at him and on the spur of the moment he wrapped his arms around her and kissed her soundly on the lips.

'Me, too.'

'Oh.' She was startled by the fervour that went into that kiss. 'What was that for?'

He grinned. 'I really appreciate what you've done here for us these last few weeks. Everyone says you've been brilliant, helping with everything from toothache to blistered toes. And I love the way you've looked over the script and offered advice on the medical stuff. Even if they're just a minor part of the film, it's important we get the hospital scenes right. And in the restaurant, when the man keels over, we needed to know how a doctor would respond.'

'Let's hope that won't be necessary at the restaurant today.' She laughed. 'It'll be great to sit and enjoy a meal in peace and quiet after all the goings-on on set.'

'Yeah, too right.' He gave her a final hug before letting her go. Then he hurried over to the lorry driver to give some final instructions.

'Going by the looks of things, it seems you and Ross are getting closer every day.' There was an edge to Connor's voice, and Alyssa looked at him in surprise as he came to stand beside her. His jaw was faintly clenched as though he was holding himself in restraint. He was wearing stone-coloured trousers and a casual, open-necked shirt, and he looked cool in the heat of the day.

'Hello, Connor,' she greeted him in a light tone, trying to counteract his disapproval. 'I wasn't expecting to see you here. I imagined you would be at work.' In fact, she'd seen very little of him these last few weeks, considering that they shared the same house, but she guessed he started work early at the hospital and he often came home late. Occasionally, he'd gone over to Florida to oversee his other project. Perhaps he'd been going out of an evening, too, once his shift ended.

As to his comment about her and Ross…she simply wasn't going to answer him. He was obviously hung up on the situation, so why make matters worse? It bothered her, though, that he had seen that kiss. How would she ever be able to convince him that there was nothing going on between her and his brother after that?

'It's my day off,' he said, 'so I thought I'd come and see how things were going here. Apparently the filming's on schedule so far.' His dark gaze moved over her. 'And I wondered how you were getting on. Has it been the quiet, relaxing time you expected?'

'Not exactly,' she murmured. 'But, then, I've been making something of an effort to get to grips with the job from the start.'

'Yes, so I heard.' A glimmer of respect flickered in the depths of his eyes. 'Ross has been singing your praises for days now. Apparently, you've made yourself known to everyone on set and managed to get a medical history from each one of them. He's very impressed with the way you've been handling things.'

Alyssa shrugged lightly, inadvertently loosening one of the thin straps of her broderie-anglaise top, so that it slid down the lightly tanned, silky smooth slope of her shoulder. 'It's what I'm paid to do, and the job is exactly what I thought it would be. I made it my business to get to know as much as I could about everyone beforehand so that I would have a good idea what I'm dealing with.'

'Very commendable.' Before she could remedy the offending strap, he reached out and hooked a finger beneath the cotton, carefully sliding it back into place. His touch trailed over her bare flesh like the slow lick of flame, causing an unexpected, feverish response to cascade through her, heating her blood and quickening her pulse. 'There,' he murmured. 'You're all neat and tidy once more.'

'I…um…have you…have you been to see every one of Ross's films being made?' she asked, disconcerted by his action and lifting a hand to push back the curls from her hot face. The movement lifted her brief top and exposed a small portion of her bare midriff, pale gold above the waistband of her dark jeans. His glance flicked downwards and lingered there for a while.

'I...uh...' He sounded distracted for a moment and then he cleared his throat. 'Most of them. I like to keep up with what's going on in the film world from time to time. Even though he's my brother, I must say Ross's work is good. He's had some notable successes. He deserves them because he works hard and pays a lot of attention to detail.'

She nodded. 'I've noticed that, too. He's been worrying about this morning's stunt, though. The timing has to be perfect. The stuntman has to jump from the bridge onto the moving lorry to escape from his pursuers, and he has to do it at exactly the right moment. They've even worked out how to make sure the lorry will be going at a certain speed when he jumps.'

He nodded. 'I guess that's what you might expect with these action adventure films. There always has to be something spectacular going on. After all, that's what the audience pays to see.'

Ross gave the signal for the camera recording to begin, and they turned to watch the proceedings. Around them, the buzz of conversation came to a halt and everyone's gaze was riveted to the scene about to take place. A lorry began to gradually pick up speed on the main road, which had been temporarily cleared of traffic while filming took place. The stuntman abandoned a wrecked car on the bridge and ran, chased determinedly by burly men who looked as though they meant business...nasty business. Coming to the concrete bulwark, he glanced around as though his character was trying to assimilate his options in double quick time.

With nowhere to go, and his pursuers gaining ground with every second that passed, he sprang up onto the guard-rail, remained poised for a moment, and then, as the men snapped at his heels, he leapt from the bridge.

The landing was perfect. He balanced, feet apart on top of the moving lorry, but a moment later a shocked gasp went up as the onlookers took in what happened next. Somehow Alex's foot twisted beneath him and the momentum of the still moving lorry flipped him onto his back, causing him to topple to the ground.

Alyssa was already on the move as it was happening, grabbing her medical equipment and racing towards the road where Alex was lying on the grass verge, groaning in agony. Her heart began to pound against the wall of her chest. This was the last thing she had expected. They'd been working so hard to make sure that nothing could go wrong. She had even checked him over to make sure that he was in prime physical condition before he attempted the feat.

'Alex, can you tell me where it hurts?' She quickly knelt down beside him, looking at him in concern.

'It's my back,' he said, his face contorted with pain. 'I think I caught it on the side of the lorry as I went over. I thought I felt something crack.'

The thought of the damage that might have been done to his spine made her sick with fear. All those old feelings of dread that she'd experienced back in the UK came flooding back to her, but she knew she had to get a grip on her emotions for her patient's sake. Small beads of perspiration broke out on her brow.

'Okay,' she said, disguising her inner fears with an

air of confidence, 'try not to worry. We'll soon have you feeling more comfortable.' She dialled emergency services, calling for an ambulance and warning them of a suspected spinal injury, and then she turned to Alex once more. 'I just need to check you over to see what the damage is.' All the colour had drained from his face, but at least he was still conscious and able to talk to her. That was perhaps a good sign, but she'd seen the way he'd fallen, and it didn't bode well.

'I can't believe I…could have messed up like that,' Alex said in a taut, strained voice. 'I thought…I thought it was going to be okay…' He broke off, and small beads of perspiration broke out on his brow.

'Are you in a lot of pain?' she asked. 'On a scale of one to ten?'

'Twelve,' he said, squeezing his eyes closed and pushing the word out through his teeth.

'All right.' Her head was swimming—the shock of this awful event was beginning to crowd in on her, but she made a huge effort to cast her feelings to one side. 'I'll give you something to take that away, just as soon as I've done a preliminary examination. Try not to move. It's very important that you stay still.'

She made a brief but thorough check of his injuries and noted his blood pressure and pulse, before injecting him with a painkiller. 'I need to put a collar around your neck to immobilise it and make sure there'll be no further damage.'

Alex didn't answer her. His strength seemed to be ebbing away, and she realised that he might be slipping into neurogenic shock through a combination of pressure on the spinal cord and possible internal bleeding.

A wave of panic swept through her. It was down to her to get him through this. What if she couldn't do it?

'Would you like some help?' Connor came over to her, and she guessed he'd been standing by, waiting to see if he was needed.

'Yes, that would be great, thanks.' Alyssa sent him a fleeting glance. His expression was serious, but he was calm, and his long, lean body was poised and ready for action. If only she could experience some of that inner composure. She said quietly, 'His blood pressure and pulse are both dropping rapidly, so I'm going to try to stabilise him with intravenous fluids.'

It was a very disturbing situation. When she tested his reflexes, Alex wasn't aware of any sensation in his legs and that was tremendously worrying, because it meant the eventual outcome could be disastrous. It was possible the damage was so great that Alex might never walk again.

She dashed those thoughts from her mind and breathed deeply to try to overcome the chaotic beat of her heart, concentrating on doing what she could for her patient. It was down to her to bring about the best outcome possible for him and the responsibility weighed heavily on her. 'I want to get a rigid collar around his neck…that's all important…and we must give him oxygen.'

He nodded. 'I'll do that for you.' He knelt down and supported Alex's neck while Alyssa carefully fixed the protective collar in place. Then he placed the oxygen mask over their patient's nose and mouth and started to squeeze the oxygen bag rhythmically. All the time, Alyssa was aware that Alex was slipping into unconsciousness.

She sucked in her breath. 'His heart rate is way too low. I'm going to give him atropine and have the defibrillator standing by, just in case.' Simply, if the heart didn't pump blood around his body effectively, her patient would die, but the atropine should help to increase the heart rate.

She quickly prepared the syringe while Connor continued with the oxygen. 'Okay,' she murmured, 'let's see if that will bring him round.' While they waited for the drug to work, Alyssa placed pads on Alex's chest and connected him to the portable defibrillator.

'It's not happening—the heart rate's not picking up enough,' Connor observed with a frown a short time later. 'Maybe it's time to deliver a shock to the heart.'

She nodded and set the machine to the correct rate and current. 'Stay clear of him while I do that.'

Connor moved back a little, and both of them waited. For a second or two, nothing happened, and Alyssa's mouth became painfully dry, the breath catching in her throat. She realised she was praying silently. This had to work.

Then there was a faint bleep, and the display on the defibrillator began to show a normal heart rhythm. She breathed a sigh of relief. The rate was still slow, but at least he was out of the woods for the moment.

The ambulance arrived as she and Connor continued the struggle to regulate Alex's blood pressure. The paramedics greeted Connor as a friend, as if they'd known him for a long time, and then they listened as Alyssa quickly brought them up to date with what was going on.

'I'm very worried about any injury to his back,' she said quietly, 'so we need to take great care when we move him. We'll help you to get him onto a spinal board.'

She and Connor knelt with one of the paramedics alongside Alex's still form, each one ready to lift and gently roll him on his side towards them on Alyssa's command. 'Okay, let's do it…three…two…one…go.'

The second paramedic slid the board underneath Alex, and then they carefully rolled him onto his back once more.

'That was well done.' Alyssa stood back as the paramedics strapped him securely in place and lifted him on to a trolley stretcher. Alex was still not speaking and she was dreadfully afraid his condition was deteriorating fast. 'I'll go with him to the hospital.'

'Okay.' The paramedic nodded and turned to Connor. 'Will you be coming along, too?'

'Yes. I'll follow in my car.'

Alyssa watched as they trundled Alex towards the ambulance, and saw, out of the corner of her eye, that Ross was hovering nearby. Seeing that she had finished working on her patient for the time being, he hurried over to her.

'Is he going to be all right? I couldn't believe what I was seeing. It's my worst nightmare.' The lively, boyish young man he'd been just a short time ago had disappeared completely. He looked haggard, devastated by what had happened.

'We'll know more after they've done tests at the hospital.' She laid a hand on his arm, wanting to comfort him. 'It wasn't your fault, Ross. All stunts carry danger, you know that. It was plain bad luck.'

'Even so, I feel terrible about it.' His face was ashen. 'Maybe I shouldn't have been directing today, but Dan had to be somewhere else, so I had to step in. I know he wanted to be here for this scene. Maybe it was an omen...'

'Ross, you mustn't blame yourself. No one could have foreseen what happened.'

His shoulders sagged. 'I don't know...I thought I had everything covered...' He pulled himself together, straightening up. 'I want to go to the hospital to be with him, but I have to get in touch with his wife, and stay here and talk to the police, and try to explain what went wrong. There will be all sorts of questions, accident reports, insurance forms to be dealt with... I'm going to be sifting through all that over the next few hours, but tell him we'll take care of his family and see to anything that he needs, will you? Anything he wants, he just has to ask.'

'I'll tell him.'

'Thanks. I'll come along to see him just as soon as I can.'

'Of course.'

She gave him a reassuring hug and then turned back to the ambulance. Connor was standing by the open doors, supervising Alex's transfer.

'It looks as though Ross isn't taking it too well,' he murmured.

'No, he isn't. He feels responsible.' She glanced at him. He looked concerned as he watched his brother brace himself and walk towards a uniformed officer. 'Do you want to stay with him while he talks to the police and so on?'

He shook his head. 'No, I think I can probably be of more use at the hospital. I'm sure Ross will cope once he's over the initial shock.'

'Maybe. Let's hope so.' She frowned, rubbing absently at her temple, where a pulse had begun to throb.

He studied her, his grey eyes narrowing. 'Are you all right? You've gone very pale all of a sudden.'

'I'll be fine. It's just a bit of a headache starting.' She had to admit to herself, though, that now her role as an immediate response medic was complete, she wasn't feeling good at all. She'd taken this job feeling pretty certain that nothing like this would ever happen. When it had, despite all the odds, she'd found herself acting purely on instinct, following the basic tenets of medical care in the way that she'd been taught, in a way that had become second nature to her.

Now, to her dismay, the adrenaline that had kept her going through those initial moments was draining away and in the aftermath she was shaking inside. She was experiencing those same feelings of dread, of exhaustion and nervous tension that had started to overwhelm her when she had been working in emergency back home. A feeling of nausea washed over her.

She climbed into the ambulance and seated herself beside Alex, closing her eyes for a brief moment as though that would shut out the memories. He reminded her so much of that patient she'd treated back in the UK. They were about the same age, the same build, with dark hair and pain-filled eyes that haunted her, and both had fallen...

The paramedic closed the doors, bringing her back to the present with a jolt, and within a few seconds they were on their way, siren blaring, to the hospital.

Connor met them at the ambulance bay. 'Welcome to Coral Cay Hospital,' he murmured, reaching out to help Alyssa step down from the vehicle. His grip was

firm and the hand at her elbow was reassuringly supportive. 'Our trauma team is all ready and waiting for
the patient. They'll take good care of him, you'll see.'

Oddly, she was glad he had decided to come here
with her. 'Yes, I'm sure they will.' By all accounts, the
hospital had a good reputation and Alex would be in
safe hands.

The registrar was already walking by the side of the
trolley as the paramedics wheeled Alex into the emergency unit, and Alyssa went with them, ready to talk
to the doctor about his condition.

'We'll do a thorough neurological examination,' the
registrar told her. 'And then we'll get a CT scan done
so that we can find out exactly what's going on.' He
glanced at Connor. 'Do you know how we can get in
touch with any of his relatives?'

Connor nodded. 'You don't need to worry about that,
Jack. My brother's already spoken to Alex's wife. He
rang to tell me on the car phone when I was on my
way over here. She's going to make arrangements for
someone to look after the children while she comes to
be with him.'

'That's good.' They'd reached the trauma bay by
now, and Jack started on his examination of the patient.
Alyssa and Connor took turns to tell him what had happened and describe the treatment they had given Alex.

'You did everything you could,' the registrar said,
'but there's nothing more you can do here. Why don't
you two go and get a cup of coffee, and I'll let you
know as soon as the scans are finished? I know how
concerned you must be, but I promise I'll keep you in
the loop.'

'Okay. Thanks. We'll get out of your way.' Alyssa

glanced at Alex, who was connected to monitors that bleeped and flashed and underlined the fact that he was in a distressing condition.

'I can hardly believe this is happening,' she said under her breath as she walked away with Connor.

He nodded. 'It's hard to take in.' He sent her an oblique glance. 'Are you okay? You don't look quite right.'

'I'm fine,' she lied.

'Hmm. I suppose all this must come as a shock when you imagined the job would involve nothing more than having to deal with a few minor ailments or lacerations.' He led the way along the corridor and showed her to his office, pushing open the door and ushering her inside, his hand resting lightly on the small of her back. It was strangely comforting, that warmth of human contact.

'Please…take a seat.' He waved her to a chair by the desk, and then flicked a switch on the coffee machine that stood on a table in a corner of the room.

She looked around. The office had been furnished with infinite care, from the seagrass-coloured carpet that added a quiet dignity over all, to the elegantly up-holstered leather armchairs that would provide comfort and ease to anxious relatives, keen to know the details of any treatment their loved ones would need. There was a leather couch, too, set against one wall, adding a feeling of opulence to the whole.

To one side of the room there was a mahogany book-case, filled with leather bound medical books, and in front of the large window was a highly polished desk made of the same rich, dark mahogany. This was topped with a burgundy leather desk mat and beautiful accessories, which included a brass pen-holder and an intricately designed brass paperweight.

'You're still look very white-faced,' he remarked as he set out two cups and saucers and began to pour coffee. 'It's not just that you're worried about Alex, is it? I can't help thinking there's something more.' He hesitated for a moment. 'Shall I get you some painkillers for the headache?'

She shook her head. 'Like I said, I'll be fine.'

He slid a cup towards her. 'Would you like cream and sugar with that?'

'Please.' She nodded, and he slid a tray containing a cream jug and sugar bowl onto the desk beside her. The bowl was filled with amber-coloured chips of rock sugar that gleamed softly in the sunlight and gave off a pleasing aroma of dark molasses.

Connor sat down, leaning back in his black leather chair, eyeing her over the rim of his cup. 'Something's definitely not right,' he said. 'What is it? You did all you possibly could for Alex, so it can't be that. Does it have something to do with the reason you're not working back in the UK?'

Her eyes widened and her heart missed a beat. 'Why would you think that?'

He shrugged. 'A few stray connections linking up in my mind. It's odd that you would leave the place where you did your training and where you worked for several years and give it all up to come halfway across the world. I can't help thinking something must have gone wrong. It's not as though you could afford to travel the world and simply take time out.'

She raised a brow. 'How do you know all that? Have you been talking to Ross?'

He smiled. 'Of course. He talks about you every opportunity he gets.'

'Oh, dear.' She brooded on that for a moment or two. She'd never given Ross the slightest encouragement to think of her as anything more than a friend, but somewhere along the way he must have started pinning his hopes on something more developing between them. Judging by what Connor was saying, she would have to put a stop to it, and sooner rather than later.

He was watching her as she thought things through. 'He thinks the world of you and would do anything for you, but we both know that you don't really feel the same way about him, don't we?'

She stiffened. 'I like Ross. I think he's a wonderful person.' She didn't appreciate the faintly challenging note in Connor's tone. It annoyed her that he should imply she had come here with an ulterior motive.

'Yes, he is…' Connor agreed, 'but that still doesn't explain why you abandoned everything to come out here with him.'

She sipped her coffee, giving herself time to gain a little more composure. 'You think I was sick of working for a living and gave up on it to follow him, don't you?'

'Isn't that a possibility?' He studied her thoughtfully. 'The idea of coming to a sun-soaked island where you could relax and forget your cares must have had huge appeal.'

She smiled briefly. 'Of course it did. But you're forgetting…in my case I'm actually here to work. Ross gave me the opportunity to try something new and I jumped at it. I don't see anything wrong with that. Do you?' Her chin lifted and a hint of defiance shimmered in her green eyes.

'When you put it that way, no…of course not.' His glance wandered over her face, lingering on the perfect curve of her mouth, the fullness of her lips made moist by the coffee and accentuated by the inviting, cherry-red lipstick she was wearing. After a moment or two he pulled himself up and shook his head as though to clear it. 'I dare say a lot of people would envy you being able to simply take off and leave everything behind.'

'I guess so.' She might have said more, but his pager went off just then, and he frowned as he checked the text message. 'Jack Somers has finished the preliminary tests. We can go and talk to him now.'

'That's good.' Her stomach muscles tightened in nervous expectation.

They went to find the registrar in his office. 'I have the CT scans here,' he said, bringing up the films on his computer screen. 'You'll see there are a couple of fractured vertebrae and there's a lot of inflammation around that area.'

Connor winced. 'It'll mean an operation, then?'

Jack nodded. 'I'm afraid so.' He glanced at Alyssa. 'We'll get him prepped for surgery as soon as possible, maybe within the hour. The surgeon will stabilise the spine with metal rods and screws and do what he can to ease the pressure on the spinal cord. Unfortunately, it'll be some time before we know what the outcome will be regarding him regaining any movement in his legs. There's so much swelling that it's hard to see exactly what damage has been done.'

'I appreciate that. Thanks for letting us know.' Alyssa was saddened, looking at those films. How would Alex take the news, having been an active, athletic man? He was in his prime, with a young family to support, and it grieved her to think of how this would affect them.

Connor added his thanks and they left the office, going over to the trauma room where Alex was being tended by two specialist nurses. Alyssa spoke to them and watched for a while as they set up drips and programmed the medication pump. He was still unresponsive, but he was being well looked after, she felt sure.

There was nothing more they could do there and she went with Connor to the car park a few minutes later.

'Time's slipping by faster than I imagined,' he said, looking briefly at the gold watch on his wrist. 'Maybe we should go and get some lunch and come back later to see how he's doing once the operation is over.' He glanced at her. 'We could go to Benvenuto, if you like. It would be a shame to let Ross's lunch reservations go to waste, don't you think?'

'I don't know. I…' His offer caught her unawares. Until that moment she hadn't even realised she was hungry, but now he mentioned it there was a definite hollow feeling in her stomach. Even so, it made her feel uncomfortable to think of deserting Ross and going out to lunch with Connor instead. 'Is there no chance he could join us? Perhaps I should give him a call…'

'I already did that.' They had reached his car, a low-slung, highly polished sports model, and now he pulled open the passenger door and waited for her to slide onto the leather upholstered seat. 'I spoke to him while you were talking to the nurses. He agreed it would be a shame to let the booking go to waste.'

'Oh, I see.' She frowned. 'I suppose he's still busy dealing with the accident reports? Did he say how it was going?'

'He's still talking to the insurers and working on his
report. Then at some point he'll have to meet with the
director and work out how they can reschedule the filming. Everything's been put on hold for the next couple
of days. Everybody's too upset to go on right now. He's
spoken to Alex's wife, and arranged for a car to take
her to the hospital.'

'I'm glad he did that.'

Connor slid into the driver's seat and set the car in
motion, while Alyssa sat back, thankful for the air-
conditioning on such a hot day. Connor had a light touch
on the controls and it seemed as though the car was a
dream to handle, smooth and responsive, covering the
miles with ease. If it hadn't been for her worries, the
journey to the marina would have been soothing and a
delight to savour.

Instead, she tried to take her mind off things by looking out of the window at the landscape of hills clad with
pine forest, which soon receded into the distance and
changed to a vista of lush orange groves and thriving
banana plantations.

'We're almost there,' Connor said a little later, pointing out the blue waters of the marina in the distance. 'I
expect the place will be quite busy at this time of the
day, but Ross reserved a table on the terrace, so we'll
be in the best spot and able to look out over the yacht
basin.'

'That sounds great.' She made a face. 'I'm actually
starving. I hadn't realised it was so long since breakfast.'

'Hmm. I'm not surprised.' He looked her over and
smiled. 'I doubt you can really give what you have to

eat the term "breakfast". Fruit juice and a small bowl of cereal is more like a quick snack, I'd say.'

She looked at him in astonishment as he drove into the restaurant car park. 'What do you mean? How do you know what I eat?'

He slipped the car into a parking space and cut the engine. 'I've seen you from the upper deck—you often go out onto the terrace to eat first thing in the morning, don't you? You're a lot like me in that. I like to be out in the fresh air so that I can take stock of my surroundings and, like you, I drink freshly squeezed orange juice. It makes me feel good first thing in the morning. Though how you can expect to last for long on what you eat is beyond me.'

He came around to the passenger side of the car and opened the door for her. She frowned. 'I usually take a break mid-morning and catch up with a bun or a croissant,' she said in a rueful tone. 'Of course, with everything going on the way it did today, that didn't happen.'

'You should enjoy the food here all the more, then.' He locked the car and laid a hand on the small of her back, leading her into the restaurant.

Alyssa was glad of the coolness of the interior. His casual, gentle touch felt very much like a caress to her heightened senses, and the heat it generated seemed to suffuse her whole body.

A waiter showed them to their table out on the terrace, and once again the heat of the sun beat down on Alyssa's bare arms. Her cheeks felt flushed and Connor must have noticed because he said softly, 'At least we'll be in the shade of that palm tree. There's a faint breeze sifting through the branches—couldn't be better.'

'It's lovely here.' She sat down and absorbed the

beauty of her surroundings for a while until gradually she felt herself begin to relax. On one side there was the marina, with an assortment of yachts bobbing gently on the water, and on the other there was the sweep of the beach, with a magnificent stretch of soft, white sand and a backdrop of low scrub and palm trees.

In the distance, the coastline changed yet again, becoming rocky, with jagged inlets, peninsulas and lagoons. There, the trees were different, smaller, and she could just about make out their twisting trunks and branches laden with sprays of yellow flowers. 'Are those the logwood trees I've been hearing about?' she asked, and he nodded.

'That's right.'

'I heard the wood yields a rich, deep reddish-purple dye,' she said. 'I've seen some lovely silk garments that were coloured with it.'

'Yes, it's used quite widely hereabouts. The flowers give great honey, too, so I guess it's a useful tree all round.'

The waiter handed them menus, and they were silent for a moment, studying them. Connor ordered a bottle of wine.

'I can't make up my mind what to choose,' Alyssa said after a while. 'Everything looks mouth-wateringly good to me.'

'I thought I might start with conch chowder and follow it with shrimp Alfredo and marinara-flavoured pasta,' he murmured. 'They do those dishes particularly well here.'

'Hmm…I think I'll go along with that, too.' She smiled and laid down her menu.

The waiter took their orders, and Connor poured her a glass of wine and asked about her family back home.

'Do you have any relatives in the UK? I know you have your cousin Carys in Florida.'

'My parents are living in London at the moment,' she told him. 'I don't have any brothers or sisters.'

He frowned. 'I imagine they must miss you, the more so since you're an only child.'

'Possibly.' She thought about that for a moment or two. 'But they're really quite busy... My mother runs a boutique and my father is a businessman, a director of an electronics company. I don't think they'll really have time to worry about what I'm getting up to. And of course I've lived away from home for a number of years, since I qualified as a doctor.'

'Hmm...that sounds like quite a...sterile...relationship.' He studied her for a while, pausing the conversation as the waiter brought a tureen of chowder to the table and began to ladle it into bowls.

Alyssa tasted her creamy soup and mulled over Connor's remark. 'I don't know about that,' she said. 'It was always that way, for as long as I can remember. In my teenage years I was what people called a latchkey kid, coming home to an empty house because my parents worked late. I didn't mind back then. In fact, I never thought much about it. I learned to fend for myself, and there were always friends that I could be with, so I wasn't lonely.'

He'd hit on something, though, the way he'd described her relationship with her family. Her eyes were troubled as she thought it over. Sometimes she'd missed that intimacy of family closeness that her friends had seemed to take for granted, especially when her career had started falling apart and her love life had taken a dive. She hadn't felt able to share her innermost secrets, even with her best friends, but it would have been good to be able to turn to family in her hour of need.

She told him a little about her mother's fashionable boutique, and how she would try on the latest designs and try to persuade her mother that she could be a good advert for the shop by wearing the beautiful creations.

'She didn't fall for that one very often, unfortunately.' She smiled, and hesitated while the waiter cleared away the first course. 'Do your parents live close by?' she asked.

He nodded. 'Reasonably so. They live in the Bahamas, but on different islands. I see them quite often, but never actually together. They divorced some years ago and my father remarried recently.'

'I'm sorry.' She frowned. 'It must have been hard for you to cope with that…for Ross, too.'

'Yes. It was difficult for Ross, especially. He was about eleven at the time, and very impressionable. Of course, you grow up hoping that your parents will stay together for ever, and when it doesn't work out that way you struggle to come to terms with all the fallout.'

'I understand how that must be a problem.' Her gaze was sympathetic. 'I've been lucky, I suppose, in that my parents are still together.'

The main course arrived, and they were quiet for a while, savouring the delicate flavours of pasta and shrimp, and then they both marvelled at the way the chef had brought his magic touch to the ingredients. The pasta was made with tomatoes, garlic and herbs, and was particularly good.

'I can see why this place is so popular,' Alyssa mur-

mured, spearing a shrimp with her fork and raising it
to her lips. 'This is delicious.' She loved the flavour of
the Alfredo sauce, made from a blend of white sauce
and cream cheese.

Connor watched her, his glance following the gentle
sweep of her hand and hovering around the full curve
of her mouth. He topped up her glass with wine, a light,
fruity complement to the superb food.

'It is,' he agreed softly. 'But, you know, there are
lots of good experiences to be had on our island.
Sightseeing, sailing, maybe even exploring the coral
reefs…though I expect you know all about those.' He
lifted his glass and swallowed some of the clear liquid.
'Have you had time to look around and get to know
the place?'

She shook her head, causing the bright curls to quiver
and drift against her shoulders. 'Not yet, unfortunately.
Ross wanted to show me around, but he's been very
busy with the film, and for my part I'm still trying to
get settled in and find my way around my new job. I
dare say there will be time to do all those other things
before too long. I have a couple more months on my
contract here, so there's no hurry.'

'I could take you anywhere you wanted to go,' he
suggested. 'It would be a shame to miss out on any of
the delights of this beautiful island, don't you think?'
His voice was silky smooth, reassuringly pleasant and
somehow intimate at the same time.

'I…uh…yes, I suppose so.' Alarm bells started to
ring inside her head. His offer was tempting, but why
was he offering to show her around? He'd made it quite
plain where they stood, on two sides of a dividing line,
with Ross in between. 'Um…it's great of you to offer,

but you really don't have to put yourself out.' She returned his gaze. 'I'm sure Ross will be free soon enough to take me out and about, and even if he isn't, I can manage some sightseeing by myself.'

'But that wouldn't be quite as enjoyable, I think.' He leaned back in his chair as the waiter came to clear the table and take their order for dessert. He handed her the menu. 'What's your fancy? There are all sorts of dishes flavoured with coconut—as you might imagine, with the number of palm trees around—or bananas, of course. Or maybe you prefer chocolate?'

'Do you know, I think I'd like to try the crêpes Suzette. Have you tried them?'

'I have. They're a good choice. I think I'll join you. One of their specialties here is to bring them to the table and flame them in Curaçao and Grand Marnier and then top them with luscious, sweet, dark cherries.' He smiled and gave the order to the waiter, then offered to top up her wine glass once more.

She covered the glass with her hand. 'No more for me, thanks. I need to keep a clear head.'

'Why do you have to do that? You're not on duty any more, are you? Filming has stopped for a couple of days, so you can relax for a while. Why not take the opportunity to ease back from work and being on your guard?' His dark eyes seemed to glint as he spoke, but it might have been a trick of the light. 'Because you are on your guard, aren't you?' he murmured.

With him, yes, she'd been constantly on her guard, ever since the moment they'd first met. He knew it, and she couldn't help but feel he was tormenting her with the knowledge.

'I've always found it best to keep an eye on what's

going on all around,' she said quietly. She'd been caught unawares with James, her ex-boyfriend, and she was determined nothing like that was ever going to happen again.

'Hmm…I wonder why?' His eyes narrowed on her, but she didn't answer him.

Instead, she took an interest in the dessert dish that the waiter prepared with a flourish before placing it in front of her. She dipped in a spoon and tasted the mix of flavours. The crêpe Suzette was hot, with a melt-in-the-mouth sauce, and the smooth, cold ice cream served with it was a delicious contrast. Connor watched her for a moment, as though he was fascinated by her absorption with the food.

'We both have some free time outside work,' he murmured, 'so perhaps you could think again about us spending it together… Maybe we could take a trip on a glass-bottomed boat so that you can see the coral close at hand. Would you like that?'

'I'm sure it would be a delightful experience,' she said softly, and he lifted a dark brow in expectation until she added, 'but somehow I don't think it would be right for you and me to be together too much outside work.'

'You don't?' He studied her thoughtfully, taking time to taste his dessert. 'Why is that? Are you afraid Ross might be concerned about what you're doing?'

'Not exactly…but I'm a bit puzzled. After all, if you really think there's something going on between us, it's a bit strange that you would think of asking me out.' She finished off her dessert and laid down her spoon, resting her hand on the table alongside her wine glass and running the tips of her fingers over the delicate stem.

He shrugged. 'I heard you say that you were through

with romance, so maybe I'm taking that statement at face value. In that case, why should it be a problem for Ross if you and I were to spend some time together?' He reached for her hand, taking it into his palm and brushing his thumb lightly over her smooth skin. Her heart began to thump heavily.

'I'd like to spend time with you, Alyssa, and get to know you better.'

'Like I said, I don't think that would be a very good idea.' Her voice was husky, drowned out by the thunder of the blood in her veins as his fingers travelled along her wrist in a subtle caress. 'I...uh...I'm not looking for any kind of involvement right now.'

'That's all right. Neither am I. Things don't have to get serious. I'm not looking for commitment.' His mouth made a wry curve. 'After the mess my parents made of things, that's the last thing I'm looking for.' His gaze meshed with hers. 'But we could have a good time all the same, you and I...no strings.'

She made a faint smile. 'That sounds...interesting,' she murmured, the breath catching in her throat. Her heart had switched into overdrive now, the beat building up to a crescendo as his fingers gently massaged the back of her hand and his thumb made tantalising circles over her wrist. 'Only...' She pulled in a deep breath. 'Only I have the feeling you're not being quite straight with me. I did mean what I said. I'm not looking for any kind of attachment right now, strings or no strings.'

She carefully extracted her hand from his. 'I'm sorry if that messes with your plans.'

He frowned. 'Not at all. It was just a suggestion, and I don't want to upset you in any way.' His glance drifted over her. 'Can you blame me for trying? You're a beautiful young woman, and I'd surely need to have ice water in my veins if I wasn't interested in you.'

She swallowed hard. 'I'm flattered, I think, but my answer's still the same, I'm afraid. I'd sooner keep things the way they are.'

'As you please, of course.' He smiled. 'Though that's not to say I won't keep trying.'

He signalled to the waiter to bring coffee, and for the rest of their time at the restaurant he was charm itself, talking to her about the island, the people and places that made up its exotic appeal. He backed off from making any more overtures and she tried to relax a little.

She didn't believe for one minute that he was interested in her for her own sake. No matter what he said, he was acting purely in his brother's interests. He thought she was involved with him in some way, and he wanted to break it up, even if it meant taking her on himself. If Ross were to be hurt in the process, then so be it, because in his mind she was the dangerous one here.

He believed she had the power to ruin his brother's happiness, and he meant to put a stop to that by any means possible. She would be as wary of Connor as she would be of a stalking tiger.

CHAPTER THREE

'I CAN'T believe we've had such a difficult day.' Ross waited while Alyssa stopped to pick up the local newspaper that lay on the porch, tossed there by the delivery boy earlier in the afternoon.

Ross followed her along the hallway and into the spacious living room. 'Do you mind if I open the doors onto the veranda?'

'Please do. Open every one you come across.' She shrugged off her light cotton jacket and kicked off her shoes. It was early evening and she was looking forward to sitting out on the deck for a while. 'I'll fix us a drink. Would you like hot or cold?'

'Cold, definitely. All I want to do is to sprawl in a chair and wind down for half an hour or so.' He ran a hand through his dark hair, leaving it dishevelled and giving him a distinctly youthful appearance.

Alyssa looked at the newspaper, scanning the headlines, and winced. 'It says here there was an accident on the highway this morning. I wonder if Connor had to deal with that? I expect he must have, unless the casualties were flown to the mainland.'

The standard of driving out here could be atrocious, she'd discovered, with people speeding and driving recklessly, or overloading their vehicles to the point where they were dangerous. According to the news report, this latest crash was as the result of a motorcyclist weaving through lanes of moving traffic.

'He most probably did,' Ross said. 'In fact, he might have been called out to go to the scene—he does regular stints as an on-call first attender. The emergency services want him there if the injuries are very serious and it's something the paramedics can't deal with on their own.' He frowned. 'I'll give him a ring,' Ross said, 'if that's all right with you? I think I heard him moving about upstairs. I want to speak to him, anyway, to see how things are going, so I expect he'll want to come down here for a while.'

She nodded. 'That's okay. I'd better set out three glasses and some sandwiches.' She didn't feel that she had much choice but to see Connor, given that she was living in his house rent-free for the duration of her contract. To object would simply be churlish, wouldn't it? Her head was aching already, though, and the last thing she needed was to be on her guard around Connor.

He walked out on to the veranda a few minutes later, bringing with him a basket of fruit. 'For you,' he told Alyssa. 'I thought you might like to sample some of the fruits of our island.'

'Wow, that's quite an assortment,' she said in an appreciative tone, gazing down at the beautifully arranged wicker basket. 'There must be almost a dozen different types of fruit in here. Thank you for this.' She was impressed. Among them there were mangoes, papaya and green sugar apples, along with pears and a large, golden pineapple. 'I don't know what I've done to deserve this.'

'You didn't have to do anything at all. Think of it as a delayed welcome-to-the-island present, if you like.'

'I will. Thanks.' She was thoughtful for a moment or two. 'Perhaps I ought to take something like this along to the hospital when I go to see Alex.'

'He already has one.' Connor's expression became sombre. 'I had one made up for him and took it in to him this morning. He's not really very interested in anything, though, at the moment. He's very depressed.'

'I suppose it doesn't help that he's not able to move much at the moment, but at least the operation went well,' Alyssa murmured. 'It's just a question of taking time to heal now, isn't it? And he'll have physiotherapy, of course, once he's up to it.' She sent Connor a fleeting glance. 'I'm surprised you found the time to look in on him if the evening paper is anything to go by. It looks as though you had to deal with a nasty traffic accident.'

He pulled a face. 'Yes, it was pretty bad. There were a few people involved, with some severe fractures, and the motorcyclist is in a very worrying condition. He went into cardiac arrest at the scene, but we managed to pull him through and get his heart started again. It's touch and go for him at the moment.'

'I'm sorry.' She frowned. 'It's a difficult job. You do what you can to patch people up, but the downside is that some of them don't make it.' Working in the emergency unit back in the UK, she had seen more than her fair share of traumatic injuries. Dealing with them day in and day out had become more than she could handle, especially when things hadn't gone well for the patient. She'd tried her utmost to help them, but occasionally fate had been against her, and that had been really hard to take.

She put down the basket of fruit in the kitchen and carried a tray out onto the deck, where they sat around on wicker chairs by a glass-topped table. She'd made up a jug of iced fruit juice and put out plates alongside a selection of sandwiches.

'Help yourselves,' she said, coming to sit down in one of the chairs. She reached for one of the filled glasses, then leaned back and stretched out her long, bare legs. Her cool, cotton skirt draped itself just above her knees. 'Mmm…this is good,' she murmured, taking a long swallow. She held the glass against her hot forehead, letting the coolness soothe her aching head.

'It looks as though you've had a difficult day, too,' Connor remarked, pulling up a chair beside her. He wore light-coloured trousers that moulded themselves to his strong thighs, and a short-sleeved shirt that was open at the neck to reveal an expanse of lightly tanned throat. His arms were strong, well muscled, the forearms covered with a light sprinkling of dark hair. For some inexplicable reason his overwhelmingly masculine presence disturbed her, and she quickly looked away.

'You name it, everything went wrong today,' she murmured wearily. 'First of all part of the prefabricated set collapsed, causing some minor injuries, and then there was a problem with some of the actors getting sick. They'd been out to breakfast early this morning and were violently ill a few hours later—gastroenteritis, I think. I gave them rehydration salts and sent them home.'

'So now we're going to be even further behind schedule,' Ross put in. 'Tempers were fraying and everyone was in a bad mood…all except Alyssa, that is.' He smiled as he looked at her. 'Somehow she managed to stay serene and patient through it all. She's a very calming influence all round.'

He sat down in a chair opposite them, by the rail on the veranda, close to the shrubbery where bougainvillea bloomed, its glorious, deep pink, paper-thin flowers bright in the sunshine. They had been planted all around the property, between showy hibiscus and the pretty, trumpet-like yellow allamanda flowers.

'We managed to keep most of the film footage where Alex did the stunt scene, which was a relief.' He frowned. 'That sounds awful, me talking like that, doesn't it, seeing how ill he is, but it could have set us back really badly. As it is, that's one worry at least off our minds.'

'Are you having problems, then?' Connor asked. 'Apart from the scenery collapsing, I mean.' He made a wry smile.

'Like Alyssa said…you name it. Nothing's going right. It's as though the whole thing is jinxed. Everything that can go wrong is going wrong. Next thing you know, we'll not be able to shoot tomorrow because there'll be a hitch with the outdoor schedule we've set up.'

'Hmm…' Connor appeared to be turning things over in his head. 'That reminds me, I had a call from Dan a short time ago. He's been trying to get hold of you but your mobile was switched off, or something.'

Ross frowned, and checked his phone. 'Wouldn't you credit it?' he said with a grimace. 'Battery's flat.'

Connor acknowledged that with a slight inclination of his head. 'Actually, he said he wanted to meet up with you at the studio. He just got in today from Florida and he wants to talk to you about the filming. He said he'll be at the studio for another couple of hours.'

Ross sighed. 'I guess that puts paid to my evening of relaxation.' He took a couple of sandwiches from the plate and stood up. 'Thanks for these, Alyssa,' he said. 'It looks as though I'll have to eat them on the move.'

Alyssa watched him go, and then looked at Connor with narrowed eyes. 'Was it really essential that he had to go over there right now? Surely a phone call would have done?'

Connor lifted his shoulders in a negligent fashion. 'I'm just the messenger,' he said. 'Far be it from me to interfere with the day-to-day work of the producer and the director.'

She looked at him from under her dark lashes. There was a smile hovering around his mouth and she didn't trust him an inch. She had the strongest feeling that he had manoeuvred the situation so Ross didn't get to spend the evening with her.

Her own phone rang just then, and she excused herself for a while, going into the living room to answer it. 'It's Carys,' she told Connor, as she glanced at the name displayed on the screen. 'Help yourself to sandwiches and salad, and there are cheese and biscuits in the kitchen if you want them.'

'Thanks.'

She handed him the evening paper, and left him to look over the headlines while she went to speak to Carys.

Some ten minutes later she went back out onto the deck, the headache considerably worse, and her mood decidedly fractious.

Connor sent her a sideways glance. 'It doesn't look as though your cousin managed to cheer you up,' he commented. 'Just the opposite, I'd say.'

She gave him a tight-lipped smile. 'She was just giving me the news from back home. She's in touch with friends over there, and they help her keep up with the latest gossip.'

'It wasn't good news, though, judging from your expression.'

'Nothing bad. My parents are as busy as ever. Apparently my father is thinking of expanding the business, and my mother has a fashion show coming up in the next couple of weeks, where she'll be able to parade some of the latest styles she has on sale.'

'That's good, isn't it?'

'I guess so.' It would perhaps explain why they hadn't had time to return her calls or answer her emails.

'Is there something more? You seem tense.'

'Nothing important,' she said. She wasn't going to tell him about James, her ex. He'd been asking after her, apparently, wanting to know how he might get in touch. That was the last thing she wanted.

She sat down and drank more of the fruit juice. 'It's another niggling headache,' she told him when he continued to subject her to a brooding stare. 'I suppose I need to learn to relax a bit more and not let things get to me so easily.'

'That would be sensible, if you could take your own advice.' He gave her a faint smile, adding on a thoughtful note, 'You could try some of the local bush medicine. That might do the trick. Do you know about the tamarind tree?'

She shook her head.

He looked around. 'See that tree over there…?' He pointed to a tree a short distance away. It had attractive leaves that billowed in the slight breeze, and there were large, reddish-coloured seedpods hanging in clusters from the branches. She nodded.

'The natives call it the jumbie plant,' he said. 'It's another name for the tamarind. You collect the leaves and boil them up in water, and then let the mixture infuse for a while. When it's cool, you drink the brew. It's supposed to make you feel much better.'

'Hmm. That sounds interesting.' She frowned. 'I wonder if it works.'

He chuckled. 'Then again, you could save yourself all that bother and just take a couple of aspirin.'

She laughed with him, and he said quietly, 'Why don't we take a stroll on the beach for a while? It might help to make you feel better. You're probably just wound up after a stressful day.'

'Yes, you could be right about that.' A walk on the beach sounded inviting, and before she gave the matter any more thought she found herself nodding. 'Okay. I think I'd enjoy a walk in the fresh air.'

She went to fetch her sandals from the sitting room, but draped the straps over her fingers as she walked barefoot along the white sand. The sun was beginning to set, casting a golden glow over the horizon, and the wading birds had come down to the shore, getting in a last meal before they retired for the night. Close by, humming birds flitted among the yellow elder flowers, sipping the nectar, and the sweet smell of frangipani filled the air. It was a magical time and Alyssa began to relax, watching the waves break on the shore, leaving behind small ribbons of white foam.

'I love this time of the day,' Connor said softly. 'Everything seems so peaceful and I find all the cares of the day begin to seep away. There's something very calming about coming down here to watch the ocean roll over the sand.'

'Mmm…that's true. I think it's because it's so steadfast. We're busy running around chasing our tails, but the forces of nature stay the same throughout, the ocean ebbs and flows and day follows night, come what may.'

They walked along the shoreline, and Alyssa felt the warm wash of water bathe her feet. Connor joined her, going barefoot by her side, so that their feet left prints in the damp sand.

As they moved further along the beach, he reached for her hand, enclosing her fingers in his palm, and at the same time he put a finger to his mouth, indicating that they should fall silent. Then he pointed ahead and she saw what he was focusing on. It was a bird, standing almost two feet high, black with a white underbelly and a large, orange bill.

'What is he?' she whispered. 'I wish I knew more about the wildlife out here.'

'He's an American oystercatcher,' he said softly, 'looking for clams or mussels, I expect. The birds migrate here in the late summer, but I've not seen any around here for a while. I think this one's a juvenile, judging from the black tip of his bill.'

'It's fascinating to see it,' she whispered back, standing still so as not to cause any disturbance that would make the bird fly off. 'I've seen so many gorgeous tropical species since I've been here.'

He smiled, drawing her close and sliding his arm around her. 'I guessed you were interested in nature from that first day. That's why I wanted to bring you down here. I know you've been busy of an evening, with one thing and another, and you haven't had time to venture very far.' His hand rested on the curve of her hip, warm, coaxing, inviting her to lean into him, to nestle into the shelter of his long body.

She was sorely tempted to do that. Here on the balmy Caribbean shore, with the sun low in the sky and nothing but the intermittent call of birds to fill the air, anything was possible. And yet it was strange that she should feel this way, considering that she was cautious now about getting close to any man. With Connor, though, everything seemed different. He confused her and set her at war within herself.

Now, as he held her with gentle, natural intimacy, she felt mesmerised by him, as though it would be the simplest thing in the world to turn in his arms and give herself up to the sheer joy of his caresses. It was what she wanted, and that was bewildering because it was as though her mind and her body were totally unconnected, her body responding to his embrace with a will of its own.

His touch was smooth, gentle, gliding over her body with infinite care. His hand trailed a path over the swell of her hip, along her waist, enticing her to him with persuasive, hypnotic ease.

She looked up into his eyes. They were dark, engrossed in her, his smile reflected in the shimmering depths. Slowly, his head bent towards her and she knew what he was about to do and for the life of her she had no will to stop it. He was going to kiss her, and it would be everything she dreamed it would be, and a whole new world would open up for her…a world with Connor at its centre.

How could that be? She gave herself a mental shake

and put up a hand, flat against his chest. 'I can't,' she said softly. 'I just can't.'

'Alyssa…' Her name was a gentle sigh on his lips. 'You and I could be so good together. There's a chemistry between us…you know it and I know it. What would be the harm?'

'It's not right. It doesn't feel right. And besides, there's Ross… I can't do that to him.'

She felt as though she was taking Ross's name in vain, but Ross was the only safeguard she had. No matter that there wasn't anything between them, it was enough that Connor would have to think twice about what he was doing. Through all this, he had his brother's interests at heart.

'You don't want him,' he said huskily. 'You've been overwhelmed by the chance he gave you to come out here. Who wouldn't be? But if you're honest with yourself, you'll see that you want what he can give you… the kudos of being with a film producer, with a wealthy man, a man who can make all your cares disappear.'

His hand stroked along the length of her spine, a slow sweep of silk that made her insides quiver and fired up her blood so that her pulse throbbed and her heart hammered against her rib cage.

'You and I are a lot alike, though you may not see it right now. Think about it. We could make a go of it, have a good time, with no commitment on either side. It'll be fun, you'll see, if only you're brave enough to give it a try.'

She shook her head and took a step away from him. 'No, Connor,' she said. 'Forget it. It isn't going to happen.'

She swivelled around and started to walk back along

the beach. She'd been badly hurt back home by James, who had sworn that he loved her, wanted her, needed her, and it had all ended in disaster.

She wasn't going to let that happen all over again, especially with a man who was only playing games with her heart.

CHAPTER FOUR

'HEY, look at you…you're absolutely gorgeous!' Ross exclaimed, his grey-blue eyes lighting up as Alyssa came out onto the deck. He gave a low whistle. 'You are fantastic.'

She gave him an uncertain smile. 'Well…thank you, but it's just a cocktail dress. I wasn't sure what I should wear for our evening out. Is this a bit over the top for a few drinks at a bar, do you think?'

'No way. But I can see I shall have to be on my guard—you'll turn the head of every man in the place.'

She made a wry smile. 'That's not exactly what I had in mind.' Ross was full of enthusiasm, and didn't seem to have noticed her worried expression. 'I just wanted to pick out something that's a little dressy to go along with the nature of the place and yet casual enough for an evening with friends.' She frowned. 'Now I'm not so sure I've made the right choice.'

'You have, believe me.' A soft, thudding sound caught their attention and they turned to see Connor climbing the steps onto the deck. 'Tell her, Connor,' Ross said. 'You must have heard what we were saying. Tell her she looks great.'

Connor was already looking at her, his eyes widening a fraction, but he didn't say anything for a second or two. He'd just arrived home from the hospital, and she could see by his expression that it had been a difficult day for him. There were lines of strain around his eyes and mouth, lending his strong features a trace of vulnerability.

He dragged his gaze away from her and nodded. 'You've pitched it just right,' he said at last. 'I'm assuming Ross is taking you to the Reef?'

'That's right.' Perversely, she didn't know whether to be disappointed or thankful that he'd made no other comment about how she looked. She was wearing a dress that faithfully followed the outline of her curves, an off-the-shoulder style, with a lightly beaded top and a skirt that finished just above her knees. 'We're having a get-together for the cast and crew, a sort of half-time rallying call. After everything that has gone wrong lately, Ross felt we needed some kind of pick-me-up.'

Connor nodded, coming to lean negligently against the rail. He looked good, dressed in pristine, dark trousers and a mid-blue linen shirt. 'Sounds good to me, but I'm not sure this is the best time to be going.'

She frowned. 'Why not? I don't know what you mean.'

'There's a storm brewing.' He looked up into the cloud-laden sky. 'I can feel it in the air. The heat was oppressive earlier, and now there's a change in the atmosphere. The wind's building up.'

Ross shook his head. 'It's a beautiful evening. There's just a bit of a breeze, that's all, and there have been no warnings issued. Anyway, we'll only be out for two or three hours. We all have to work in the morning.'

'Even so...' Connor stood his ground.

Alyssa sent Ross a troubled glance. 'It's not too late for us to cancel, is it, just to be sure?' For some reason she trusted Connor's judgement, and if he was cautious, perhaps they ought to take his concerns seriously. 'We could ring round and let everyone know, couldn't we? We can easily arrange a different date.'

'It's too late for that, I think,' Ross said. 'Some people will already be there. Besides, I don't think there's anything to worry about. The wind's coming in off the sea, it's true, and it feels a little chillier than we're used to, but it'll be fine, I'm sure. We might get a heavy rainstorm, but it should blow over fairly quickly.'

'Okay…' There was a hint of doubt in her voice. 'If you think so.' She looked at Connor, but he made no further comment. He was watching her, his gaze brooding, and she wondered if he was thinking about the day's events. 'Would you like me to get you some coffee, Connor? You look as though you could do with a cup.'

'Thanks. That would be good.' His gaze travelled to the mass of coppery curls that framed her face, lighting on the beaded clips that held her hair back and then dipping down to the silver necklace at her throat. For a moment she thought he was going to say something more but he stayed silent, and she turned to go into the kitchen. Both men followed her.

'Have you had a bad day?' she asked Connor as she switched on the coffee maker and set out mugs on the island bar. 'You look weary.'

He frowned. 'Let's just say, I've known better. I lost a patient today…a road-accident victim.'

Her green eyes clouded with compassion. 'I'm so sorry.' Despite her ambivalent feelings about him, Alyssa was torn by the tinge of raw emotion she saw on his face. She knew what it felt like to come home after a particularly bad day at the hospital.

Seeing those same feelings echoed in Connor's demeanour made her want to go to him and put her arms around him to offer sympathy and support. But after what had happened on the beach the other day, she had to steel herself to keep some distance between them.

He pressed his lips together briefly. 'We did everything we could, but it was hopeless from the start, really. His injuries were too severe, and he'd lost a lot of blood.'

She nodded, understanding what he was going through. 'You try to tell yourself you've given your best, but it doesn't help when the outcome is bad, does it? That awful sense of loss is always going to be there.' She sent him a quick glance. 'Was it the motorcyclist from the other day? You said he had multiple injuries.'

'No, fortunately he's recovering after surgery. It'll be a long job, but he's on the mend.' He accepted the mug of coffee she offered him and took a slow, satisfying sip. 'It's the same with Alex. He's recovering, but he has a long path ahead of him.'

'Yes, I realised that when I went to see him at lunchtime.' She recalled Alex's mixed feelings, pleasure at having visitors, and frustration with his situation. 'He wants to walk, but the signals from his brain are not getting to his legs properly and so he's finding it very difficult. It may be that the spinal cord is badly bruised and perhaps things will improve with time.'

'We're doing what we can for his family, in the meantime,' Ross said. 'There will be an insurance payout, but until that's finalised we're making sure that they can pay their rent and put food on the table.'

She smiled at him and laid her hand on his in acknowledgement. 'That must be a huge relief for him.'

'It is.' He returned her smile and squeezed her hand. 'It's one less pressure on him, anyway.'

'So how have things gone for you this week?' Connor dragged his gaze from where her hand was engulfed in Ross's larger one, and looked Alyssa in the eyes. 'Have you managed to steer clear of any major casualties?'

'It's been good.' Conscious of his narrow-eyed scrutiny, she carefully extricated her hand. 'I haven't had to do much at all, except to soak up the sun while I've watched the film being made. I'm looking forward to spending a few more weeks doing that.'

'Hmm.' Connor studied her thoughtfully. 'Doesn't it ever bother you, the fact that you have great medical skills at your fingertips and yet you're not using them? You showed your expertise when you worked on Alex. Doesn't it ever occur to you that you're wasting years of expensive medical training by opting out?'

She sucked in a sharp breath. He'd delivered a thrust that had gone directly to her heart. She hadn't been expecting it, and the way he'd said it, in such a straightforward, matter-of-fact way, somehow made it seem all the worse.

'I don't see it that way. I felt I needed a change of direction.' There was a faint quiver in her voice. 'I'm doing what's right for me at the moment.' She shook her head. 'I don't expect you to understand.'

Ross wrapped his arms around her. 'Don't let my brother get to you. He's sometimes very blunt and doesn't realise how he might hit a nerve.' Glaring at Connor, he said in a terse voice, 'You shouldn't judge Alyssa that way. You don't know her well enough.'

'Obviously not.' Connor's gaze darkened as Ross kissed Alyssa lightly on the temple and hugged her close. He straightened up and moved away from the worktop. 'I'm going up to my apartment to take a shower. Enjoy your evening…if you still insist on going. Just take care, and make sure you watch out for any warning signs. You might find you need to stay at the bar until things settle down.'

'I doubt that'll be necessary,' Ross answered. 'We'll be home by ten-thirty at the latest, because we have to get an early start tomorrow. We're shooting the scenes that take place at sunrise.'

Connor acknowledged that with a nod and left the room, but Ross kept his arms around Alyssa for a moment or two longer.

She looked up at him. 'Could he be right? I mean…'

'You worry too much. We get used to these tropical storms around here.' He smiled and dropped a gentle kiss on her mouth. 'You should try to relax a little.'

She sent him a cautious glance. 'Ross…you know Connor has the wrong idea about you and me, don't you? He thinks we're involved with one another, and it doesn't help when he sees you hold me this way. It's bound to make him think there's something going on.'

Ross sighed. 'Yeah, I know.' He looked into her eyes. 'And there isn't anything between us, is there? Not on your part, right?'

Alyssa frowned. She had to deal with this, once and for all. Ross had to understand the way she felt. 'You know how I feel, don't you? We're friends, Ross…great friends, but that's all. I can't think of you any other way. Besides, after the way my ex treated me, I'm not even going to think of getting involved again. It's just too painful. I'm sorry.'

'I know.' He ran a hand down her bare arm, his expression filled with sympathy and understanding. 'As for Connor, I know he has the wrong idea about you and me, but that annoys me. He's my big brother and he's always looked out for me since I was small, but it's time he realised I can make my own decisions for good or bad.' He laid a finger beneath her chin. 'I can't resist tormenting him a little, just to teach him a lesson. You're a good person and he shouldn't let his prejudices rule him.'

She shook her head. 'Even so, I want you to stop. It isn't helping and I don't like him getting the wrong impression.'

'Okay.' He slowly released her. 'I'm not promising anything, but I'll try.'

They left for the Reef Bar a short time later, and met up with friends in the lounge area where doors had been opened onto a covered terrace to let in the fresh evening air.

The atmosphere was boisterous and happy, with heavy beat music coming from a group of men playing drums, cowbells and whistles, along with a brass section made up of horns, trumpets, trombones and tuba. It was lively and very loud so that Alyssa had almost to shout to make herself heard.

'I'll get you a drink,' Ross said. 'What will you have? They do all sorts of cocktails here.'

She studied the list, written up on a board at the side of the bar. 'Hmm…let me see… Tequila Sunset sounds good…a mix of vodka and Cointreau…and so does Yellow Bird.' That was made from a herbal liqueur called Galliano and added rum. She mulled things over. 'But I think I'll go with Brown Skin Girl.' It was a mix of rum with crème de cocoa, cranberry and orange juice, and when Ross handed it to her it was in a wide-rimmed cocktail glass filled with ice and topped with a cherry.

'Mmm…this is delicious,' she told him, taking a sip. She noticed he wasn't drinking anything alcoholic, probably because he would be driving later. It didn't seem to spoil his fun, though, because he joined in with the general chatter, laughter and dancing, pulling her out onto the wooden dance floor to move to the rhythm of the Caribbean.

They danced and chatted with members of the film crew and cast, and the time passed so quickly that Alyssa was taken by surprise when it was time to leave.

'Do you want to stay on?' Ross asked. 'I could arrange a lift, or a taxi, for you.'

'No, don't do that. I'll go home with you,' she told him, and together they went to say their goodbyes to everyone.

'I've had a wonderful time,' she murmured, as they left the bar a short time later.

'So have I.' He pushed open the side door that led on to the car park, and for the first time that day Alyssa felt the chill of the breeze on her bare arms. She shivered a little, and Ross put his arm around her to warm her. Looking about her, she noticed the branches of a nearby casuarina tree shaking wildly in the breeze, its thin, needle-like leaves tossed about with casual ease.

'It's going to rain,' Ross said, looking at the leaden sky. He frowned. 'Let's get to the car before it starts.'

His car was a sleek silver saloon, and Alyssa was

glad to slip into the passenger seat as his prediction came true. Her bare arms were already wet and within a few seconds the initial individual raindrops had turned into a lashing downpour. She could hear it beating down on the roof of the car.

'Do you think we ought to follow Connor's advice and stay at the bar until the storm passes over?' she asked, looking out of the window at the growing turbulence all around. The wind had become almost violent in nature, and there was a noise, an ominous sound in the background, that she couldn't quite fathom.

Ross frowned. 'That could mean we're stuck here for hours,' he said. 'We're only about twenty minutes' drive away from home, so we could probably make it back before things get too bad.'

'I suppose so.' She wasn't convinced, and she was still worried about that loud, booming sound she could hear, even from within the relatively safe interior of the car. She saw that the Reef's bartenders were beginning to close the doors and draw the shutters over the windows. 'What's that noise I can hear? Do you know?'

'It's probably the sea,' he answered. 'The danger from these tropical storms isn't to do with the wind so much as the sea. It gets whipped up and the waves build up and the water starts to encroach on the land. Any inlets or streams quickly get swollen with flood water.'

'That doesn't sound too good.'

'No. But we're some distance from the ocean here, so we probably don't need to worry too much.'

A thought struck her, and her brows drew together in a frown. 'But we're right next to the sea back at the house. Doesn't that mean Connor's in danger?' The fact that he might be in trouble made her want to rush back right away.

Ross shook his head. 'We're on the leeward side of the island, so we're relatively sheltered there. And the trees and shrubs tend to act as a windbreak. We're on quite a raised plot, too, which is why you can look out over the sea from there. Connor will be all right.'

She was relieved. 'That's something, at least.' She wasn't happy about going on but, then, she wasn't used to life on the island, whereas Ross had lived here most of his life. She'd follow his lead.

He started up the car and they headed out along the road towards the main highway. Alyssa was apprehensive, watching the branches of the trees that lined their route sway dangerously in the wind. Some of the less sturdy ones would lose their branches if things became much worse, she felt sure.

Ross turned the car onto a quiet, rural road. 'This should be the safer option, I think,' he murmured. 'It's less open to crosswinds.'

She nodded, following his logic, but she was cautious about the tall trees that stood like menacing sentinels on either side of the road. The sky was ominously dark, and the trees appeared as black figures against the skyline, their branches dipping and swooping in a frightening way.

There was a sudden creaking and a crashing sound as one of the smaller trees seemed to uproot itself and she stared at it in horror as it started to fall across their path. Ross was quick to take evasive action, turning the steering wheel vigorously and driving towards the opposite side of the road, but Alyssa had the dreadful feeling that it was too late. Her stomach clenched in fear as a massive branch fell across the front of the car, smashing into them. At the same time the car came to a sudden stop as Ross slammed on the brakes.

Alyssa instinctively bent her head and covered her face with her arms as the thick windscreen glass groaned and shattered. Small pieces of laminated glass fell over her, but as the car shuddered to a halt, she gradually came to realise that, apart from some possible bruising from the emergency braking, she was all right. She wasn't hurt. She sat up, brushing blunt fragments of glass from her hair, and turned to look at Ross.

What she saw left her rigid with shock. Some of the tree's branches had speared the windscreen, coming through on the driver's side, and Ross was slumped over the wheel. There was a gash to the side of his head, and even in the darkness she could see that blood was trickling from it down his cheek.

Heart thumping, she felt for a pulse at his wrist. It was beating, an erratic kind of rhythm, but it was there and he was still alive. She sighed with relief, but it was short-lived. What would she do if his condition began to deteriorate? How would she cope?

'Ross, can you hear me? Can you talk to me?'

He mumbled something, and she tried again. 'I need to know if you're hurt anywhere other than your head,' she said slowly. 'Talk to me, Ross.'

Somehow, she was going to have to get them out of this mess, but for now she couldn't think what to do. It wouldn't be wise to move him, because he might have sustained a whiplash injury or worse when the branch had struck him. She flipped on the car's interior light and looked around to see if there was anything she could use to make a neck collar that would prevent him from sustaining any more damage.

In the back seat of the car she saw a newspaper, quickly leaned over to get it and began to roll it with trembling hands into a serviceable, tight wad. There was some tape in the glove compartment, and she used this to secure it around his neck. Then she gently eased him back in the seat so that the headrest supported his head. Blood oozed from his wound and he started to retch.

She searched in her handbag and found some tissues. They weren't much use, but they would help to contain things a bit if he was sick.

She breathed deeply and tried to pull herself together. Foraging in her handbag once more, she found her mobile phone and dialled the emergency services' number, only to discover that there was no signal. Dismayed, she thought through her options. Judging from what had happened to her, the ambulance and rescue services would probably be overrun with calls right now. She'd heard about the nature of these storms and could only imagine the damage that would have been caused to property, especially in the poorer areas.

She sat back in her seat and fought to stem the tide of panic that ran through her. The front of the car was completely destroyed, rendering the car out of action, even if she'd had the strength to move the tree.

She had never felt so completely alone. On a dark, stormy night she was stranded on a lonely road in the middle of nowhere, in a strange country, and for a second or two she felt a wave of panic wash through her. Her heart was thumping wildly. If only Connor was here. He would know what to do.

Only he wasn't here, and he was way too sensible to

ever have risked coming out on a night like this. Would he even know that they were in trouble?

All she could do was to sit things out and wait for the storm to abate. They were off the road, as far as she could see, so they should be safe from any traffic at least. It seemed that when he'd seen what was about to happen, Ross had swerved onto a verge on the opposite side of the road. The tree was a worry, though, a danger to other road users.

'Ross, how are you doing? Are you able to talk to me? Please try to answer me.' Somehow she had to get him to respond.

He mumbled something once more, words that she couldn't make out, but at least it meant he was semiconscious. He didn't appear to have any other wounds, just the nasty gash on his head.

She didn't know how long she sat there, but lights suddenly dazzled her, coming from straight ahead. Was it another motorist heading towards them? She had to warn the driver about the fallen tree blocking his path. Ought she to stop whoever it was and ask for help? At least he might help them to get to a hospital.

The other car was still some distance away so she might yet be able to catch the driver's attention. She reached over and switched on the lights, flashing them on and off several times. Then she pushed open the passenger door and tried to step out into the road.

The force of the billowing, gusty wind almost knocked her over and she fought desperately to keep her balance, holding onto the car door. In the gloom she saw that the other driver had stopped and was getting out of his vehicle.

'What on earth are you doing? Get back inside the

car.' It was Connor's voice and she was so stunned to see and hear him that she stayed where she was and stared at him, wide-eyed and open-mouthed.

'In the car,' he said again, taking her by the arm and urging her back inside. Making sure she was securely settled in her seat, he came and sat in the back of the vehicle.

He must have been shocked by what he'd seen as he'd driven towards them, but he steeled himself now to reach forward and examine his brother, quickly assessing the damage.

Alyssa struggled to gain control of herself. Relief had washed over her when she'd seen him, but now the enormity of the situation was bearing down on her. Her heart beat a staccato rhythm. 'He has a head injury,' she told him, 'but he's semi-conscious. I've been trying to talk to him, to keep him awake.'

He nodded. 'We'll have to get him to the hospital. It's not too far from here.'

'I wanted to do that, but I knew, from the size of it, that I wouldn't be able to shift that tree on my own.'

'Of course you couldn't.' He studied her, his expression taut. 'Are you all right? Are you hurt in any way?'

She shook her head. 'I'm fine,' she said.

'Are you sure?' He reached out and touched her cheek as though he would physically check her out. 'You were shaking when I first got here.'

'Really, I'm okay.' She frowned. 'What are you doing here, anyway? How did you know we needed help or where to find us?' That had to be the only reason he was out here on a night like this. He'd come specially to find them.

'When you didn't come home when I expected you

I tried to call both of you on your mobiles. I guessed there was no signal, which made me all the more concerned. But I managed to get through to the Reef Bar on a landline, and the bartender told me you had left there almost an hour previously. I was worried.' His expression tightened. 'I didn't like to think what might have happened to you.'

'So you came to find us.' Thank goodness he had cared enough to do that. The brothers might have their differences from time to time, but Connor's loyalty was unshakeable. She frowned. 'You took a big risk coming out here, knowing what conditions were like.'

'I had to find out what had happened. Anyway, I have a solid, four-wheel drive that I keep for times like these. I assumed Ross would have avoided the main highway.'

He looked around. 'Okay, you stay here. I'm going to try to move the tree to make things safer for anyone else who comes this way. Then I need to get Ross out of here.'

'I'm coming with you.' She'd already started to slide out of the car, and when he started to object, she said quickly, 'You'll need help.'

Perhaps he could see from the determined tilt of her chin that there was no point in arguing with her. 'Make sure you keep hold of something at all times,' he said.

They set to work. Between them they attempted to pull the tree from the car, battling all the while against the raging storm. Rain drove into Alyssa, drenching her, and the wind took her breath away.

'Here, give me your hand,' Connor said when he was satisfied the road was clear. 'I'll help you back to the car.' She did as he asked and they huddled together against the driving force of the wind.

'Sit back in the car while I move Ross,' he said, but she shook her head.

'I'll give you a hand. We don't know if he has any other injuries, and we need to be as careful as possible,' she warned him. 'I'll hold the door open for you.'

He pressed his lips together. 'All right… But, as before, make sure you keep hold of the car, or me, at all times.'

'Okay.'

He went around to the driver's side and slowly, carefully, eased Ross over his shoulder in a fireman's lift. Alyssa helped to keep Ross's body from twisting or jerking in any way, and between them they managed to transfer him to the back of Connor's car. Even in the darkness she could see it was a top-spec model. There was no time to dwell on that, though. The gale howled all around them, whipping the branches like a maddened beast. Alyssa's teeth started to chatter.

Connor made sure that his brother was securely fastened into his seat, and covered him with a blanket that he retrieved from the boot of the car. Alyssa went to sit beside Ross, talking to him the whole time, trying to get him to answer her. Connor took off his jacket and draped it over her.

'But you'll need it,' she protested.

He gave her a wry look. 'I think right now you need it more than I do.'

He went around to the boot of the vehicle once more and came back a moment later to hand her a first-aid kit. 'There are dressings in there, and bags in case he's sick.' He frowned. 'He's badly concussed.'

Then he slid into the driver's seat and started the engine. The car purred into action and a moment or two later heat began to waft around Alyssa as he engaged climate control. It was one small comfort after what they'd been through. Very soon they were on their way to the hospital.

They'd gone a mile or so, and had emerged from the leafy lane to turn on to a road leading to a small settlement area. A creek ran alongside a cluster of wooden houses, and Alyssa guessed it had burst its banks and flooded the area, because the land all around was awash with water. She could see the moon glinting on the surface ripples. Flimsy roofs had been torn off the wooden outhouses, and here and there doors were missing.

She peered through the gloom. Even with such conditions causing havoc all around them, a group of people huddled in the wide, covered entrance to what she guessed was an old, brick schoolhouse. One of them, a man in his thirties, she guessed, started to wave frantically, trying to get them to stop.

Connor carefully drew the vehicle to a halt, glancing at Ross in the back. 'Are you still with us, Ross?' he asked.

Ross mumbled a reply. His eyes were closed and he seemed oblivious to what was going on. Alyssa had covered the gash on his head but the dressing was soaked with blood.

Connor wound down his window a little. 'What's the problem?' he asked.

'It's my little girl—she was swallowed up by the creek—it swept her away and she nearly drowned. We rescued her, but we can't get her to breathe—she needs to go to hospital. Can you help us?'

Alyssa wondered what the child was doing up at this time of night. Whatever the reason, it was a horren-

dous situation these people had found themselves in—
she doubted that any of them had transport that would
withstand the journey to the hospital.

She glanced at Ross, wondering if she dared leave
him, because Connor was already climbing out of the
vehicle to go and see what he could do to help. 'I'm
a doctor,' he told the distraught man. 'I'll see what I
can do.'

Now that she focussed more clearly, Alyssa could
make out a small figure lying in the covered porch.
The child couldn't be much more than five years old,
she guessed.

Connor knelt down beside the girl and checked her
breathing and her pulse. Then he looked in her mouth
for any obstruction and made a finger sweep search.
Alyssa guessed he found something because he shook
the debris free of his hand and started to press down on
her chest, with steady, rhythmic movements.

Alyssa made up her mind what she had to do.
Turning to Ross, she said urgently, 'I'm sorry, Ross,
but I have to go. I won't be long, but I think Connor
might need some help. I promise I'll be back with you
in a few minutes.'

Keeping her head down, she struggled through the
storm to get to Connor. Hands reached for her, and the
small assembly drew her into the relative safety of the
archway.

She knelt down beside Connor. 'What can I do?'
she asked.

'Take over from me. I'll go and get the oxygen kit
from my car.'

'Okay.' She took his place, going on with the CPR,
while Connor searched in the boot for his medical kit.

The little girl wasn't moving. She was deathly white, her lips taking on a bluish tinge, and Alyssa's heart turned over with dread. How could this happen to such a small, helpless child?

'Can you do anything for her?' the father pleaded. 'She isn't breathing, is she?' His voice broke. 'We were having a birthday celebration. That's why she was up so late. But then she wandered outside...'

Connor returned and straight away checked the little girl's pulse. 'It's very faint, but she's still with us...' He looked down at her frail form. 'Just a little more effort, sweetheart. Breathe for me. Try to fill your lungs, you must breathe.'

He placed the mask over her face and then looked up at the child's father. 'What's her name?'

'Bijou. It means "jewel".'

Connor smiled. 'That's a lovely name.' Then he turned back to the child and said softly, 'Breathe for me, Bijou. You can do it, I know you can.'

Alyssa watched him. He cared so much that this tiny girl should live. He wasn't going to give up on her while there was the remotest chance, and she desperately wanted him to succeed. She was numb inside, scared about what might happen, but she went on with the CPR without interruption as Connor rhythmically squeezed the oxygen bag.

Bijou suddenly spluttered, turning her head to one side and dislodging the mask. She coughed and seemed to choke, and then after a second or two she tried desperately to suck air into her lungs. When she settled once more, Connor held the mask over her nose and mouth. 'That's it. Good girl. Take your time. Breathe in...that's it, nice and deep.'

Alyssa smiled, overcome with joy. 'She's going to be all right.' She glanced up at the parents. 'We must take her to hospital all the same, to make sure everything's as it should be.' There could be some irritant after-effects of having water in her lungs, and the hospital would be the best place to make sure she received the right support.

Connor agreed. 'We can take her, along with one parent. I'm sorry, but I've no room for any more because my brother's injured and I have to take him to hospital. Who will it be?'

'I'll go with her.' The child's mother stepped forward. Her face was drained of colour, etched with the strain of seeing her daughter struggle for life. 'Thank you so much for what you've done. I don't know what to say. I can't thank you enough.'

Bijou's father joined in. 'Yes, yes…a thousand thanks. We owe you so much. Thank you.'

The small crowd of people helped them back to the car. The little girl was very cold but they managed to find a blanket for her, and Alyssa removed her wet dress and carefully wrapped her up warmly before placing her beside her mother in the back of the car.

Both she and Connor checked on Ross. He was still quiet, sitting with his eyes closed, occasionally retching.

Alyssa was glad of the warmth of the car once more. Connor drove carefully, looking ahead for signs of trouble but keeping on a steady path towards the hospital. It was hard to believe the evening had turned out so badly.

'We're here. Let's get everyone inside.'

Alyssa looked around, startled to find that they were at Coral Cay Hospital already. Her mind had wandered, thinking about Connor's calm, assured actions as he'd battled to save the small child, and how careful he'd been to make sure his brother came to no harm. She didn't like to dwell on either outcome if he hadn't turned up when he had.

He made his report to the on-duty registrar, and Bijou was whisked away to the paediatric ward. The registrar spoke soothingly to the child's mother. 'We'll make sure she's thoroughly warm and then we'll examine her to be certain there's no ongoing damage,' he said. 'She may need a chest X-ray and antibiotics, or possibly even medication to stop any spasm of the airways. That can sometimes happen a few hours after the event, so we'll keep her in for observation.'

Ross was wheeled to a treatment bay, where one of the emergency doctors started to check him over, looking for signs of neurological damage. 'We'll get the wound cleaned up and apply a fresh dressing,' he told Connor. 'He'll probably be glad of some painkillers, too. Leave him with us for a while.'

He looked Connor over and then glanced at Alyssa. 'You both look as though you could do with getting out of those wet clothes. We could find you some fresh scrubs to wear and then maybe you'd like to warm up from the inside. Our cafeteria is still open.'

'That sounds good to me. Hot soup would be just the thing.' Connor sent Alyssa a questioning glance, and she nodded, her mind somewhere else, watching the small girl being wheeled away.

It was beginning to dawn on her how close she had come to seeing a child die. The thought hit her like a hammer blow, leaving a heavy, aching feeling in the pit of her stomach. She felt faint. She didn't know how to handle the emotions that rippled through her like a shock wave.

Connor held out his hand to her. 'I'll show you where you can change,' he murmured. He gave her a sideways glance, a questioning look in his eyes.

She nodded, unable to answer him just then. The events of the night were beginning to crowd in on her and she had an overwhelming feeling that she was about to cry. The responsibility of being a doctor was awesome, and she didn't think she could cope with it for much longer.

He showed her to a room where she could dress in private, and handed her a large, white towel and a set of scrubs.

'Thanks.'

He left her, again with that thoughtful, musing glance, and once she was alone she stared at herself in the mirror that had been fixed to the wall.

She looked a mess. Her dress clung to her, and her hair had reverted to a mass of unruly curls, the way it did whenever it was wet. Connor, on the other hand, had looked as good as ever, with his shirt plastered to his chest and a damp sheen outlining his angular features. He was strong and capable, and she didn't know how she would have managed without him.

She removed her dress and towelled herself dry then put on the hospital scrubs, loose-fitting cotton trousers and a short-sleeved top. As for her hair, she did what she could with the towel and then used the hot-air machine next to the sink to get rid of the worst of the damp.

There was a comb in her handbag, and she ran it through her curls, restoring as much order as was possible. A smear of colour on her full lips made the final

touch, and she braced herself to go and meet with
Connor once more.

'Are you feeling a bit better?' he asked, and she nodded.

'Yes, thanks.'

'Good. I had some food brought down from the cafeteria. It's all set up in my office. I thought it might be
a bit more private in there. You don't feel much like
company, do you?'

'No, you're right. I don't.' She tried a smile. 'That
was thoughtful of you.'

He led the way to his office, putting an arm around
her waist, the flat of his hand splayed out over her rib
cage. 'Here we are. Do you want to take a seat on the
couch? You might be more comfy there.'

She sat down on the luxurious leather couch, and
he brought a tray over to the small table in front of her.
A coffee pot and cups had already been set out there,
along with cream and sugar, but on the tray there was
a small tureen of soup, together with bowls and an assortment of bread rolls. He lifted the lid from the tureen,
and the appetising aroma of chicken and vegetables
filled the air.

'This will warm you through and through,' he said,
ladling the rich mixture into the bowls. Then he came
to sit beside her and for a few minutes they sat in silence, appreciating the food and waiting while the hot
soup helped to make the chill of the night disappear
from their bones.

'You seemed very upset after we treated the little
girl,' he said when she finally laid down her spoon.
'Perhaps the events of the night were beginning to catch
up with you. You must have been shocked by what hap-

pened, with the tree coming down and everything that followed.'

She nodded. 'I was. You don't realise it so much at the time, but afterwards it comes home to you.'

'And looking after the child was the clincher, perhaps?' He opened up a box from the tray and produced a couple of glazed fruit tarts for dessert, gloriously exotic, with small slivers of strawberries, kumquats and kiwi, topped with raspberries and blueberries.

'I suppose so.' She accepted the tart he offered, but didn't begin to eat. He obviously wanted to know what had happened to suddenly make her become so emotional, and perhaps she owed it to him to tell him the truth after the way he'd risked everything to come and find her and Ross.

'The thing is, I don't seem to deal very well with those kinds of situations any more.' She frowned. 'That's a bad thing for a doctor to say, isn't it?' When he didn't answer, she pressed her lips together briefly and went on, 'I worked in emergency back in the UK, and for a time everything was fine. I was good at my job and people respected me. I always did what I could to make sure I pulled people through and helped them back on their feet.'

She hesitated, lost in thought for a moment or two, and Connor began to pour coffee, sliding a cup across the table towards her. 'Go on, please…you were saying you worked in emergency…'

'Yes. Then, one day I witnessed an accident. I was there when it happened, sitting at a table in an open-air café, watching the traffic go by. A man was at work, up a ladder, painting the window frames of the building next door to the café. His wife and children were sitting at the table next to me, talking to him as he worked, enjoying a light snack. It was a beautiful summer day and they seemed such a lovely, happy family. I think they'd been out on a shopping trip and had come to the café especially to see him. Every now and again he would stop what he was doing to pass a comment or two.'

She thought back to that time and a vivid picture filled her mind, blanking out everything else.

She sipped the coffee and realised that her hand was shaking so badly that Connor reached out to cup her hand in his, holding it steady and keeping the coffee from spilling over. 'It's all right, I have you,' he murmured. 'Are you able to go on?'

She nodded and pulled in a deep breath. 'He was in his early thirties, I think. Perhaps it was because I saw it happen that it made such an impact on me. Usually, in emergency, we see people as they come in to hospital. We treat them, patch them up, and we don't really get deeply involved in their lives and relationships, do we? We can be a little bit impartial.' She frowned. 'Does that sound bad? I mean, we do care, but...'

'I know what you mean,' Connor said. 'We don't know them when we're treating them. It's only afterwards, when they're recovering, that we begin to feel the impact.' He looked into her eyes. 'Did something happen to this man?'

She nodded again, swallowing hard. 'The café was situated on a bend in the road. All of a sudden a car came around the bend, going way too fast, and mounted the pavement. It crashed into the ladder and took out part of the wall of the building. The young man fell and went through the windscreen.' She closed her eyes briefly.

Connor helped her to put her cup down on the table. 'That must have been awful,' he said quietly.

'Yes, it was.' She clasped her fingers together in her lap. 'The driver escaped with just a broken arm and whiplash, plus a few cuts and bruises. I did what I could for both of them, but the decorator suffered a head wound and arterial bleeding. I managed to stop it and I tried to stabilise him on his journey to hospital. I even thought he might stand a chance…but it turned out that he was bleeding internally, and we couldn't do anything to stop it. The…the damage was too great.' Her eyes filled with tears.

He wrapped his arms around her. 'Here, let me hold you. I think maybe you need to let this all out. Have you never talked to anyone about this before now? I mean, properly talked about it, about how much it upset you? I get the feeling you haven't.'

She shook her head, taking up his invitation and nestling against him, letting the tears slowly trickle down her cheeks. There'd been no one she could talk to, no one who would really understand how she felt. 'No one had any idea what it felt like.'

Her parents had frowned, alarmed to hear about what had happened, but they had soon forgotten about it and moved on. To them, it was a moment of conversation. And James… James hadn't been able to understand why she wasn't able to shake off the images. 'Put it behind you,' he'd said. 'You deal with injured people every day. You'll get over it.'

It was expected of her that she would carry on. And she had, for a long time, until one day it had all become too much for her. There had been too many critically ill

patients and she had found it more and more difficult to
go on. Soon after that, Ross had stepped into her life.

Connor comforted her, his hand gently stroking her
back, her arm, as she wept into his shirt. She felt secure
in his embrace, as though he was sheltering her from
the world. He didn't say anything but waited patiently
until she became still, until she managed to pull herself
together and started to dash the wetness from her eyes.

'I'm sorry,' she said, straightening up. She shouldn't
be burdening him with her problems. Why would he
care? 'I know I should be stronger. I despise myself for
being so weak.'

'You shouldn't worry about that. Take your time.
Take a few deep breaths and you'll start to feel better.'

She nodded, sitting up and sweeping her fingers
across her cheeks to clear away any remaining damp-
ness. Then there was a knock at the door of the office
and the registrar came in. Alyssa picked up her coffee cup, holding it in both hands to enjoy the warmth,
and she sat with her head down, absorbed in her own
thoughts. She didn't want to face anyone right now.

'Your brother is coming round,' the registrar told
Connor. He smiled. 'I thought you'd like to know. He's
going to be okay.'

'That's great news. Thanks. I'll be along to see him
in a minute.'

'Okay.' The registrar left the room, and Connor
turned to face her once more.

'I'm glad Ross is recovering,' she said.

'So am I.' He pushed the fruit tart towards her. 'Eat
it,' he said. 'They're delicious. I think you need something tasty and exotic right now.'

'They look wonderful, almost too good to eat, don't

they?' She looked up at him, suddenly concerned. 'I shouldn't have loaded all my troubles onto you. I'm sorry about that. And anyway, you have other things on your mind. I know he's going to be okay, but even so Ross needs...'

'It sounds as though he's going to be absolutely fine. I expect they'll keep him under observation for a few hours, maybe overnight, and then let him go.' He dipped a spoon into his tart and tasted the fruit. 'Mmm...fantastic.' She had the feeling he was eating in order to encourage her to do the same.

She followed his cue and started to eat. When they had both finished, he stood up and said, 'I'm going to see how my brother is doing. Do you want to stay here for a while and relax with another cup of coffee?'

'No, thank you. That was really good, but I'm full up now. I'll go with you.'

'Okay.'

They left the room together. Connor made no mention of what had gone before, and she couldn't help wondering what he thought about what she'd said. She wished she'd never given in to her feelings that way. How could she represent her profession when she was emotionally vulnerable and clearly unfit to practise? He must think she was weak and not fit to be a doctor. Wouldn't he have even more reason for doubting her now?

CHAPTER FIVE

'HAVE I called at a bad time? It sounds as though you're a bit breathless, or in a hurry, maybe? Are you getting ready for work?' On the other end of the line, Carys was keen to know what Alyssa was up to, and Alyssa paused for a moment, peering into her wardrobe and taking stock of the situation.

'I'm trying to decide what I should wear for a trip into the mangrove swamps.'

'The mangroves?' Her cousin was intrigued. 'That sounds interesting. What's that all about? Anyway, I'd have thought jeans and a light top would do the trick.'

'Yes, you're probably right.' Alyssa reached into the wardrobe and drew out a pair of white jeans and held them in front of her while she looked in the mirror. 'We're filming there later today, and I need to look okay because…guess what…' She paused for effect. 'I'm going to be on film! Can you believe it? I've been roped in as one of the extras.'

'Wow! And here I was worrying they were working you too hard!'

Alyssa laughed. 'Of course I'll be there in my medical capacity, too. But with any luck everyone will be fine and I'll be able to sit back and enjoy the ride.'

'It sounds great. I'd love to be there with you…' Her voice sounded wistful. 'Maybe we could meet up one weekend? I could come over and visit you, if you like.'

'Oh, Carys, that would be great. How about next weekend?' She chatted with Carys for a little longer and then hurried to get ready for the day ahead. The sun was out in its full glory this morning, and the sky was a tranquil blue. It was all so different from a couple of days ago when the storm had wreaked havoc over the island.

Since filming had been stopped for a couple of days, she'd been out with the teams that had been hastily set up to help clear up after the devastation, and at times she'd found herself working alongside Connor, when he'd been able to grab a few hours away from work.

Today, though, everything was serene as usual. The palm trees swayed gently in the breeze, and bordering the beach everything was rich with vibrant life. From the open doors of her bedroom Alyssa could see the pretty pink flowers of the oleander, and on the veranda itself there was a terracotta pot filled with the flamboyant orange and yellow blooms of poinciana. Just looking at them made her feel cheerful.

Strangely, since that evening when Connor had held her in his arms, she'd felt an odd sense of release. She didn't understand it at all. But it was definitely there, this lightening of spirit.

'Are you about ready to be off, then?' Ross came into the kitchen as she was doing a last-minute bit of tidying up. He'd been staying with his brother in the apartment upstairs for the last couple of days, as Connor insisted on keeping an eye on him while he was recovering from concussion. 'I wish I was coming with you as we planned, but I suppose Connor's right—the company's insurance people would have all sorts of problems with that.'

'I think it's probably best if you stay at home and rest up for a few days more,' Alyssa told him. 'You certainly look better today than you have done these last couple of days.' Apart from a dressing on his head wound, he seemed to be in reasonably good shape. He'd had an ongoing headache since the accident and some slightly blurred vision, but he'd finished taking painkillers now, and that was hopefully a good sign.

'I'd still rather I was going with you on this trip. I hate sitting back and leaving everything to other people.'

'That's because you simply don't know how to delegate,' she said with a laugh. 'Dan *is* the director, you know. You have to let him handle things.'

'Hmmph. Maybe.' He was in a grumpy mood, and that wasn't like him at all.

She patted his hand. 'Take some time out to lie back in the hammock,' she told him, pointing to the canvas that was strung up outside between two palm trees. 'It'll do you the world of good.'

'Yeah, right. Anyway, I'm sorry I won't be able to take you to meet up with the cast and crew—Connor has a day off, though, and he said he'll take you, so there won't be any need for you to call a taxi.'

'Yes, he mentioned it to me last night,' she said as she stacked crockery into the dishwasher. She'd been surprised by his offer. 'I really didn't want to put him out—he leads such a busy life and I'd have thought he'd welcome the chance to stay home and do nothing for a change. He even had to go out somewhere this morning. I heard his car start up as I was thinking about getting out of bed.'

Ross nodded. 'He went to see my father. He rang up this morning, complaining of stomach pains, and said he didn't want to call his own doctor.'

She frowned. 'I'm sorry to hear that. Do you think it's something serious?'

He shook his head. 'The beginnings of an ulcer, probably. I expect Connor will give him some tablets. I don't think it helps that my father's constantly at odds with our stepmother—his second wife. She's turned out to be a feisty individual. But, then, his judgement was never very good where women are concerned. He had an affair while he was married to our mother—not a great move, because she divorced him after she found out.' He was quiet for a moment or two, thinking about that. 'We were still quite young when it happened...I think I was about eleven.'

He pulled a face. 'So we became part of a divided family, going from one parent to the other throughout the year. And, of course, after the divorce my father became very attractive to other women who liked the idea of his wealth and the lifestyle it could bring them. I was upset, I remember. I wanted my parents to stay together, and I wanted to protect my mother from being hurt, but I didn't know how. So I poured out my worries to my big brother, and he tried to find ways to make me feel better...when all the time he must have been going through it, too.'

She tried to imagine how Connor must have felt, being torn by the disruption to family life and suddenly worrying about his little brother's well-being. She frowned. 'I can't begin to guess what that must have been like. It must have been so difficult for both of you.'

No wonder Connor was so protective of his brother even now. Back then, being some three years older than Ross, he must have taken it upon himself to shield him from any upsets that might come along. Her heart went out to those young boys struggling to come to terms with the break-up of their family.

'Yeah.' Ross absently massaged his brow with his fingers. 'It was hard when we were young, but that's all in the past now.'

'Is it?' She wasn't so sure about that. 'These things probably leave scars of some sort or another.'

'Well, you could be right. I suppose it was bound to leave some kind of legacy, and we were both at an impressionable age. That must be the reason Connor avoids getting deeply involved with anyone. If things start getting too close for comfort, he tends to bail out. And according to him I go after all the wrong kinds of women.' He made a faint smile.

'He's probably right—I've had a few near misses over the years. I tend to be too trusting, I suspect, and then I realise too late that some women are wowed by the prospect of being with a film producer. I'm just me, but they see me as something else.' He sighed. 'I guess all the upheaval in our lives was bound to affect us in some way.'

She thought about that when Ross left a few minutes later. It wasn't really a surprise to learn that Connor was reluctant to get involved in relationships in any meaningful way. There had been rumours amongst the cast and crew and people she'd spoken to at the hospital about women who'd loved and lost him. They'd been kccn for something more to develop out of the relationship with Connor, but in each case apparently he'd chosen that time to gently engineer a parting of the ways.

But she didn't want to dwell on any of that right now. Thinking about Connor only left her confused and distracted. So, instead, she carried on with her chores, wiping down the work surfaces and making sure that everything was spick and span.

Connor arrived back at the house a few minutes later as she was watering the houseplants.

'Is everything all right?' she asked, checking the soil around the base of a fern. He looked ready for the day, dressed in casual clothes, dark trousers and a crisp linen shirt that was open at the neck. He glowed with health, and his keys dangled from his fingers as though he was ready to be on the move again. He was full of vibrant energy, and she resisted an urge to put her arms around him and slow him down. 'Ross told me your father wasn't well…he said he thought it might be a stomach ulcer.'

He nodded. 'I think he'll be okay. At least he seems to be feeling much better now. I gave him some tablets and told him I would speak to his doctor to arrange for tests to be done. There could be a bacterial cause, but he's suffered from ulcers before, and I don't think the atmosphere at home helps. I expect Ross told you about that?'

'A little.' She put away the watering can and turned to face him properly. 'It sounds as though your father and stepmother have a fairly volatile relationship.'

He shrugged. 'Well, you know what they say…he made his bed, now he has to lie in it.'

She frowned. 'You don't seem particularly sympathetic.' Maybe that wasn't altogether unexpected, given the circumstances. 'Ross mentioned that you went through quite a bit of upheaval when your parents split up.'

'Yes, we did, but these things happen. You learn to be philosophical about it in the end. Anyway, I expect they're happy enough. Some people enjoy living life on the edge.'

'Hmm. That wouldn't do for me.' She wondered how much of what he said was bravado. After all, that fourteen-year-old boy, shielding his brother from upset, was very much still part of the man.

'Or me.' He looked around and saw her bag on the table. 'So, are you about ready to leave?'

'I am.' She smiled at him. 'I'm looking forward to this trip. Though I do have a few misgivings. I hope we don't…' She frowned as a sudden thought struck her. 'I mean…we're not likely to come across any nasty creatures, are we? Like crocodiles, maybe? I'm not sure quite how I'd cope with them.'

He laughed. 'No, nothing like that. You'll be quite safe. It's really very tame out there. You might see a few crabs scuttling about in the water, but that's about as dangerous as it gets.' He studied her thoughtfully. 'How are you on the water? Do you think you'll get on all right in a kayak?'

She pondered on that for a moment or two. 'Um… actually, I don't know… I imagine I'll be okay. I've been in a rowboat before, and I can swim, if that's what you're asking.'

He smiled. 'I don't think swimming will be necessary. If by some remote chance you manage to overturn the boat, you'll be able to stand up in the water. It's not very deep.'

'Hmm. That's all right, then.' Her shoulders relaxed as relief washed over her. 'But I was hoping I wouldn't be on my own. These are two-man boats we'll be using, aren't they?' She walked with him to the door.

'That's right. But you'll be with me, so you shouldn't have any problems.'

Her eyes widened. 'You mean…you're coming along on the trip?' Her pulse leapt in response to the unexpected news. 'I didn't realise—I thought you were simply taking me to the meeting point.'

'Oh, no. I'm definitely along for the ride.' His gaze meshed with hers. 'I wouldn't miss out on the opportunity to spend the day with you, would I?'

Warm colour flushed her cheeks. He wanted to be with her?

'And besides,' he went on, 'as one of the partners in the company I've always thought it a good idea to see how things are going with the filming. I need to take an interest and have some say in what goes on.'

Her jaw dropped. 'You're a partner? I didn't know. Ross never said…'

'Did he not? Ah, well…' He opened the passenger door of his car and waited for her to be comfortably seated. 'I helped to set up the company with Ross some years back, but I'm more of a silent partner, so to speak. I'm so busy at the hospital that I don't have time for anything more.'

'I wondered how it was that you came to see the filming whenever you had the chance.' She looked at him as though she was seeing him for the first time.

'What was it that made you get into film production? It's a long way from medicine.'

'True.' He gave it some thought as he started up the car. 'We've always been interested in films—as boys we went to see all the latest blockbusters, and Ross had a knack for seeing how scenes were set up or how things could have been done better. For myself, I thought there was a brilliant opportunity for basing production on these islands. There's a whole lot of glamour and excitement here, all the things that filmgoers want to enjoy.'

'It's not everyone who has the money to contemplate starting such an enterprise. Were you just fortunate that way?'

'I guess so.' He drove along the coast road for a while, so that the vista of the deep blue ocean washing up onto an unbroken stretch of white sand stayed with them along the way. 'My grandfather made a good deal of money from exporting fruit, and he set up a trust fund for us. My father runs a financial consultancy business, and I learned from him how to invest any money I managed to save.' His mouth curved. 'I did pretty well out of it, all things considered.'

'So it seems.' Her eyes were wide with admiration. He'd done more than well. 'I suppose Ross must have done much the same.'

'Yes, he did.' Connor sent her a brief, sideways look. 'Where is he, anyway? I thought he would have been around to see you off.'

'He was. He came down to the apartment for a while, but then he took himself off back upstairs. I think he's feeling a little out of sorts.'

'Poor Ross.' His mouth made a crooked line. 'He hates it when I get to spend time with you.'

'No...no, it isn't that.' She shook her head to emphasise the point. 'He just hates to be away from the filming.'

'Sure he does. He'll get over it soon enough.' Connor was still smiling as he turned the car onto the main highway.

Alyssa sank back in her seat, deep in thought, contemplating the day ahead. Was it true, what he'd said earlier? Was that really why Connor had decided to come along today, because he wanted to be with her? After the way she'd opened up to him the other evening about her failures as a doctor, she hadn't expected him to be at all interested in her. After all, how could he have any respect for her when she didn't respect herself? But now...despite her misgivings about getting involved with him, she couldn't deny that the idea of spending time with him made her insides tingle.

Still, doubt crept in once more. Ever since her ex-boyfriend had let her down and proved untrustworthy, she'd had a problem taking things at face value. Was it actually the company business Connor was most concerned with today? And his reaction to Ross's grumpiness had been a little strange, too. Was he simply taking the opportunity to keep them apart whenever possible? It was all very puzzling.

'Here we are. This is the meeting point,' Connor murmured a few minutes later, and she quickly brought her attention back to the present. They had arrived at a coastal stretch of the island, where a brackish creek flowed into the sea, and people were already beginning to gather by the water's edge. Sliding out of the car, Alyssa went with Connor to join them.

All around everything was green, rich with lush vegetation, and an overhang of densely populated, leafy trees countered the heat of the sun.

They exchanged greetings with everyone who was taking part in the filming, relaxing for a while ahead of the day's events. Then the director stepped forward and spoke to them all for a few minutes, cast and extras, about the course the filming was to take. Dan was a well-built man, florid and exuberant, with brown hair that had been bleached by the sun.

'Okay folks, listen up,' he said. 'You'll be going through the mangrove swamps at a leisurely pace. Try to forget that the camera is on you. You need to be as natural as possible. Take in the scenery all around you as if you're on a pleasure trip. Our leading man will be trying to blend in like one of the tourists, and his major activity won't start until we reach the cave system, so you've no need to be anticipating anything untoward. Is that all clear?'

He looked around, and everyone nodded. 'Good. We'll be heading for the landing point—just follow the lead kayak and ignore the cameras. From there you'll take the boardwalk to the cavern system and the beach, and that's where your part ends. You'll have lunch there. It's all laid on.'

A small cheer went up. 'I hope you've provided something for us to drink,' one bright spark piped up. 'Something of the alcoholic variety would be good.' There were a few more cheers in support.

'Yes, yes, it's all arranged. Along with a bus to take you home again.' Dan clapped his hands together. 'Okay, shall we get on? Time's wasting, and the light's perfect right now. I don't want to lose it.'

Alyssa gazed around her. The mangrove swamp was

a truly magnificent sight. Huge trees seemed to walk on the water, their gnarled, tangled roots above the surface and below. Everything was verdant, bustling with life, and through the canopy the sun glinted down on the salt creek.

Connor helped her into their kayak. They were seated one behind the other, with Alyssa at the back, and slowly they edged out into the water, dipping their paddles in unison.

As they moved deeper into the swamp, she was overwhelmed by the serenity of the place. 'It's beautiful here, so peaceful,' she murmured. 'I wasn't expecting that, but it's perfect.' Birds called to one another, darting from tree to tree or gliding leisurely on the wind currents. And when she looked into the forest on either side she saw glimpses of broad-leaved ferns and, here and there, flowers, delicate, beautiful blooms in bright colours. 'They're orchids, aren't they?' she said quietly, her voice full of awe.

'Yes, that's right.' Connor stowed his paddle for a while, allowing them to drift and take in their surroundings, and Alyssa followed his example. 'They grow wild out here,' he said, 'in small pockets in the trunks of the trees or in crevices in the rocks.'

'Somehow I didn't imagine there would be flowers. It's all so lovely, it's breathtaking.'

Connor smiled. 'I thought you'd like it here. It's something we have in common, don't we...a love of nature? Ross and I often came here when we were teenagers, kayaking through the lagoons. I really appreciated it when we moved from Florida and came to live here. I loved everything about the islands. There's so much variety.'

They paddled idly through the water, passing by billowing seagrass and oyster beds, where molluscs had fastened themselves to the underwater tree roots.

They chuckled as a sandpiper teetered along the bank, in his distinctive wobbling gait, his tail bobbing up and down while he searched for titbits with his orange, pointed bill. And a few minutes later they were startled by the sudden loud call of a green heron that came to settle on the opposite bank.

'That's a bonus for us,' Connor said softly. 'You don't usually see them in the daytime, unless they're hungry or feeding their young.'

Once again they stopped paddling and remained still for a while, following the bird's movements as it picked out insects one by one and then dropped them in the water to attract any passing fish. Then, as soon as he spied his prey, he swooped, triumphant.

Soon, perhaps too soon, Alyssa thought, they reached the landing point, and tied up the kayak, stepping out onto the wooden boardwalk. On either side of them the mangrove forest became a thick, green wall of leaves and branches.

Connor put his arm around her. 'I'm glad you agreed to come along today,' he said quietly. 'I wasn't sure, after the night of the storm, whether you'd still be up for it. Those winds can be scary and they leave a wide trail of damage behind them, one way and another.'

'With people, as well as property, you mean?' She tried not to think about that arm that circled her shoulders and protected her from any stray, encroaching branch as they walked along. 'I was just so glad you came to find us that night. I don't know what I'd have done without you.'

'You'd have found a way to get him to hospital, even if it meant waiting for the next driver to come along. I was fortunate in that I found you first.'

'Yes.' She smiled up at him. 'Thank you for what you did, anyway. I was so impressed by the way you saved that little girl.'

'Ah...that was a joint operation, I think. And by all accounts, she's doing well now.'

'I'm glad about that.' She frowned. 'But what will happen about all the damage to their village? They looked like poor people, so even though things have been cleared up, it might be difficult for them to get the repairs started. I heard of other villages, too, where there were a few slight injuries and property was wrecked.'

'Yes, that's true. A number of settlements were hit, and people need help, but we've organised workers to go on with the clearing-up process.' He hugged her briefly. 'I thought it was great how you pitched in to help. Anyway, at the end of filming we'll give a gala dinner and invite people to donate to the fund we're setting up to help with rebuilding.'

She looked at him with renewed respect. 'By "we" you mean you and Ross?'

He nodded. 'We couldn't just stand by and do nothing.'

'No. I think it's great, what you're proposing.'

They walked along the pathway to a sheltered area of the rock-strewn beach, where the cast and crew were assembling for a picnic lunch. To Alyssa's surprise, someone had set up a gas-fired barbecue beneath the palm trees and a chef dressed in traditional white jacket and dark trousers was there, already busy preparing food. The cameraman turned his attention to the inlets and caves some distance away where the film action was taking place.

Connor found a patch of smooth, white sand a little apart from the crowd, shaded by the branches of a tropical sea grape tree. He sat down, reaching for her hand and pulled her down beside him. The fruits of the tree hung down in clusters above them, purplish-red in colour, as though inviting someone to pick and eat them.

'Mmm…something smells good.' Alyssa's mouth was beginning to water as the appetising aroma of chicken and barbecue ribs filled the air. 'I was expecting something like sandwiches, definitely not hot food.'

'We aim to please.' Connor smiled, and just then a couple of catering staff came around with plates, inviting people to help themselves.

Alyssa was handed a plate and Connor helped her to pick out a selection of crab cakes, served with tangy zucchini and cucumber coleslaw, along with smoked chicken wings and conch fritters. These were served with a spicy dipping sauce, and there was rice and salad to complete the dish.

A table had been set up in the shade of a cavern, where wine bottles were chilling on a bed of ice, and Connor went to fill two glasses with sparkling white wine. He came and sat beside her once more and she realised he'd brought the bottle with him, along with a bucket of ice.

'I think,' Alyssa murmured, after a while, leaning back against a sun-warmed rock, 'this is what I came here for—to the Bahamas, I mean… Sun, sand and sea, and the most delicious food ever.' There had been a wonderful selection of fruit for dessert, a perfect accompaniment to the meal. 'I sometimes think I must have died and gone to heaven.'

Connor laughed. 'Heaven here on earth, perhaps,' he murmured, filling up her glass once more. 'You might as well relax, because we're free for the rest of the afternoon, as the man said.'

She nodded dreamily as she sipped her wine. 'I will. You don't need to encourage me. I can't think of anything I'd rather be doing.'

'You can't?' He moved closer, his hand coming to rest on the soft curve of her hip, and she cautiously set her glass down on a nearby flat rock.

'Connor, I...'

'Maybe I could help you with a few ideas.' He dropped a kiss onto her unsuspecting lips and murmured softly, 'Mmm...you taste of spice and summer fruit...pineapple, I think, and plump, juicy peaches, luscious...just like you.'

She gazed up at him, eyes widening, her lips parting in startled awareness after that dreamy, soft-as-thistledown kiss, while her whole body had begun to fizz with heightened expectation. He'd kissed her just once, and to her shame she wanted more. She wanted to feel his lips on hers all over again and his hands to stroke along the length of her body.

'I...uh...'

'You...uh...need me to show you how to let go of your worries and enjoy being cosseted, don't you?' he said with a smile. 'I can do that, Alyssa. I can make you feel good about yourself. Let me show you...'

He kissed her again, slowly, thoroughly, his hand splayed out over her rib cage, warm, tender, inviting her to lean into the protective curve of his body. And she was sorely tempted. More than anything, she wanted to feel his long body next to hers, to have him hold her and to have him transport her to some magical, sensational world where nothing mattered but the two of them and their slow, sweet exploration of each other.

But something in her resisted, some faint vestige of self-preservation managed to rise above his sensual on-slaught. So, instead, she shifted in his arms and even before she pressed the flat of her hand against his rib cage, he had come to realise that all wasn't well.

'What's wrong, Alyssa?' he murmured. His cheek brushed hers, teasing her with his closeness, his lips so near, yet so far, and to her dismay she felt her resistance crumbling at the first hurdle.

'Connor, I…uh…I don't think this is a good idea.'

'Are you sure about that?' he demurred softly. 'That's a great shame because, you know, I'd really like to kiss you again.' His head lowered, his mouth coming dangerously close to hers. 'Why don't you want me to kiss you?'

She made a soft groan. 'I do…but I can't let it happen. I can't get involved. Besides, there are way too many people around. It wouldn't be right. It wouldn't feel right.'

'Should we talk about conflicting signals here?' He gave her a rueful smile. 'Anyway, nobody's taking any notice of us. We're in the shade, away from where all the action is. And they'll be gone soon. The bus will be taking them back in a few minutes.'

'Won't we be on that bus with them?'

He shook his head. 'I've a boat waiting to take us back to the meeting point. I thought you might like to spend some more time here. Was I wrong about that?'

She shook her head. 'No, I love it here.'

'But you don't want to be here with me, is that it?' His features darkened, something bleak flickering in the depths of his eyes. 'Are you still hankering after my brother?'

'No, you have it all wrong, Connor. You don't understand.'

'No, I don't.' He sat up and wrapped his arms around his knees. 'Perhaps you should explain it to me.'

She pulled in a deep breath. 'You said I was giving conflicting signals, and perhaps you were right about that. I like being with you, I can't deny it. But you have to know, one of the reasons I came to the island was because I was in a relationship with someone and it all went wrong.' She swallowed. 'I thought we had something going for us, but it fell apart, and in the end I felt I needed to get away from my ex. He hurt me, and I don't think I'm ready for the dating scene again.'

'I'm sorry he hurt you,' he said softly. 'But it doesn't have to be like that with us. I'm not looking for anything heavy. I told you once before, I don't want commitment, Alyssa, but you and I could have fun together. What would be wrong in that? I like being with you. You're gentle, kind, fun to be with…intelligent… I look forward to seeing you, and whenever I'm with you I want to hold you close and cover you with kisses. Is that so wrong? I get the feeling you like being with me, too.'

'I do. But when it comes down to it, you're talking about sex,' she said in a flat voice. She shook her head. 'I don't go in for meaningless relationships, Connor. I don't sleep around, and I couldn't accept the kind of situation you're suggesting. Besides, maybe things start off that way, leisurely, friendly, no strings attached, but

sooner or later, more often than not, the situation begins
to change, and someone gets hurt.'

'Like you and your ex?' His glance skimmed over
her, tracing a line over her taut features. 'Do you want
to tell me what happened?'

She moved her shoulders in an awkward gesture. 'We
were together for a couple of years.' She sucked air into
her lungs. 'It started off as a mutual friendship and grew
into something more as time went by. But then I found
I was working more and more hours in A and E as I
specialised, while he was left with time on his hands.
He worked at the hospital, doing research, and his was
more or less a nine to five kind of job. I think he grew
tired of waiting for me to finish my shifts, and sometimes, when we had something planned, I had to let him
down because I couldn't leave my patients in the lurch.'

She frowned. 'I think we might have made a go of
things, all the same, but then I started to suffer from
burnout. I needed someone to talk to, but suddenly he
wasn't there for me. He didn't seem to understand. And
for my part I began to wonder what kind of man he was
if I couldn't count on his support when I needed him.'

'So you broke up with him?'

Her mouth turned down at the corners. 'Not then,
not right away. We talked things through and decided
to try to put things right…only perhaps I was trying
a little bit harder than he was. I went over to his flat
early one day, planning to surprise him with a special
dinner for his birthday and tickets to a concert…but I
found he was already celebrating, with a girl from his
research department.'

He sucked air into his lungs. 'I'm sorry. That must

have come as a killer blow.' His eyes had darkened, his gaze moving over her.

'Yes, it was.' She lifted her chin. 'I suppose you imagine that's par for the course, the kind of thing that happens sooner or later when two people get together.'

He shook his head. 'I'm thinking the man was a fool for playing around when he could have you as his girlfriend.'

She pulled a face. 'Perhaps, deep down, he didn't believe in commitment. Like you.'

'Ouch!' He winced. 'I suppose I deserved that. But the truth is, up to now I've never met anyone that I wanted to commit to. It's not much of a defence, I know.'

He looked so deflated that she couldn't help but smile. 'Shall we just agree to enjoy the rest of the time we have here on the beach? There's more wine in the bottle—I notice you haven't been drinking much—and then I'll look forward to a ride in that boat you said you have waiting.' She frowned as a thought crossed her mind. 'It isn't a rowboat, is it? I really don't fancy paddling my way home along the coast, not after all that delicious food and wine.'

'Oh, it definitely isn't a rowing boat,' he said with a chuckle. 'It has a motor, and a cabin with a galley...as well as all the mod cons that a girl like you might like.'

'I guess that's all right, then. Everything for a girl like me...' What kind of girl did he think she was? She gave him a teasing smile. 'You seem to know me pretty well—but, then, you must have had me more or less sussed out when we first met and you decided I was after Ross for my own mercenary reasons.'

'Ah, but that was way back...an age ago,' he protested, his brows lifting. 'Are you going to keep on holding that against me?'

'Oh, yes,' she said, a glimmer in her green eyes. 'You're definitely not off the hook, by a long way.'

He held a hand to his chest as though she'd wounded him deeply, and she smiled and sipped the wine he poured for her.

The moment had passed when he would have held her close and kissed her, and she mourned its passing. But it was for the best that she'd held him at bay, wasn't it? It didn't feel too good right now, but she'd get over it soon enough. She hoped.

CHAPTER SIX

'THAT'S a really nasty sunburn you have, Ryan.' Alyssa examined the cameraman's back and shoulders, and frowned. 'How did you manage to get yourself into such a state? Your skin is very red and it's peeling, so there's a risk of infection if it's not treated.'

Ryan winced. 'I was stupid, I know. I didn't think a couple of hours out in the sun without my shirt would hurt. Only we stayed on the beach longer than I expected, and I fell asleep on my front while the others were messing about in the sea.' He moved his hands in a helpless gesture. 'I never knew sunburn could hurt so much. I've been feeling really light-headed and sick.'

'Second-degree burns can be very painful.' She went over to the sink and rinsed a cloth with cold water, giving it to him to hold over his forehead. 'That should cool you down a bit and help take away the sick feeling.'

She checked her medicine cupboard for silver sulfadiazine ointment and used the sterile applicator to spread a thick layer of the cream over the damaged skin. 'This is an antibiotic ointment, to prevent infection,' she told him. 'You'll need to come in every day for the next two or three days so that I can treat you. But I'll put

a dressing on the shoulder for you, in the meantime…
that's looks to be the worst bit of all.'

'Thanks, Alyssa. You're a gem. It's beginning to
feel easier already.'

She smiled. 'It's the coolness, I expect. It's very
soothing, but you can help yourself by drinking plenty
of fluids—not alcohol but lots of water, juices and so
on, over the next day or so to prevent dehydration. And
make sure you wear a shirt at all times to keep the area
covered.'

'Okay. Thanks again.' He left a few minutes later,
clutching a prescription for ibuprofen, to help him deal
with the pain.

'Another satisfied customer?' Connor put his head
round the door of her makeshift surgery as she was
washing her hands at the sink. The company had provided a mobile unit for her, complete with desk, couch
and everything that she would need.

'I hope so. He had a nasty sunburn.'

'It must have been serious if you were using that,'
he said, watching her replace the lid on the tub of ointment. 'The natives around here use something natural…gamalamee.'

She sent him a puzzled look. 'I can't say I've ever
heard of it.'

'No? It's a bush medicine—the bark of the gumbo
limbo tree, or gamalamee, as they call it hereabouts,
cut into strips and boiled. When it's cool, they place the
strips on the burn to soothe the skin and help it heal.'
He smiled. 'It's sometimes known as the tourist tree.'

'Really?' She lifted a brow. 'Why's that?'

'Because the red bark peels, just like the skin of the
unfortunate tourists.'

She chuckled. 'I can never be sure whether or not you're teasing me,' she said.

'Not at all. It's quite true. They say it helps a lot with sunburn.' He peered inside her fridge and lifted out a jug of orange juice. 'Is it okay if I help myself?'

'Of course. Glasses are in the cupboard on the wall.'

'Thanks.' He was still smiling as he poured juice for himself and offered a glass to Alyssa. 'It's also true that it's one of the main ingredients in a bush tea called Twenty-One-Gun Salute.' His eyes took on a devilish gleam. 'It's said to be a great aphrodisiac.'

'Hmm. I think maybe we'd best not go there,' she said with a laugh.

'Perhaps you're right. Anyway, you look cool and fresh,' he said, looking her over as she accepted the cold drink. She was wearing a short-sleeved blouse and a loose-fitting skirt that floated lightly around her legs as she walked. 'It's in the high eighties out there.'

'So you've come in here to escape the heat?'

He nodded, taking a long swig from his glass. 'It's my lunch break. I had to go and visit my father to see how he was doing, and this place was on my way back to the hospital, so I thought I'd stop by and see how you were doing.'

'Everything's going fairly well here, up to now, I think. How's your father doing?'

'He's fine. The tests showed some ulceration, nothing more serious than that, and he has medication to clear it up.' He studied her. 'So what's new here?'

She tasted the refreshing juice and took a long swallow. 'Ross is back on site—he looks fit and well, so it seems he's completely over the injury to his head. He's so much back on form that he's getting in Dan's way, I think.'

He chuckled. 'Is he?'

She nodded, giving a faint smile. 'He was talking to Dan about needing to find a stand-in for Alex. There's a water-skiing stunt coming up and they need to get it sorted quickly. Anyway, he told Dan he wants to do the stunt himself.'

He frowned. 'So soon after a head injury? That's definitely not on.'

'Well, everyone seems to think Dan will agree to it. That's the talk around here today. The thing with this job is that people tend to drop in here and I get to hear all the gossip. They confide all their niggling worries and problems in me.'

'Well, I can see why they might want to do that. I notice that Ross, in particular, calls in on you fairly often.'

'And how would you know that?'

'As you say, people gossip. They know that he's besotted with you. I only have to walk on the set and people are ready to help me catch up on the news.'

She absorbed that while he finished his drink and glanced at his watch. 'Perhaps I should be getting back—' He broke off as someone knocked on the door, and then Ross came in, supporting one of the stagehands, who appeared to be ill. He was also limping badly, and leaning on Ross as best he could.

'Bring him over to the couch,' Alyssa said quickly. She recognised the young man as one of the workers who had helped with the clean-up after the storm a few days ago. She'd stood alongside him in the flooded area of a small settlement and piled debris onto a waiting truck.

'What's wrong, Lewis?' she asked. 'How can I help?'

'It's my foot,' he said, struggling for breath. 'The pain is really bad.' He was shivering, too, and looked as though he might pass out at any moment. This couldn't simply be a problem with his foot, she realised. The man was sick.

'Shall I take off his shoe and sock?' Ross asked, when the man was settled on the couch. She nodded.

'Please. I need to take a look.' She put on a pair of latex gloves and examined the badly swollen area around Lewis's ankle and part of his foot. 'This is very red and angry-looking,' she told him. There were blisters all around the area, as well as bruising beneath the skin, but in the centre there was an area of dead tissue. 'Have you any idea how this happened? Did you graze your ankle at any time?'

Lewis nodded, sinking back against the pillows of the couch. A thin film of sweat beaded his brow, yet his body was racked with cold tremors. 'I caught it on a rock some days ago. It was nothing really, but after the storm it really started to get bad.'

Alyssa reached for her stethoscope and listened to his chest. His lungs were rasping, and when she took his blood pressure she discovered that it was dangerously low.

'Okay, Lewis, I want you to lie back for a while and rest, and I'm going to give you some oxygen to help with your breathing.' She placed an oxygen mask over his nose and mouth and connected it to an oxygen cylinder. 'Take it easy for a while,' she said. 'I'm going to have a word with Dr Blakeley, if that's all right with you.'

He nodded and closed his eyes, and she turned

quickly to Ross. 'Would you get him something to drink while I talk to Connor for a moment?' she asked.

'Of course. He's really ill, isn't he?' he said, under his breath.

'I think so, yes. It's good that you brought him to me.'

She glanced at Connor, whose expression was sober as he checked the results on the blood-pressure monitor. 'His pulse is very high,' she murmured, moving away from the couch so that Lewis couldn't hear what was being said. 'And combined with the low blood pressure, I believe he's going into shock. I think we should get him to hospital right away.'

Connor nodded. 'He's dehydrated. Can we get an intravenous line in? And I think it would be wise to give him a strong broad-spectrum antibiotic. We're looking at sepsis here, and we need to act quickly.'

'Yes, I think you're right about that.' It looked as though Lewis's whole body was inflamed by some sort of infection. 'I'll see to it.'

She'd recognised straight away that it was a grave situation, and for a moment or two she felt the familiar rapid increase in her heartbeat and the knot in the pit of her stomach. Somehow, though, having Connor close by made her feel much stronger, and his presence was reassuring, helping her through this. After a while her hands became steadier and she started to think more clearly.

She said thoughtfully, 'But what could have caused the wound to flare up like that? What kind of organism are we dealing with here? Something waterborne? I know he was standing in flood water next to me the other day, and his legs were bare.' She shook her head. 'I've never seen anything quite like it before. There's an area of dead skin that will need surgical debridement.'

'It could be Vibrio,' Connor said. 'Sometimes after tropical storms it blooms quite profusely in flood water. Molluscs feed on poisonous plankton, and the bacteria can be passed on to people, either through being eaten, if the shellfish aren't prepared properly, boiled, and so on, or they thrive in water and can infect wounds, which is what I think might have happened in this case.'

'And it's more dangerous this way?'

He nodded. 'Extremely so. Lewis is already in a bad way, near to collapse. I think we should take him to hospital now—we can go in my car. It'll be quicker than waiting for an ambulance.'

'Okay. I'll get him ready.'

She set up an intravenous line in Lewis's arm to remedy the dehydration and try to restore the balance of his blood pressure and heart rate, and at the same time she explained to him that they needed to get him to hospital. 'They'll do blood tests and make sure you get the right antibiotic to deal with the infection,' she told him. 'In the meantime, I'm going to inject you with the strongest one I have, and that should help to stop it in its tracks.'

Between them, Ross and Connor helped him out to the car, while Alyssa held the fluid bag of normal saline aloft.

She sat with him in the back of the car while Connor started up the engine. 'Thanks for your help, Ross,' she said, giving him a light wave before the car moved away. Ross was subdued, shocked, she guessed, by what was happening. 'Try not to worry. We'll take care of him.'

Once they arrived at the hospital Connor went into action, hooking Lewis up to a cardiac monitor and checking his vital signs once more. Then he took samples of his blood for testing.

'His breathing's pretty bad,' he said, turning to Alyssa, who was looking on. 'I suspect there's a lot of inflammation there, so I'm going to put him on corticosteroids to try to reduce it. And as soon as I get the test results back, I'll give him electrolytes to restore the acid balance of his blood.' He frowned and turned to the nurse who was assisting him. 'We'll put him on a vasopressor drug and see if that will bring up his blood pressure some more. It's still dangerously low.'

'Okay, I'll get things ready for you.'

A porter took the samples over to the lab and Connor called for a surgeon to come and look at Lewis's wound.

'All we can do now is wait for the results to come through,' Connor told Alyssa some time later. 'It shouldn't take too long for some of the simpler ones to come back from the lab, but he won't be able to go to surgery until we have his condition stabilised.' He glanced at her, taking in her worried expression. 'How are you holding up? Are you okay? I know these situations are worrying for you.'

'I'm all right.' She frowned. 'It's very strange, but for the first time in a couple of years I haven't had that awful, prolonged sick feeling in my stomach when I've had to deal with an emergency. It was there, but it was over very quickly. I can't explain it.' She looked at him. He was so calm, so thorough in everything he did, reliable, capable…everything she dreamed of being.

'Perhaps it was because you were with me,' she murmured as the thought dawned on her. 'I can't think of any other reason why I should feel this way. But around you I feel more secure somehow.'

'Then I'll have to arrange it so that I'm with you more often,' he said with a smile. He wrapped his arms around her and gave her a hug, but it was over almost as soon as it had begun and she mourned the loss of that comforting embrace.

He was called away a few minutes later to deal with another patient, but he urged Alyssa to go and wait in his office. 'I'll come and find you as soon as I have anything for you. I know you're concerned about Lewis. Help yourself to coffee, or whatever. Make yourself at home.'

'I will, thanks.'

She went to his office and made coffee, as he'd suggested, and then sat down to glance through some magazines she found on a low table. She was too anxious about what was happening to Lewis, though, to be able to concentrate for long, and restlessness soon overcame her. She stood up and went to stare out of the window at the fig tree that provided shade in a corner of the landscaped gardens. Everything about Connor's place of work, including the area outside, was designed to be luxurious and peaceful, to put people at their ease.

She turned away and looked around the room. In a corner, on top of a mahogany filing cabinet, she found a child's toy, a lightweight, wooden horse and cart. The wheels on the cart turned when she gently spun them. On the seat of the cart there was a jointed, carved figure of a little girl. Engrossed in the beautiful simplicity of the toy, she took a moment to react when Connor came into the room.

'Oh, you've discovered my secret hobby,' he said, his mouth curving. 'I wasn't sure whether or not to paint it. Do you think it might look better?'

'You made this?' Her eyes widened. 'No, you should leave it. I think it's perfect as it is. I love this sort of thing—in fact, I was just thinking that I'd like to buy something hand-crafted to send home to my mother.' She looked at him with real admiration. 'So this is your hobby?'

'One of them,' he said, nodding. 'The wood's particularly easy to carve. It comes from the gamalamee I was telling you about. It's a kind of balsa wood, so it's really easy to work with. I thought I'd give this toy to the little girl who was nearly drowned. Apparently she lost her doll in the flood—I thought this might help to make up for it.' He frowned. 'What do you think? I wondered if perhaps it's not girly enough?'

She went over to him and laid her hand on his arm, looking up into his eyes. 'Oh, Connor, she'll absolutely love it. I think that's a wonderful idea.' It was such a thoughtful gesture that it brought a lump to her throat and she wanted to reach up and kiss him…and for a moment or two she was poised on the edge of doing just that. But even as she warred within herself, his arms went around her and he dropped a kiss lightly on her mouth.

'I'm glad you think so,' he murmured.

Flustered, she stayed where she was for the time being, not stirring but watching him, her lips gently parted, stunned by the intimate gesture and desperate for him to sear her mouth with flame once again.

'If you go on looking at me like that,' he warned softly, 'there'll be nothing for it except to kiss you all over again.'

'Um…' She pulled herself together and gave herself a mental shake. What on earth was she thinking? For a second or two she'd been reckless enough to think of throwing caution to the wind and basking in the shelter of his arms. That would have been sheer madness. He would lead her along the same path as all his other conquests and then disentangle himself when he judged things were liable to get out of hand. And she could see them getting out of hand very quickly.

'Did you...?' She tried to collect her thoughts. 'Did you have some news about Lewis? You seem to have been gone for ages.'

'Sorry about that. Yes...' He slowly released her. 'I had some of the results back and added some more drugs to his list of medication. His blood pressure's up a little, so that's a sign things are moving in the right direction, but his heart rate is still very fast. He's not out of the woods yet by a long way. And we need to get that infection under control.'

'I suppose it's something, at least, that his condition isn't getting any worse.'

'Yes. Anyway, he'll be admitted to one of the wards, and another doctor will go on with his treatment.'

He glanced briefly at the wooden cart and then turned back to her. 'How do you feel about going to the market in town to look for that gift you mentioned? My shift's finished so I could take you there, if you like... unless you have to get back for some reason? I can't see that either of us will do any good by staying here any longer—we'll be leaving Lewis in good hands.'

She nodded. 'The filming was due to finish over an hour ago, so I'm through for the day.' She smiled at him. 'I think I'd like that. Thanks.'

They left the hospital a few minutes later after she'd taken a quick look at Lewis to see how he was doing.

He was sleeping and his wife was at his bedside. 'I'll leave you two alone,' Alyssa murmured, laying a comforting hand on the woman's shoulder.

'Thank you—both of you—for taking care of him and bringing him here,' the woman said.

'You're welcome. We're very concerned that he should get better.'

They made their way to the car park and set off for the market. It was a short ride away, a bustling place filled with wooden stalls where all kinds of wares were set out. Nearby was an open square bordered with bars and cafés and dotted around with tables and chairs where people could sit to eat and drink. In the middle of the square a traditional steel band was playing. The whole atmosphere was lively and entertaining, and Alyssa felt her spirits lifting.

'I love this market,' she told Connor as they walked around. 'There are so many lovely hand-crafted items for sale—I don't know how on earth I'm going to choose what to buy.'

'It's true, they're very big on straw crafts here—handbags, hats, and souvenirs. It depends what you're looking for... Something for your mother, you said?'

'That's right. It's her birthday next week, on Saturday, so I thought I might get her something personal.' There were jewellery stalls full of wonderful necklaces and bracelets made from beads or seeds polished to a high gloss, and some were made of oyster pearls. They stood for a while, watching a woman thread glass beads on to a wire and fashion it into a pretty spiral bracelet.

'She makes it look so easy,' Alyssa said, 'but some of the necklaces she made are very intricate. My mother bought me something similar for my birthday last

year...' She smiled. 'It was funny, because her birthday was a week earlier than mine and I'd bought her a
bracelet that would have gone with it perfectly. She said
it gave her the inspiration for my present.'

'You like jewellery?'

She laughed. 'I do. Show me a woman who doesn't.'

'Well, yes...' He smiled. 'But I meant, you like
beaded necklaces?'

'Oh, yes. I sort of collect them. I see something
pretty like that, and I can scarcely resist buying it.'

They wandered around the stalls, checking out the
goods, and in the end Alyssa chose a handbag made
from woven palm leaves and decorated with coloured
beads. 'I think my mother will like that,' she said. 'It's
lined with silk, and there's a purse to match.'

'She must look forward to hearing from you, I expect,' Connor said. 'After all, you've been here for some
time now, and you're a long way from home.'

'Maybe. I don't really know about that,' Alyssa answered, a fleeting expression of sadness moving over
her features. 'I've tried calling her a few times, but she's
usually out—I think she's been especially busy lately,
putting together a collection for her boutique.'

'What about your father? Have you spoken to him?'

'A couple of times. He's been away a lot, checking
on different subsidiaries of the company, so I've tended
to leave email messages instead of phoning these last
couple of weeks. That way they get back to me whenever they can.'

He put his arm around her and drew her close. 'I
wonder if they know how much you need them to be
there for you,' he said softly.

She stared at him, her green eyes troubled. How did

he know? It was something she'd tried to keep to herself, this feeling of disconnection from her family. Was he so perceptive that he saw through the outer shell to her inner being?

'I'm a grown woman,' she said. 'They know I'm independent and they probably respect me for it.'

'Maybe.' His arm was reassuringly steady around her, and his hand lightly cupped her shoulder. 'Let's go and get a cold drink and listen to the band for a while.'

'Okay. Just for a half an hour or so, and then I should get back.'

They walked over to the cobbled square and sat at a wooden bench table under the shade of a parasol. A waiter took their order for drinks and Connor ordered a platter of sandwiches. When it arrived a few minutes later Alyssa's eyes grew large. It looked surprisingly appetising.

'I was expecting straightforward bread with a filling,' she said, 'but these look delicious.' Among the sandwiches to choose from there were chicken and bacon with mayonnaise, cheese and sun-dried tomato with a herb dressing, and surrounding it all was a bed of crispy, fresh salad. 'This is wonderful.'

They ate, and drank, and listened to the music, watching as men carried two support struts and a cane into the centre of the square. Then supple limbo dancers dipped and dived, moving around to the heavy beat of the music and taking it in turns to bend beneath the horizontal cane, which was gradually lowered to within a few inches of the ground. The crowd whooped and cheered in delight.

When the show finished, Alyssa glanced at her watch. 'I ought to go back,' she said on a reluctant note.

'Do you have to?'

'I'm afraid so. I've arranged to see Ross later on, back at the house. He said he wanted to talk to me… about the filming, I think. He's very taken up with how it's all going. And he seems to be obsessed with taking on this water-skiing stunt.' She frowned. 'Has he done this sort of thing before?'

Connor nodded. 'He's pretty good at all kinds of water sports.' His mouth made a wry curve. 'I think that's how he managed to hook up with quite a few young women—they were very impressed with his prowess…as well as his six-pack.'

'Oh, dear. Even so, even if he's quite skilled, I still wish he wouldn't do it. I wish Dan had put his foot down and refused to let him take it on.'

She frowned. 'Apparently the scene in the film calls for a race across the water, and I can't help but worry about it. All sorts of things could go wrong—there are bound to be other people and boats on the water, and he could be turned off course by the swell from other boats—not to mention that he's just recovered from a nasty head injury.'

She looked earnestly at Connor. 'Can't you persuade him not to do it? He might listen to you.'

'I can try, but I doubt if he'll take any notice.' His eyes glittered. 'I suspect he's only doing it because he wants to try to impress you. He thinks the world of you.'

'But that's the last thing I want,' she protested, appalled at the thought. 'I hate to think of him risking life and limb for the cameras.'

'Because you care for him, don't you?' Connor's features were in shadow as the sun dipped behind a backdrop of trees. 'You can't bear the thought of him being hurt.'

'Of course I care for him… I think the world of him. He helped me when I was down and encouraged me to come over here—how can I ignore all that now and watch him put himself at risk? He's your brother, don't you want to steer him away from doing anything reckless?'

'There are a lot of things I want,' Connor said darkly, his eyes glinting with some unfathomable emotion. 'And my brother's well-being is one of them. But there are also times when being my brother's keeper can be a bit like wielding a double-edged sword.'

She wasn't quite sure what he meant by that, but she had the feeling that she was at the root of his brooding manner. Was there an inherent rivalry between the brothers that he'd tried to suppress, or was he merely concerned by Ross's apparent foolhardiness?

Either way, she didn't want to be the cause of any dissension between them. What could she do to keep this from happening?

CHAPTER SEVEN

'WELL, there's a sight for sore eyes.' Connor's voice sounded close by and Alyssa woke with a start. She'd been dozing in the hammock outside in the sunshine, and as she looked around, the hammock swayed gently with her movements.

Connor looked as though he was on top form, long, lithe, energetic, dressed in dark trousers and a linen shirt that showed the flat line of his stomach and emphasised his perfect physique.

'I was just... I didn't expect to fall asleep,' she murmured, her voice husky from the heat. It was still before noon, after all, though she glanced at her watch to make sure she hadn't been sleeping for too long. 'I just came out here to take the air for half an hour or so, and before I knew it I must have been well away.'

'Mmm. Perhaps you needed the rest. You looked so beautifully relaxed, it seemed a pity I had to wake you.' His gaze swept along the length of her, coming to rest on the expanse of her bare thigh, which must have been exposed when she'd wriggled into a more comfortable position. Flustered, she tried to cover herself by quickly tugging down the skirt of her dress.

He pulled a wry face. 'That is such a shame,' he

mused on a reflective note, 'I could have stood here and watched you for hours.'

Hot colour ran along her cheekbones. 'You said you had to wake me? Is something wrong?' She sat up, still a bit groggy from sleep, and readied herself to swing down from the hammock. It was the weekend, so there was no work for her to be worrying about, and she wondered what could possibly be the problem.

'Is this to do with Ross? He was going to pick up his new car this morning. He said he would bring it over here to show me…has the deal fallen through somehow?' Ross's car had been a write-off after the accident on the night of the storm, but he'd quickly set about organising a replacement.

Connor shook his head. 'No, it's nothing like that. Your cousin rang…Carys. You left your phone out on the deck, so I answered it for you in case it was anything urgent. She said she's getting an earlier plane and wonders if you could meet her at the airport—she should be arriving in about an hour.' He frowned. 'I'd offer to take you but I have to leave for the hospital around that time. I'm on call with the emergency services this afternoon.'

'Oh, that's all right, don't worry about it. Thanks, anyway. I have my little runabout and I'm sure I'll manage to find my way to the airport, even without sat-nav.' She smiled. 'You know Carys, don't you? Ross said you and he were her neighbours when you lived in Florida, though I expect you were all youngsters back then.'

He nodded. 'We've kept in touch with the family over the years—and we both still go back there quite often.'

'So you'll both probably enjoy seeing her again. Oh, wow… It's great that she's managed to get an earlier flight. I wasn't expecting her to arrive until this evening, but now we'll have a bit more time together. She'll be going back late tomorrow evening.' She pulled in a quick breath. 'I ought to go and give her a ring.'

She went to get down from the hammock, but it started to swing from side to side and she hesitated for a second or two.

'Here, let me help you.' Connor reached for her, his strong arms sliding around her waist and bringing her up close to him. As he lifted her down her soft curves brushed against the length of his hard body, and a whole host of wild and wonderful feelings started up inside her. Blood pumped through her veins with lightning force as she found herself being drawn into his firm embrace, and her whole body was suddenly vibrant with thrilling sensation.

Her feet finally touched the ground, but he went on holding her, and she realised she was in no hurry at all to move away from him. He was tall and strong, impressively masculine, and his powerful arms were locked around her in a way that had every nerve ending clamouring for attention. Delicious tremors shimmered through her. Her breasts were softly crushed against his long, tautly muscled frame, and his strong thighs were pressuring hers, so that a flood of heat began to pool in the pit of her abdomen.

He eased her against him, his hands gently caressing her, gliding along the length of her spine and over the swell of her hips, stirring up a firestorm of heat inside her. Then he bent his head towards her, and she knew that in the very next moment he was going to kiss her. Her heart began to tap out an erratic rhythm, and elation rose up in her. All she could think about was her desperate need to feel his lips on hers.

She didn't have to wait long for her wish to be granted. In the next instant his mouth covered hers, gently coaxing, teasing her lips apart so that in a heartbeat she yielded to the sweet, tender onslaught. Her body was supple, fired up with need, and she moulded herself to him, wanting this moment to never end. Out of the blue, it dawned on her that she'd never felt this way before, never wanted any man the way she wanted him.

'Sweet, sweet girl,' he murmured, nuzzling her throat and trailing a line of flame all the way down to the creamy slope of her shoulder. 'What am I to do? I can't resist you. I'm heady with wanting you, Alyssa. It feels as though I'm drunk and off balance.'

That was how she felt, too, as though her world had been tilted off its axis and she was spinning out of control. It was a strange, breathtaking feeling, and for once in her life she didn't know how to handle things.

She didn't have much time to think about it, though. His head dipped down and in the next moment his lips brushed over the smooth swell of her breasts where they escaped the confines of her lace-edged bra. His kisses were gossamer-light, thrilling her through and through until her whole body tingled with feverish pleasure.

'Heaven knows,' he said in a roughened voice, 'I've tried to keep from doing this, from getting close to you, but it's just too much…it's virtually impossible. You tantalise me…every time I see you, I'm lost…'

His breathing was ragged, his gaze absorbed as his hands moved over her, making a slow, sensual exploration of her rounded curves. Alyssa revelled in his touch. Under the golden blaze of this idyllic island sun everything was perfection and she wanted this moment to last for ever. But she didn't understand what was happening to her. Why did she feel this way? Wasn't it madness to let this go on? Things could very soon get out of hand...

Perhaps she'd been out in the sun too long and the heat had affected her way of thinking. Hadn't he said that all he wanted was a fun, no-strings kind of affair? Was that what she wanted? Would that really be such a bad option? At least she would have him to herself for just a short while.

'I don't know what's happening to me,' she said huskily. 'I've never felt this way before...'

'I know. It's the same for me,' he murmured, his voice rough around the edges. 'I think you've cast a spell on me. I can scarcely think straight when I'm around you.' He gently lifted her hand and placed it over his heart. 'See what you do to me? I don't understand it, no other woman has ever made me feel quite like this before.'

His heart was thudding heavily, a chaotic, thundering rhythm, and she felt its beat ricochet along her arm. Had she really made him feel this way, his emotions raging out of control, just as was happening with her? A short burst of elation spiralled inside her, until she realised her thoughts were taking a hazardous course. Should she stop this right now, or was it already too late? Her heart and mind were at war with one another.

Then the roar of a car's engine sounded in the distance, breaking the spell, and Connor half turned to glance in the direction of the road. 'I guess that must be Ross, coming to show off his new car,' he said on a soft sigh. He ran his hands over her arms. 'Perhaps I should have known I wouldn't get you all to myself for very long.' He lowered his head towards her and kissed her tenderly on the lips. 'Just one more kiss to keep me going…then I'll have that to remember when I'm at work.'

She wound her arms around his neck and kissed him in return. What would it hurt to give way to her feelings just this once?

They drew apart as a car swung onto the driveway of the property. Ross parked by the side of the house and cut the engine.

'What are you two up to?' he said in a suspicious voice, looking them over as he walked towards them. 'You're getting very close all of a sudden, aren't you? Is there something going on that I should know about?'

'You know everything there is to know,' Connor murmured, sliding an arm lightly around Alyssa's waist. He looked at the shiny, metallic grey convertible on the driveway. 'So this is the new dream machine…very nice. From the way you roared in here, I guess you've already put it through its paces.'

Ross smiled, nodding. 'It purrs like a kitten, and the acceleration is so smooth.' He turned to Alyssa. 'I'll have to take you for a spin in it. You'll love it with the top down and the feel of the wind in your hair. Couldn't be better.' He checked his watch. 'How about now? There's no time like the present.'

'Sorry, but I have to get ready to go and meet Carys at the airport,' she said. 'Perhaps some other time.'

He frowned. 'I could take you there—it's no problem. It's a two plus two seater, so there's room for Carys in the back. She's only a slim slip of a girl, so she should manage okay with a small amount of leg room.' His mouth quirked. 'That's the thing with sports cars… they're built for speed, not space.'

Alyssa thought it over. 'Are you sure you don't mind

taking me? It would help as you know the roads better than I do. But I should warn you—I might have to hang around for a while if her plane comes in late. And the journey's more than just a short trip, you know. It will take at least half an hour for us to get there.'

'Or twenty minutes in my new baby.' He gave her a beaming smile.

'Are you planning on writing off this car before you've even had a chance to run it in?' Connor was frowning. 'You'll have Alyssa in the passenger seat— if you're going to drive like a maniac she'll do better to drive herself.'

'Oh, but he wouldn't do that,' Alyssa put in quickly, 'would you, Ross?'

'Of course not, sweetheart.' Ross turned to Connor. 'As if I would do anything to put her at risk. Believe in me, brother. I'll bring her back safe and sound.'

'You'd better. The problem is, I know you too well.' Connor's expression was serious. 'I've been wondering if that knock on your head didn't set off your wild streak, especially after you started to talk about doing the water-ski stunt. You're meant to be the film producer, not the stuntman. The company doesn't insure you to put yourself in the frame.'

Ross reached out and patted him on the shoulder. 'You worry too much, bro. It'll all be fine, you'll see.'

'Hmm.' Connor was still frowning. 'It had better be. Remember, you have Alyssa to think about—you don't need to be showing off in front of her—she already knows who you are.'

Ross laughed. 'I'll take care of her, I promise.' He looked curiously at his brother. 'Is this a protective instinct coming out in you? I guess I have competition.'

He made a crooked smile. 'Still, she already knows you don't have any staying power. I warned her about you and your reputation a long while ago.'

'I'll just bet you did.' Connor's dark eyes glinted, flint-sharp.

Alyssa decided it was time to interrupt. 'Look, you need to put your differences to one side for a while, both of you. And there's no competition going on here. I'm not looking to get involved with anyone. I've been there and it wasn't good, and I'm not likely to be trying it again any time soon, especially with a man who thinks he's the next James Bond and another who thinks the dating game is just that—a game.' Those few minutes in Connor's arms had been a mistake, she could see it now. Why would he think of her differently compared to any of the women who had gone before? She was deluding herself if she thought otherwise, wasn't she?

She was frowning now, and both men were looking at her with alert expressions. She glanced at her watch. 'And I really think I should be setting off or I'll be late. I'll go and get my bag.'

A short time later she slid into the passenger seat of Ross's convertible and watched him set the sat-nav. 'Okay, we're off,' he said, and the engine growled into life. She glanced at him. 'Just kidding,' he murmured. 'Connor's watching, and I wanted to make him sweat.'

'You're such a child,' she scolded. 'Behave yourself, for heaven's sake.' She turned to look at Connor, who was standing by the house, his features taut, his body rigid. She waved, and mouthed silently, 'See you later.'

Ross shot the car along the road, gathering speed until they had left the isolated property behind them. Only then did he slow down and turn to look at her in triumph. 'That gave him something to think about, didn't it?'

'That doesn't even deserve an answer,' she said, flicking him a cool glance. 'You need to grow up, Ross.'

'Yeah, I know. I will.' He slid the car onto the main highway. 'I wouldn't take any risks with you. He ought to know that.' He shot her a quick look. 'But I think you must have crept under his skin somehow and found a soft spot. He's definitely hot and bothered where you're concerned.'

'I doubt it,' she murmured. 'Anyway, could we talk about something else?'

'Sore point, eh?' He smiled. 'Sure. So what do you think of my new beauty? She even has cameras to help with parking. You just switch on the screen on the dash, press "camera", and away you go.'

Alyssa was suitably impressed, and Ross pointed out all the finer features of the car while they drove along. Traffic was building up on the roads, as might have been expected this close to midday, but Ross stayed calm and headed towards the road junction ahead. He glanced in his rear-view mirror.

'Some people are unbelievable,' he murmured, and Alyssa pulled down her courtesy mirror to see what was going on behind them.

A driver in a white saloon was weaving in and out of traffic, as though he was determined to get to the junction ahead of anyone else. He was a young man, in his early twenties, Alyssa guessed.

'He'll end up causing all kinds of mayhem, the way he's going,' Ross murmured. 'I don't see why he can't just…' He let out a mild curse as, without warning, the driver pulled out into the far lane to overtake and then swung back in front of him.

Ross touched his brakes, conscious all the time of the cars closing the gap behind him. 'Now, why on earth would he do something like that?' he murmured, frowning.

'He's obviously in a hurry.'

Too much so, because in the next minute the driver shot across the junction and there was an almighty crash and the awful sound of grinding metal as he ran straight into a car that was already travelling towards the middle of the road.

Alyssa's heart seemed to turn over. 'Oh, no... Stop the car, Ross,' she said in a shocked voice. 'Is there anywhere you can pull over? I need to go and see if anyone needs help.' It didn't look good. The left side of the other vehicle, a black coupé, had caved in, and the white saloon had lost its front end.

'I can't pull over. I'm completely boxed in,' Ross answered, searching around for a solution. 'The way people drive out here can be awful at times. I'm sorry you had to see this.' He stopped the car next to the crashed cars, and Alyssa slid out of the passenger seat. All the other traffic had come to a standstill and car horns were blaring.

'I don't suppose you have a first-aid box in the car, do you?' she asked, reaching into her bag for her phone as she pushed open the passenger door.

'I do. Connor tells me I always have to be prepared. I'll get it for you.' He stepped out of the car.

'Thanks.' Fumbling around in her bag, she pulled a face. 'I left my phone back at the house. Will you call for an ambulance?'

'Of course. I'm already on it.' He took the first-aid box from the boot of his car and handed it to her, then pulled out his mobile phone and began to punch in numbers.

Alyssa went over to the black car. At first glance that appeared to be the one where there was likely to be the most damage to the occupants.

The woman driver was bleeding badly from a chest wound and appeared to be in deep shock, though she managed to give her name. 'My name is Raeni,' she said. 'My children—' She broke off, struggling to breathe.

Alyssa glanced in the back of the car. There were two children there, a boy and a girl, aged about ten and eight, both white faced and crying quietly. 'Mama's bleeding,' the boy said in a panicked tone, his face crumpling. 'She's bleeding.' The children were very distressed by the sight of the blood.

'I know, but we're going to look after her.' As far as she could tell, neither of the children was injured, but it was clear they were very badly shaken.

'He came out of nowhere,' Raeni managed to say, gasping between each word. 'I don't know what he—' She was very agitated. 'My children—'

'They're all right,' Alyssa assured the woman. 'Try not to upset yourself. Help's on the way.' She took a dressing pad from the first-aid kit. 'I'm going to put this dressing pad against your chest. Perhaps you could hold it there to help stem the bleeding. I have to go and check on the people in the other car, but I promise I'll be back in a minute or two.'

The woman nodded, and Alyssa hurried over to the white saloon. She found the young man slumped over the wheel, but he was still conscious and able to answer Alyssa when she spoke to him. He said his name was Malik. He was alert but breathless, and complained of abdominal pain. There were some cuts on his forearm, too, but nothing that appeared major.

'Try to stay still, Malik,' Alyssa said softly. 'The ambulance will be here soon.' She wished she could give him oxygen, but without her medical equipment she was severely hampered. Added to that, she couldn't split herself two ways and had to decide which person needed attention most of all. She opted to go to the woman in the black car. She was losing blood fairly rapidly and her condition could deteriorate at any moment.

Ross came over to her. 'Can I do anything to help?'

'Yes, please,' she said in a low voice. 'Will you stay with Malik while I see to the other driver? Perhaps you could put a couple of dressings on his arm.' She gave him some dressings and a bandage from the first-aid kit. 'Try to keep him calm, if you can. If he gets agitated it will make his breathing worse.'

'I can do that. Don't worry. I'll stay with him.'

Alyssa went back to the black car but was alarmed to find that Raeni was by now unconscious and the dressing pad was soaked through with her blood. She quickly felt for the pulse at her wrist, but to her dismay it was barely discernible.

She was stunned by what had happened, and it was the worst kind of situation she could have had to face. If Raeni's heart stopped, or was at a virtual standstill, no oxygen would flow around her body, and she would be brain dead within a very short time unless something was done to save her. What could she do? Where was the ambulance? The thought that she was the only one who could help this woman weighed heavily on her. Was she up to it?

Turning to the children, she said softly, 'I need you to go and sit with my friend for a little while so that I can look after your mother. Will you do that for me? I promise I'll take care of her.'

She bit her lip as she made that promise. Would she be able to save their mother? She shook off the negative thought. She *had* to save her. She couldn't bear the thought of these two innocent children being left motherless.

They tried to object but under her gentle insistence they gradually gave way and she quickly helped them out of the car. Ross gave her a concerned glance. He seemed to understand that she didn't want them to see what she had to do and said, 'Don't worry, they'll be fine with me.'

Alyssa went back to Raeni. Acting on instinct, she lowered the back of the driver's seat so that she was lying as flat as possible. Then she opened the woman's blouse and checked the wound. What she saw almost made her gasp out loud. It was nasty, deep, wide and gaping. How on earth could she bring her through this? She was so badly injured, there was hardly any chance of her being able to pull through.

She was guessing that the wound must have penetrated the heart, but even with the dire prognosis that presented, she couldn't give up, could she? Recalling the children's pinched, tear-stained faces was enough to spur her on. There had to be some way she could restore the woman's circulation.

She switched on the car's interior light so that she would be able to see a little better. She removed a pair of disposable gloves from the first-aid kit, along with a small bottle of antiseptic lotion, then took a sharp pair of scissors from her bag. After dousing the scissors in the solution, she began to clean Raeni's skin. She could only pray that the scissors would be strong enough and sharp enough to do the job in place of a scalpel.

In the distance, she heard the sound of the ambulance as she cut into the woman's chest. There was no anaesthetic she could give her, but in Raeni's present state that was probably the least of her problems. Within a minute or two Alyssa had opened up the area and could see the cause of the problem. The pericardium, the sac around the heart, was swollen and stiff with blood, putting pressure like a clamp around the heart and preventing it from pumping.

She heard the ambulance draw up and soon the paramedics were talking to Ross. She looked around and knew a huge surge of relief as she saw Connor coming towards her.

'Oh, Connor, thank heaven it's you,' she said. 'I'd forgotten it would be you coming out with the ambulance... I'm so glad to see you. I really need your help.' A wave of nausea washed through her as the strain of the last few minutes started to make itself felt on her.

'It's okay, Alyssa... Take it easy... Slow down and take a deep breath...' He laid a reassuring hand on her shoulder. His voice and his calm, soothing presence were instantly comforting to her, and she felt some of the tension ease from her. It was only then, as she looked up at him, that she realised Connor might not be as composed as he seemed. His face was devoid of colour and his body was taut, as though he was steeling himself in some way.

'Are you all right?' she asked, and he nodded.

'Tell me what the situation is here.' His manner was brisk, and that was surely understandable. They were dealing with an emergency here.

'I need to remove the blood clot that's formed in the pericardium,' she told him, 'but she'll need anaesthetic and a fluid line, preferably before I do that. We have to act quickly. She may need medication to force the heart muscle to contract.' She'd find out later what was wrong with Connor. For now, their patient had to be their main priority.

Connor was already opening up his medical kit and pulling on disposable gloves. Within a very short time he had put in an intravenous line so that Raeni could be given life-saving fluids, as well as an anaesthetic and other medication. He put an endotracheal tube down her windpipe and connected it to an oxygen supply.

While he did all that, Alyssa carefully began to remove the blood clot and drained away some of the fluid from the pericardial sac. Slowly, as the pressure was eased, the woman's heart began to beat once more, and at the same time blood began to spurt from the wound site. Alyssa placed her finger over the hole to stem the flow.

'We should get her to hospital right away,' she said. 'I'll keep my finger over the hole until we can get her to a surgeon. Will you phone ahead and arrange for a surgical team to be waiting for us?'

'Yes, I will. Are you going to be okay staying with her like that? I could take over for you if you like.'

Alyssa shook her head. 'I'll be fine. I'm just anxious about our other patient. He was very breathless. I didn't get a chance to do anything other than check him out.'

'I think the paramedics started to give him oxygen when we arrived, but I'll go and take over from them while we get this lady transferred to the ambulance. Sit tight and I'll send the paramedics over to you.'

'Thanks, Connor.' On an afterthought she said, 'Will you ask Ross to take care of the children and see that they're handed over to their father?'

'I will.' He smiled at her. 'You're doing a great job. You amaze me, Alyssa. You're a brilliant doctor. I'd be more than glad to have you at my side if I were in dire straits. I can't think of anyone else I'd sooner have with me.'

Her heart jumped a little. It was great that he had faith in her. 'Let's hope that's never put to the test.' She stayed where she was, keeping her finger in place to stop the blood from escaping, but his words warmed her through and through.

A couple of minutes later, the paramedics had placed Raeni on a stretcher, and wheeled her to the ambulance, with Alyssa staying constantly by her side, her hand still in position.

Malik travelled with them, propped up a little by pillows to ease his breathing. There was an oxygen mask over his nose and mouth and his eyes were closed, but it was plain to see that he was suffering a considerable amount of discomfort.

'Did you manage to examine him?' Alyssa asked quietly as the ambulance driver started up the engine and they sped away.

Connor nodded. 'I think there may have been some disruption to the diaphragm,' he said in a low voice. 'When I listened to his chest with the stethoscope I could hear sounds that you wouldn't usually expect to hear.'

'You mean there might be a tear in the diaphragm?'

'That's right. So some of the abdominal organs might have been pushed upwards into the chest cavity. We'll do a chest X-ray and MRI scan to be certain, but I'm pretty sure he'll need surgery.'

Alyssa winced. 'They're both in a bad way.'

'Yes.'

She studied him thoughtfully for a moment or two. 'I didn't realise it straight away, but you weren't quite yourself when you came out of the ambulance. What was wrong?'

'I was fine.'

'No, you weren't. I could tell. What was it, Connor? It couldn't be that you were bothered by the crash, could it? You must have seen things like that many times in your career.'

He nodded, and perhaps he realised that she would persist in her questioning because he said, 'But never when Ross's car was at the scene. When I first stepped out of the ambulance, it looked as though his car was part of the accident. I felt sick to my stomach, imagining that you and he might be injured.'

She sucked in a quick breath. 'I didn't know... I'm so sorry. That must have been awful.'

'It was, but then I found out that you were both okay. That was a tremendous relief. I couldn't bear the thought of either of you being hurt. I don't know how I would have gone on if—' He broke off. He looked uncomfortable, as though he'd said too much.

'If what?' Alyssa prompted him, but he shook his head.

'Nothing. It doesn't matter.'

She thought about it. Was he wondering about how he would go on if anything happened to Ross? Or maybe he was thinking of her...was it possible? Might he care for her more than she dared hope?

Their conversation had to come to an end, though, because by now they had arrived at the hospital and medical teams were waiting in the ambulance bay.

There were separate teams for each of the patients. Raeni was whisked away to the operating theatre and Malik was taken to the radiology department. Alyssa walked with Connor to the emergency room and saw that Raeni's children were there with their father. Ross, it turned out, had gone on to the airport to see if Carys was waiting.

'Heavens, I'd forgotten all about Carys,' Alyssa said in a stunned tone. 'She must be wondering what on earth's going on.'

'I expect Ross will look after her,' Connor murmured.

'Yes, you're probably right.' She was relieved at the thought. 'Perhaps he'll take her for lunch somewhere. That's what I planned to do.'

Connor nodded. 'Don't worry about it—I'm sure Ross will explain the situation to her and help to make her feel welcome. They always got on well together.'

'Good. That's a relief, anyway.'

He led her towards his office. 'I'm still on call for a few hours so I might have to leave at any moment, but I think you should sit down and rest for a while. That must have been a terrible ordeal for you, and yet you stayed in control, doing what you had to do. I'm really proud of you, Alyssa.'

She pressed her lips together. 'I didn't really get a

chance to think about it—until you arrived, and then it hit home with a bang.' They went into the room and he switched on the coffee machine.

'You're a wonderful, skilled doctor,' he said, a few minutes later as he handed her a reviving cup of hot coffee. 'It would be a tremendous waste to the profession if you were to give up on it.'

'I did what I could…but we don't know yet what will happen to her. I may have been too late…'

'At least you gave her a chance of survival. If you hadn't acted as you did, she wouldn't be here now, in the operating theatre.'

Alyssa sipped her coffee. It was good to know that he had faith in her, but could she live up to those expectations? Perhaps it was too early yet to say. She was still very shaken by what had happened.

His pager bleeped and he checked the text message briefly. 'I have to go,' he said. 'Will you get a taxi back home when you're ready? I can give you the number of a reliable company.'

'Yes, I'll be fine. Don't worry about me,' she murmured.

He studied her, his gaze dark and brooding. 'But I do worry,' he said. 'That's the problem.'

CHAPTER EIGHT

'IT MUST have been a terrible shock for you—coming across an accident like that.' Carys shook her head, making her blonde hair swirl silkily around her pretty, oval-shaped face. 'Such awful injuries. Ross has been telling me all about it. And those children—they must have been scared half to death.'

'Yes,' Alyssa agreed, 'that was worrying, seeing how upset they were. It's hard not being able to give them any real news about their mother, but she was still in the recovery room when I left the hospital, and we won't know how she'll be for some time yet. She lost a lot of blood and there are problems with her lungs because of the extent of the injury.'

'At least she came through the operation.' Ross poured drinks for the girls as they sat on the deck, looking out over the sparkling blue ocean. Brown shearwaters swooped and dived for fish, their white underbellies glinting in the sunlight, while black-headed terns cheekily tried to steal their catch.

Alyssa sipped her fruit punch, listening to the clink of ice in her glass. It was good to have Carys here at last. 'Anyway, I'm sorry we had to leave you high and dry at the airport,' she said. 'You must have wondered what was going on. Perhaps you thought we'd abandoned you?'

Carys laughed. 'Oh, no. I knew something must have gone wrong. Ross phoned to tell me he was on his way, and then he took me to the Oasis Club for lunch and drinks. We had a lot of catching up to do, and he told me all about the filming.' She frowned. 'Apparently it will all be over with soon… I expect life will seem fairly drab after all the excitement of the film shoots.'

'You're probably right. I think Ross will feel it quite badly—he thrives on the adrenaline rush.'

Ross nodded agreement. 'Once one project finishes, I'm on the lookout for another.'

As for herself, she would have to think through her options once her contract with the company came to an end. Instead of the relatively easy time she had been expecting, this stint of work in the Bahamas had given her a lot of food for thought.

They chatted through the afternoon, until Connor arrived home from his shift with the ambulance service.

'Hi, there, Carys,' he said, coming on to the deck and greeting her with a warm smile. 'It's good to see you again.' He bent his head towards her.

'You, too.' Carys lifted her cheek for his kiss and, watching them in such a warm, tender embrace, Alyssa felt a sudden sharp stab of jealousy. It was an unexpected reaction and definitely one that she didn't want. It was upsetting that she should respond this way, and it bewildered her. After all, there was no call for it— Carys was her cousin, they'd been close friends all their lives, like sisters almost, and it was perfectly natural for her and Connor to be close to one another.

Even so, she bent her head to hide her frown. Had

her cousin kissed Ross that way, or were these special moments reserved for Connor?

Annoyed with herself, she swallowed some more of her ice-cold drink and put on a smile. 'We were wondering what to do this evening,' she told Connor. 'We thought it might be good to take Carys somewhere special.'

He straightened up and nodded. 'I've been thinking about that. There's a beach barbecue and fire-eating show going on tonight at Smugglers' Cove. That should be well worth a visit.'

'It sounds great,' Carys said, her blue eyes bright with anticipation. 'I vote we go for the fire-eating—just as long as I don't have to try it out myself!'

'I doubt there's much chance of that.' Connor laughed. 'But it should be fun, and there's usually dancing and a whole variety of cocktails to try out.'

'You're leading me down the path to devil-may-care, I can see that,' she told him with a smile. 'But I'm not worried. I'm here to relax and have a good time, and I want Alyssa to do the same.'

'Oh, I will,' Alyssa murmured. 'I'm there in spirit already.' She shot Connor a quick look. 'Why is it called Smugglers' Cove—were there dark and dangerous goings on there at some time in the past?'

'There certainly were. It was the hub of rum-running in the prohibition era. There are lots of caves around there where sailors could hide their booty.'

She smiled. 'It's getting to sound more and more interesting.'

'You'll enjoy it, I'm sure.' Connor went to shower and change, and later, as the sun started to set on the horizon, they all set off to walk along the headland to

Smugglers' Cove. Rounding the bay, they were met by
the sound of drums beating out a fast, heady rhythm
and by the sight of islanders dressed in vivid costumes,
dancing to the feverish beat.

The aroma of barbecued chicken greeted them, and
a buffet table had been laid out on a terrace filled with
platters of pork, ribs, rice and peas and bowls of salad.
It was colourful and appetising, and Alyssa realised
she was hungry.

Connor and Ross went to get drinks while the girls
found seats at a table and sat down to watch the dancers. Men, bare-chested and athletic, moved to the music,
their bodies supple and toned, while the women dancers wore tube tops and flouncy short skirts that flicked
up and down as they shifted to the rhythm of the band.
There was a fire at the centre of the group, and they
took it in turn to light torches, swirling them around,
making patterns with the flames.

Alyssa drank tequila sunrise, a flamboyant cocktail with brilliant red and orange colouring, and felt
the music deep down inside her, so that when the floor
show finished and Connor held out his hand to draw
her to her feet, she was ready to dance with him in the
traditional hip-shaking, foot-stomping way of the fire
dancers. They laughed together, buoyed up by the cheerful atmosphere, and when Carys and Ross came to join
them they danced as a foursome.

'I'd no idea you could move like that,' Alyssa remarked, and Connor smiled and tugged her to him.

'You don't do so badly yourself,' he murmured huskily against her cheek. 'You've been tantalising me all
night long with those swaying hips and that gorgeous
body.'

'Have I really?' She laughed, snuggling up to him. Perhaps the alcohol had gone to her head because all she wanted right now was to be in his arms and it didn't matter to her that there were people all around.

'Yes, you have, Jezebel.' His eyes were dark, glittering with smouldering intent. 'I've been wanting to get close to you all night. I need to have you all to myself.' He looked around. 'What do you say we give these two the slip and go for a walk along the beach?'

'That sounds good to me.' She glanced over to where Ross and Carys were engrossed, deep in conversation. 'I don't think they'll miss us, do you?'

'It doesn't look like it. They've really hit it off, haven't they?'

So they set out to walk back along the beach in the moonlight, kicking up the sand with their bare feet, laughing when the waves rolled in and tickled their toes.

'I think I've had too much to drink,' she murmured, gazing up at the clear night sky. Stars shimmered like diamonds and in the balmy evening the whole world seemed magical. 'My head is swirling, and it's filled with music.'

'That's because we can still hear it, even from this distance.' They rounded the headland and stood for a while, looking out over the bay. A heron was silhouetted against the moonlit horizon, standing on a rocky outcrop, preening itself.

Connor took her in his arms and kissed her tenderly, and it seemed to Alyssa just then that it was so right that they should be together like this. No one had ever made her feel so good, so perfectly at ease with herself and the world.

'Have you had a good time tonight?' he asked

softly, and she nodded, blissful in his arms, not wanting to move.

'I have. I think I've fallen in love with this island, its people and their traditions.' She'd probably fallen in love with him, too, and maybe that was what coloured her judgement, but she couldn't tell him that. He might feel it was time to gently extricate himself, and she wanted to stay close to him for as long as was possible.

'I'm glad. I want you to be happy, Alyssa. You were so sad when you first came here… Not outwardly, but I think inside you were hurting, though I didn't realise it at the time. You talked about how you felt about your work, your relationship with your parents, and your ex… Do you still feel bad about breaking up with him?'

She shook her head. 'I haven't thought about him in a long time.' She frowned. 'It's strange, isn't it, how someone can take up so much of your thoughts and be so great a part of your life, and yet after a while they fade into the distance?' She thought about that for a while.

'I think perhaps we were never really suited. He didn't understand me and how important my work was to me back then. And, of course, when everything went wrong for me in my job, he wasn't there to support me. I suppose I started to look at him with different eyes then, even before he cheated on me.'

Thinking about that was a salutary reminder of how things could go wrong. She looked up at Connor, his face shadowed in the moonlight. Could she let herself love him and put her trust in him? She wanted to, so much.

He cupped her cheek in his hand. 'I shouldn't have doubted you when you first came here. I had such pre-set ideas about the women who'd set their sights on

Ross in the past, and I was judging you without even knowing you.'

'And you don't have those same worries about Carys?' She smiled. 'He seems to be very taken with her.'

'He's always had a place in his heart for Carys. Nothing ever came of it because she sees him for what he is—a man who enjoys life to the hilt and jumps at every opportunity without thinking first.'

'Perhaps he's changing.'

'Maybe.'

'So you don't need to be his protector any more?'

'Probably not. It's a habit I should have left behind long ago.' He smiled. 'I wonder why we're wasting this moonlit night talking about Ross?'

She knew the answer to that. 'Because I've had a little too much to drink and I'm afraid if I let you kiss me I'll do something foolish like fall in love with you.'

He inhaled sharply. 'That would never do, would it?'

'No.' She shook her head. 'You know what they say, "once bitten…"'

'True. But not all relationships have to end badly, do they? Perhaps I hadn't thought about it properly before. I mean, just because your ex let you down, and my parents made a mess of things, it doesn't have to follow that all love affairs follow the same course, does it?'

He swooped to claim her mouth once more and kissed her, deeply, passionately with all the fervour of a man whose emotions were rapidly running out of control. His hands shaped her and drew her to him, tracing the lines of her body with tender devotion.

'I want you so much…' he said raggedly '…so much that it's like an ache deep inside me.'

Her heart seemed to flip over. It was good to know that she could make him feel this way... It made her blood fizz with excitement and filled her with exhilaration to know that he wanted her, and in her heady, dreamlike state she was almost ready to throw caution to the winds and tell him she felt the same way. But self-preservation was a powerful deterrent and just a hint of caution remained, a tiny spark of doubt left to torment her. Perhaps his view of things was changing, but he still talked about affairs, and not about a lasting commitment, didn't he?

It would hurt her so badly if he were to cast her aside once she had committed herself to him. She knew it and there was no escaping the fact. The distress of having to end the relationship with James would be nothing compared to how she would feel if Connor was to go out of her life. She realised now that her feelings for him went very deep, deeper than she'd ever thought possible, and she didn't think she could cope if he were to let her down.

'Alyssa...'

'I know,' she said softly, on a breathy sigh. 'I want you too, but I need to get my feelings straight. I can't let you sweep me off my feet.'

'Are you sure about that?' His lips gently nuzzled the curve of her neck, and slid down along the bare slope of her shoulder. 'It's a very tempting idea. You know there's nothing I'd like more. Ever since the accident, I've been thinking about you and me...how we might be together...'

But before he could kiss her again they heard the sound of voices in the distance, coming ever closer, and Connor sighed and rested his cheek against hers for a second or two. Then he straightened and reluctantly eased himself away from her, still holding onto her hands and looking around to see who was coming along the path towards them.

Alyssa's mind was in a whirl. What did he mean, how they might be together?

'I might have known,' he said, under his breath. 'Ross's timing has always been atrocious.'

'I suppose they decided it was about time to set off for home,' Alyssa murmured, watching his brother and Carys coming closer. 'The music has stopped. It must be very late.'

He laid an arm around her shoulder. 'You're right. I guess we should be thinking about what we can do to entertain Carys tomorrow…unless you want to keep her to yourself?'

She shook her head. 'I think she'd enjoy the four of us being together.' She felt the loss of his arms around her intensely, and she was churned up inside at the interruption, but Carys had come over here especially to see her, and now she felt guilty because of her own dismay at seeing her turn up on the footpath with Ross. She wanted to be alone with Connor right now…but maybe that was not the most sensible idea around.

They went back to the house with Ross and Carys, and since it was so late Ross decided to stay in his brother's apartment overnight.

In the morning, they all had breakfast together on the deck outside Connor's apartment.

'I thought you might like to take a trip around the islands,' Connor suggested, looking first at Carys and then at Alyssa. 'My yacht's moored not far from here—

we could spend the day seeing the sights from on board, take a picnic lunch with us. What do you think?'

'That sounds wonderful.' Carys glanced at Alyssa and she nodded in agreement.

'I think so, too. Perhaps we'd better start getting some food together...and maybe a bottle or two or three...'

Connor shook his head. 'There's no need for you to do that. I'll organise things. You two can just relax and spend some time together while Ross and I see to everything.'

'Well, I'm all for that,' Carys murmured, smiling. 'I'll go and put on some sun cream in readiness.'

'Me, too.' Alyssa turned to go downstairs with Carys, picking up her phone as its ringtone sounded.

She was startled to hear her mother's voice on the other end of the line.

'Hi, Mum, how are you doing?' She signalled to Carys that she was going to take the call out in the garden, and Carys gave her a cheery wave in return.

'I just heard all about the accident you were caught up in,' her mother said, sounding vexed. 'Why on earth didn't you tell me about it?'

'The accident?' Alyssa was puzzled. How would her mother come to know anything about what had happened? Which accident was she talking about?

'On the night of the storm. The car was a write-off, but you didn't say a word. Heavens, Lyssa, you could have been hurt...but you didn't tell me. I'm your mother, and I knew nothing at all about it.'

'I'm sorry. I was fine and I thought it best not to worry you.' She frowned. 'How did you get to hear about it?'

'Well, you know how it is. Your Aunt Jenny heard it from Carys...and Jenny is my sister, after all, so she phoned me and asked, did I know? Of course I didn't. You never tell me anything.'

'That's not true,' Alyssa protested. 'I email you lots of times and tell you all the gossip—I just don't mention anything that might worry you unnecessarily, that's all.'

'Well, you should have told me about that.' Her mother was indignant. 'I need to know that you're safe.'

'I am. Honestly. I'm fine. You've no need to worry about me. It was poor Ross who came out of it with concussion, but he's okay now.' Alyssa was touched that her mother had taken the trouble to phone her. 'I miss you, Mum. It's great to hear from you.'

'We miss you, too, Lyssa. Maybe your dad and I could have a video chat with you when it's your birthday next week? We must arrange a time that's good for the three of us.'

They talked for a few more minutes and Alyssa promised she would let her mother know straight away if anything out of the ordinary happened. In turn, her mother said she would try to keep in touch more often.

'We'll choose a time each week when we can be sure we're both able to get to the phone,' she said. There was a wistful note in her voice as she added, 'Though it would be good if we were able to see you again properly. I couldn't quite take it in when you suddenly upped and left, but your father and I didn't want to stand in your way.'

It was strange, hearing things from her parents' point of view, and when she cut the call a short time later, Alyssa was deep in thought.

'Is everything all right?' Connor asked, on his way

from the house to the car with a large wicker hamper. 'Did I hear you say it was your mother on the phone?'

'Yes, it was…and everything's fine. She heard about Ross's car being written off and wanted to know what happened. She said they miss me. She and Dad are going to call me on my birthday—they want to do a video call that morning.'

His mouth curved. 'That sounds good. Perhaps it won't seem so bad being far away from them if you can hook up by video and actually get to see one another.'

She nodded. 'I suppose so. Though with my contract coming to an end soon I'll have to decide what I'm going to do…whether to stay on here and look for work or maybe go back home. I think my parents would like that.'

He set the hamper down on the ground. He appeared to be stunned. His body became rigid, his shoulders stiff and his whole frame was tense. 'You're not really thinking of going back home, are you?' he said in a shocked voice. 'I thought you said you loved the island?'

Her eyes were troubled. 'I do. But I have to be practical and think about the future. When I came here I needed a break, time to sort myself out. I was trying to decide whether I should give up on medicine altogether. I'm still not entirely sure, but I don't think I can go on straddling the fence for much longer. And if I choose medicine… Well, the fact is I did my training in the UK, so it would seem sensible to go back there to work.'

She didn't tell him the one true factor that would underline her decision-making. She wanted to be near to Connor, to spend her days—and nights—with him. But his track record wasn't encouraging where women were concerned and she'd already seen for herself that things could go badly wrong. Maybe she would feel differently if he gave her some idea that he wanted more than a fleeting affair, but why would he change the habit of a lifetime?

'I can't imagine how it would be without you here,' he said huskily. 'I've grown so used to having you around. You can't mean it...'

'I have to consider it as a real possibility,' she said. She was surprised by how much her words seemed to have affected him. The colour had drained from his face. 'But I still have a week or so before I need to make my decision.'

He nodded, and she said quietly, 'I suppose I should go and get ready for this boat trip. I'm already running late, from the looks of things.' She gestured towards the hamper. 'Have you filled that up already? Surely, you haven't had time?'

'No. That's true, we haven't.' He seemed to make a conscious effort to relax his stance. 'I phoned the catering service in the town and they're going to fill the basket for me. It's only a ten-minute run in the car, so I'll be back before you know it.' His gaze wandered over her. 'You look as though you're ready for the day ahead, anyway. You're perfect as you are.'

'Well, thanks for the vote of confidence.' She smiled. She had chosen to wear white jeans and a lightly patterned blouse that was gently nipped in at the waist. 'I'll just put on some more lipstick and pin back my hair, and then I'll be ready to go. We won't keep you waiting.'

'That's all right. Don't worry about it...but your hair looks great as it is. It always looks good, whether you leave it loose or pin it up, or whatever. I've always thought it was beautiful…that glossy, deep chestnut colour and those gorgeous curls. You look fantastic.'

She felt warm colour run along her cheekbones. 'I'm glad you feel that way. Somehow, with Carys around, looking so lovely, I sometimes feel as though I fade into the background. She's truly beautiful.'

He reached for her, his hands lightly clasping her bare arms. 'So are you. You could never fade into the background. Don't even think it.' He frowned, looking her over. 'You don't have much self-confidence, do you? And yet you have so much to be proud of. All that nonsense about leaving… Maybe I can help you to change your mind.'

She shook her head. 'I don't think that will work,' she said.

'No?' A challenging glint came into his eyes. 'I can see I'm going to have to take you in hand.'

She glanced at the fingers curled around her arms. 'Did you mean that literally?'

'Oh, yes. Definitely.' He had started to pull her towards him when Ross shouted down from the upper veranda.

'Are you going to get that hamper filled,' he said with an amused twist to his mouth, 'or are we going to hang about all morning? Stop fooling around, bro, and get a move on.'

Connor's mouth quirked in mock annoyance. 'I knew I should have sent him back to his own place last night.'

Alyssa chuckled, faintly relieved by the diversion. After all, she couldn't be certain she would be able to withstand Connor's gentle coaxing. 'There are times when I think I must be lucky not to have any siblings.

People talk about rivalry, and you expect it when they're young, but when you grow up…?'

'Yeah, well, a lot of testosterone gets thrown about where men are involved.' He let her go and went to load the hamper in the car. 'I won't be long,' he promised.

He was as good as his word, and it was around mid-morning when they set sail from the marina where Connor's yacht was moored. They climbed into the boat and within a very short time they were cruising the crystal clear waters around the island, with Connor at the helm. Ross mixed rum punch and offered the girls the chance to look through his binoculars at the startling white cliffs in the distance.

After a while, Alyssa went to join Connor at the helm. She handed him an ice-cold lager and he swallowed the drink gratefully.

'Thanks, I was ready for that.'

'I thought you might be.' She pointed to the island in the distance. 'Is that where we're headed?'

'Yes, Ross and I thought it would be a good place to stop for lunch. There's a lovely stretch of beach in a sheltered bay—it's fringed by coral reefs, so it's really one of the most beautiful places around.'

'From what I've seen, the coral is spectacular,' she murmured. 'I didn't think we'd be able to get so close to it, but in these calm waters you can see everything.' She'd seen swaying purple sea fans, pink sea anemones and myriad brightly coloured tropical fish.

'I hoped you would like it,' he said, smiling.

'I do.' She sighed contentedly. 'I'm so glad we came out here today. I wanted to see as much as I could of the reefs and the fish that swim around them. Carys said she was keen on doing that as well.'

'You should have a good chance of that this afternoon.'

They moved slowly through the sparkling turquoise water for an hour or so, and then dropped anchor in the bay of the island they had seen some time ago through the binoculars.

From the deck of the yacht Alyssa looked out at the pristine white sand that bordered the cliffs. Long-billed pelicans made their nesting ground near rocky outcrops, and overhead they could hear gulls calling to one another.

Connor opened up the hamper and produced a wonderful selection of food. There were spiced meats and rock lobster, along with pâté and savoury biscuits, salad and a variety of mouth-watering dips. For dessert they ate fruit tarts with fresh cream—everything had been kept chilled in a cooler and had then been transferred to the fridge on board the yacht.

'Mmm…I could get used to this life,' Alyssa murmured, leaning back in her seat and sipping the highball Ross had handed her.

'Me, too.' Carys stretched out her long, slender legs. 'I've eaten way too much.' She gave Connor a mock glare. 'You're using this weekend to ply me with food— I shall soon be totally fat.'

He laughed. He was sitting by the deck rail and now he cast a glance over her lithe body. 'Oh, I don't think so,' he said. 'You've had that same figure for the last several years—I doubt you're going to start piling on the pounds now.'

'Huh. So you say. How am I supposed to do any work tomorrow? I shall still be stuffed by morning, and it's all your fault for providing such luscious food.'

'Ah, well, I dare say the events management team can do without your input for a few hours…if the local sports club doesn't get their programme for the charity fete for another day or so, it's hardly going to matter, is it? And if Ross's film schedule's held up for half a day because he can't get out of his chair, no one will worry too much.'

'Don't you believe it,' Ross interjected drily. 'The finance department will be on my tail for a week or more.' He made a wry smile. 'Still, I don't suppose it's quite the same as you and Alyssa not turning up for work, is it?'

'I'm not so sure about that,' Alyssa murmured. 'We're not indispensable. There will always be someone skilled and capable who can look after the patients for us.' She looked at Connor. 'Not that I'm suggesting we leave them to it,' she added.

'I don't know,' Ross said. 'If you hadn't been there when those two cars crashed, I doubt Raeni would still be with us. How is she? Do you know?'

'She's still sedated and recovering from the loss of blood,' Connor said, 'and from the fact that her heart actually stopped beating at one point. They haven't managed to restore her heart to a normal rhythm yet, so that's a worry, but she's in Intensive Care, so everything's being done that can be done.'

Alyssa swirled the colourful juice in her glass. 'Did you get to hear anything more about Malik? I rang up yesterday to try and find out, but the consultant was still deciding on the best course of action.'

'There was a tear in his diaphragm,' Connor told her. 'They've decided to operate tomorrow, so we should know a bit more by late afternoon.'

Carys frowned. 'I could never do that job,' she said quietly. 'It would worry me way too much.'

Alyssa nodded. 'That's how I felt when I came over here. I didn't know if I would be able to go on working as a doctor—I thought these last few months would give me the break I needed to help me recharge my batteries.' She frowned. 'But then we had to deal with some real emergencies—something I never expected to happen—and I began to think my career was over. I didn't think I could cope.'

'Do you still feel that way?' Connor was standing by the deck rail, watching her closely.

She shook her head. 'I think I've discovered that I would far rather try to save lives than not to try at all.' She was thoughtful for a moment. 'Things don't always work out the way we want them to in this job, but at least we have the satisfaction of doing everything we possibly can.'

He came over to her and reached for her hand. 'I'm really glad you feel that way,' he said, going down on his haunches beside her. 'I think you've made the right decision.'

She made a faint smile. 'I wasn't so keen when Alex fell from the lorry,' she said quietly. 'But he's beginning to make good progress with his walking, so I guess things are looking up for him at last.'

Lewis hadn't been quite so lucky, though. She'd looked in on him a couple of days ago and the consultant in charge of his case was still searching for a strong antibiotic that would knock the septicaemia on its head. The ones they'd tried so far weren't bringing about the response the team had hoped for.

'Alex should come out of this without any lasting effects,' Connor said. 'He looked really cheerful when I last saw him.' He stood up, glancing out over the side of the yacht and began to tug on her hand, urging her up from her seat. 'Come and see this... I think a shoal of fish must be heading our way. You, too, Carys. You might want to see this.'

They all went with him to the deck rail, Ross coming to stand beside Alyssa, while Connor pointed out the shoal to Carys.

'They don't usually come this close to the surface,' he said softly.

'What are they?' Carys asked. 'Do you know?'

'They're parrotfish—they call them that because of their parrot-like beaks.'

'Oh, I've heard about them,' Carys said, intrigued. 'They use the beak to scrape off coral so that they can feed on algae. They're beautifully coloured, aren't they?' They were blue, yellow and red, flashing brightly as they swam through the water in search of coral. 'I heard they can change sex,' she added in an awed voice. 'That must cause some confusion among the ranks.'

They all laughed and went to sit back on deck. They sipped cocktails and chatted for some time, until Carys reluctantly mentioned that she had a plane to catch in a couple of hours.

'Okay, we'll up anchor,' Connor said. 'I'll drive you to the airport, if you like.'

'Okay, thanks.'

Ross frowned, and Alyssa wondered if he was troubled by his brother's offer. He didn't say anything, though, and when they arrived back at the house some time later, Ross went into the study in Connor's apartment and left Connor to make the arrangements for the journey to the airport. 'I have to make a phone call,' he told Carys. 'You won't leave without saying goodbye, will you?'

'Of course not.' Carys went with Alyssa to the ground-floor apartment. 'I'll be ready in a jiffy,' she told Connor. 'My bag was almost packed before we went out this morning, so I've only a few things to add to it.'

'That's okay. I'll be out on the deck when you need me.'

Alyssa's phone bleeped and she checked the text message that had arrived as they'd walked into the sitting room. 'My mother's arranged a time for us to link up by phone once a week,' she said, looking pleased. 'I wondered if she would remember.'

She chatted with Carys as her cousin finished putting last-minute items into her bag.

'Connor's gorgeous, isn't he?' Carys said, looking around for her make-up bag. 'I was thrilled to bits that he took us out on the boat today. I really wasn't expecting anything like that—just you and me together and a few take-away meals was what I thought when we planned the weekend—and then he went and produced that luxury hamper. Wow, that's the life, isn't it? It'll seem so mundane, going back to my little home in Florida.'

'Yes, I know what you mean.' Alyssa could well understand her cousin's enthusiasm. 'But you do love your home really, and your family is there…that must count for a lot.'

'True.' Carys sighed. 'But he is great, all the same.'

Alyssa chuckled. 'Don't tell me you're smitten. It seems to happen to an awful lot of women, from what I've heard.'

'Yeah…fat chance I'd have there.'

'Anyway, Ross is just as dishy, and he's very keen on you, or hadn't you noticed?'

'Ross?' Carys's eyebrows shot up. 'No way. You're joking.'

'I'm not.'

'You are, too.'

Still exchanging banter, the girls set off to meet Connor up on the deck.

'Oh…I think I left my phone somewhere,' Alyssa said. 'I'd better go and find it.' She was thinking of going with Carys to the airport, so she would need to have her bag as well. 'I'll catch up with you,' she said.

'Okay, no worries.'

It took a few minutes for Alyssa to find her phone, but eventually it turned up beneath a couple of magazines that Carys had put to one side while she was collecting her things together.

She dropped it into her bag and went upstairs to join Connor and her cousin.

She'd expected to hear them talking, but as she approached the veranda from Connor's sitting room she saw that they were very quiet, talking in hushed tones and standing by the rail, their heads close together. Connor put his arm around Carys's shoulder, bending his head towards her, and it seemed at one point as though their bodies almost meshed together.

Alyssa watched them, her mind reeling in stunned surprise. Connor's expression was serious, and Carys was looking up at him with rapt attention.

Alyssa felt a wave of nausea wash over her. Was this really happening? She hadn't mistaken what she'd seen, had she? Now all her dreams were dissolving in the light of that close embrace.

Was he exactly as people had implied, a man who went from one woman to the next? How could he do this? How could he tell her how much he wanted her, make her yearn for him in return, and then casually move on to try his charm on another woman?

He was treating her feelings as if they were of no account, trampling all over them.

She couldn't bear to watch. This hurt went deep, like a knife wound to the heart, and her whole body froze in pain. Her world had collapsed in an instant. What was she to do now?

CHAPTER NINE

'I'LL miss you, Alyssa.' Carys stood beside Connor's car and gave Alyssa a hug. 'We'll have to meet up again soon.'

'We will.' Alyssa was still hurting inside from the shock of seeing her cousin in such an intimate embrace with Connor, but none of this was her cousin's fault so she made an effort to put on a show of cheerfulness. 'I'll come over to Florida for a weekend before I go… and there's always the gala dinner in a few days' time, on Saturday. You have to come over for that.'

Carys nodded with enthusiasm. 'Yes, I'll be there.'

Ross came to say his goodbyes, and Alyssa noticed he held onto Carys's hand for a fraction longer than necessary. 'I was going to offer to take you to the airport myself,' he said, 'but Connor beat me to it. I think I hate him.'

Carys laughed. 'Don't feel so bad about it. There'll be other times. Anyway, I think he wants to talk to me about something—events management stuff for the hospital, and so on, and we can do that on the way.'

'Oh, boring stuff…' Ross grinned and kissed her lightly on the cheek. 'Bye, Carys.'

'Bye, Ross. And if you even think of doing that stunt

with the water-skis, I shan't speak to you. It was bad enough hearing that you'd been virtually knocked unconscious. You've been warned.'

Ross's brows lifted. 'So you do care about me after all? Okay, I won't do it, then. I promise.'

Smiling, Carys slid into the passenger seat beside Connor. Alyssa didn't think for a minute that Connor planned to talk to her about events management, but there was definitely some reason why he'd been so quick to offer to drive her to the airport. She had no idea what that might be, but she was determined now that she wasn't going to go with them to find out. There was the problem of two's company, three's a crowd, to make her think twice about doing that.

But she was still deeply troubled by what she'd seen earlier. Connor had obviously been concerned when she'd said she was thinking about going back to the UK, and perhaps he'd taken that to mean he would have no chance with her. It seemed a bit odd that he should turn his attention to Carys so soon, though, especially since it was clear that Ross was interested in her.

She waved Carys off and went to her bedroom. There, she lay on the bed and tried to think things through. Connor had never looked at another woman in all the time she'd been over here. It just didn't add up that he should start doing it now.

Could it be that she'd misinterpreted his actions? Perhaps she was letting her ex's behaviour influence her unduly. She had a huge problem with trust, and it had coloured all her judgement. But she couldn't rid herself of that image of Connor with his arm around Carys. It had shocked her to the core.

The situation tormented her, and she had no idea how

to resolve the problem. She loved Connor, she realised that now, but it was like a festering wound, believing that he had let her down so badly.

Over the next few days, she couldn't eat, she couldn't sleep, but she tried to lose herself in work, anything to blot out the picture of Connor and Carys together. She couldn't bring herself to talk to him about her worries because he might tell her it was true, and she didn't know how on earth she would handle that without falling apart. It would be a crippling blow.

She went through the motions at work, putting on a brave face for the occasional patient who came into her surgery. When she had some free time she went over to the hospital to look in on the people she had treated.

'Raeni's on the mend, I believe,' the registrar told her. 'Her breathing's improved, and her heart is pumping much more strongly. She seems to have turned the corner.'

'That's brilliant news,' she said, relieved. Apparently Raeni's children went to see her every day with their father, and were beginning to talk about the day when she would go home.

'It shouldn't be too much longer now,' the registrar added, 'two or three weeks, maybe. Of course, she'll have to take things easy to begin with, while everything continues to heal.'

'That's much better than I expected, anyway.' Alyssa thanked him and went to check on Malik, who was recovering on the men's ward after his surgery.

'How are you doing?' she asked him. 'I hear the operation went well.'

'I'm okay...a bit sore, but the doctor said that's to

be expected. I got them to take me over to see the lady who was in the other car. I'm really sorry for the way she was hurt.' He pulled a face. 'I was in a hurry that day because my wife rang to say she'd gone into labour. I was trying to get back home to her.'

'I'm sorry things turned out the way they did.' Alyssa frowned. 'What happened when you didn't get home?'

'A neighbour took her to the hospital.' He grinned, showing white teeth. 'We have a little girl. She's beautiful.'

'I'm glad it worked out all right, in the end, Malik. Congratulations.'

Back on the film set, things were winding to a close. They finished filming the water-ski chase, and she was glad to see that Ross stood back and let a professional stuntman do the action scenes.

'I didn't have much choice,' he told her in a mournful voice. 'I'm pretty sure Carys meant what she said when she told me she wouldn't speak to me. I guess my wild days are over.'

'Poor you.' She patted his shoulder and sent him a commiserating glance. 'You'll have to settle for being a top-notch film producer instead.'

'Yeah.' He laughed. 'I guess that's not so bad.'

A couple of days after that Alyssa closed down her medical centre and locked the door on what had been her sanctuary for the last few months. In a way, she was sad to see it come to an end, but she'd learned a lot about herself and her vocation as a doctor since she'd been here. It had given her a good breathing space and allowed her to sort out what she needed to do next.

On the day of the gala dinner she awoke to a glorious, sun-filled day and decided to go for a walk along the beach before breakfast. It would give her time to think. She needed to sort things out, once and for all.

She gazed around her at the gently swaying branches of the palm trees and let her glance wander over the magnificent sweep of the bay, where the blue water of the ocean met smooth, white sand. It was flawless, a true paradise island…all it needed was for her to find her soul-mate and to live with him here in perfect harmony.

She smiled wistfully and watched the waves break on the shore, leaving lacy ribbons of white foam. She desperately wanted Connor to be there with her.

Over these last few days she'd had plenty of time to think about what had happened on the day when he had taken Carys to the airport. Wasn't it possible she'd got the wrong end of the stick and come up with a false idea of what was going on? Back home, her ex had cheated on her, and ever since then she'd found it hard to put her trust in anyone.

But James was a totally different person from Connor, wasn't he? He'd never been particularly supportive, or understanding, whereas Connor had been there for her every step of the way. He'd never let her down. In fact, he'd gone out of his way to make sure she was safe, happy, and even that she was secure in her work.

She loved him, and surely that meant she had to learn to trust him? Somehow or other, she had to take risks with her feelings, because she didn't want to miss out on being with him.

'Alyssa…'

It was as though, by thinking of him, she'd somehow managed to conjure him up. She shielded her eyes against the sun and looked towards the house, to see Connor coming down the path that led to the beach.

'Hi.' She waved, and waited for him to come closer. 'You're up and about early,' she said. 'I thought this was your day off? I expected you'd be having a lie-in.'

'It is.' He caught up with her and came to stand alongside her, looking out over the sea. 'I heard you moving chairs about on the deck and I realised you'd been going off for early morning walks since your work here finished. I wanted to come with you and wish you a happy birthday.'

Her eyes widened. 'I didn't think you would remember.'

He smiled. 'I did. I was hoping you'd let me take you to the gala dinner—I realised I'd been taking it for granted that we'd go together, but I haven't asked you formally. Will you let me take you? It will be a good way to celebrate your birthday. I'd like to make it special for you.'

She gazed at him, drinking in the sight of him. 'Thank you, I'd like that, very much.' She studied him thoughtfully, hardly daring to say what was on her mind. 'Actually, I wondered if you might ask Carys.'

'She's going with Ross.'

'Ah.' She looked at him from under her lashes. 'How do you feel about that? Do you mind?'

He seemed puzzled. 'I think it's great—she's perfect for Ross.'

She frowned. 'So it doesn't bother you, her being with him?' She couldn't quite take in his easy answers. She hadn't expected this response at all. How could he be so casual and unconcerned if he'd fallen for Carys?

'Why would it bother me?' He was genuinely mystified by her question, and she finally began to relax a little. Had she misjudged him? 'Am I missing something here?' he said. 'You've been acting oddly ever since Carys went home. Is it because you're missing her?'

'I am,' she admitted. She wasn't ready to tell him the true reason. 'We always get on so well together. I sometimes wish we lived closer to one another.'

He wrapped his arms around her. 'She's only a short flight away—or even a boat ride. I could take you over there whenever you wanted to see her.'

She smiled at him. 'That's really thoughtful of you,' she said softly. 'Thank you for that.' It was typical of him that he should make the offer and she was beginning to feel ashamed of herself for doubting him. Surely there was a logical explanation for his behaviour with Carys? The trouble was, she was too embarrassed to ask him about it.

'You're welcome, any time. I want you to be happy, Alyssa.' He frowned briefly. 'Have you decided what you're going to do about staying on in the Bahamas? I hate the thought of you going away. If it's work that worries you, I know there's room for another doctor in the emergency department at the hospital here. There would be no problem getting you in there.'

'Do you think so?'

'I know it,' he said firmly. 'Everyone talks about how much you did for the patients who ended up in the hospital, and because of you they're all recovering. You know about the car-crash victims, they're both doing well. And Alex has been discharged and is walking again with just a stick to help him—sooner or later he'll be able to cope without that.'

'Yes, I saw him the other day. He came on to the film set to say hello to everyone.'

'You see what I'm saying? He's doing fine. And so is Lewis, now that they've found the right antibiotic. Admittedly, it was touch and go for a while, but now he's getting better every day.'

'It just goes to show what a marvellous hospital system you have here.'

He hugged her to him. 'Seriously, Alyssa…it gave me hope when you said you would go on with your work as a doctor. It would have been such a waste if you'd let it all go. But you could just as easily do that work here, couldn't you? You don't need to go back to the UK, do you?'

'I suppose I could stay…but what is there for me here? Why would you want me to stay? You've never wanted to get deeply involved with anyone before this, have you?'

'Things are different now.' His hand smoothed over the length of her spine. 'I dread the thought of you going away. I want you to stay here, with me. Ever since the accident last week, since I saw Ross's car there and thought you were involved in the crash, I've been churned up inside, imagining what it would be like if you weren't around. It was the same when I saw the tree through Ross's windscreen and thought you might be hurt—I couldn't understand why I cared so much. I'd never felt that way about any woman before.'

She lifted a hand to his cheek, scarcely able to believe what he was saying. 'Do you mean it?'

'Of course I do.' He wrapped her fingers in his and kissed the palm of her hand. 'You can't imagine what it was like for me, thinking that you might be injured.

It struck me like a blow to the stomach that I couldn't bear it if you weren't with me.'

Her heart leapt. 'I didn't think it was possible for you to feel that way.'

'Believe it.' It was a heartfelt admission, and she felt his body shudder next to hers. 'And then when you said you were going away, it was like a double blow.' He frowned. 'Alyssa, I know your parents miss you and you miss them—but they could come and visit any time, couldn't they? There's plenty of room for them to stay at the house.'

'You wouldn't mind that…them coming over to stay in the apartment? I mean, it was different with Carys, because you already knew her.'

'Of course I wouldn't mind.' He kissed her tenderly on the lips. 'I want you to stay on and think of the apartment as your own—' He broke off, suddenly intent, searching her face for her response. 'In fact, I'd sooner turn it back into a house and do away with the two apartments.'

'I don't understand,' she said, suddenly confused. 'Are you saying you want me to live with you?'

'Yes, that's exactly what I'm saying.' He ran his hands over her arms, thrilling her with his gentle caresses. 'I want to keep you close, Alyssa. When you told me you were thinking of leaving it made me realise how badly I needed you to stay.' His fingers trailed lightly over her cheek. 'I can't bear to lose you, Alyssa. Will you stay here and marry me so that we can be together for always?'

She pulled in a sharp breath. She wanted to believe that he meant what he said, but her head was reeling from the sudden shock of his proposal. 'But you—you said you didn't believe in commitment… You've never wanted to settle down with any woman.'

'Because I'd never met the right woman until now.' His arms circled her once more and he kissed her, a long, thorough, fervent kiss that left her breathless and sent sweet ripples of ecstasy to flow throughout her body.

'I just know we'll be perfect together,' he said, coming up for air, his voice rough around the edges. 'It won't be like it was for my parents—I'm not the same person as my father. I don't need to go looking at other women because I know you're the one for me. I love you. I thought—' He broke off. 'It felt as though you loved me, too.' He looked at her, his eyes shimmering with passionate intensity.

She smiled, her lips parting in invitation. 'I do, Connor. I do. I wasn't sure you could love me in return.'

'What's not to love? You're gentle, thoughtful, caring…I've never met anyone like you, and I know we make up two halves of the whole. We're right for one another. I just needed to get my head right and see past the mistakes my father made, that's all. That's not going to happen with us. I know that we're right for one another.'

'That's how I feel, too.' She wrapped her arms around him and he gave a deep sigh of contentment, holding her close for a long time while the birds called to one another overhead and the sea lapped desultorily at the fringes of the beach.

After a while, he stirred and said huskily, 'I'd almost forgotten your birthday present. It's in a drawer in the apartment.' He clasped her hand firmly in his. 'Come with me and I'll get it for you.'

They walked back along the beach towards the

house. 'I wasn't sure what to do for the best, but then I talked to Carys, and she said what I had in mind would be just right.' He frowned. 'I hope you like it. I'm still not sure… I mean, I could have…' He stopped talking as she came to a halt and placed her fingers on his lips.

'Whatever it is, I know I'll love it, because you gave to me.' She sent him a thoughtful glance. 'Is this what you and Carys were talking about that day—before you took her to the airport?'

He frowned, and she said, 'I saw you both on the deck. Your heads were close together, and at first I thought…well, it doesn't matter what I thought, but perhaps that was when you were discussing it? Is that why you wanted to drive her there?'

He nodded, but studied her cautiously. 'What went through your mind when you saw us?'

She wriggled her shoulders. 'Nothing. It isn't important.'

He curled his fingers around her upper arms in a firm but gentle clasp. 'You thought I was making a play for her, didn't you?'

She tried to escape from his grasp but he wasn't letting her go until she answered him.

'Okay, yes… It did cross my mind. Only I gave it a lot of thought and decided I had to learn to trust you. If I couldn't do that, we were doomed, and I really wanted us to have a chance.'

He gave a shuddery sigh. 'Next time you have any doubts or worries, talk to me about them. Promise me?'

'I will. I promise.' She gave him a tremulous smile. 'It was hard for me, Connor. I was badly hurt when James cheated on me, and I could see the same thing happening all over again.' She breathed deeply. 'Then

I came to my senses and decided that I was willing to risk everything by putting my faith in you.'

'I will never, ever let you down, Alyssa. Believe me.'

He tugged on her hand and they started towards the house once more. 'Mind you,' he said, almost as an afterthought, 'I had to explain my motives to Ross when I arrived back home. He wasn't at all happy that I'd pipped him to the post by driving Carys to the airport.'

Alyssa laughed. 'Yes, I remember he was very quiet that night.'

They went into Connor's apartment and he went straight over to a bureau in the sitting room and took out a box that was about half the size of a shoebox. He held it out to her.

'Happy birthday,' he said.

She took it from him, gazing at it in wonder. It was beautifully wrapped in gold foil and tied with a pretty silver ribbon. 'It's so lovely, it seems a shame to open it,' she said softly.

'Please do. I really need to know if you like it, if I've done the right thing…I could always…'

She stopped him with a glance and a slight rise of her eyebrow. He laughed. 'Okay, I won't say any more. I've never felt so nervous…'

Carefully, she undid the wrapping and there inside was an exquisite, hand-carved jewellery box, heart-shaped and decorated with an inlaid pattern and delicate enamelling in the shape of a rose.

'Oh, Connor,' she gasped. 'This is beautiful. You made it yourself, didn't you? That's why you were anxious. You shouldn't have been. It's absolutely lovely.'

He breathed a sigh of relief. 'Open it up,' he urged her.

She did as he asked, lifting the lid to reveal a velvet lined interior with sections for necklaces and rings. And in the centre there was another small box, again with an enamelled flower decoration. She lifted it out, and Connor took the jewellery box from her, putting it to one side on a table.

Alyssa's heart began to pound. 'Is this what I think it is?'

He nodded but didn't say anything more, and she carefully opened the box.

Nestling on a bed of silk was a sparkling diamond ring. The gemstones were dazzling, reflecting the sunlight, and the flawless setting took her breath away.

'I've never seen anything so lovely,' she said huskily. 'It's stunning…'

'That's another reason I had to have Carys's help,' he murmured. 'I needed to get the right size, and she said she had a ring that fitted you. We took the measurement from it.'

'No wonder you were so secretive,' she breathed. 'I'd no idea.'

'Let me slip it on your finger,' he said. He smiled. 'Third finger, left hand…' He held up the ring and pulled in a deep breath. 'Will you marry me, Alyssa?'

'Oh, yes. I will. I do love you, Connor,' she said, her voice husky with emotion.

'I love you.'

He slipped the ring on her finger, and they stood by the open doors of his sitting room, arms around one another, gazing at the ring and looking out over the vista of the ocean. Alyssa sighed happily. This was truly their paradise island, and a dream come true.

* * * * *